CAMELOT'S QUEEN

BOOK TWO OF GUINEVERE'S TALE

NICOLE EVELINA

Camelot's Queen

© 2016 Nicole Evelina

Lawson Gartner Publishing
PO Box 2021
Maryland Heights MO, 63043
www.lawsongartnerpublishing.com

Printed in the United States of America
First Printing 2016

ISBNs
978-0-9967631-3-4 (print)
978-0-9967631-4-1 (e-book)

Library of Congress Control Number: 2015959040

Publisher's Cataloging-In-Publication Data
(Prepared by The Donohue Group, Inc.)

Names: Evelina, Nicole.
Title: Camelot's queen / Nicole Evelina.
Description: Maryland Heights, MO : Lawson Gartner Publishing, [2016] |
    Series: Guinevere's tale ; book 2
Identifiers: ISBN 9780996763134 (print) | ISBN 9780996763141 (ebook) |
    ISBN 9780996763158 (audiobook)
Subjects: LCSH: Guenevere, Queen (Legendary character)--Fiction. | Great Britain—
    History—To 1066—Fiction. | Queens—Great Britain—Fiction. | LCGFT: Arthurian
    romances. | Historical fiction. | Fantasy fiction.
Classification: LCC PS3605.V424 C36 2016 (print) | LCC PS3605.V424 (ebook) |
    DDC 813/.6--dc23

Editor: Cassie Cox, Joy Editing
Cover Design: Jenny Quinlan, Historical Editorial
Layout: The Editorial Department

1. Fiction 2. Historical Fiction 3. Historical Fantasy 4. Myth and Legend 5. Arthurian Legend

To Courtney and Jen,
who believed before anyone else

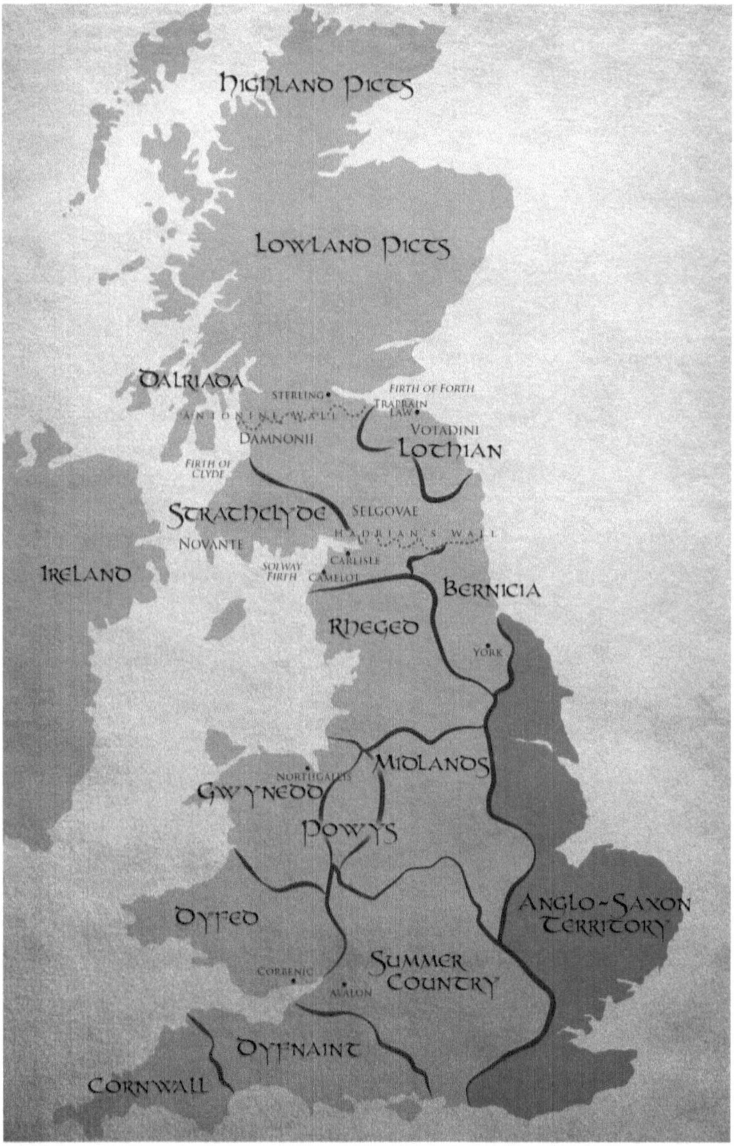

HIGHLAND PICTS
LOWLAND PICTS
DALRIADA
STERLING
FIRTH OF FORTH
TRAPRAIN LAW
ANTONINE WALL
DAMNONII
VOTADINI
LOTHIAN
FIRTH OF CLYDE
STRATHCLYDE
SELGOVAE
HADRIAN'S WALL
NOVANTE
IRELAND
SOLWAY FIRTH
CARLISLE
CAMELOT
BERNICIA
RHEGED
YORK
MIDLANDS
NORTHGALLIS
GWYNEDD
POWYS
ANGLO-SAXON TERRITORY
DYFED
CORBENIC
SUMMER COUNTRY
AVALON
DYFNAINT
CORNWALL

PART ONE

Fledgeling

Chapter One

Winter 497

The sigh of a reed pen across parchment, one jagged line of ink. That was all it took to betray my king and myself.

My signature, made with trembling hands, may have made me Arthur Pendragon's wife, but it couldn't change my heart. He'd asked for my assent to this marriage, and I gave it, but it was a lie.

Marrying him was my duty. That much I had resigned myself to in the two months since Arthur proposed, shattering my dreams of a life with Aggrivane of Lothian.

I watched with hollow detachment from my place next to Arthur as our marriage contract was sealed in the snowy courtyard of the old Roman fort of Carlisle, the stronghold of Arthur's father, the previous high king, Uther.

Arthur stood facing my father, back to the gate of the castle. His breaths were small puffs of white in the frosty air. "King Leodgrance of Gwynedd, by the signing of this contract, I bind myself to you and your kin through the hand of your daughter, Guinevere. As proof of my fidelity, I bestow upon you the price of her honor." Arthur extended a wooden box of coins, ornately wrought gold brooches, and jewels—my bride-price, the money that assured Arthur's sincere backing of our union but which would become mine should we ever part ways.

"I thank you, Your Majesty," my father said with a humble bow. "You are now my son as well. My gift to you is a symbol of my tribe, the people who are your most loyal servants."

My father held out his hand, and a servant placed the reins of a bridle into them. He passed them to Arthur. At the other end was a coal-black steed, a reminder of the days when brides were sold for cattle or land rather than gold. The stallion was muscular and strong but calm, indicating he was well trained and would be a valuable addition to Arthur's growing cavalry.

Arthur handed the reins to one of his attendants and clapped my father on the shoulder. "All of Britain is indebted to you for the most precious gift of your daughter, who, in a moment, will become our queen. I thank you for giving her into my care."

My eyes welled with stinging tears. To anyone in the assembled crowd, I likely appeared overwhelmed now that the deed was done, but my heart burned with a mix of emotions. Some small part of me knew this was the same transaction that would have taken place had I married Aggrivane as I'd intended, but my heart said this was all wrong. I should have been standing next to a man I loved, one with whom I couldn't wait to share my life, not the stranger who had stolen my dreams.

But those were the ruminations of a lovesick, petulant girl, not a level-headed ruler. As Merlin approached me with a pot of fragrant rose oil in one hand, the crown of Britain in the other, I forced myself to think like the high queen I was about to become. I was married to the High King of Britain, a position most women would kill for, and I'd had to do nothing to obtain it thanks to my father's willingness to use me as payment of his life-debt to the king.

I glanced at Arthur. His kind gaze held not a hint of temper or malice; he would not abuse me. Plus, he was allowing me to be crowned queen instead of simply naming me his royal wife, which meant we would rule as equals. Those facts had to be enough to trump whatever hurt and pain I still felt. Besides, though I would never openly admit it, part of me wanted to be high queen. I had been raised to rule and govern, and now I had a chance beyond my wildest imaginings.

I fell to one knee before Merlin, touching my right thumb to my forehead, lips, and heart—the sign of Avalon—in acknowledgement of his office as Archdruid.

Merlin's smile reflected our long friendship, forged from my years in Avalon under the tutelage of the Lady of the Lake. He leaned in close, his voice soft in my ear as he said, "No one is more deserving of this role than you. But take care your heart does not lead you astray."

I pulled back, regarding Merlin quizzically. I had no idea what he meant. For a moment, his eyes held the glassy, faraway look of prophecy, then he blinked, and it was gone. Before I could be sure I had really seen it, Merlin turned away as though nothing had ever passed between us.

To the waiting crowd, he proclaimed, "Guinevere of North-gallis, priestess of Avalon, and now wife to High King Arthur

Pendragon in accordance with his will, this day I anoint you High Queen of Britain."

Bowing, I willed myself not to shake, though my legs felt as if they would give way beneath me.

"May you be blessed with purity of mind and judgment by the Maiden"—he anointed my hair—"with love of your people from the Mother"—he drew small, sticky shapes on my cheeks—"and with the wisdom of the Crone"—he covered my hands in the warm oil—"and may she of a thousand names bless you and keep you always."

He placed the glittering circlet upon my head, secured a heavy braided metal torque around my neck, and knelt. "May I be the first to pledge my loyalty to you, High Queen Guinevere."

The crowd genuflected as one with a soft rustling of furs and other fine materials.

Arthur came and stood by my side, taking my gloved hand. Loudly enough to be heard by all, he said, "These are your people, my lady. From this day forth, they are in your care. You are my equal in war as in peace. Will you fight by my side to defend their honor with your person and your very life?"

The full weight of responsibility was a stone in my stomach as I looked over the bowed heads of Britain's nobility—the kings and queens of our thirteen kingdoms and countless tribes—along with Arthur's most trusted warriors and advisors. A flurry of movement caught my eye, and I glanced over just in time to catch my father yanking Father Marius, his confessor and advisor, to his knees. The pious troll had never borne me any affection. In fact, he had tried to ruin my life a few years earlier, so seeing him forced to prostrate himself before me gave me no small pleasure.

I turned my gaze back to Arthur. "I will. From this moment on, I honor and care for them as I would my own children, for they are children of the gods. I am privileged to lead them."

A cheer went up, growing louder as the group rose to their feet. In a moment, they would come forth one by one to pledge their allegiance to me, but there was one thing left for me to do—our union must be sealed with a kiss.

I turned to Arthur. My stomach clenched as I looked into his deep blue eyes. I saw naught of malice, only affection and hope—hope for the future of Britain, for us. As our lips met for the first time, I told myself the past was done. What mattered now was our future and the future of our kingdom.

⁂

As the sun set on the old Roman fort, nobility from across the country and emissaries from all of the surrounding lands toasted our health and welfare. Arthur and I were seated above the rest, on a dais at the center of a long table. Our families trailed off like ribbons on either side.

The hours sped by in a haze of ale, music, laughter, and good cheer. Dish after dish of delicacies were placed before us and removed, finely dressed pheasant giving way to fish in pungent sauces, roasted boar with herbs followed by sweetmeats, candied nuts, and baked apples. All the while, wine and ale flowed freely—so freely some even said the fountain in the courtyard dedicated to the god of victory spurted wine in our honor.

Amid the clatter of plates as courses changed, Isolde, heir to the throne of Ireland and my dearest friend, came to my side and embraced me tightly.

"See, I told you my queen would bring you good fortune," she teased, referring to her piece from the game of Holy Stones we'd played on and off for over a year.

I reached into the pouch beneath my gown and retrieved the gleaming red orb. "Is this occasion enough to return it to you, or do you wish to win it back?" I held it out to her on my open palm.

She considered for a moment, green eyes dancing with mirth. "I believe you have better things to do tonight." As though the implication in her voice were not enough, she threw a longing look at Arthur. "It is my turn to be jealous, I suppose."

My elbow caught her ribs just as she snatched up the stone. "Speaking of jealousy, how is Galen?" Galen was the one-time betrothed of our friend Elaine whose heart Isolde had broken when she ran away to Ireland with him.

She rolled her eyes and sighed. "It is far too long a story to relate tonight, but I will tell you this—I knew what I was doing when I agreed to let him come with me. He has proven to be valuable leverage for my family."

Slightly fearful of her thirst for justice, I wondered what fate she planned for him.

She read my expression and continued, "I have plans that will benefit both his country and mine."

I shook my head, in awe of her determination and strategy. "You are a formidable ruler already, and the crown has not even passed to you yet."

She flashed her impish smile. "I learned young it is never too early to read your allies and enemies and uncover what each one most needs. If you can provide it or deny it, you hold the power." Her gaze flickered across the room to the lanky, fair-haired warrior called Tristan. I remembered him from the tournament as part of the house of Cornwall. "Speaking of which, I have allies to make."

I wasn't sure if she meant politically or personally. Knowing Isolde, it was probably both. We gazed at each other for a long moment, knowing we likely wouldn't see one another again before she returned home.

"I will write as often as possible. You will make a great queen." She squeezed my hand and glanced at Arthur. "Do yourself a favor. Forget about what is past and enjoy the role fate has given you." She arched an eyebrow. "I certainly would."

Her laugher trailed behind her, and I couldn't help but echo it.

Arthur turned toward me. "This is the happiest I have seen you since the night we were betrothed," he said, sounding slightly astounded.

I dropped my gaze to my lap, embarrassed. "Isolde brings out the best in me."

Arthur raised my chin softly with his finger. "If the roles were different and I could have her at court, I would command it in a heartbeat, if only to see more of your beautiful smile."

I blushed, uncertain what to say. Since our betrothal, we had been under the same roof less than two weeks, so the awkward tension of strangers had yet to melt into familiarity.

I fidgeted with the torque encircling my neck. Made of intricately twisted strands of gold, silver, and copper, it was the symbol that proclaimed me queen to all who held to our people's beliefs; the crown I wore was mere pageantry. Tipped on one end with a highly polished black lodestone and on the other with an opaque orb of moonstone, it was a constant reminder of the light and dark responsibilities of queenship while also acting as a conduit to the wisdom of the gods.

I lifted one of the finials from the skin I was convinced it was bruising. "Please tell me we don't have to wear these every day."

His gaze followed my hand, and he smiled. "Only on formal occasions." He adjusted the weight for me.

We were so intent on each other neither of us noticed a visitor had approached until she spoke. "Patience, brother. You'll have time enough later for undressing your new bride."

We both looked up, startled, into the placid eyes of Ana of Lothian, Arthur's older sister. Her expression was playful.

"I swore my loyalty to Guinevere earlier, and now I would like to offer you both my love." She fixed her gaze on me. "And my apologies. I am truly sorry for the circumstances surrounding your engagement. If I had known your intentions—"

Arthur's brow wrinkled. "Ana, what are you apologizing for?"

My eyes snapped to him, and I searched his face for some hint of malevolence or deception, some indication this was a cruel joke. But all I found was genuine confusion.

"You didn't know." The words were a gasp, hardly above a whisper as they escaped my lips. I'd assumed he was aware of the circumstances but had simply done as he pleased. This turn of events shook my perception of him, prodding my reluctant heart toward compassion.

Ana covered her mouth with her hand. "I thought—I thought for sure you knew, that Leodgrance told you and you overruled him." She looked at the floor, unable to face either of us. "Guinevere and my son Aggrivane pledged their troth shortly before you asked for her hand. My husband was supposed to secure her father's consent, but you succeeded first."

Arthur looked between Ana and me, surely searching for something in my eyes to confirm or refute her words. Then his gaze became distant, as though he was envisioning his own stolen future.

A moment later, he gave me a sorrowful look. "I did not know. I am sorry. I do not ask your forgiveness, for an offense of such a nature will take a long time to heal, but I beg you to try not to hold this misunderstanding against me."

I looked at Ana, pleading with her to give me a sign or tell me what to say, but her gaze was still on floor, her cheeks flushed with embarrassment. So this was to be my first test. How would I respond to an impossible request without anyone to guide me?

I cleared my throat before placing my hand on Arthur's and giving him a soft smile, just as a queen should. "Of course I forgive you, husband. It was a tragic misunderstanding but one that brought us to this night. Let us dwell not on it but enjoy our feast."

Those pretty words were required of me. In my heart, shock, confusion, and misery warred. I had no idea which one would win out.

◦ઓ℮ ℮ઓ◦

The long meal finished, our guests reveled in earnest. Musicians filled the hall with lively song while jugglers, bards, and entertainers of every ilk roamed among the guests, delighting and mystifying them with colorful tricks and witty verse. The tables were pushed against the walls to create an ample dance floor, which quickly filled with tipsy couples.

Arthur led me into a lively round where we stayed side by side for most of the dance. Something had been bothering me since our conversation with Ana, and I took advantage of the situation to unburden myself.

"Arthur, if you intended to ask me to be your wife, why did you award the stag's head to Elaine?"

His expression showed he thought the answer was obvious. "Pellinor was my host; I could not insult him. Besides, he is a valuable subject."

"I thought you were going to ask her to marry you."

He laughed. "So did almost everyone else. Perhaps I was a little too charming, but she is a sweet girl and thrived on my attention. What was I supposed to do, warn her ahead of time?"

I narrowed my eyes at him. "A hint would have been polite. The poor girl was crushed." Arthur grunted, and I glanced around his shoulder at Pellinor, who certainly didn't appear upset that his daughter had been passed over. "Her father looks to be quite recovered from the disappointment."

Arthur winked at me. "Gold cures most ills, trust me."

The song ended, and we milled among the crowd, accepting even more well-wishes. Within a few minutes, I felt as if the false smile I had maintained all day would stiffen and set, as permanent as the crescent mark of Avalon on my brow.

A young couple approached us, and my stomach twisted. He was Lord Malegant of the Summer Country. I had learned his identity when he pledged his fealty to me during my coronation. Then I had been dazzled by his handsomeness, but all night something had needled at me, a tiny voice insisting I had seen him before.

Malegant was tall and muscular, wavy dark blond hair tied at the base of his neck with a royal blue cord identical to his cloak. His skin was ruddy with drink. He led a small woman by the arm—a child really, perhaps all of fourteen—and gracefully maneuvered her in front of him as they reached us. She dipped into a low curtsey, and he bowed.

"Well met, Lord Malegant." Arthur clapped him on the shoulder.

"My king, allow me to introduce my wife, Fiona."

Fiona raised her head, revealing amazingly large hazel eyes. "I am honored to be in your presence, my lord." She smiled shyly at me and added, "Yours as well, my lady."

Malegant took my hand and kissed it, his slight beard gazing my skin. "Your Majesty." His eyes glinted with a look that was truly magnetic.

With a sharp intake of breath, I realized I knew that look, and the memory came flooding back.

It was during my third year in Avalon, before I had attained priestesshood. Normally I wouldn't have been allowed on the other side of the mists, but one of the marsh women had gone into early labor and I was asked to accompany one of the priestesses as her assistant midwife.

I had been standing on the shore of the lake, waiting for my companion to finish her business inside, when he emerged from one of the little huts at the base of the Tor. I'd expected to see one of the wild hermits who were part of the community of Joseph of Arimathea, but instead this well-groomed noble fixed his irresistible eyes upon me. I remembered thinking I would melt and be swept away by the waters of the lake.

When I described him to my priestess companion, she knew immediately who he was and warned me in a motherly tone to stay far away from him. He was known to cause trouble for women, especially those vowed to the isle, she said. But I never understood why because she refused to say more.

But before I could speak, Malegant led the doe-eyed girl away, his hand clasped just a little too tightly around her arm. Caught up in my own thoughts, I had missed the whole conversation plus any opportunity to find out more about the Lord of the Summer Country. Uriens called Arthur's name, and my husband excused himself.

I was heading back to my chair, still wrapped up in half-remembered rumors about Malegant's questionable reputation, when a voice stopped me in my tracks.

"Well, well," it said.

I could almost see the catlike smile in the lilting voice. It was a sound straight out of my nightmares. I knew the speaker even before I turned. "Hello, Morgan," I said as cheerily as I could manage.

We regarded one another coldly, each taking the other's measure. She was little changed, the candlelight making her skin glow and highlighting the crescent mark of a priestess on her forehead. Wherever she had fled couldn't have given her too hard a life.

She settled into a mock curtsy. "Your Majesty." She nearly choked on the words.

I gave her a triumphant smile. "Last I heard, you slipped Avalon's guard and went missing. What ill star directs you to darken this happy occasion?"

Morgan shook her head and clicked her tongue disapprovingly. "Still bitter about being second best, I see."

"You know my role, yet you dare call me second best?"

She was nonplussed by my outrage, which only irritated me more. "I've always been better at understanding the will of the Goddess than you."

I sucked in air to reply, but then I noticed how her hand hovered protectively over her abdomen, which, now that I looked closely, was swollen. She was pregnant.

I tried to cover my astonishment. "And whom did the Goddess direct you to marry? Or do you just rut like a sow and see who the child most resembles?"

Morgan's smile was indulgent, as if she was dealing with an especially simple child, but her tone was frosty, biting. "My husband is Uriens of Rheged, brother-in-law to the king. Welcome to the family, Guinevere."

ふだ だふ

I plopped down in my chair with a huff, mind still reeling from Morgan's revelation. An orphan who did not know her lineage had managed to infiltrate the highest levels of Briton nobility—and now she was my sister by marriage. That meant I would be spending much more time in her presence, no doubt the subject of her constant conniving. I'd thought I left that behind when we parted ways in Avalon, but the Goddess had willed us together again whether I liked it or no.

Sensing my displeasure, my life-long attendant, Octavia, flitted to my side and replaced my cup with a fresh one. I smiled, grateful for her constant concern and friendship. I brought the cup to my lips, intending to drain it in one gulp, but the sharp smell stopped me. It was unlike any wine or ale I had ever encountered, nor was it cloying like mead. I sniffed it warily, its bitter bouquet stinging my nose.

Octavia saw my confusion. "It is a drink from your mother's native land. Some of the Votadini ambassadors brought it to toast your queenship. You *are* one of them after all. Your father and some of the knights are partaking of it liberally in the adjoining room—and enjoying themselves immensely, I might add."

I raised an eyebrow at her and took a slip. It was bitter but slid smoothly down my throat, its peppery tail burning like a comet. I shuddered, intending to push the cup away. But the warmth that followed made me reconsider. This strange drink heated me from the inside out, making me feel comfortable for the first time all day, as though I was wrapped in my mother's old blanket. A few more sips and I barely remembered talking to Morgan or any of the pain of the last few months.

Lost in this tingling fog, I scarcely noticed when the crowd began to thin. Eventually Arthur returned to my side, a little worse for the wear. He was laughing and smelled of the same strange brew. I wondered when they had pulled him into the other room.

The tone of the music changed, becoming slow and sensual, and with it, the entire tenor of the room shifted. Now it felt more like a Beltane ritual than a wedding feast. Arthur's closest friends and many of his knights were teasing us, telling lewd jokes with base gestures that openly indicated what was to come. Soon the entire room descended into debauchery.

Kay was more than happy to fulfill his duty as Arthur's first man. When the appointed hour came, Kay wriggled his eyebrows at me, picked me up, and threw me over his shoulder, symbolically kidnapping me. He carried me into the bridal chamber as I flailed and screamed with laughter for him to put me down. His bravado faded, however, as soon as he set me on my feet. He took his leave with a stiff bow, but not before swatting me on the backside. I thought I heard him stifle a drunken giggle as he passed over the threshold.

Turning into the room, I froze. The bed, with its double-layer feather mattress, was finer than anything I had ever seen. The expensive sheets were strewn with rose petals and fertility herbs, and a bough of mistletoe hung over the pillows, prepared to receive the newlywed lovers.

Octavia slipped in to prepare me. She lovingly removed my clothes and bathed me in perfumed water, whispering advice and a few pointers I was embarrassed she knew. She clothed me in a simple white shift and quietly ducked out of the room, leaving me alone to wait for my husband.

I heard the horde of men even before the door opened to a chorus of whoops and whistles, and Arthur stumbled in, having been shoved by his enthusiastic friends.

"No listening in the hall," he called after them as the door closed and the lock clicked. He regarded me uncertainly, the firelight glinting off his freshly oiled chest.

Nervous laughter escaped my lips. "You look ready for a wrestling match."

Arthur lifted an eyebrow. "If that is how you would like it." He stepped closer and removed the chaplet of flowers from my hair. "And you are fit for a ritual, not a wedding bed."

"Is it not every man's dream to lie with the Goddess?" I teased, the drink making my tongue bold.

His face darkened, and he looked away, mumbling, "I prefer my partners mortal."

Silence stretched on for a few moments as we each tried to

decide how to proceed. I finally decided to be honest with him, to tell him all the things building in my heart since the fateful night he had proposed. If the truth wasn't spoken now, it might not ever be.

"You really didn't know?" I asked, barely above a whisper. "About Aggrivane?"

Arthur shook his head, watching me carefully. "If you had it to do over again, would you choose me?"

How could he even ask me such a question? He was the king. What was I going to say—no? "Would I have a choice?"

Arthur stepped toward me, hand outstretched. "Of course. You've always had a choice."

I stepped away from him. "Have I? You asked for my hand in front of the entire court of Dyfed, already having secured my father's agreement."

Arthur dropped his hand, balling it into a fist at his side. "Guinevere, I understand your pain. You are not the only one who has lost something. I had a completely different life before I became king—plans, dreams which will never be fulfilled. This is a duty I never asked for."

"Neither did I."

"But you're here now." His smile was tender.

Before I could respond, he leaned in and kissed me gently. Then he pulled back and searched my eyes as if looking for permission to continue.

My tension eased, shoulders sagging as I realized he was right. I was here now, with my husband. No matter what had come before, I'd made my promise to him. I had a duty now, to him and to my people. In answer to his questioning eyes, I kissed him back, with equal tenderness and no small amount of awkwardness.

He ran his hands over my hair, down my neck and shoulders, to my waist as our lips danced, gradually learning one another's pace and preferences. When his hands reached my hips, he removed my shift and lifted me effortlessly. We made love with the uncertainty of strangers, the act slowly forming a bond between us even as we struggled to find pleasure in our forced coupling.

When it was over, Arthur lay his head on my chest and his breathing slowed to the even pace of a dreamer. I kissed the top of his head.

"I suppose being married to you will not be so bad," I whispered before closing my eyes.

Chapter Two

A week later, we set off for Camelot, Arthur's permanent home some miles west of Carlisle. We took the two-day journey at a leisurely pace but rose early on the third morning at Arthur's insistence. We arrived just as the eastern clouds were slowly breaking, the first light of dawn glowing rose and gold in their underbelly.

Arthur lowered my hood and kissed the top of my head, whispering into my hair, "Behold your kingdom, my queen."

My breath caught in my throat as we rounded a bend and the land ahead came into view. High above, on a lofty hill, a massive fortress made of gray stone held court. Its elegant square turrets reached like arms into the sky while graceful arches stretched across courtyards like limber sinews and glazed windows winked in the morning light.

This was nothing like the fortress I had called home as a child or even Pellinor's vast estate. Out of necessity, we had fortified our wooden palisades with stone, but it was not meant to enhance the appearance of our homes. This castle, on the other hand, with its ethereal beauty, looked as though it had grown right from the mountainside at the command of some otherworldly force. Some might say it looked like an imagining out of a bard's tale or an enchanted palace built by the fey, but to me, it was the star castle of the goddess Arianrhod, who rules the heavens.

My eyes followed the zigzagging line of ramparts separating the living quarters from the town, the town from the market, and the market from the military defenses. A burgeoning community spilled out from the castle's inmost walls in a patchwork of thatched and timber roofs. Along the sides of the road and in the main courtyard outside the castle gates, merchants stacked the last of the orchards' apples in precarious piles, butchers hung the remnants of their slaughtered charges in attractive displays while others arranged baskets, bread, and other wares in rows of stalls.

As trades were made, wagons rumbled through the outer gates and down to the docks on the edge of a large harbor. There, trade ships prepared to cross the waters to do business with the Caledonii, who lived on the distant northern shore. Miles away, the bay gave way to the Firth of Clyde, and the Firth melted into the sea.

The woodland through which we had passed embraced the entire area, stretching all the way from the shore to the farthest reaches behind the castle. As I took in the dense stands of wooly fir, emerald pine, and the shivering branches of oak and elm, I could scarcely believe this breathtaking place was real.

Dizzily, I clung to Arthur, searching his face for some sign I was dreaming.

He merely smiled softly. "Welcome to Camelot, Guinevere."

෧෩ ෨෨

We followed a hidden path to the castle and entered through a private side gate so as not to attract the attention of the townsfolk. There would be time to meet them later.

I couldn't help but crane my neck in awe, taking in the vaulted ceilings, towering columns, and Roman arches that defied nature as they held up massive stone blocks heavy enough to crush a man should they fall. Arthur led me through the maze of corridors into the heart of the castle.

"My father had long dreamed of a fortress to rival even the greatest built by Rome," Arthur explained, "one none of our enemies would dare attack."

I heard his voice but couldn't tear my eyes away to look at him. He didn't appear to mind, guiding me as patiently and gently as one leading the blind.

"He spent most of his life studying Roman and Greek architecture and even the engineering of the strange lands far to the east of Rome. This place was his life's work, but even had he lived one hundred years, he could not have completed this alone."

"He had Merlin's help," I said softly, as sure of that as I was of my own name.

I had seen Merlin's powers of persuasion firsthand. The Archdruid had a way of convincing people to do his bidding, yet he left them with the certainty that it was their idea, that they had volunteered for whatever backbreaking task he had in mind.

"How many years did it take to build?" I looked at Arthur for the first time.

"Several decades from what Merlin has said. I was living with Lord Ector, so I know little of what occurred in the royal family before my father's death."

We stopped in a circular portico that stretched out beyond the main walls of the castle. Watching over it at even intervals were four giant statues, each several times larger than any mortal man.

"Your tribal gods?" I asked, thinking this room was a sort of shrine.

Arthur shook his head. "My family." He pulled a large golden ring from the smallest finger of his left hand and held it out for me to see. "This ring tells their story."

The band was thin, capped by a square with rounded corners. The square was divided into twelve triangles filled with smoky quartz. A large round sapphire dominated the center, braced at four corners by smaller blue stones. Encircling the whole was a wreath of ornately wrought gold resembling eight crescents of lace. At the center of each, capping the spokes of the triangles, was a large gold orb.

"It's beautiful," I exclaimed, holding the ring up and turning it this way and that in the sunlight.

Arthur nodded. "Indeed. It was hard won over many generations."

He took my hand and approached the first statue, a stoic man with sharp features and a hawklike stare. He wore a Roman toga, its dark gray marble nearly purple in the shadows, and a wreath of laurel was chiseled around his head.

"This is the Emperor Constantine the Third, my grandfather, the last Roman ruler of this isle. He was proclaimed emperor by the Britons, but he had quite a bit of trouble with your mother's people, I'm told," he said.

My mother had come from the Votadini, one of the four tribes who lived just north of Hadrian's Wall. "We don't enjoy being told what to do," I said matter-of-factly.

Arthur grinned. "So I've noticed." He pointed at the center stone in the ring. "This sapphire was part of the booty Constantine collected upon conquering the city of Arles, which was part of Gaul, southwest of Brittany. But at that point, it was only a stone."

"How did it come to be like this?" I asked, touching the ring and letting my hand rest on his.

"Ah, to answer that, I must introduce you to my uncle."

Passing a wide window that reached from floor to ceiling, we came to the next statue, a man with slightly gentler features and a pleasant expression. He held a book and a map.

"This is Aurelius Ambrosius, second eldest son of Constantine. Aurelius was considered a great diplomat, and he was the first to try to unite the ancient tribes. To a certain extent, he succeeded. Were it not for him, my father would not have been able to claim the title of high king."

"But Vortigern held the throne between Constantine and Aurelius, did he not?" I asked, turning from the statue to my husband.

Arthur was pleased. "They taught you well in Avalon." Then his face clouded, and he clenched his jaw, making a muscle jump. His eyes hardened, turning as cold as the marble statues. "The tyrant Vortigern. . ." Arthur exhaled. "He usurped the throne in the chaos surrounding Constantine's death. You see, Constantine's sons were too young to rule, so they fled to Brittany to seek safe haven, and Vortigern swooped in to fill the void. He was king of Powys at the time. Idiocy must run in the blood, for from what you tell me of your encounters with him, Vortigern's current progeny, Evrain, is no wiser than his great-grandfather. All Vortigern got in return was a knife in the gut, betrayed by the Saxons at his own peace council. Some say he died—"

"Others say he sleeps still under the mountains of Snowdonia," I whispered. In my mind's eye, the icy peaks rose to the north of my childhood home, and I recalled the fanciful tale that said Vortigern's breath melted the snows in spring each year. I also remembered it was he who had convinced my maternal grandfather to settle in Gwynedd, an act that eventually led to my mother marrying my father. Because of that, I was in some small measure happy Vortigern had had his moment of triumph.

Arthur interrupted my reverie by continuing his tale. "Vortigern's son, Vortimer, reigned for a few months before being poisoned, but I can promise you my family had no hand in that. We simply took back the title that was rightfully ours. Aurelius had the sapphire set in a brooch. The story goes that the triangles represent the ancient tribes, those who held the most power during Aurelius's time."

Arthur led me onward around the room. Another window, a twin of the first, separated Ambrosius from his brother. I looked up into features that bore a distinct resemblance to my husband's. I knew before Arthur even spoke that this was Uther Pendragon.

Arthur put an arm around me and gently urged me forward. "Father, may I present to you my wife, Guinevere of Northgallis."

Smiling with a mixture of embarrassment and admiration for my husband, I curtsied before the mute figure. "My lord, I only wish I could have met you in this world."

As I raised my head, I took in the image next to Uther, the only woman in the group. I recognized her immediately for I had met her only a short time before. This was Queen Iggraine. In her full regal regalia, strong and confident, she stood in stark contrast to the docile nun who had witnessed my marriage and coronation while shrouded in heavy black robes.

Arthur seemed to understand my musings. "My mother was a mighty queen, or so they tell me. She ruled her family's ancestral kingdom of Dyfnaint with her first husband, Goloris, for several years. When my sister was about seven or eight—I can't remember now—Uther visited Tintagel. As Ana tells it, Uther was smitten with my mother when he first laid eyes on her. I'm not sure how Ana could have known that at such a young age, but to this day she maintains her certainty.

"Uther called on Goloris and his men to help defend against the Saxons as they were pushing west from the old Regni lands and soon would threaten Dyfnaint. Uther's army was victorious, but Goloris perished. My mother eventually wed Uther, becoming high queen. This ring was his gift to her, forged from the brooch, as a wedding present." Arthur took the ring and slipped it onto the largest finger of my right hand. "And now I wish you to have it. You are part of this family and part of its story now." He kissed both of my hands. Arthur's gaze turned from me to the image of his mother. "I hadn't intended to tell you my whole family history today, but there you have it. I hope to come to know yours sometime."

"You will," I assured him. My attention was drawn to an empty niche beyond another pair of windows. "What is this for then?"

Arthur looked into the shadows of the alcove. "That place

is reserved for my own statue." He turned to me. "And I hope yours as well."

My cheeks flushed as I embraced him. "I would be honored."

"Come." He tugged on my arm. "I want to show you why I did not bring you here for the wedding."

We traversed yet more hallways leading deep into the center of the castle. Arthur paused before opening a single door. As we stepped into an enclosed courtyard, a rush of cold air raised my skirts, bringing goose pimples to my legs.

I gasped. Before me was a perfect replica of the labyrinth that coiled around the Tor in Avalon. Borders of stone and bush formed the boundaries of the gravel pathway, which wound inward rather than up as the one on the Tor did. Outside the circle was a carpet of grass bordered on three sides by the castle. A high wall guarded the fourth side, affording complete privacy.

"The garden was just completed. I was waiting for word before bringing you here. I have no doubt it will be prettier during the growing season," Arthur said by way of excuse for the plants that had long since turned inward to become reedy skeletons during the cold months.

"I think it is wonderful," I gushed as I pulled him along the path behind me.

"Viviane told me how much walking the labyrinth in Avalon helped you think. I fear that as queen there will be much on your mind, so the least I could do was provide you with a place of sanctuary."

I stopped, turned, and kissed him.

After some time, he pulled away, grinning, and urged me onward. When we reached the center, I clapped a hand over my mouth. A lone apple tree shivered in the breeze, waving a few stubborn pieces of withered fruit at us in greeting.

"From Avalon's own orchards," Arthur proclaimed proudly. He drew up close behind me so I felt his warm breath on my ear.

"Viviane?" I asked.

"And Merlin," he added.

"Of course."

Arthur bent forward and embraced me tightly. "I hope you will feel welcome here, Guinevere."

"I already do."

☙ ❧

Once the Yule celebrations were over and I had met the entire court, as well as half the populous—or so it felt—Arthur and I retreated into the warmth of his study. The small room was located above his bedroom and accessible only by a hidden staircase that led from one room to the other. Here we would not be disturbed.

As the snow fell deep and ice coated the land below, I set about learning all I could about the vast island for which I now had responsibility. On the table, Arthur had spread out a large map depicting each of the kingdoms, their intersections with ancient tribal boundaries, and areas of possible conflict. I traced the carefully drawn lines with my fingertips—green land, blue water, red battle lines—remembering the large tapestry map that hung in my father's council chamber. The borders had changed little since then, and unfortunately, neither had the conflicts.

"The Saxons have all but given up fighting for the winter," Arthur explained, "but we do have a small contingent holding out near Badbury Hill. Our men are well supplied at the fort there, so I believe they will make it through the winter with few casualties. But I can't say the same for the Saxons. They know if they cripple us there, they will have a clear path into the Summer Country and Salisbury Plain. That's why they are willing to starve. And starve they will." He growled the last sentence like an irritated bear.

He stabbed a finger at one of the many forts lining Hadrian's Wall to the northeast of us. "The tribes between the walls appear to be our next concern. My men at Corastopitum report increased activity in the area and believe Chief Caw of the Damnonii is planning something." He sank back in his chair. "As for our western foes, the Irish are quiet for now, and if King Mark follows my advice, they are likely to remain placated."

I raised an eyebrow at him. "What advice?"

Arthur's smile was full of mischief. "I told him it would be wise for him to make alliances—of the marital variety."

I considered the possibilities. I knew of several unmarried noblewomen Mark could choose from, including the docile Elaine, whose neighboring kingdom of Dyfed could possibly present a united front with Cornwall against the Irish. But even that didn't suggest a strong enough alliance to keep them at bay. Surely Arthur couldn't mean Isolde, could he? Mark was handsome, but she would never suffer his arrogance. I imagined the arguments that would surely arise from that union and smiled.

I was still giggling as I readied the board of Holy Stones, a divination tool of the Druids that most people considered merely a game. As I set the two clusters of twenty-one stones in their places, I said a quick prayer of gratitude I had been taught how to use the sight to draw deeper meaning from the game. Even if I didn't know the politics of the realm as well as Arthur yet, at least I could prove my worth this way.

I arranged the stones to mirror a battle with the Damnonii. The four tribes that made up the area between the Hadrian and Antonine Walls were normally peaceful, allied with us even though they weren't subject to Arthur. But like anywhere else, it only took one poor decision to plunge them into war. If Arthur thought they were a threat, they likely were.

I stared at the stones, letting the sight take over. Flashes came to me as I moved the pieces, which represented different groups of warriors, trying over and over to find the point of greatest advantage for our troops. Our men were more formally trained than the Damnonii, but the northerners were quick and fiercely determined. They knew if they could get our men off their horses, they evened the fight. Plus, they had been raised on the land, felt it their souls, and could use every hiding place and ambush point to their favor.

"I've been thinking," Arthur said some time later, jolting me out of my trance.

I blinked, forcing my mind back to him. "About what?"

"We are fools if we don't learn from our predecessors," he said, flicking away the latest missive from one of his advisors.

"I agree. But to what end? What are you proposing?"

He rose and came to stand beside me, studying the board. "Claudius just completed his survey of the old Roman forts. He sent a report by messenger. It made me think we are lacking something in our defenses." His hand hovered over the defending army, and he moved a company of spearmen.

I swatted his hand and moved the pebble back; my plan would

be completely derailed if I lost that group of men. "My visions are showing the same." I gestured to the board. "I'll show you."

Arthur leaned forward on his arms, and the table groaned.

"Our horsemen should be our strongest asset." I indicated a group of blue stones currently clustered around the queen. "They are powerful, fast, and difficult to defend against, so why do we lose so many? From what I can see, they have two main limitations—they are easily unseated and those who are not are often grievously wounded. If we could give them a more secure base from which to fight and strengthen their armor, they could truly be a force to be feared."

Arthur sat next to me, studying the stones. "I see your point. The Breton boy who won the tournament—what was his name?"

"Lancelot."

"Yes. Lancelot had some interesting thoughts on modifying saddles that I am curious to test. He pointed out that some of the strongest armies in the world employ a foothold on either side to keep their men from slipping from their steeds. It's in part how the Scythians and Sarmatians earned their fearsome reputation."

I shivered at the mental image of the wild horsemen who had many times terrorized Rome and most of the continent, leaving a bloody trail in their wake. If we could learn from them, we stood a better chance of keeping our attackers at bay, perhaps even defeating them for good.

My thoughts turned to Lancelot and how he had shocked everyone at the tournament by turning down the honor of being named Arthur's second. Arthur had politely accepted his refusal, but it was an embarrassment, so I'd expected Arthur to treat it as an insult. But here he was waxing poetic about Lancelot's wisdom. I shook my head. I still had a lot to learn about my husband.

Beside me, Arthur rambled on, oblivious to my musings. "Claudius also reports there may be some advantage to returning to the old tribal armor. Have you ever seen it?"

I nodded, remembering the weight of the thick layer of interlocking metal rings on my chest and shoulders as I learned weaponry from my mother. A few tribes still used it, but in general, it had been abandoned because of the expense and time it took to produce.

"We could never afford to outfit every man with it," Arthur said, "but I think it may be worth trying on our most elite forces even though they will need a little time and training with it. I am certain we still have some metalsmiths left who know the craft."

I looked at the pieces on the board, seeing men in their place. "Arthur, I think you are on the right track. Look."

I shuffled pieces across the board, engineering an escape to open land for the mounted army. They fanned out, keeping the queen safe behind their impenetrable line. They swallowed up the contingents of footmen, easily deflecting blows from spears and other missiles, cutting down whole ranks in mere moments. A few perished, but only a few turns later, they had captured the king and were in striking distance of the opposing queen. It was only a matter of time before she was taken.

I looked up at Arthur, proud to have finally found the path to victory. "If this army had the improvements you suggest, they would easily overpower their opponents."

"And with your strategy, they would be certain to win." His eyes were alight with hope and satisfaction.

Slowly, I realized he was proud of me, his battle queen and partner, his wife. I had gained some measure of respect, passed a test neither of us had known was looming.

I pushed myself up, standing just enough so I could kiss him gently, tacitly, as I measured his interest. His kisses were warm, but the nails he ran down my arms suggested he was in the mood for something more sporting than our usual soft lovemaking. I nipped his lower lip in answer and moved my hips against his.

Groping blindly behind me, Arthur shoved the contents of the tabletop to the floor, letters falling like autumn leaves in my peripheral vision. He bent me backward until I was half standing and half lying on the table. Before he could even grab my dress, I went for his trousers, peeling them off to expose his swollen manhood. Starting at his knee, I ran my tongue up his inner thigh and took him into my mouth. Arthur grunted his pleasure.

When he could take no more, he stopped me, leaned me back again, and entered me with such force I cried out. My body, more than wakened by the act I'd just performed, accepted him willingly. It wasn't long before we were both panting and spent, lying in each other's arms on the floor.

But that didn't last long. As soon as he recovered, Arthur kissed each of my breasts and rose to his feet, fastening his trousers.

"Where are you going?" I called as he bounded down the stairs to his bedroom.

"To find the Breton boy. We have to get the men and horses trained before anyone else attacks."

I flopped back down, using my arms as a pillow. So this was the life of a queen, abandoned by my husband for his men and horses. Yet I smiled. I was happy after all.

<h1 style="text-align:center">Chapter Three</h1>

Spring 497

By the time the first blossoms appeared on the trees, I was pregnant. I was wary of telling Arthur for I had already lost one child over the winter. I went little more than a month without bleeding then had a harder time of it when it did come. But there were signs any priestess would recognize, and I knew.

I had been using certain herbs to encourage conception, the antithesis of those I had used to prevent it when I was with Aggrivane. It appeared they were working, but I was still frightened this one would not last, so I kept my happy little secret and spent time every night praying to Brigid, the divine midwife and healer, that the child within me would grow strong and live to open his or her eyes to the world.

Finally, I could wait no longer. My breasts had swollen, along with my belly, and it looked as though the child was destined to live. One clear evening near Beltane, Arthur and I stood on one of Camelot's many terraces, watching the sun settle to its rest in the bosom of the mountains. As I watched him contemplating the peaceful land below, my mind ran through a million ways to tell him, hundreds of phrases, but none of them conveyed the growing sense of hope within me.

I took his hand, and he looked at me, immediately noticing the preoccupation in my eyes. Before he could ask, I put a finger to his lips.

"My love, I am with child," I said quietly.

A flicker of confusion then the dawn of clarity came into his eyes. A wide smile lit up his face. "Truly?"

I nodded, my eyes filling with tears. "By the end of the year, you will have an heir."

He picked me up with a whoop of joy and spun me around then set me gently on my feet. He embraced me with a tenderness I would not have expected from a man of his tall, broad stature.

I stood with my head resting on his chest, listening to his heartbeat. This was supposed to be a moment of great joy and anticipation, but I already felt panic dulling the happiness. It coiled around my heart and slithered down my spine, leaving an icy trail in its wake. I grabbed Arthur's hands and squeezed them.

"I have never been so scared," I admitted in a small voice.

Arthur leaned back and tipped my face up toward his. "Why?"

I pulled away from him and paced, willing my heart to slow though it seemed determined to beat faster with every step. "My mother bore thirteen children—did I ever tell you that? I was the only one to live more than a few years. Most died shortly after birth and some well before. And my mother"—my voice cracked—"she died in childbirth. They tell me she screamed for days before my father finally had the child cut from her body in the hope of saving him, but it was too late. What if the same fate befalls me? The goddess of fertility is not kind to the women in my family, Arthur."

To his credit, Arthur listened to my rambling patiently and didn't try to stop me.

My eyes fixated on a puffy pink cloud as the ghost of a memory danced in the back of my mind. "I remember having a brother. I wasn't much older than he when he succumbed to some sort of illness. The saddest thing is that one day he was prattling at my feet, and the next he was dead. All that life, all of his potential, gone in the blink of an eye."

Arthur wrapped his arms around me from behind and rested his chin on the top of my head. "The same misfortune will not befall you. It is terrible your parents suffered so, but your life is your own. You are young and strong and nothing bad will happen to you. I will not let it. I promise."

I tipped my head back to look at him. He was beaming with pride. I forced myself to smile, letting the panic ebb away under his touch. "So who do we tell first? Your family or mine?"

He grinned. "We tell the world."

⁕⁖ ⁖⁕

As the weather warmed and buds began to dot the trees, I set out to get to know my people. I longed to visit the innkeepers, midwives, blacksmiths, carpenters, bakers, tanners, and families of all trades. Just as Pellinor had on Candlemas, I wished to introduce myself personally and hear about their daily needs not important enough to lay before the court in formal petition.

Just before I left the fortress for the town, Arthur broke away from a conversation with Kay, Bedivere, and Malegant to catch my arm.

"Since you have not yet named your champion and have no one to guard you, you should take one of my men with you," he said.

"Why? I can defend myself if need be."

Arthur looked down, scratching the base of his neck. "Oh, I am well aware. But it's not just you I am concerned with." He placed a hand on my belly. "We have enemies all around, my love. I would feel better knowing you had someone watching over you. Plus, you could devote more of your attention to listening to the people if you didn't need to constantly be on your guard."

"He makes a valid point," Kay put in.

"I volunteer to accompany you, my queen," Malegant interjected with a slight bow and a gracious smile.

"Do you now? And why should I choose you over the other men here?"

"Because I speak three languages and am knowledgeable in trade from the diversity of my own kingdom. Think of me more as an advisor."

"One with a very sharp sword." Arthur snickered.

"Indeed. Plus, it will give us the chance to get to know one another better. After all, I too am one of your loyal subjects." Malegant's eyes sparkled with mirth.

I laughed despite myself. "That is what I asked for, is it not? Very well." I eyed Malegant with mock suspicion. "But do not get in my way," I teased.

It didn't take Malegant long to prove his worth. By noon, he had already physically turned away one man whom he'd deemed a threat to my safety, discussed the competitive price of shellfish up and down the coast with a fishmonger, and by nightfall had taught a young apprentice how to load amphore without spilling the contents.

"How does the Lord of the Summer Country know such things?" I asked the next day as we wandered through the town again.

Malegant raised a tawny eyebrow at me. "Do you think I've spent my years only yelling commands and counting my wealth? I have had many adventures, lived many lives." He took my forearm and guided me through a particularly crowded lane. "You see, my family has a bit of a turbulent past. When my father was killed, I was forced to flee my tribe and seek fosterage elsewhere. When I came of age, I had the skill but not the power to defeat those who sought my blood. So I worked where I could, learning and gaining respect as I went. Now I know a little about a great many things."

With his vast knowledge, Malegant became an advisor to the people in addition to my personal guard. We spent many mornings together, seeking to learn the ways of those who lived in the shadow of Camelot.

Once the rains ended and seeds were sown, the market returned, and I spent most of my spare time among the milling crowds, visiting vendors from the surrounding countryside. I quickly learned it was they, not the townspeople, who were the most reliable source of information. Free of Camelot's walls, they came bearing news from three kingdoms in every direction.

Those glorious, sun-dappled spring mornings, when the harbor breeze carried the scent of lilacs and salt and the world felt full of possibilities, were also perfect for loosening lips as everyone wanted to bask in the sunshine and spread the latest gossip. In one morning, I learned from a woman selling freshly picked greens that Morgan had given birth to a son, a tanner told me of rumors that a new Christian missionary was due in town, and a hunter setting up shop to peddle his pelts relayed that the Saxons were recruiting any mercenaries and outlaws they could find. That was chilling confirmation of what Arthur's spies had long suspected. Arthur's attempts at diplomacy had failed; soon there would again be war.

But that was not the only disturbance pricking at my mind. Malegant's behavior was beginning to concern me. When he'd first taken to defending me from those who would clamor for a piece of their queen––those who rushed at me or if a crowd pressed in too close––I attributed his zeal to overprotection. But as the weeks passed, I noted he was enjoying his role of enforcer a little too much, sometimes shoving and tossing men aside when a polite word would have done.

When I spoke to him of it, he promised to reign in his temper, but I wondered if he could hold to it, especially after the heated argument he had instigated that very morning with another nobleman who offered to take his place at my side.

The memory was still fresh in my mind when a group of young men, chieftains' sons judging by their finery, called to Malegant to join them in the alehouse.

Malegant waved them off. "I'm afraid that must wait for another time. For today I am the queen's protector."

All eyes turned to me. It didn't take long for one of the boys to kneel, his friends following suit. The first looked familiar, tall and lanky with big brown eyes that made him appear younger than he likely was. Something in his awkward gestures tugged at my memory. Perhaps we had met before.

"Please, my lords, rise. I do not require such gestures every time someone lays eyes on me."

They stood, and the tallest ambled over to Malegant. "How does *Pudicitia Fur* become the queen's guardian?" He elbowed Malegant. "Who did you have to bribe to get that position?"

I turned to Malegant, who had gone rigid, his nostrils flaring. "These are your friends, yet they call you 'the virtue thief'? Pray tell me how you came by that name."

"He is known for taking what he wants," one of the men answered for Malegant, either not catching or ignoring the joke in my voice.

"That's an understatement," snorted another. "Liked Fiona so much he stole her right out from under her father's nose."

The familiar man tensed. "You speak of my sister. Show some respect," he said through gritted teeth.

"I could say the same to you," Malegant stated. "Show your betters their due, Fergus."

Fergus. It all clicked into place. The familiar man before me was the grown-up version of the Powys boy to whom Lord Evrain had tried to match me nearly two years earlier. Being the youngest son, he was of lower rank than Malegant, who ruled his own kingdom, thus Fergus was expected to demonstrate deference.

"You are no better than I and certainly not worthy of Fiona," Fergus growled.

"Hey, little pup, don't get your hackles up over me," Malegant taunted.

"Gentlemen, that is enough," I warned them.

Fergus paid me no heed, advancing on Malegant. "And why not? You kidnapped my sister, forced her to marry you, and now you ensure her allegiance through fear. I've seen her bruises. I know what you do to her. What you've done to them all."

I didn't like the way this was going. Soon they would come to blows. I should have just left them to it for it was no business of mine what they did, but Fergus's words stirred something in the back of my mind. What was it the priestess had said when I first sighted Malegant outside of Avalon all those years ago—that he had sullied more than one priestess and was not to be trusted?

Malegant leaned toward Fergus, so close his breath stirred Fergus's beard. "Be careful what you say, boy, or I shall be forced to put you in your place."

"And where is that? At the bottom of a bog with your last wife?"

Malegant's face turned scarlet. Before I could step between them, he was grappling with Fergus like a wrestler. His friends were no help; rather than helping me break up the fight, they cheered Malegant and Fergus on.

A crowd gathered around us, yelling and placing bets, as I looked for an opening to put an end to this childish behavior. Malegant knocked Fergus to the ground and landed a blow to his gut. Fergus kicked back, and I was able to wedge myself between them, shoving hard at the shoulders of both men.

"That is enough, both of you. You are lords in your own right, not children." I shouted Fergus and his friends away. "Go on about your business. If you don't, I will have you imprisoned for endangering my welfare."

The three of them scampered into the crowd.

I turned to Malegant. "I shall require a new protector, one

who can hold his temper. Rest assured Arthur will hear of this. You have proven yourself an embarrassment to the crown."

Malegant opened his mouth, presumably to defend himself, but I didn't let him.

"Move," I commanded the onlookers, who dutifully parted to let me through.

As I stormed back to the castle, I was certain of two things: Arthur would not deal kindly with Malegant's transgression and Malegant's anger toward me would take a long time to flare out. He was a proud man, and I had just publicly shamed him. Were I any other woman, I might have feared his wrath, but my position protected me from any revenge he might seek. Or so I chose to believe.

Chapter Four

Summer 497

Combrogi—that's what he called them. It was an ancient word meaning "fellow countrymen," but to Arthur, it meant much more. Those men were his most trusted advisors, his brothers. They were also the strongest warriors in the land. Led by twelve prime members, each represented his own tribe and took Arthur's decrees back to their lords. It was a relationship based in mutual trust. He hid nothing from them and listened to their thoughts, in return expecting them to respect his decisions and be open with their opinions. If that bond were broken, so too would be the tenuous peace that united us as one land.

They were more than a war council and something other than a team of advisors. Together the decisions the Combrogi made had to take into account the temperament of their lords, the needs of the peasants, threats from within and outside our borders, and still reconcile conflicts between generals in such a way they would supply Arthur's needs for men, horses, and supplies.

As queen, I was now one of them, attending my first of their quarterly meetings held on each of the solar festivals. The Combrogi gathered in Arthur's circular meeting hall, the area I had mistaken for a shrine on my first day at Camelot. Arthur and I sat in thrones raised slightly above the other seats. All others were equal in their places. A few chairs stood empty, waiting for the return of men who were out on assignments for the king.

Today my father occupied one of the open spaces. He was not technically a member of the Combrogi, but since he was visiting, he had insisted on sitting in. Arthur wasn't pleased by this, but because Northgallis's support would be crucial in the upcoming war, he'd acquiesced. He had, however, drawn the line at allowing Father Marius to accompany my father. Arthur had explained that not even Merlin attended these meetings and if Leodgrance felt the need for spiritual direction, he could obtain it in private, just as Arthur did.

As Gawain began his report on how the adoption of the stirrups and chainmail was progressing, I caught sight of a shadow drifting from left to right, right to left beneath the chamber doors. If I listened closely, I could hear the almost imperceptible sweep of fabric across the stones followed at even intervals by the whisper of Latin.

Marius. I smiled. It must have been killing him to wait outside, two armed guards barring his entrance. At least this was the last time he'd darken our doors for a while. He was leaving for Rome in the morning, called there by the leader of his religion to report on the spread of Christianity in our fair isle. With any luck, they would keep him there.

"The men are adapting to the new armor much better than

the horses are to the new saddle and stirrup, my lord," Gawain was saying when my attention returned to the room. "We are having some difficultly training them to it."

"Perhaps if you didn't beat them into submission, they would respect you rather than fear you," I answered, temper rising quickly.

Horses were sacred to my family as a symbol of the Goddess. Call her Epona, Rhiannon, or any other name, horses were her animals, and I could not bear to see them harmed. I had never seen them mistreated until I came here. In Gwynedd, we loved our horses, letting them warm to us, and earned their trust over time. What resulted was a lifelong bond that was broken only by death. During one of the Irish attacks, I had even seen a horse turn on an enemy soldier when his rider was threatened.

In contrast, these northern men knew no way to get an animal to do their bidding other than to break its spirit. Horses, oxen, dogs—it didn't matter; they wanted to dominate them all with whips and brands. I suspected they used the same tactics on their women.

I had hoped my position would help end their barbaric practices, but I could do little to make Arthur see reason. I had even demonstrated to the Combrogi how I'd learned to train my own horse and showed them how he could be taught to tolerate the modified saddle. But my advice had fallen on deaf ears, and the reason was always the same—"It takes too much time. Time we do not have."

Arthur shot me a reproachful look. "Guinevere, we have discussed this. If anyone can show me an effective way to tame the stallions that does not take months of work, I will gladly employ his methods, but until then, we must continue with what we know. It is imperative that both horse and rider learn to accommodate our new offenses as quickly as possible."

Gawain wisely moved on to another subject before I could respond. But he wasn't talking for long before the chamber doors burst open and my heart stopped. Sweeping through the door with great agitation was my former fiancé, followed by a man whose angelic gaze took my breath away.

Aggrivane bowed before Arthur, ignoring me completely. "Your Majesty, my lords, I apologize for the interruption. But word reached me you were looking for this man." He jerked his thumb over his shoulder at Lancelot. "I have found him, and I now happily deliver him to you."

Something in Aggrivane's voice told me he was still smarting from Lancelot's victory at the tournament in Dyfed two summers before. The pair had obviously not bonded on their journey here.

Lancelot bowed, first to me then to Arthur. "I am pleased to be of service to you, High King. Please tell me how I may help." His accent made every word sound as though it tumbled on a light breeze.

Arthur gestured for the two men to sit. The only empty chairs left were on either side of Tristan, directly opposite me, so I had no choice but to look at the two of them. Lancelot smiled warmly at me, but Aggrivane still refused to acknowledge my presence.

Arthur addressed Aggrivane. "I thank you for doing what no other of my subjects seem capable of—" He nodded at Lancelot. "Harnessing the wind. As a gesture of my thanks, Aggrivane, you may take a place among my Combrogi, if you wish."

I stopped breathing. *No, no, no, no, no. This isn't happening.*

This can't be happening. Arthur knew our history. He couldn't be so thick as to name Aggrivane one of his most trusted men, could he?

But then I remembered Arthur's deal with Lot, who had led an unsuccessful rebellion shortly after Arthur came to power. As punishment, Lot's sons were forever under Arthur's control, and Arthur preferred to keep them as close as possible. I let out a silent sigh, sagging in my chair. It looked as though I would have to get used to having my former lover around, something I was not comfortable with. As much as I had learned to be happy with Arthur, part of my heart still belonged to Aggrivane.

Aggrivane looked at Arthur with great surprise. Apparently he hadn't expected so kind a reception either. "My Lord, I am honored to accept."

Arthur narrowed his eyes to steely darts directed at Aggrivane. "My offer is, of course, based on the provision that you have kept your word to me."

I looked from the man I'd thought would be my husband to the one who was. As far as I knew, they hadn't seen one another since the night Arthur proposed to me and sent my life crashing down around me. I had no idea what promise Arthur could have extracted from Aggrivane.

Arthur's features relaxed as Aggrivane nodded slowly. "Good. I look forward to seeing proof of your fidelity." He turned his attention to Lancelot. "I assume my lord Lothian has told you I have taken your advice on how to improve our forces? You are well-known for your skill with horses, are you not?"

"*Oui,*" Lancelot answered, somewhat perplexed.

"Then you will join us in the stable yard at noon. We are all eager to see what you can do." Arthur banged his fist on the table three times, and the meeting was adjourned.

ෲ ෧

"What did he mean, 'proof of your fidelity?'" I demanded as the door boomed shut behind me.

Aggrivane didn't look up from where he sat, drinking deeply from a cup of what smelled like strong red wine. The shutters were shut, blocking out the daylight, so the only illumination came from the fire pit. But in that subtle glow, I saw him wince.

"Why do you not ask him yourself? He is your husband." The words were forced through gritted teeth.

"Aggrivane, do not do this. Do not behave like this," I begged.

"How am I behaving? Like a jilted lover? No, I have no right to that title."

His sarcasm stung. I crossed my arms defensively, as if to ward off his anger.

"Tell me, how long after I left that night did it take you to fall into his arms? Or his bed?"

I ignored his question. "Need I remind you that *you* left me? You left me to face my unwanted fate all alone. The least you could have done was stand by my side and fight for me."

He wrenched the cork from a bottle and poured himself another glass of wine without looking up. "What good would that have done? He is High King. I am nothing in comparison. From what I hear, your fate was sealed long before that night. You were never intended to be with me."

"Arthur was not aware of our relationship. Did you know that?"

Aggrivane met my gaze then, apparently speechless.

"If you had stayed, if we had faced him together, none of this would have happened. We might be together now."

Aggrivane swallowed hard, the shadow of what could have been darkening his eyes. "*Might* is the operative word. He could just as easily have dismissed me and taken you to wife anyway. He bears no love for my family, remember? Even now he uses my father's attempted rebellion to hold me to foolish promises."

I bent in front of him to grasp the arms of his chair. "Exactly what proof does he expect to see?"

"You do not want me to answer that, my queen." His face was only inches from mine, but he kept his eyes trained on the crimson bottom of his cup.

"Aggrivane, please stop with the formality. It is only the two of us here. Remember us?" My mind flashed back to the night we were reunited at Corbenic and our frantic lovemaking. My cheeks flushed, but I doubted he saw it. "Answer the question."

"Fine." He let the silence stretch out before meeting my gaze with cold, emotionless eyes. "Arthur wishes to meet my wife."

I recoiled as though he had punched me in the gut. "You are married?"

The words hung in the air like a bird gliding on the wind.

Then he shot them down with the only arrow that would find the mark. "And you are pregnant."

My hands automatically went to my belly. It wasn't yet obvious through my clothing, so someone must have told him. "Yes, I am."

I moved away and opened the shutters.

He squinted at me through the bright light. "Well, we make quite the pair, do we not? Both married to people we do not love and you with a child on the way."

"I never said I do not love Arthur," I said automatically, then the full meaning of his words hit me and my stomach clenched. "Wait—you are not in love with your wife?" I sat across from him, unconsciously leaning toward him.

"Do you really think I could fall in love with someone in such a short time?" He sounded hurt. "I do love Camille but not the way I loved you."

I cringed. Camille? What sort of name was that? It sounded fitting for a cat or maybe a prize dairy cow.

"When my father sent me away, it was back to the Saxon border where he knew my mind would be preoccupied with other things, like staying alive. Sometime later, I heard of your wedding. That was a grim time for me, and I will not insult your intelligence by saying I spent that night alone. It was easy to find comfort in the arms of a stranger."

Hurt bubbled up inside me. Telling me he had been with a whore or his wife was a whore, whichever the case may be, was not helping.

"A short time later, a messenger from the king arrived, instructing me not to return to court for at least six months, and even then I could not return without a wife." He cocked his head at me. "It seems your husband wanted to neutralize any threat I may be to his new marriage."

I glowered at him, silently willing him to get to the point.

"Once the snows cleared, I'd had enough of battle and decided to visit the court of my uncle Uriens. Aunt Morgan says hello, by the way." He raised his glass to me mockingly.

I gave him a derisive smile. He was clearly enjoying himself.

"I walked into a hornet's nest there, but it all turned out well."

He swung his feet up onto a footstool, set his glass down, and laced his hands together on his abdomen, waiting.

He clearly wanted me to ask him to continue, but I wouldn't give him the satisfaction. Moments passed as we stared at one another, neither willing to budge. I considered the appropriateness of labeling anywhere Morgan was a hornet's nest. She would have been their queen bee.

Finally, I gave in with a heavy sigh. "And what was so interesting in Rheged?"

For the first time since he'd arrived, Aggrivane smiled. "My wife."

I thought I was going to vomit, and it had nothing to do with my pregnancy.

"I will wager you did not know Uriens had a daughter, did you? Well, she is adopted. Her parents died in a fire when she was a child. She still has scars on her hands. She spent some time in a convent, but with no family to provide for her expenses, they could not let her stay. So Uriens took her in. It is a shame the nuns could not keep her; she would have made a great nun, wanted nothing more in the world.

"Anyway, she was caretaker to Accolon's sons and Morgan's new baby when I arrived. She was content too, but Uriens insisted she marry. He said without a husband, she was a drain on the family's resources."

"So she married you," I concluded, happy to have his drawn-out tale finished.

Aggrivane wagged a finger at me. "Eventually yes, but not yet. Let me finish the story."

"I wish you would."

"You see, Camille is a Christian." He waited for me to blanch, but I carefully kept my face neutral. "She believed she belonged to Christ just as much as if she had taken vows in the convent. She refused to marry and, in an act of rebellion, cut off all her hair."

My mouth dropped open. "But the only women who wear their hair shorn are slaves. It is sign of bondage."

"Yes, it is. For Camille, it was a sign of bondage to Christ. She was his slave, so she made certain no man would want to marry her."

"But you did."

Aggrivane dropped his eyes to his cup again. "When I arrived, Uriens was threatening to sell her into a brothel or let her starve on the streets. I couldn't let that happen."

Don't act as if this was all charity on your part. I almost said it, but something in his expression stopped me.

"But you also saw a solution to Arthur's provision," I reminded him.

"Yes, it worked out well for us both."

My browed furrowed. "How did you convince someone so bonded to Christ to give up her virginity to you? That is still a condition of marriage in her faith, isn't it?"

A small rumble echoed in Aggrivane's throat. "Religion be damned. The marriage was not consummated, so it is not valid in that way, but it is still legally binding. However, if you tell anyone what I have shared with you, Camille and I are ruined."

I briefly considered shouting it from the rooftops. Slowly, I understood that his risky admission was Aggrivane's way of apologizing. If I wanted to ruin him and have him removed from court—and Arthur's good graces—I could. He'd willingly given me the key.

Aggrivane rose and slowly advanced on me. "I allow Camille to live as a spouse of Christ, and she enables me to be here. Once Arthur has met her, she will return to Rheged and help raise Uriens' children and grandchildren. Do you understand? We live a lie because it suits us. She is there, and I am here. I am here because I—"

He was interrupted by a light rapping on the door.

"Enter," I said, thinking it was one of the guards calling me to the stables.

The door swung open, and a young woman with dark hair and eyes entered. Her face lit up at the sight of Aggrivane, but she immediately dropped into a curtsy when she noticed me. Her short, uneven hair prevented her veil from lying flat on her head, and she wore thin gloves. This was obviously Camille.

"Your Grace, they told me I might find my husband here. I am—"

Her voice was as placid as her eyes, but in spite of Aggrivane's confession, I couldn't stop jealousy from surging through me. I cut her off. "I know who you are. Your husband was just telling me *all* about you."

The threat was meant for Aggrivane, but Camille's frightened expression said she'd perceived its meaning as well.

They both bowed as I swept from the room.

⁊⁊

The sun was shining merrily, birds were chirping, and people were joyfully calling to one another as they readied for the midsummer festivities beginning at sundown. After my encounter with Aggrivane, I was in a foul temper, and the last thing I wanted to do was stand around with the Combrogi and watch some boy charm horses, no matter how attractive he was.

As Arthur approached the stables with Lancelot, his arm slung around the Breton in friendship and their heads close together in conference, I reconsidered my assumptions. Maybe it wasn't fair to call Lancelot a boy. He had to be near my age, perhaps a few years younger, but he had a face so open, an expression so innocent, I doubted even the most evil spirit would dare assault his virtue. Not that I was under any illusion he was as unsullied as he appeared; enough wandering warriors has passed through Northgallis and Corbenic for me to know better. In his years on the road, chances were good Lancelot had warmed the fur-lined beds of queens and lain down in flea-ridden brothels— and chances were equally good he was at home in either place.

The Combrogi, a few of their wives, and a smattering of servants, stable hands, grooms, blacksmiths, and the like were gathered round as Kay led one of the more troublesome young horses out into the courtyard beyond the stalls.

"Ho there, handsome. Let us see you work your magic," a woman called to Lancelot from deep within the crowd.

Lancelot did not respond, only smiled self-consciously.

Arthur bid him to begin. "Her name is Danu," Arthur told him of the horse.

Lancelot stood still for a long moment, watching the animal, noting her every move from the flick of her ears and the twitch of her tail to the way she pawed the ground and how her muscles rippled as she took in his scent. It reminded me of the way he had sized up his opponents in the tournament.

Slowly, Lancelot raised one arm, holding his hand out to the horse as though asking her to dance. The filly snorted and pawed the dirt again, but Lancelot moved forward, never taking his eyes from the animal's. He approached at an angle so as not to frighten the beast, pausing if the horse backed away, and when he was nearly in front of her, Lancelot crooned to the animal in his native tongue.

"Aw, isn't that sweet? He's whispering sweet nothings in her ear." Malegant laughed derisively while someone else made kissing noises.

Arthur shushed Malegant and his friends with a warning glare, but Lancelot didn't notice. He was stroking the mane and muzzle of the filly. Several men muttered amongst themselves in disbelief at how quickly the two were taking to each other.

"The only misunderstanding that ever comes between horse and rider is born from spoken language," Lancelot spoke to us. "Believe me, they understand your intention, know your every move before you do. Nothing is lost on them, but we fail to have a way to clearly communicate our desire through words.

"Your king tells me many of you resort to violence to make your wishes known." He shook his head reprovingly. "How many of you would beat your wives if they did not understand you?"

A ripple passed through the crowd.

"Ah, perhaps that is the wrong question to ask here. Let me put it to you another way. How many of you would harm a child who was only learning to speak?"

The crowd was silent. Lancelot had their attention now.

"Horses are much like children," he explained, not bothering to look at us as he stroked the horse. "Though I have known several who surpass men in their intellectual capacity"—he glanced at the pair who had made fun of him and fixed them with an unfriendly stare—"we must approach them as we would a child. Because as with our young, we cannot simply tell horses what we wish them to do. We must show them, earn their trust, and they will learn from us."

Lancelot motioned for Kay to hand him the saddle. Lancelot opened his palm to the horse, who greedily snuffled something out of it, and I swore she looked at Lancelot with appreciation. "You are all experienced riders. Certainly you know a treat will put your horse at ease just as a sweet pacifies an ill-tempered child."

Lancelot held up the saddle in front of the horse, showing it to her and motioning his intention to heave the burden onto her back. The horse snorted and her nostrils flared, but she only stamped in place. Lancelot whispered to her again, and the animal steadied. Slowly, with all the care of a mother dressing her child, Lancelot secured the saddle on the filly's back, giving her another handful of oats to reward her good behavior.

Lancelot stepped back. "It is not the stirrup they fear but you. A saddle is a saddle, but because of the way you introduced it, they associate it—and you—with pain and humiliation. I tell you this—if you continue in this way, your horses will rebel and you will lose your cavalry completely."

"Arrogant arse. Thinks we do not know our own horses," Malegant muttered.

"I think he makes some good points," Gawain replied.

I rolled my eyes. I had told them the exact same things only weeks before. But would they listen to a mere woman? No. But a foreigner whom they barely know? Of course. He had proved himself worthy of attention by besting them all at the tournament. Plus, it was clear he had Arthur's backing, something I could not manage.

After another few words of encouragement, Lancelot slipped his boot into the stirrup, mounted the horse, and led her in a tight circle.

"Bollocks!" Malegant cried, still firmly on the side of flogging.

Lancelot raised an eyebrow at him. "Indeed? You have not seen enough? Would you like to try, or shall I show you again?"

Malegant only crossed his arms and grimaced.

The horse shied and bucked slightly when Lancelot urged her forward, and Lancelot was smart enough to know when it was time to give the animal a break.

"I will see to her myself," he said to the grooms. "Continuing the flattery into routine grooming is very important. It lets her know you are there for her in all things, both unusual and mundane." He smiled. "Somewhat like a romance."

Several of the women giggled, and a blush warmed my own face. Try as I may to dismiss his charms, I was smitten. Lancelot began to lead the horse inside, ignoring the tittering onlookers.

Arthur called after him. "Lancelot, wait. A moment of your time, please."

"Wait for me inside," Lancelot instructed the grooms who led the horse away.

Arthur clapped Lancelot on the shoulder. "What you have done here today is nothing short of miraculous. You have accomplished more in mere moments than we have in months, all with no harm to anyone. Will you do me the great service of staying on at Camelot as my master of the horse? My men will learn much from you."

Behind Arthur, I made a face. If he had listened to me, we'd have had no need for this new prodigy and would be well on our way to having the horses trained by now.

"Ah, *oui*," Lancelot answered with a humble smile. "Yes, gladly."

"Excellent. Tonight at the festival, you will swear allegiance to me and my queen and take your place as a member of the Combrogi."

Malegant scowled. He had been jockeying for that position since Arthur was crowned. He huffed away through the crowd, a bitter grudge taking shape with each step. Lancelot was proving quicker to make enemies than friends.

Lancelot stared after him. "Perhaps we did not get off to the best start," he said as I neared.

I watched Malegant's receding figure stalk back toward the castle.

"I think not." I placed a reassuring hand on Lancelot's arm and took a deep breath, trying to decide the most delicate way of saying what was on my mind. "Malegant is a proud man. He does not take kindly to correction, so you will need to be diplomatic in your dealings with him. You should be gentle in your interactions with all of the Combrogi. Brothers in arms though they may be, they eye one another suspiciously even on the best of days, so think how much less trust they have for a foreigner, especially one who begins by telling them they are wrong."

"She is right, you know," Arthur put in.

Lancelot nodded, apparently seeing my line of reasoning. "I fear I have painted myself a fool."

We advanced slowly toward the great stables so Lancelot could finish his work.

"I would not say that, but it would be wise for you to try a different tack, something less chastising and more encouraging," Arthur said.

"As you noted, they are experienced soldiers and horsemen, not green squires who do not know their way around a saddle," I said. "In your new role, they will be forced to look up to you, like it or not, so it is important you give them a reason to respect you." I glanced at Arthur. "We will do everything we can to help persuade them toward you."

Chapter Five

It hadn't rained in weeks. Not a single drop had fallen since after midsummer, and soon Lughnasa would be upon us. In the withering fields and cramped stables, cattle and horses swatted at biting flies, and dogs lolled in alleyways or nipped at one another in the streets, irritated to restlessness by the oppressive heat.

Indoors, the Combrogi were little better. Malegant picked yet another fight with Lancelot, who was being vigorously defended by Garheis, Aggrivane's youngest brother and Lancelot's strongest devotee. At least Tristan wasn't there to stir the pot. King Mark's decision to call him back to Cornwall was fortuitous. Tristan disliked Malegant but regarded Lancelot even less kindly, so he would have done all he could to egg them both on.

Today was pleading day, the one day of the month when anyone—slave, servant, freeman, or noble—could lay their suit before us in open court. Because of Arthur's continued time in council with them, the majority of the Combrogi also were present, ready to accept any complaint of behalf of their lords. Most months saw an onslaught of petitioners who waited hours to stand before the throne, but on this day, few arrived to make their cases. The nobles most likely didn't wish to sully their trousers with sweat by leaving their dwellings while the poor were in the dehydrated fields, scratching in vain at the unyielding ground for some source of water to quench the thirst we all felt.

I had tried several times to call down a shower from the clouds to no avail. Some part of me knew it would take more than my power alone to break the stranglehold of this heat, but I had to try. I had summoned rain when I became a priestess and a hundred times before, but it seemed the baby was diverting my energy. The most I could muster was a few wispy clouds that dissipated as quickly as they gathered. So I was awaiting word from Avalon, where I had sent Viviane an urgent request for a rain ritual on our behalf. I didn't know how the rest of the country was faring, but if Camelot's condition was any indication, we were all well on our way to ruin. I prayed that was not the case.

From my seat on the dais, I watched Gawain charming, or rather harassing, one of the courtiers on the far side of the room. At first she seemed taken in by his smile and whatever seductive words he spoke softly into her golden hair, but when his hands roamed a little too freely, she turned and smacked him hard across the cheek.

Peredur burst out laughing, applauding her courage, and Arthur snarled for all of them to settle down. Sometimes I felt as if I was living in a castle full of overgrown children. Finally Arthur kicked them all out, saying he and I would wait out the last of the pleading hours alone.

Lancelot and Malegant slunk out down opposite hallways as soon as Arthur's tirade ended. Peredur and Gawain were making plans to meet in the tiltyard when we heard the alarmed voices of the guards outside.

"Messengers for the king," one cried while the rest was garbled by chaos we could not see.

We all jumped to our feet and advanced toward the door, but it opened with a thud before any of us could reach it. A body slumped into the room, another slightly less injured man following and hovering over the prone figure before us. Arthur swore, and I recognized the distinctive uniform worn by the soldiers from the milecastles, small forts along Hadrian's Wall. Arthur circled the bleeding husk of a man, and I knelt to examine his wounds.

"It's a miracle he survived the journey, but I fear he will not live to tell his tale," I said, shaking my head sadly as the soldier's life drained out at my feet.

"He doesn't need to," Arthur said grimly, pointing the toe of his boot at the man's uniform, which was more toga than tunic. "Nor was he meant to. This was the message we were meant to receive. He is Tremonium's general, so if he is here, chances are good there is no one left to save at the fort." He rounded on the mute second man, clearly the horseman who had carried the general to us. "How did you escape with your life?"

The man looked at Arthur with a mixture of horror and shock etched into his ashen features. He was shaking and could only stare. I fetched him some wine, and he drank what he could with unsteady hands. The rest spilled onto the floor where it became indistinguishable from the general's blood.

"Chief Caw," he sputtered, unable to say more.

Even behind the emotion, the horseman's voice had a familiar inflection it took me a moment to place. He was Votadini. Why would the Damnonii chieftain send a Votadini man as a courier from a fort mostly populated by Strathclyde Britons? The hair on the backs of my arms raised. It made no sense yet could not be without meaning.

The solider had found his voice again but only just. "Dead, every one—men, women, horses too."

Arthur growled and struck a vase with his fist, sending it shattering to the ground. He ignored the shards grinding into the stone beneath his boots as he paced. "He would have known that fort was more than a garrison. It was a shelter for lowland villagers in times of distress. If there had been any whiff of trouble—and I promise you he gave them one—they would have headed for the safety of its walls like sheep. Heartless bastard."

The servants around us stood like statues, shocked by Arthur's outburst.

Recovering myself, I gestured to the women nearest to me. "Ladies, please take our wounded messenger to the infirmary and see he be tended to."

As for the general, there was nothing anyone could do.

"We ride to Tremonium then," Kay resolved, already heading toward the stables.

Arthur put out a hand to stop him. "No. Not now. That is exactly what Caw expects us to do. He's counting on us to swoop in on a rescue mission. It would make us easy targets, well-contained for his hordes. No, I will play this out in my own time." He continued to pace. "Now we wait. Let them grow restless, unsure.

Let them wonder. Did the general die on the road to Camelot? Did Caw's dramatic message fail to make it to the king? Was the king unmoved? Better yet, does the king now lie in wait for him? I want all of these questions, all of these fears, to be chasing their tails around his mind before we move to retaliate."

When he finally halted at the base of the dais, I expected to see the familiar gleam of triumph in his eyes, but instead he turned a look of great distress upon me.

"He's heading to Lothian," Arthur said. "Why else send a Votadini with the general? They share tribal bounds with Lot and are his strongest allies. This was no random act of terror but a show of power to indicate what is to come. He's plotting to overthrow the kingdom and seize power for himself."

I was struck dumb by Arthur's words. If that was true, then Chief Caw had gone mad. The Votadini and the people of Lothian wanted nothing of war. I highly doubted this move had Damnonii backing either. The peace they had built was far too precious for any of them to risk.

Bedivere must have been thinking along a similar track. "Arthur, do you see what he is doing? If Lothian falls and the Votadini cower, nothing is stopping him from marching south to sack York, which is already weakened thanks to repeated Saxon attacks. From there he would have free rein into Brigante territory and would have amassed a force great enough to bring down even Camelot. It's not an original plan, another fool tried it about three hundred years ago, but it is a formidable one."

Arthur moved into action. "Then we have little time. Gawain, Aggrivane, send our fastest messengers on the most direct route to your mother and make her aware of the situation. Caw has a few days on us, and I do not want Ana taken by surprise. Follow the messengers with our strongest forces and meet us at Traprain Law, but do not take the main roads. I don't want to risk the Damnonii anticipating our movements. And summon Tristan from Cornwall. Tell him to ride night and day. We will need his skills."

He turned to Kay and Bedivere. "Since the two of you know the area the best, I am sending you as scouts up to Tremonium. Look around and see if you can gauge what we are in for, where the threat is greatest. I'm not sure if they will have moved on to Lothian yet, and if so, with what percentage of their forces. Even if they have split, if we can take down part of their army, we will be stronger for it."

"Best not appear as soldiers though," I warned. "Disguise yourselves as farmers or shepherds. Pretend to be picking around the ruins for scraps of stone or whatever else you can find to enlarge your pens. If the Damnonii insurgents even suspect who you are, their archers will pierce you through before you can draw breath."

For the first time since the general's arrival, Arthur relaxed a little as he recognized the advantage of having a battle-trained wife to relieve some of his burden. "A very wise bit of advice you'd do well to heed. I would like to see you both returned to my presence alive."

The two men regarded each other with familiar humor, and Bedivere looked down at the stump of his deformed left arm. "I guess this means I am your servant again. Just once I would like to be the master but have yet to find anyone who believes me a proper threat."

"Until they have your javelin sticking in their gorge, that is," Kay added with a hearty laugh. He was clearly looking forward to the adventure.

"The rest of you," Arthur addressed the remaining crowd, "brief your men, make your preparations, and say your farewells. We ride with the morning star."

◦◦◦

It took me all night to convince Arthur to let me come with him to Traprain Law. He sought to exclude me only out of love and concern, but it rankled me nonetheless. These were my mother's people, and her influence had made me loathe to be kept out of any situation in which my skills could be of use. Even more, I had to admit I feared being left home alone, useless like a dairy maid, while Arthur and everyone I cared about risked their lives. I was a battle queen, and I was going to act like one, pregnant or no.

"You are in no condition to make such a long journey. We will be riding fast and hard, and I will not risk the life of our heir to appease your self-worth," he said, seeing my intentions for what they were.

I should have been more concerned about the fate of my baby, but I believed that as long as I stayed out of the thick of battle and atop my horse, we would both be fine. And like it or not, Arthur needed me there as strategic collaborator.

"I am not yet so heavy with child that I cannot sit upon a horse. Even Octavia will attest to that," I retorted.

Arthur's look warned me he was growing tired of our argument. "Would you have me trundle across the country in a chariot with you? Or perhaps you would prefer a cart? I will not slow us down or place you in any danger, Guinevere." His voice was laced with the guilt he would feel should any misfortune befall us.

But in the end, he succumbed, and I took my place next to him at the head of the line. Following my warning to Kay and Bedivere, Arthur split up our forces into reasonably sized groups and had us all outfitted to appear as bands of pilgrims on holiday to the holy springs and lakes that dotted the northern lands. He kept us off the old Roman roads and led us down a series of ancient byways and trails, navigating based on the expertise of a Combrogi named Bors who had spent his life in the area.

After an exhausting three-day journey, we rested at Traprain Law, a little more certain of our safety with our two armies combined. But now there was the question of how to proceed. We had anticipated a quick confrontation with a definite outcome, but that did not appear to be the way things were working out.

Kay and Bedivere returned from Tremonium the same day. They found the fort exactly as we had feared—torched to the ground with no survivors and very few clues left to tell what, or who, had brought down the once-mighty citadel. Although they had spotted a few lightly armed warriors patrolling the area, Kay and Bedivere were left in peace and did not think they were followed.

So it appeared Caw's war band had moved on, but Ana had not had any overture from him that indicated he was near. Much like with the undying heat, we were at an impasse, unsure of how to force the arm of change and even less certain how to ensure it came down in our favor.

Arthur grew more and more frustrated with each passing

day. I wondered if part of Caw's plan was to drive Arthur to rash behavior, but I didn't dare voice it. Penned inside the fortress walls, Arthur behaved very much like the bear for which he was named, and I had no desire to feel his wrath.

As soon as Tristan arrived, he ordered the Cornish knight to accompany the scouts on a tracking mission. They returned with news that Caw and his men were holed up somewhere within the outskirts of the Caledon forest.

The seam of the wood was just visible from the guard towers on the northeast side of the castle. Arthur, Kay, Bedivere, Lot, Ana, Tristan, and I met in one of the larger square rooms while the rest of the household slept, trying desperately to think of some solution to the quagmire.

"They won't attack the castle," Tristan declared. "I didn't see any evidence of siege weapons or any indication they were building any, so I doubt they have the manpower."

Lot shook his head. "So why come all this way, exert all this effort, if they're unwilling to do the one thing necessary to overthrow us?"

"You forget," Arthur said, "that they need not destroy the town to claim victory. In fact, it is to their advantage to keep it as intact as possible for their own use. All they need is one of our heads."

Lot snorted. "So what are you suggesting, that we walk out there and let them take their pick? Or should I dispatch you right now and save them the trouble? Perhaps if I presented your corpse to them politely, they would show me mercy."

Ana's face reddened in a rare display of anger. Lot's swagger made it easy to forget that she was still in charge, as Arthur had long ago decreed. "Enough, both of you. This is not a boyhood brawl we are facing. It is the future of our kingdoms. The way I see it, if you do not think they will attack, we have three options." She ticked them off on her fingers. "One, we could try to wait them out, which does not seem wise considering the drought has already undermined our resources and they have the water of the swamps and bogs at their disposal, disgusting as they are. Two, we could do as our frustration bids us and charge in blindly, but that gives Caw the advantage of not only seeing us coming but being able to savor the chaos in which we die. Or. . . we can find a way to flush them out."

"I still favor standing at the edge of the wood and shouting, 'Here I am. Come and get me,'" Lot whispered to me, and I had to suppress my laughter.

Though amused by her husband, I was proud of Ana for her level-headedness and ability to see clearly through the emotionally charged situation. But then again, she was the daughter of Queen Iggraine and the famous warrior Goloris.

I turned her words over and over in my head. "Flush them out," she had said. But how? I tried to think of every angle, to see the impending clash from their point of view and determine what would drive me out were the roles reversed, but my mind moved in the same maddening circles. Arthur, Lot, and Kay's ideas grew more and more fanciful as the night wore on. I closed my eyes and tried to block out their voices, to summon the sight or call upon the Goddess, but it seemed that avenue of inspiration was as closed to me as my ability to draw down rain.

I opened my eyes with a sigh just in time to see a sheet of heat lightning illuminate the eastern horizon, revealing the contours of tall puffy clouds that looked like ship's sails. Suddenly a thought shifted in my brain, a single grain of sand set free to tip the whole balance. The sky flashed violet once again, and I knew Ana was right. We could force them out. And the earth was telling us how.

"What would happen if that lightning were not contained within the clouds, if it were set free?"

For a long moment, no one responded to my peculiar question. Six pairs of eyes blinked at me blankly.

"It would strike something," Ana answered warily.

"And say it struck a tree. It would catch fire, right?"

"I presume so, yes."

I turned away from the window, a plan rapidly forming in my head. "So why can we not be the fire? Burn them out. I have seen it used on small game in the hunt, so why not extend the metaphor and make it a little bigger?" I rushed over to Arthur, eager to make him to share in my excitement. "Think about it. They are shielded from our sight and our weapons by walls of trees—dry, brittle wood, thanks to this merciless summer. What difference is there from the fort they just destroyed? What would you do if they were hidden within a wooden castle?"

"Burn it down," he said, slowly beginning to understand.

"But there is a serious flaw in your plan," Lot protested. "Caledon Wood is not a defined structure. You cannot simply set it ablaze and let it burn. You would destroy the countryside for miles with absolutely no control over where it burns. You would be risking the lives and livelihoods of my people."

From his solitary perch on the northern windowsill, Tristan watched me carefully, green eyes narrowed in concentration. "Not necessarily. Ana, you said there are bogs and swamps hidden within the trees, right? Has anyone ever mapped them? Do we know where they lead?"

"To the river and then to the sea," Lot said. "A series of canals more or less connects the heart of the wood to the water. My family has been ruling this land for countless generations. There is not much about it we do not know. Yes, the marsh would divert the fire and perhaps control its spread, but it also would provide Caw with a safe place for shelter and a possible method of retreat."

"Not if we block it off." Tristan was on his feet now, bent over the table, fingers rapidly sketching out a drawing of the areas he and his team had surveyed. Lot supplemented what he could recall of the locations of the marshlands. Tristan stabbed a finger at one edge of the map. "If we wait for a night with a southern wind and focus on this area, it will carry the flames exactly where we want them to be, forcing Caw to retreat into this clearing just beyond the periphery of the woodland. If we can get our troops in place before we start the blaze, we will have the best chance of ambush as they flee from the flames."

᧞ᧉ ᧉ᧞

We moved contingents out of the fortress over the next three nights, when the moon hid her face and the land was shrouded in darkness. Placed at key points around the wood, each was a self-contained unit of fighters comprised of cavalry and infantry, equally capable of success as a cohesive entity or as highly skilled individuals. The weakness of our army was the strong individual pride that ran in veins more used to clan allegiance and self-reliance than the precise formations demanded by Roman strategy. We had to be certain that even if the unit broke, the men would survive to defeat their attackers.

I agreed to remain behind with Ana and her family, far from danger, while Arthur, Lot, and their forces plunged in headlong. Occasionally an eagle-eyed Damnonii would spot our army's movements and leave camp to investigate, but not one of them returned. I had to wonder what Caw made of his slowly dwindling numbers or if he even noticed.

As the feast of Lughnasa passed, still without a single rain shower, a strange pressure built in the land as if the earth itself would soon begin to boil. If we were restless within the relative safety of Traprain Law, I had to wonder how the foot soldiers in the field, exposed to the elements and all their heat-induced hallucinations, were faring.

Then one evening, in the dead of night, the winds shifted, their southern heat unmistakable. Huddled in the highest level of the hill fort, Ana and I watched as Caledon Wood went up in flames. The trees themselves seemed to combust, some as though set off by the very dirt in which they grew as torches were flung into their roots, others with hair on fire from flaming missiles. I said a silent prayer for forgiveness to the spirits of the trees that were now sacrificing their lives for our cause.

Smoke rose rapidly, obscuring any view of the pandemonium we might have glimpsed. For once I was thankful for the loss of sight, both physical and mystical, for I had no desire to know the suffering that must have been taking place below. All I could do was pray that Arthur and our men were safe and that our destruction of this magnificent wood would not be in vain.

The people housed within Traprain Law had been instructed to stay within the well-guarded walls of the castle, but they quickly clogged the ramparts, climbing on anything they could find to get a better view of the spectacle. Their shouts and exclamations only added to the madness.

Confusion reigned until the air cooled as dawn approached. I watched the eastern sky for some sign of light and soon realized that though the night was done, no brightness was forthcoming. It was as though the ash had choked out the sun. Then the first cool drops stung my skin, rapidly increasing until they created tiny rivulets in the ashy grime that coated me from head to toe. The sun was not gone, merely masked by clouds. At long last, it was raining.

Ana and I hugged as the drops became a downpour. The Goddess, and perhaps the priestesses in Avalon, had heard our prayers and deigned to help us dampen the fire. As the clouds continued to pour forth their libation, we all waited to learn the final outcome of the battle—anxiously at first, then with increasing dread as time dragged by. I clung to the damp window, praying with all my heart I would not return to Camelot a widow or spend my remaining days grieving for the Combrogi, certain in the knowledge I had orchestrated their deaths.

By the time the smoke cleared and sky lightened, most of the fire had been dowsed. The remaining trees, bereft of their leaves, stood in somber silence like tombstones, marking the loss of life for both their kind and ours. The quiet stretched on, interrupted at odd moments by a crack as a charred branch gave way and tumbled to the blackened brush below, a sharp cry as a crow spotted carrion or a confused songbird sought an incinerated nest.

Slowly the wood stirred as men emerged, some seemingly unharmed, others limping, blackened with soot or stained by dark splotches of blood. They appeared one at time or in pairs, but occasionally a group would stumble into the clearing, car-rying a fallen brother or dragging an inert prisoner. At first they were all strangers to me, probably Lot's men, but then came faces and bodies I recognized. I was somewhat shocked and slightly mortified by the gratitude I felt that I didn't personally know any of the dead.

One by one, the Combrogi returned, shaken but relatively unscathed. Peredur was limping, Malegant and Gawain were clutching bleeding wounds, and Tristan held a broken arm, but none appeared to be in danger of death. The worst of the fighting had to be over because more and more men followed, their spirits buoyed by the sight of safety and shelter. They called out to loved ones on the ramparts and swooped them up in joyous embraces at the gates. A few held aloft the remains of their enemies, cursing and taunting the spirits of the dead.

The knot in my stomach tightened as I scanned the outline of the once-great forest for any sign of Arthur. Every few moments, my gaze swept the mounting crowd below, hoping I had missed him. *Where is he? Has he been injured? Or even. . .* I couldn't dare think the word.

My heart sank as I watched Kay and Bedivere guide an injured Lot through the gates. I rushed down to meet them, Ana close at my heels. She was making an odd choking sound by the time we reached them.

Lot held up a hand to calm her. "It is all right. I will be fine. It is only a broken leg."

"Had a tussle with one of the bogs," Kay explained in my ear, "fell right in."

So much for knowing everything about them. "And Arthur? Where is he?" I couldn't keep the edge of hysteria out of my voice.

Kay and Bedivere exchanged a glance I couldn't read.

"He'll be along," Kay said.

Ana left me so she could attend Lot, and the two soldiers headed for the barracks for some much-needed rest. I found myself standing alone in the midst of the crowd, uncertain what to do or even what to think. I hugged myself protectively and watched, unseeing, as the jubilant armies of Camelot and Lothian rejoiced at the Damnonii defeat. As more time passed, I fought the urge to sink to my knees in the mud and give in to the terror that threatened to engulf me.

"The living grieve only for the dead, and I do not think many tears will be shed for him."

My head snapped up when I heard the familiar gravelly voice that held just a hint of irony. Astonished, I peered into Arthur's twinkling eyes, dumbly processing in some part of my mind that he was here, safe and alive. As this awareness dawned, I realized that Caw's severed head was dangling from Arthur's raised hand, twisting to and fro like a child's toy.

Shoving away Arthur's burned knuckles and, with them, his trophy, I pulled him to me, caressing his sodden, blistered skin. As the reality of Arthur's safety and our victory dawned, I felt another very intimate shock. I gasped as the babe in my womb moved, landing a sharp kick beneath my ribs followed quickly by a second further down in my abdomen.

Arthur bent over me in alarm. "What is it? Are you unwell?"

In his expression, I read the manifestation of all the anxiety he had put aside to allow me to accompany him here.

I shook my head, laughing. "Hardly." I placed his broad palm along the curve of my belly and waited. It wasn't long before he flinched in surprise as the child moved again, a second flutter following shortly after. "Arthur, I believe we have sired warrior children."

"Children?"

"Yes, I feel two distinct presences. I believe I am carrying twins."

Chapter Six

Autumn 497

A fiery shower of reddish-orange leaves fluttered from the oak trees surrounding us as I looked out over the assembled men, many of them my friends, all of them my sworn subjects. From their number I had finally chosen my champion, and they were here, in a sacred grove protected by the Druids, to hear his name declared in one of our few rituals that mingled the secular with the sacred.

It had been my right, or more accurately, my responsibility, to choose a champion from the moment I was crowned queen. Arthur could not serve as both king and champion because doing so would have divided his loyalties between his wife and his realm, so I needed to choose a protector. But a champion was more than a bodyguard; he was in essence an extension of my will, vowed to follow me in all things. I had to trust him with my very life for he was sworn to protect me above all else, even the king. Together with Kay, Arthur's champion, this man would protect my children as they were fruits of my body. I could have chosen randomly from the strangers I'd met at my coronation, as some queens had done before me, like a child drawing lots for a game. But I didn't want to make such an important decision before I'd had the chance to get to know the temperaments and proclivities of those from whom I chose.

Some of them had openly courted me for the position, which had the opposite of the intended effect. I could not entrust my life to a man who desired the position for its status; I had to trust him implicitly, which I could not do with knowledge of his ulterior motives. Even those who'd employed more subtle tactics—I firmly believed that was the reason behind Malegant's early efforts to accompany me in public—had hurt their chances. With each meeting of the Combrogi, and even some chance personal encounters, the pool of possible contenders had dwindled.

I'd made my decision that summer. I couldn't say that a single event had cemented my choice, nor could I tell exactly when it had been made, but one day I looked at him and I knew. Perhaps it was the sum of a string of small moments, a kind word here, a gesture there, but as I thought back over our time together, the answer was clear. He was a dangerous choice, and one that likely would prove unpopular, but my mind was made up.

One thing still haunted me as I began to chant, letting go of myself and calling the Goddess into me—Merlin's reaction when I had disclosed my choice the day before. He had turned his sapphire gaze on me, and I suddenly felt chilled. His pupils contracted as his gaze retreated inward, and a brief shadow clouded his face. It was a look I knew well—it signaled a flash of the sight.

Merlin's eyes had focused on me as he came back to himself,

but they lost none of their iciness. "Tell me, how can you be sure you've made the right decision?"

"Are you saying it is not?" I countered with equal steeliness. As much as I cared for and respected him, I could not abide his meddling in my personal affairs. It was my right to choose whom I willed. He was Arthur's advisor, not mine, and I preferred him to stay out of my business.

He stood directly in front of me, towering over me. "I am saying all actions have consequences, and I have seen the result of the one you are contemplating. You tread a slippery hillside, Guinevere. If you do not guard yourself well, you may go tumbling down and drag us all into the mire with you."

I pulled myself to my feet, no easy task with my protruding belly, and faced him down. Most people wouldn't have dared challenge the Archdruid, but sometime in the last year, I'd lost the awe that had held me in fear of him. Maybe it was the familiarity of spending so much time with him or the fact that I now held a position of power as well, but I no longer felt compelled to cower in his presence.

I stepped toward him, forcing him to retreat slightly. "If you have seen something of such great import, *Archdruid*"—I laced his title with as much contempt as I dared—"tell it to me in plain terms; do not hide behind the vaguery of visions and prophecy."

Merlin shook his head. "Alas, I cannot. You know as well as I that the future is fluid, ever changing as the sea. If I name what I have seen, I risk impugning innocent men *and women*"—his tone made sure I knew he was referring to me—"for trespasses they may never commit. I can only warn you that this reaches well beyond who carries a sword in your name."

That was his last word on the subject. Now, with my eyes closed, I could feel him to my left, but I no longer sensed any hostility. He was doing his job as Archdruid, submitting to the will of the gods and no doubt praying they would change mine.

I made myself forget the past and focus on the present. This was as close as I would ever get to experiencing the power of the Lady of the Lake. Today, I was the Goddess in her role of Sovereignty, she who grants and removes temporal power. I was to invoke her just as fully as during any Avalonian ceremony but without the aid of the sacred drink for I still needed my human faculties. I was to be at once goddess and queen, the supreme symbol of womanhood, both mortal and divine.

I said a silent prayer for guidance and let my consciousness slip downward in the quiet. At first, nothing happened, then a silver glow, like liquid moonlight, filled me with warmth. I felt her within me, a quiet, gentle, reassuring presence.

I opened my eyes, and the awe on the assembled faces made me realize I must appear to them every bit the Goddess incarnate. Merlin had dressed me in the pure white gown of the Maiden, which was cinched by a thick black cloth belt, symbolizing the wisdom of the Crone, and covered in the rich crimson cloak of the Mother. That I was nearing the end of my pregnancy only added to the effect.

I opened my arms wide and addressed them. As I spoke, I wasn't sure if it was in my own name or that of the Goddess or both. I had the strange sensation of remembering the ritual, rather than reciting it, as though it were as familiar to me as breathing. "I have called you here today for one purpose—the arming of a champion. This role is second only in sacredness to that of kingship. As such, it is a privilege only I can grant, and once sanctified, none may contest.

"Many of you are worthy, but only one can hold the office. I have searched my own heart and endeavored to know yours. Know the one whom I have chosen is not peerless, nor should he seek to place himself above the rest. I choose him because he is, to me, best suited for the role. It is an honor, yes, but the man who takes on this mantle also shoulders a great burden, so do not be envious of his station."

In unison, the assembled men knelt. I regarded each man with new perceptiveness, seeing them with the vision of the Goddess. My eyes passed over Kay and Bedivere, whom I could never choose because they were Arthur's men through and through and their loyalty would always be to him; to Bors, Malegant, Accolon, and a few others I liked but mistrusted for reasons I could not name; past Aggrivane, with whom my tangled past would forever be a stumbling block; and finally to Owain, Tristan, and many others I knew had greater loyalties to their lords than to me.

Finally I found the face I sought. "Lancelot du Lac, arise and stand before me."

Merlin closed his eyes and bowed his head in disappointment and submission. I gestured Lancelot forward, and the men murmured to one another uneasily. Hesitantly, and slightly self-consciously, Lancelot did as he was bidden.

"I have chosen you for my champion. Do you accept this office?"

He smiled and dipped his head humbly. "I do."

Before I even had the chance to ask, Aggrivane was on his feet, shouting, "I invoke the right of challenge."

His words were greeted by an audible gasp from the crowd, followed by cheers of support. Lancelot hadn't made many friends since his arrival. Many of the men would have been happy to see him publicly defeated.

When I'd made up my mind, I foresaw this might happen, but challenge was Aggrivane's right. At the time of first investiture, any man might challenge the chosen one and the two had to do battle. The winner would be the queen's champion, but the loser was allowed to renew his petition each year on Lughnasa for seven years. If the challenger was ever successful, the title would pass to him. If not, the title would remain for life with the original winner. I could only hope Aggrivane wouldn't hold a grudge for long.

The human part of me was mortified and afraid that Arthur would take Aggrivane's outburst as a sign of lingering affection for me, but the Goddess within saw the justice. I had no choice but to let them proceed.

I nodded, speaking the words of the Goddess. "Men have long fought for love of me. Lay on, but draw no blood within this sacred circle."

Weapons were not allowed within the sacred grove, so they would have to fight hand-to-hand, a skill I knew Aggrivane possessed. I was unsure of Lancelot as I had only seen him do battle with a sword. Amid cheers from their supporters, they both removed their shirts and shoes and rolled up their trouser legs. The crowd quieted and formed two camps, leaving the combatants in full view of where I stood.

As they circled each other like wolves, Lancelot taunted Aggrivane. "I have already bested you in front of the king and court once. Do you really wish to have me humiliate you in front of the Combrogi and the Goddess as well?"

Aggrivane's answering grin was thick with malevolence. "It will be all the more sweet to avenge that affront before such an audience."

Then he lunged at Lancelot and grasped him around the shoulders, seeking to throw him off balance. Their brawl reminded me of two spiders fighting, an indistinguishable tangle of limbs. They struggled not only against one another but against nature herself, unable to find true purchase on the wet, leaf-strewn ground. One moment one seemed to have the upper hand, then fickle Fortuna would smile upon the other and he would rally, flipping his opponent and pinning him but never for long.

Their grunts and groans were nearly drowned out by the cheering Combrogi, who had forgotten they were still at a ritual rather than a game of sport. Most supported the son of Lothian, but a few were on Lancelot's side. For my part, I held my breath and tried to abandon my will to the Goddess who floated unperturbed inside me.

Finally, Lancelot wrestled Aggrivane to the forest floor and held him down. Merlin begrudgingly declared him the victor. Aggrivane snatched up his shirt and returned to his place, growling. I thought it cruel that he now had to watch as another man yet again took his place by my side, but I was powerless to change tradition.

Brushing leaves, dirt, and acorn shards from his hair and pants, Lancelot dressed and once again took his place in front of me.

"Lancelot du Lac, so named as the son of the Lady of the Lake in the forest Broceliande, you have declared your willingness to serve as my champion; now swear your allegiance to me."

Lancelot knelt and touched his thumb to his forehead, lips, and heart in recognition that his vows were to both queen and Goddess. "My lady and my queen, I thank you for selecting me as your champion and defender. Though I know I am not worthy, I humbly accept this honor and pledge myself to you. I vow to use all that I am, all that I know, and all that I may acquire in your service. Anything you ask of me, I will do. If you are in peril, I will rescue you; if you are reviled, I will defend you; if you are threatened, I will fight for you, even unto death. My life is now forfeit; do with me as you will."

Arthur stepped forward and drew his sword, the legendary Caliburn, one of the treasures of Avalon given to him by the Lady of the Lake when he became king. He held it flat, shining blade resting against on his open palm, hilt of intertwined golden dragons in the other. He held it out to Lancelot, saying, "Know that you defend my queen in my name and with my power. Anyone who opposes you opposes me."

Lancelot bent his head to receive Arthur's blessing. As Arthur sheathed his sword, I handed another to Lancelot. It was a specially forged replica of Caliburn, the only difference being that the jewels in the dragons' eyes were a bright emerald rather than ruby. The similarity was meant to remind Lancelot, and anyone unfortunate enough to face his might, that he fought in defense of the house of Pendragon. As Lancelot accepted the weapon, the sun bounced off the blade, illuminating its inscription: "In Her names and by Her power, I defend this land." A reminder of these very vows.

As Merlin blessed Lancelot and consecrated his sword, the

Goddess departed from me, her purpose fulfilled. The tranquility and peace left me in a rush like an exhalation, and just as quickly, my usual worries flooded back in. I looked over the Combrogi, wondering how they were reacting to the news that Lancelot was now not only master of the horse but my champion as well. Part of me wished I could hear their thoughts, but I knew it was best I could not. They were no doubt filled with resentment. Every one of them hoped to be elevated to a higher position in Arthur's court, and as far as they were concerned, its two highest honors had been given to an unworthy outsider. I hoped they would come to understand in time.

I couldn't help but watch Aggrivane. Even as Merlin said the closing words, Aggrivane shifted from foot to foot, understandably uncomfortable. After Merlin's final blessing, Aggrivane shot through the trees and out of sight just as he had the night he lost me to Arthur.

Merlin shooed everyone out of the grove so he could purify the site for its next use by the Druids. The men dispersed, some talking excitedly in groups, others striding off to the horses, anxious to begin the long ride back to Camelot. But Lancelot lingered at my side.

"Thank you for this honor, my lady. It is truly unexpected, and I will be forever grateful," he said as we followed others to the horses.

I kicked up leaves like a child as I walked. "You are best suited to defend me in all things, and I trust you implicitly."

As we passed Merlin, I expected him to ignore me, but to my surprise, he put out a hand to bar my path. He glanced up at Lancelot and then back to me.

"What is done is done," he said without preamble. "I suggest you find Aggrivane and try to make him see reason. He stormed off in that direction." He pointed east. "You are the only person he will listen to right now, and we cannot afford to make an enemy of him."

Without another word, he entered the circle and began paying homage to each of the oak trees as though I did not exist.

I gave Lancelot an apologetic look. "He's right. I should go and find him. Please wait for me here. I will not be long."

⚬⚬ ⚬⚬

Aggrivane had made no effort to cover his tracks. Following his footprints, deep and unmistakably stamped with rage into the muddy depths of the forest, I picked through clumps of mutilated leaves and swept past decapitated branches, the innocent victims of his anger, until I came to a small clearing at the edge of a stream.

His back was toward me as he faced the water. "You should not have come."

"But you knew I would." I couldn't see his face, but I imagined how he would close his eyes and smile ruefully by way of answer. He was determined to ignore me, so I crossed the clearing in a few purposeful strides then tugged on his shoulder in a vain attempt to force him to face me. "What would you have me do, Aggrivane? Choose my former lover as my champion? How would that look to Arthur? To the court?" I was almost yelling, my voice raw.

He had to see reason. He had to know I'd had no other choice. Because I hadn't, had I? I wrapped my arms protectively around myself. Suddenly I wasn't so sure.

For a long while, Aggrivane said nothing, and sounds of the forest returned as the birds decided my outburst was not aimed at them. Then slowly he turned, his face a stony mask, but I saw pain reflected in his eyes.

"Yes," he whispered. "That is exactly what you should have done—selected the one you wish to have always by your side, not a substitute to distract you from your true feelings."

The candor of his words struck me to the core as surely as if he had buried an arrow deep inside my heart. Tears dampened my cheeks before I could find my voice, and I turned away. My mind was working feverishly to deny the truth of his words.

"I am no longer the girl you met in Avalon. My actions. . ." I took a deep breath. "Are watched by everyone." I winced inwardly as I realized how close I had come to repeating Merlin's words about my actions having consequences. "To have named you my champion would only have given my detractors something to use against me."

"Did Lyonesse teach you that, how to make excuses for any subject?" Aggrivane spat, referring to the malicious woman I had lived with during the latter part of our courtship.

I whirled around, ready to retort, but he stopped me by holding up his hand.

"Everything you have said to me since I returned has been one gigantic justification." His eyes narrowed, inspecting my face. Then he firmly gripped my shoulders, forcing me to look directly into his eyes. "Why do you refuse to acknowledge that you are still in love with me even to yourself?" His eyes searched mine so thoroughly I felt naked before him. "Do you know what I was about to say to you the day Camille interrupted us?"

I was about to reply, but he rushed on. "I was about to tell you that I was still in love with you. Married or no, neither of us can deny what flickers deep within no matter how hard we try to hide it or snuff it out."

Aggrivane cradled my cheeks, and my heart cracked all over again, just as it had when my father separated us, just as it had when I futilely searched for his face in the moments after Arthur proposed. I closed my eyes, trying to deny what my heart so readily understood. My head spun with a million thoughts, the loudest being a voice shouting, *No, this cannot be happening. He did not just say those words.*

You are dreaming; this is not real, I kept repeating, but I knew it wasn't true. I tried to force the feelings down, and I let out a strangled gasp as they nearly choked me. I did still love him, but to admit it, to say it out loud, would have been treason. And once I gave voice to those feelings, there would be no going back—no controlling the torrent that came with them.

The words were hanging on my tongue, each beat of my heart bringing them closer to my lips. I pulled away, head bowed and eyes on the grass slowly dying beneath my soles. I knew what I had to do, what had to be said, but every fiber of my being railed against it. I swallowed hard and forced myself to speak, my voice sounding foreign to my ears. "This has to end, Aggrivane. We can't continue to live like this. I do not want to lose you, but there can be no illusions about what is or ever will be between us."

Aggrivane cleared his throat and shuffled his feet. I didn't dare look up. I knew by his silence that his expression would rend me beyond repair.

"If that is what you wish," he said, clearly struggling to keep his voice steady. "But promise me one thing."

I answered without hesitation, "Anything."

I suddenly remembered how he had looked the night we first kissed, the way the wind rippled his black locks into shining waves and how his dark eyes twinkled like the stars in the midnight sky. I would have given anything to be able to go back to that moment, to start things over and live the life destiny had stolen from our grasp.

"Promise me no matter how much you love your husband or esteem your champion, no matter how many others you burn with passion for, you will reserve a small place in your heart only for us. It can be in the darkest depths of your soul, but I need to know there is some part of you no one else can touch, a place that is purely mine."

I stared at him, wishing I could tell him such a place already existed, sealed from all others by wounds that would never fully heal, scars that marked me as his as clearly as if he had carved his name into my heart. But all I could do was nod and wipe away the tears as they fell. "I promise."

His smile was as tender as his touch as he ran his fingertips down my cheek from my temple to jaw. "So do I."

As he embraced me one last time and kissed my forehead, I knew my love for him would haunt me forever.

Chapter Seven

Winter 498

With one sharp stab, my entire world changed.

We were in the middle of a cordial dinner with Cador, lord of the western kingdom of Bernicia, when I felt the first sign of distress. At first I thought I'd just eaten too much venison or the leek soup had disagreed with me, so I continued my conversation with Cador's wife, laughing heartily at her impression of an impudent servant.

But then a second twinge bit at my ballooning belly. I sucked in air and dropped my knife, hands instinctively fluttering to the sore spot in my side. I looked at Arthur in alarm, and he slowly ceased chewing as understanding dawned across his features. A moment later, I felt a soft trickle of warmth ooze down my thigh.

I grabbed Octavia's arm as she leaned over my shoulder to refill my goblet and whispered in her ear, "I think my time has come."

Ignoring the sudden silence and alarmed expressions of

Cador and his wife, I allowed Octavia help me to my feet and usher me toward the door. I prayed my womb would hold the remainder of its waters until we were out of their presence.

"Lord Cador, it appears you and your wife may have the honor of being present at the birth of my first children . . ." Arthur's voice held a mixture of astonishment and pride.

Halfway down the hall, I had to grip the wall near a window as another spasm caught me off guard, and the seal of my womb broke in a watery rush. I had just enough time to notice the large flakes of snow falling in the deepening shadows before another of my maids came running to support my other arm. She and Octavia helped me shuffle the rest of the way to the room prepared for the royal birth.

Chaos broke out all around as soon as I was safely ensconced in childbed. Octavia called for the servants and sent one to fetch Grainne, who, on Arthur's orders, had been staying at Camelot for the last month so she could assist when my labor pains began. He had originally insisted that Viviane act as midwife, but she'd successfully argued that the High Priestess of Avalon could not be withheld from her duties to wait on the whim of unborn children, no matter how royal. Arthur's expression of consternation that someone would dare disobey his orders had been so outrageous it made me smile even to remember it.

But my joy was short-lived. I grimaced and took a deep breath as another cramp began, though I willed myself through it. I had been present at enough births to know this was just the beginning. But I could already feel tiny fissures of fear breaching the calm I endeavored to maintain.

The pain rose and abated as the evening progressed. Servants flitted about me, preparing reams of cloth, heating water, and fussing over details real and imagined. Outside, the snow mirrored their frenzy, coating treetops and turrets in a thick white blanket as the sky hardened from lead to pitch. All the while, Octavia sat by my side, holding my hand and cooing encouragement as the pain rose along with my screams and my determination diminished.

As the birthing process took hold, everything became hazy, disjointed like when I'd had the fever in Pellinor's house, except this time, instead of being numb, I was acutely aware of every nerve in my body. My throat was raw from screaming, my legs cramped from holding the muscles taut, and I could scarcely take a breath between the spasms in my womb.

I wasn't sure when I began calling for my mother—it must have been sometime between when a servant told Octavia a crowd of townspeople had gathered to hold vigil in the courtyard and when Grainne said it was nearly time to push. Even though I cried out for her, the thought of my mother did little to calm me because with it came the memory of her many trials in childbed. I tried not to give in to the terror that threatened to consume me, but pain had weakened my resolve. Soon I lost all grip on reality.

I was oblivious to the world around me, lost in a thrumming buzz that was everywhere and nowhere all at once. Eventually Octavia's voice cut through the din, commanding me with every ounce of her Roman authority to push. I took a deep breath, gritted my teeth, and bore down hard.

"The baby's head is nearly out. Push again, my love," Grainne encouraged.

I grunted and pushed harder, again and again, until an odd sense of relief and release washed over me, and the child slipped out from between my thighs.

"You have a son," Grainne shouted jubilantly.

But just as quickly, her face fell. Instead of a lusty cry, there was silence. No one spoke as I searched each face, each one more concerned than the last. I knew something was terribly wrong.

"What is it? What is wrong with my baby?" I croaked.

Grainne only shook her head and handed the child to the young priestess acting as her assistant. She clutched my son, patting his back and holding him as near to the fire as she dared. It was then I noticed there was no rise and fall in his chest. My baby was not breathing.

Before I had a chance to protest, to beg my child to draw breath, a new wave of pain rocked my weakened frame, and I cried out.

"Guinevere, you have another baby who seeks the light of life. You must find the strength to push again."

My mind was in tatters, hardly able to comprehend what she was saying, torn between my silent son and his sibling waiting to be born. I gave a mighty heave that felt as though it broke me entirely.

"Very good, Guinevere," Octavia coached. "I know you are tired, but this little one cannot be born without your help. Try just one more time."

I tried to focus on what she was saying, but my mind kept wandering to the hearth, trying to understand what was happening to my son. Somewhere in the lucid recesses of my mind, I recognized what the young priestess was doing. My child had been born dead, and she was cleaning him, swaddling him not for his first hours of life but for the grave.

I hardly noticed as another convulsion shook my deflating belly. All around me, Octavia, Grainne, and the other women urged me on. I pushed one final time. Then there was nothing left to give.

Grainne was cursing at me in several languages as she struggled to pull my second child free. I shook my head weakly, tangled black locks whipping the sides of my face, and sank into the sweat-soaked sheets, utterly defeated.

I was numb, and my spirit was slowly detaching from my body. Soon I swam in a sea of darkness as soft as gosling down. Higher and higher I flew until nothing remained of my former life.

The last sound I heard was the fragile, mewling cry of my daughter.

⚬⚬⚬

Where I was was utterly silent, calm and peaceful like the quiet of a soft winter snowfall when the whole world is at rest. But I was not in the world; that much I knew. I was somewhere in-between and outside, not unlike the ethereal borderland of mists shrouding Avalon. But I was not there either. This place had none of the humming vibration that was felt rather than heard as the boat slipped through the mists. No, this place was somewhere else entirely.

I was moving forward yet standing still at the same time. I had no sensation of walking or even thinking that I wanted to move, yet there was motion all around me. I tried to close my eyes and reopen them to balance myself and refocus, but it made no difference. I looked down to find I had no arms to guide me, no legs supporting me.

I had the vague sense I had been somewhere similar to this before, perhaps in one of my many meditative journeys as part of my training in Avalon. Slowly, like a babe opening its eyes for the first time, I realized this was the land of the spirit, where no corporeal body could follow. If I'd still had lungs to fill with air, I would have sighed in relief. Never before had I realized what a burden it was to carry around a body or retain a lifetime of thoughts and memories. Gone were the worries and anxieties of life, the expectations, misplaced priorities, anger, and grudges. All that was left was the true essence of myself.

I had always expected to come face-to-face with the dark aspect of the Goddess when my soul departed this life, to have a terrible moment of reckoning before meeting the mighty Ceridwen and her cauldron of death and rebirth where I would either be granted access to the eternal joy of the Otherworld with my ancestors or plunged into the depths of her cauldron to be reborn again.

When I heard my name called, it was as though the sound came from both outside myself and within my mind at once. Still following my human instincts, I turned, expecting to behold the Goddess. But there was no one there.

Like a dreamer gradually waking from slumber, I began to sense dull colors and formless shapes, though I could make no sense of them. It was as though my inner eyes were adjusting after the transition from the physical world. Slowly, the world formed around me, or rather, revealed itself to me one sparkling grain of light at a time.

As the jumble of hues and wild figures coalesced, I found myself in a grassy sunlit meadow dappled with bashful violets, stately poppies, and clusters of tiny golden wildflowers. Their colors were so much more intense than anything I had seen on earth, their scent more heavily perfumed.

And suddenly I was no longer alone. The presence I had sensed from the first moment of darkness but had not dared to name took form before me. A woman with glistening raven hair, slightly lined pale skin, and gentle green eyes that were straight out of my memories stood before me. After all of my tears and pleading, she had come at last—too late to save my body but perfectly timed to soothe my bewildered soul.

"Mother," I breathed, instinctively rushing toward her, wanting to embrace her.

"My sweet daughter," she crooned just as she had when I was babe. I was certain she would have embraced me if it was within her power in this incorporeal state.

"Mother, I missed you so much. Where am I? Is this the Otherworld? Where is the Goddess?" The words tumbled out in a rush.

My mother smiled, a lovely, luminous gesture that filled my whole being with the sunshine of loving acceptance. "She is here. She is everywhere." She regarded me with appraising eyes. "But you are asking the wrong questions. It matters not whether your heart still beats. What you should be asking is do you wish it to? Are you ready to leave your life behind and stay with me?"

I began to shake. My mind whirled through everything I had

lost in the last few years—her, Aggrivane, and for all practical purposes, my father. I could abandon it all because there was nothing left for me in the world. But then I thought of Arthur, and for a brief moment, I could see him, collapsed by my bedside next to the pale, fragile body I barely recognized as my own. His head was bent as if in prayer, his hands clasped so tightly over the motionless bones of my arm that his knuckles were white. Long strands of hair, flecked gold at odd intervals in the somber candlelight, curtained his face from sight, but I could tell from the quaking of his large frame that he was sobbing, grieving for the wife he thought was dead.

Perhaps I was. I looked back at my mother in confusion, more uncertain than ever what was happening.

"Can you leave him?" she asked as two children appeared next to her.

One was a confident, proud young boy, perhaps two years old, the other an angelic girl of the same age. Both had identical bright green eyes and long tawny locks.

"Your children are safe and happy here. I will take care of them just as I did you."

A bittersweet blend of joy and sadness washed over me. So they had both died. I was certain I would have been crying if I'd had tears to shed in this world between worlds.

"May I see them?" I asked tremulously, almost afraid of the answer.

My mother nodded, and they scampered to me, so calm and comfortable I was certain they knew I was their mother. I sank down so my eyes were level with theirs, and to my great astonishment, I felt two small, sticky hands around each of my arms, and I was able to hold them against my heart, which I now felt beating faintly.

Somewhere in the back of my mind, I knew what was happening. Without realizing it, I had made my decision as soon as I had witnessed Arthur's pain, and I was slowly returning to life. It also meant I was slowly losing my children all over again.

I looked into their eyes, determined they would know just how much I loved them. Somehow being able to hold them and gaze into their eyes was all the communication I needed. The spirit spoke without words.

After a long while, the boy squeezed me tight, and the girl placed a dainty kiss on my cheek. Then a host of other children appeared—the brothers and sisters I had never known. Some had the stormy gray-blue eyes and defined chin of my father, while in the faces of others, I saw my mother or even my paternal grandmother looking back at me. With a final look at me, my twins darted off to the edges of the meadow to play, shrieking the earsplitting yelps of joy only children can produce, tumbling over one another but never getting hurt.

My mother took a few steps forward and encircled me in her arms, warmth radiating through all my limbs. "You must return now. But know I love you for all time. I promise to watch over you and welcome you to the Otherworld when your time comes. Have faith and trust in the God and Goddess to whom you have pledged your life."

I nodded, tears scalding my cheeks. "I will. I love you."

A dull humming noise, like the crescendo of a wordless chant, rose in my ears, and the edges of my vision blurred. I turned, facing a portal of shimmering golden light. All I had to do was step through, and I would be back in my body.

I glanced over my shoulder in time to catch one final glimpse of her, now holding my children like an image of the Mother Goddess.

"Good-bye, Mother." The words I had been deprived the chance to say in life echoed behind me as I fell through golden rain into the darkness of unconsciousness.

⁂

They told me Arthur kept vigil at my bedside from the moment Octavia's call of distress had brought him to the birth that had gone badly. As the servants replaced the bloody bed linens, he lifted my lifeless body, begging me in strained whispers not to abandon him. Long after the servants had slipped back to their quarters, eyes red-rimmed and shoulders sagging with fear, grief, and guilt, long after Grainne had prepared my babes for their burial and placed a soft hand on Arthur's shoulder, telling him my spirit was all but gone, Arthur remained. Stubborn as the bear for which he was named, he refused to accept my death.

When I surfaced from the black depths separating the worlds, eyelids fluttering in the golden light of a new day, Arthur stirred, disbelieving. He lifted his head from where it rested on my belly and stared at my face, rubbing his eyes like one convinced he dreamed still. I smiled weakly, raising the first three fingers on my right hand in an attempt to reach him.

"Guinevere," he breathed, tears sliding down his cheeks. "The gods be praised. My prayers do not go unheeded."

He embraced me as gently as he dared and called for Grainne, who appeared prepared to conduct a funeral, if her somber expression and lowered eyes were any indication. She nearly dropped her candle at the sight of me sitting up and blinking, weakened but very much in the realm of mortals.

Once she had given me a thorough examination and declared I would live, her attention returned to the most dreaded of all priestess' duties—a child's funeral. I had been unconscious a full two days, but they had delayed the royal burial out of concern I would need to be interred with my children.

They were to have their funerary rites at sunset as was custom. Arthur had decreed his children should be entombed with his father in a nearly inaccessible valley at the base of the highest of the Western Fells. It was an ideal royal resting place for few would be brave enough to venture in and do the graves harm, and it was fast becoming Camelot's royal cemetery.

I wasn't well enough to travel to the funeral, and truth be told, I didn't want to. I had said good-bye to my children in the Otherworld. But that wasn't enough to keep the sight at bay. Weakened by grief and my childbed travails, I was defenseless against it. Against my will, it transported me to that final, terrible ritual as clearly as though I were at Arthur's side.

Most of the city, as well as nobles from three neighboring kingdoms, turned out to bid farewell to the future of the realm, the prince and princess they'd never know. From Camelot's gates to the entrance to the valley, noble and peasant stood shoulder to shoulder. In more populated areas, people lined the streets so thickly the Combrogi had to ride ahead of the bier, cutting a path for the wagon to pass, and guards lined every side, doing their best to keep villagers from touching the caskets, which the peasants believed held some magical power.

Still, by the time its wheels stilled in the muddy, snow-dappled basin, the funerary cart was laden with gifts from the people: sprays of late season flowers, berries, and leaves; evergreen boughs symbolizing life after death; and bracelets and trinkets of gold, bronze, and silver. They were offerings made on the children's behalf, which Arthur dropped into the sacred stream that sliced through the valley.

When the time came, Merlin led the prayers over the bodies with Grainne acting as his assistant. With gentle, trembling hands, Arthur placed our babies in their graves, arranging their bodies in the traditional posture—pointing north on their left side, knees curled up and arms crossed over their chests in an attitude of sleep, heads facing east to look toward the promise of rebirth. He folded the funeral shrouds over them but could do no more. Sinking to his knees, he wept so hard his entire body shook. It was left to Kay and Bedivere, his trusted companions, to place our funerary gifts at their sides and fill in the graves.

Arthur kept watch with our son and daughter as day faded into night.

Finally, when the moon had risen and the frigid air made icicles in Arthur's beard, Merlin put an arm around him. "It is time to depart, old friend. Let them rest in peace. You kingdom awaits your return."

Throughout the long visions, my eyes were dry. My heart clenched in agony, but silent sobs were the only outward sign of my grief. As I lay curled in bed, seeking to hide from the visions and the pain, my body betrayed me, breasts leaking milk for mouths that would never taste it. I felt the emptiness of loss with every movement, keenly aware that those who had so recently inhabited my body now rested in the womb of the earth.

PART TWO

Hunted

Chapter Eight

Summer 500

I didn't need to hear the words to know what everyone was saying. I sensed it in their pitying glances, saw it cloaked in the eyes of courtiers, scented it on the wind that carried the servants' secrets beyond the alleyways, and in my darkest moments, I even tasted it on my husband's tongue. In the alehouses and barracks, ripening fields and desolate moors, they all whispered the same refrain—"the queen is barren."

Two years had passed since my children were born dead, and still my womb refused to allow life to take root. Grainne had assured me from the moment I regained consciousness that there was no reason I could not have many more children, but even then I had been suspicious. As a midwife, I had on occasion lied to a grieving mother, especially when I sensed that telling her the truth would mean taking away all she had to live for.

If that was the case for Grainne, I would not hold it against her. It was my highest duty to produce an heir. If she saw some merit in giving me false hope, then I would credit the cloud of deception in her gray-blue eyes to my own untamed imagination.

For a while, I was able to convince myself she was right, especially when, a few months after I had recovered, my moon time came and went without a drop of blood for three straight months. In that small bloom of anticipation, my world was right once again. But hope was drowned in a rush of crimson that returned with every new moon to remind me of my failure to my husband and my country.

"Arthur, we must decide what to do if this continues. We cannot leave the country without an heir," I told him late one night as we lay in bed.

He grunted his agreement. "I have thought upon that much since our children died. We could pick up the plan my father abandoned and name one of Lot's sons to the throne. Gawain would make an excellent king."

"But what of those who believe the throne should pass through my line? My nearest relative is my cousin Bran."

"Does he wish to take the throne?"

I thought hard. As a member of the Combrogi and ruler of Gwynned, Bran was known well to both of us. Though he was a capable fighter, he had not the stomach to take on a larger kingdom, much less the entire country. "No, I do not believe so."

"Then we must approach the house of Lothian and, failing that, pick another of the Combrogi. I would like to watch Mark's nephew Constantine. Like Tristan, he is a strong strategist and a capable fighter. After Gawain, he may be our wisest choice. Let us allow time to reveal the answer."

As we grappled with the real possibly of a childless future, life at Camelot continued. This month we held pleading day outside in the courtyard rather than in the Great Hall to capture the blessed relief of occasional breezes tossed up from the harbor. However, the winds could scarcely reach us, blocked as they were by the sour bodies gathered around us. The crowd was attracted by the oaths and screeching of our last case, a loud quarrel between two lordlings who came to blows before Arthur and I could render judgment.

Before we could call forth the next petitioner, a man emerged from the crowd, the ragged, coarse material of his tunic dragging behind him. Sobbing, he fell to his knees at our feet, mumbling something that sounded like "forgive me" over and over. He clutched and clawed at our legs as though we could save him from whatever plagued his mind.

I clambered back in my chair, seeking to move out of his reach. I sent Kay and Lancelot a warning glare, ready to call them into service to remove the intruder.

He was trembling, eyes rolling about uncontrollably as he begged, "Mercy, my lord, have mercy."

Arthur leaned toward him, placing a hand on his bony shoulder. "What crime have you committed? How may I show you mercy?"

The man looked up, and his eyes cleared for one awful moment, holding in their depths the chilling resolve only madness could create. "Murder."

Kay and Lancelot inched closer, but Arthur paid them no heed. His deranged subject held all of his attention. "Whom have you killed? Why come before me?"

The man shook his head as if loathe to confess the nature of his crime. He stared at us for a long moment. Then slowly he pointed at Arthur, speaking so softly we had to lean forward to hear him whisper, "You have the eyes of the dead."

My skin prickled, and I caught the flash of steel, but before I could react, a dark-haired woman leapt out of the throng and tackled our claimant, sending him sprawling with a cry of pain. The crowd let out a collective gasp and backed quickly away. Arthur and I were on our feet, weapons drawn, while half the Combrogi surrounded our attackers.

"What is the meaning of this?" Arthur roared.

"I have just saved your life," the woman announced.

We stepped cautiously toward where she lay, still holding our claimant. She lifted his left arm, which dangled uselessly in her grip, and revealed a thin blade pressed against his palm and wrist, concealed beneath a tattered sleeve. It was the same hand he had held out to Arthur.

"This was inches from your throats, and neither of you saw it." She looked at us, accusation plain in her stunning black eyes.

For a moment, neither of us moved. Then involuntarily, my hand went to my throat.

"How do we know you are not involved, merely part of the trick?" I asked.

"Because if I were," she said with a look of disdain, "you would be dead by now."

Arthur recovered himself, expression blossoming as though he had just been made party to the plot of some elaborate joke. "Indeed, Sobian can be lethal when she puts her mind to it."

I stared at him, openmouthed. "You know this woman?"

Arthur laughed, a hearty sound that began in his chest and escaped as a joyous rumble. He extended a hand to the woman and helped her to her feet. "Kay, take this man away." He kicked the madman with the toe of his boot.

"Gladly." Kay pulled our would-be killer roughly to his feet. "I have additional business with you." His voice held the promise of dreaded things to come.

I was still speechless, trying to comprehend what had just taken place. This woman had come out of nowhere to save us from a madman bent on killing us both but whom neither of us, trained in the arts of war, had suspected. Now it appeared Arthur knew her.

I took Arthur's hand, suddenly unsteady. "What is going on? Who is this woman?"

Arthur's smile brightened. "Guinevere, meet Sobian, Scourge of Sidhe."

Sobian brushed off her deep golden cloak and sank into a curtsey. "I am honored to be of service, my queen."

I took in the stunned crowd standing around us, as unsure of how to react as I was. "I—how do you know one another?"

Arthur's gaze followed mine. "That is a story best told in private."

Bedivere and Lancelot set about dispersing the crowd while Arthur invited Sobian inside. He sent servants ahead with orders for strong ale and water so Sobian could wash. I followed on their heels, still confused and feeling suddenly displaced by our guest.

Arthur and I sat in a small meeting room just off the main hall, waiting as Sobian cleaned the dirt from her clothes and skin. Octavia brought in the ale then hovered protectively at my side, just like the second mother I'd always felt her to be. I put a hand reassuringly on the one she laid on my shoulder.

"I am fine," I told her between long draughts of ale. "Really."

Her eyes narrowed. "Keep telling yourself that and eventually you may believe it, but I don't. I can feel you trembling."

Was I? I stilled myself for a moment. Wild energy still coursed through my veins from the attack, but beneath that, yes, I was shaking. And why should I not be? Some lunatic had just tried to kill us both, and I never saw it coming. I took a deep breath and tried to arrange my thoughts. Best start with the most pressing issue. "Arthur, who *is* this woman? Why do you trust her so?"

Arthur smiled, his face taking on a dreamy air as though he recalled a cherished memory. "Let's just say that during my time in Uther's army, I grappled with her on more than one occasion. Sobian is, to this day, one of the most fearsome creatures I have ever encountered."

"More fearsome than I?" I quirked an eyebrow at him, daring him to give the wrong answer.

His smile widened, and he leaned forward to kiss me. "Of course not."

I gestured for him to continue. "Get back to your story. I want to know who this woman is before she returns."

"This woman, as you call her, has always gone by the name Sobian, though I've never believed her to be Irish. She used to be a river pirate. I first encountered her when I was stationed at Caerleon near the Bristol Channel. Uther sent a contingent of men because she was causing a lot of trouble on the Sabrina. If you were foolish enough to fall for her charms, you'd lose your purse faster than your pants." Arthur chuckled. "They called her the Scourge of the Sidhe because she had the ability to slip on and off of ships with her crew as stealthily as the fey and the charm to convince the captain he'd given her his goods of his own free will."

"It's hard to believe one woman could possess such charm," I said dryly.

"Oh, I assure you, she does. Wait a bit. I'm sure she'll turn it on you. Women certainly aren't immune."

"Immune to what?" Sobian entered the room as Octavia quietly slipped out.

"I was just telling my wife about your reputation."

She gave me a dazzling smile. "I knew I was not ever far from your mind, my king." She curtseyed to Arthur, lowering her long lashes at same time as her bosom.

I did my best to hide the glower her shameless flirting brought to my face before she looked up.

"Please sit with us and have a drink. It is the least we can do for you." He held out a cup to her, and she obliged his request. Arthur leaned toward her across the table. "How did you know what that man was going to do? Do you think him genuinely mad?"

Sobian's reaction was guarded as she watched me over the rim of her cup. "Let's just say I had been tracking him for some time and knew better than to believe what I saw."

Her vague answer did nothing to improve my opinion of her. "How exactly does a river pirate know how to spot an assassin?"

"I left that profession many years ago. Now I earn my keep in many ways."

Arthur arched an eyebrow. "So you are an honest woman now?"

Her amusement came out as a trilling laugh. "I would not say that, but I am no longer a criminal if that is what you mean."

"What *do* you do?" I asked.

"I have been a warrior, a spy, and even an outlaw for a time."

"And an assassin," I added.

Sobian's eyes grew wide, and she made to protest.

I held up a hand to silence her denial. "Don't bother. I was trained by one of the best warriors on this isle and know you have to be aware of what to look for in order to spot someone as convincing as our criminal."

Sobian was dumbstruck. She turned to Arthur. "I would never—"

"I know. Please forgive my wife's rudeness." He shot me a scathing look. "She does not know you as do I. In fact, I was thinking that we can use a woman of your skills."

It was my turn to be incredulous. I set down my cup with more force than I intended. "We can?"

"Yes." His tone brooked no argument. "Today has shown us our security is weak, and I cannot have that. Sobian, you have seen the law from both sides. You know its holes. I believe you can help me improve my ability to protect myself, my wife, and my people."

Sobian took a long drink. "What exactly are you asking of me?"

"I would like you to lead my cadre of spies. You will learn everything you can of our friends and enemies."

I cringed at the thought of having this woman around regularly. "Kay already acts as your second, and I have Lancelot as my champion. What more protection do we need?"

Arthur's exasperation came out in a flare of temper. "Guinevere, you have a strategic mind. If you let go of your petty fear that I will give you up for Sobian—which will not happen, I assure you—you will be able to see the wisdom in my choice.

Kay and Lancelot protect us daily, but someone needs to be in command. Until now, I have filled that role, but it is becoming clear I cannot handle that duty in addition to governing my country. Sobian has already proven her loyalty to us. Who better to employ?"

My cheeks reddened. I could not believe he would call me jealous in front of her, no matter what their history. "First of all, *husband,* I have no fear of this woman. If need be, I will prove that to you in the sparring ring. Second, will it not appear strange that a woman is suddenly in charge of our guard? I do not think your men will take kindly to taking orders from her."

Arthur regarded me calmly, a challenge in his eyes. "Nor do I. That is why her true role will only be known to us and our champions. Sobian, you are well versed in subterfuge. Do you believe you could pretend to hold another role while acting in this one?"

Sobian looked back and forth between us, chewing the nail of her littlest finger as she weighed her options. "Of course."

Arthur stood, motioning for us to do the same. He placed my hand in Sobian's. "Meet your new lady's maid."

I coughed, choking on the ale I was swallowing. "Arthur, you must be joking."

"Not at all. It is the perfect disguise. She will have every right to be near us."

"I already have Octavia. What do you suggest I do, turn her out? And what will people say when Sobian is seen meeting with you in private?"

"Octavia will continue to fulfill the same duties she always has. She will simply appear to have more help." He cast a flirtatious look in Sobian's direction. "As for what people will say, kings have had dalliances with maids since time began. The more they believe that, the less likely they are to suspect the truth."

I shoved Arthur with both hands, knowing the act wouldn't budge him, but it made me feel better. "I am simply supposed to go along with this, is that right?"

Arthur said nothing.

I looked from one to the other, knowing I was trapped. Arthur's plan was sound, but I did not like the idea of living in close company with a woman Arthur had obviously befriended in the past any more than I liked knowing people would think he was disloyal to me. Arguing with him would do no good. Perhaps I could tolerate the situation until I found a reason to have Sobian removed. "If you two will excuse me, I would like to lie down."

I was halfway out of the room before Sobian came trailing after me. "Let me assist you, my lady," she offered, amusement clear in her voice.

"I do not require your services," I spat over my shoulder.

⁂

I made it to my room and slammed the door. Alone at last, I leaned against the door, struggling to catch my breath. Tears spilled over as the enormity of the day finally sank in. I slid down to the floor and ran my hands through my hair. How could my life have changed so much in only a few hours? I thought Arthur had grown to love me, but he had just accepted a former lover back into his confidence after only having been reunited with her for a few hours. What did that mean for my marriage?

I didn't know how long I spent contemplating my situation, but just as quickly as the tears had come, I started laughing. I was being ridiculous. Arthur had had to learn to live with Aggrivane at court long ago. Granted he'd sent my former betrothed on missions away from Camelot as often as possible, but he had still learned how to cope with his presence. I was behaving like a child. Galen had been right the day we argued in the forest so many years before. I really was as bad as a fisherman's wife. And worse, I had changed little with the passage of time. I stood, straightening my dress and mentally preparing myself to apologize to them both.

After a few deep breaths, I went back down to the meeting room, expecting to find Arthur and Sobian discussing the finer points of her new role. But to my surprise, the room was empty. Octavia came in, holding a tray to collect the ale pitcher and our used glasses.

"Do you know where Arthur went?"

She eyed me carefully. "He is in his room. Alone." She emphasized the word, knowing I would wonder. "They told me about her new role. Are you in agreement that it is wise?"

"I will be," I reassured her.

Octavia made a noise indicating she wasn't so certain then busied herself cleaning up the table. That was when I saw the lone sheet of paper. Thinking it to be notes from Arthur and Sobian's discussion, I bent over the table to get a better look.

My blood turned to ice. The letters were formed of patterns made by varying lengths of horizontal, vertical, and diagonal lines. It was written in Ogham, the ancient language of the Druids, so it could not have come from Arthur. He hadn't studied with them long enough to have learned it. Plus, its message was not one a husband leaves his wife.

I ran to Arthur's room, rubbing my hand over the goose-pimpled flesh of my arm. "You may wish to rethink your decision," I said as I entered.

He looked up. "Why is that?"

I held the paper out to him. "This was left in the meeting room." I shivered again.

He plucked the paper out of my hand and turned it in several directions, trying to figure out how to read it. "Ogham. That's unusual. What does it say?"

I grabbed it back, irritated beyond decorum. After what had happened with the madman and Sobian, I didn't think I could take much more.

"That's the problem. I think it's a threat. *'My queen, you may close your eyes to the one you scorned, but that will not keep me away. I will breathe your last breath so that you will live on forever in me.'*"

Arthur's face darkened. "Only one man could claim such a thing."

I looked at him quizzically, brow furrowing. "How do you know Sobian isn't party to this? It appeared right after she did in the very room she last occupied."

Arthur sighed, clearly frustrated that I didn't trust Sobian implicitly as he did. "Because this isn't her way. As she said, if she wished you dead, you would be. She has no need for idle threats."

"Who then?"

"Think about the message." His tone took on a condescending air I did not care for. "Someone you once rejected? Who did you give up to marry me? You may not want to see it, but the answer is right in front of you."

He didn't have to say the name. Suddenly I knew exactly who he blamed. His menacing gaze was fixed on my former lover.

Guilty or not, Aggrivane was in serious trouble.

◦◦◦

Within the week, Aggrivane was given a special assignment as an envoy in Brittany, and Camille chose to go with him. In many ways, it was easier for me not having him around, not being reminded of what would never be, especially with Camille's recent pregnancy. That had been a surprise given Aggrivane's insistence on their love being chaste. Plus, while I'd never suspected Aggrivane, I breathed a little easier knowing he was out of easy reach of Arthur's wrath.

But despite this move, the notes continued appearing as summer progressed, which meant Aggrivane couldn't have sent them. They came at odd intervals, frequently enough that the sender had to be nearby—messages didn't travel that quickly from Brittany—but inconsistently enough that I could never anticipate them. Or rather, I was *always* anticipating them, always on edge, as I was sure my hunter intended. Each one was more threatening and found in a more intimate location than the last. The fear they provoked built along with summer's heat. These were no mere mind games; whoever was doing this had a point to prove—he or she had, or could gain, personal access to me. It had to be someone in our inner circle, but I had no idea who it could be or why this was happening.

Then on the night of the full moon, after Grainne and I completed our ritual, I found a tattered page tied to the apple tree in the center of the labyrinth at the very heart of Camelot. Without reading its sinister message, I crumpled it with a snarl and marched straight to Arthur's quarters.

"I cannot take any more of this. I am the queen. I will not have one of my subjects threatening me. If you will not act to find out who is doing this, I will."

Arthur stood. "What will you do?" he asked with a mocking chuckle. "Interrogate each man of the realm until one finally confesses? I'm already doing everything that can be done, wife. Sobian is investigating. Give her time." He marched over to me, towering above me. "And if you ever speak to me like that again…"

I looked up at him, steel in my eyes. "You'll what? Divorce me? Hit me? In the former, you cannot, and in the latter, you forget I can and will take you on any day."

"Is that so?" He picked me up and carried me to his bed. "Let us see how well you fare."

⁂

It was Sobian's idea to gather the kings of the tribes, their lordlings, and the Combrogi at Arthur's southern power base, a scarred hill fort called Cadbury. Officially, we were together to celebrate Samhain—the night the old year gave way to the new—but what only those closest to the crown knew was that Sobian had reason to believe this area was linked to the source of the chilling notes.

"When I was a pirate, I amassed a vast collection of valuable paperwork along with the other booty," she explained. "Naturally,

I kept any correspondence written by those in power in case it would ever prove useful leverage. In time, I noticed these pages had common characteristics, such as the way the vellum was prepared or even the color of the ink, little signatures that betrayed a common maker. By matching those with the name of sender, I could usually narrow down the location of origin." She tapped one of the threatening notes against her hand. "I believe this came from somewhere in the south-central part of the Summer Country."

We couldn't accuse anyone based on that idea, but it was a place to start. Sobian suggested we gather everyone in the area and observe them in the abandon of the feast when they would be most at ease.

Situated atop a towering hill overlooking the Somerset Levels, Cadbury had one of the most impressive views I'd ever seen. From its walls, farmland, bogs, and untamed wilderness stretched to the horizon in every direction. Anyone foolish enough to attack this fort would be seen long before they glimpsed the castle and its four terraced earthen banks and ditches surrounded by thick stands of trees. Even if they did manage to overcome those obstacles, the castle itself was ringed by a wooden palisade with several gatehouses full of archers and armed troops. Arthur had chosen his location well.

Cadbury was even more impressive from the inside. The great hall, a massive structure separate from the fortress's other buildings, was larger than any I'd ever seen, even Camelot. Above me, its support timbers stretched like ancient oaks into darkness even hundreds of candles could not penetrate. Based on the number of bodies milling about, I was fairly confident it could hold nearly a thousand people without strain.

At a signal from Arthur, Kay rapped on the underside of the table, indicating to the crowd they should quiet down—and for a moment, I was back in Corbenic the night Arthur had proposed and turned my life upside down. I shook my head to clear it and pushed my goblet out of arm's reach. Whatever Arthur had them serving was too strong for me to consume without measure. I needed my wits about me if I was to observe whatever actions Arthur suspected would be brought out as our guests drank themselves into unsuspecting candor.

Arthur stood, watching imperiously as his guests settled and turned their faces to him. "I promise you will not have to listen to me overmuch this night—"

"Aye, we all know how you love making speeches," Bedivere interrupted from his table below the dais, brotherly grin bright enough to light the night.

Arthur acknowledged him with an expression colored by a mix of amusement and annoyance before turning back to the assembly. "It is by no coincidence I picked this night to bring you together. It is the new year, and as the wheel of time turns once more, it is a time for celebrating, a time for new beginnings and unity. In that same spirit of brotherhood, I wish to introduce all of you tonight to our newest member. As many of you know, Mark of Cornwall has ruled the kingdom of Dyfneint in addition to his own land since his brother's passing into the Otherworld. This night, he wishes to formally pass control of Dyfneint to his nephew, Constantine." Arthur raised his hand, indicating the two men should rise.

Mark looked around at the assembled lords. "I could have passed the crown to my nephew in private, but I wanted all of you to know he takes this throne with my blessing." He stepped forward and kissed his nephew, removing a golden torque from around his neck and placing it around Constantine's throat. He turned back to the crowd. "My fellow lords, regardless of your quarrels with me, if you recognize my nephew as the rightful ruler of Dyfneint, please stand that I may see you."

Arthur remained standing, and I joined him, offering Mark a compassionate smile. One by one, each of the lords, including Ana, silently rose.

Mark nodded his thanks. "In that knowledge, I bid you all peace." He and his nephew took their seats.

Before Arthur could speak again, Malegant stood. "My king, if we are using this feast as a public stage for private matters, I wish to speak."

Beside me, Arthur stiffened. He still hadn't forgiven Malegant for his embarrassing tussle in the market all those years before, for which Malegant had been banished from court for three months. "Lord Malegant, I remind you this is not pleading day. If you have a case to lay before the court, I suggest you come to Camelot on the next full moon with everyone else."

"But this isn't just any case. And I too wish the full witness of the court to its outcome."

Arthur pursed his lips behind folded hands. "I have a feeling if I forbid you to speak you will do so anyway, and I have no desire to eject you from my court *again*. You may proceed, but be brief." He sat down hard on the bench, hunched shoulders and taut muscles clearly displaying his displeasure.

Malegant bowed with dramatic flourish. "Thank you, my king."

Arthur made an impatient gesture, commanding him to get to the point.

"Quite simply, I am here to lodge a formal complaint that Lord Uriens still holds approximately one hundred of my men captive in his lands. I have petitioned this court multiple times against him, and still they languish rather than being reunited with their families."

Before Arthur could issue a rebuttal, Uriens was on his feet, rushing toward Malegant with the virility of a man half his years. "You attacked me, remember? Do you truly expect no punishment for your breach of peace? Did it ever occur to you that our king has taken no action because he feels me justified in my acts?"

Malegant shot Arthur a disdainful look. "If that is so, then he is not only cowardly but a disgrace to his role."

The collective intake of breath in the room was audible. Many of the men in the crowd stood, loyalty and instinct bidding them to protect their king.

Before I could blink, Uriens had his eating dagger drawn, blade at Malegant's throat from behind. "I could split you open from ear to ear here and now, and no one would lift a finger to stop me, you traitorous bastard!"

Weapons were not allowed at the quarterly meetings, but still Combrogi rushed forward to do what they could to prevent any further violence.

Malegant grinned evilly. "Go ahead, old man."

Uriens flicked his wrist and blood ran from Malegant's throat, but the younger man spun away before the blade could do any serious damage. Malegant picked up his own utensil and caught Uriens in the side. Blood blossomed in a crimson stain on Uriens's tunic.

Malegant laughed, a cruel sound of dark glee. He wielded his dagger at the others. "Who else wishes to oppose me?" He turned his manic eyes on Arthur. "Do you dare challenge me, king?"

"Surrender or I will kill you myself," Arthur yelled.

Malegant made a show of thinking. "I rather like my odds."

He turned and melted into the now turbulent crowd, most of whom were trying to stop him. He dodged bodies and gloved fists as though he had trained for this very moment, shoving some men aside, tripping and punching others until he was free.

Arthur motioned to Kay, Lancelot, and Sobian. "Take your troops and be sure he leaves this city in worse shape than he entered it. And if he happens to stop breathing in the process, bring me his head on a pole."

⁂

I sat dumbfounded in the chaos that followed, unable to do more than watch as Morgan tended to her injured husband and groups mobilized to ensure Malegant was apprehended.

Arthur sat equally silent, a vein in his neck pulsing rapidly.

"Owain and Accolon will kill him for that," I finally said.

Arthur grunted, a masculine sound I had grown to associate with disapproval. "If they can find him. That slippery bastard has more holdings in this part of the country than there are chambers in a beehive."

"Do we still hold the feast, or would it be better to postpone?" I asked.

"No, we will proceed. Sobian still wants to see how everyone acts when deep in their cups. Now I must be her eyes." Arthur motioned Bors over. "Tell the servants to bring out dinner. That should tempt everyone back to order." He winked at me. "If I know one thing, it's that rumbling stomachs sooner obey the call of food than ears listen to any order. Uther's army taught me that."

Arthur was right. At the first whiff of food, the remaining lords who had chosen not to chase after Malegant turned their attention from their plans and arguments to peer over one another's shoulders, hoping to catch a glimpse of what delicacies were being laid on the table. Soon, all were seated, their earlier proclamations quieted to a hushed buzz of conversation.

I had just taken my first bite of roasted meat when a serving maid approached us from behind.

The girl bowed her head. "Forgive me, my king, but I am sent to find the queen."

"I am here. What need have you?"

The girl kept her eyes on the ground. "My lord Aggrivane has need of your skills for his wife and child lie ill in the next building."

I wondered why I had not seen them among the crowd. As much as I disliked Camille, I wouldn't have wished her ill health. I looked at Arthur, trying to gauge his reaction.

He nodded. "Go, but take Gareth with you. I will not have you alone with so many revelers and madmen about."

I touched his hand in thanks. "If Morgan returns, send her as well. We may have need of her. . . specialized skill." I choked out the compliment. "I will meet you back here when I am finished."

The girl and I found Gareth then fled into the cool night, a fine spray of mist falling from the moonless sky. I shielded my eyes from the unexpected brightness of dozens of leaping bonfires. As my eyes adjusted, the courtyard came alive with dancers, hundreds of people packed into the confines of the thick castle walls.

"Forgive me, my lady," the maid said demurely then grabbed my wrist before leading me into the fray, Gareth following close behind.

I quickly understood why she had risked touching me. If she had not, I would have quickly lost her in the shifting throng. Everywhere I looked was a whirl of light, color, and sound. The flash of a blue cloak gave way to the giddy laughter of a group of young girls enjoying their first festival and the cry of a vendor hawking skewers of meat. Faces whirled past, some painted into masks, others unrecognizable under hoods, everyone's eyes gleaming wildly. We veered to the left, and a cup of some rank drink was thrust into my hand, but before I could see who had given it, they were swallowed up in the press of people. We wove right, dodging a knot of rowdy men, and I yelled my apologies as I stepped on someone's foot. I turned back just in time to narrowly miss colliding with a brazier.

I was panting by the time we reached the doors of the next building, a long, low structure like the ones in which we lived in Avalon. Gareth took up his post outside. Without pausing, the maid—whose name I still did not know—opened the door and led me to the chamber where Camille and her young son were staying. His cries were audible before the door more than cracked open.

The poor thing must be miserable.

Camille was visible as soon as I entered the room. She leaned against the windowsill, clad only in her shift despite the cool dampness of the breeze. It clung to her, fixed in place by sweat. She held her screaming son on her right hip, propping herself up with the other. The strain in her features said she was using all her energy to stand upright.

Camille looked up, her face pale and drawn, hair plastered to her forehead and neck. "I can't get him to stop crying." Her voice was thin and weak.

"Here"—I reached out to take him—"let me try."

Her hands barely brushed mine, but it was enough to confirm she was burning with fever. Her son's forehead was equally hot, his tiny, clenched palms clammy as he beat against my shoulder.

"Shhh. . . all will be well, little one," I cooed, stroking his hair, careful not to bounce him and upset what likely was a delicate tummy. "Camille, please lie down." I pulled the sheets back from the bed. I turned to the maid. "Has she anything else to wear?"

The maid removed another thin tunic from a chest and helped Camille into the dry clothing.

Camille lay back. "I wonder why you bother when I will just sweat through it too." She spoke through cracked lips that looked painful even from a distance.

I turned to the maid. "Water some wine and bring it back here for her. Then go to the kitchen and bring back some yarrow and feverfew, honey, a flagon of wine, a small cooking pot, a mortar and pestle, and as much willow bark as you can find."

The maid curtsied and scampered off without a word.

I smiled at Camille. "I will make a tea that will hopefully help both of you sleep and bring the fever down. How long have you been ill?"

Camille's eyes fluttered closed as she lost her battle to keep them open. "I felt strangely upon rising this morning and grew weaker throughout the day. Llew became restless only a few hours ago. He is why I did not attend the feast."

I looked at Llew, who had finally stopped screaming and

trying to beat me into making him feel better. He was worn into submission, a cranky mew the only indication he was still fighting whatever illness held him in its grip.

The maid returned with the wine and some of the supplies. She helped Camille drink while I struggled to grind the herbs with one hand and keep Llew secure in my other arm. Once the maid was gone again to fetch the rest, I looked at Camille, who had sunk into sleep, her breathing shallow but even.

"Your mother needs her rest, little Llew. And so do you. Sleep now." I abandoned the mortar and rubbed the top of his head, willing his tiny eyelids to grow heavy. "The Goddess guard you as you slumber." I kissed his tiny limp hand as he finally drifted off.

I didn't know how long I sat there holding him before a voice cold as ice woke me from my reverie.

"Does it pain you to know he could have been yours?"

I looked up to see Morgan draped in the doorway, arms crossed defensively.

She was right. He could have been my son had Aggrivane and I married. I shifted Llew's weight in my arms. Now that she mentioned it, it did hurt, but I wouldn't let her know.

"Does it pain you to be such a shrew?" I snapped back.

Morgan pushed off the doorframe and moved back to let the maid through. "Suit yourself. I don't have to help you."

I would have let her go if Camille hadn't woken right then, mumbling incoherently. I handed Llew to Morgan and rushed to her side, cupping her forehead. "Her fever is worsening."

Morgan laid Llew next to Camille in the bed. Without a word, she stripped off her cloak, rolled up the sleeves of her tunic, and rattled off yet another list of supplies for the poor maid to fetch.

Then she hung the pot over the fire and poured in the honey, which caught the light and reflected it onto her face, making her glow like some Otherworldly being.

Like the fey they say she hails from. That rumor had been around before I set foot on Avalon's shores and had dogged her ever since. Sometimes I wondered if it was true.

I picked up the mortar and pestle and continued grinding. "How is your husband?"

She threw me a look that clearly questioned my motives for asking. "He is resting nearby. The wound is serious, but there is nothing else I can do for now." She stirred the honey before setting the spoon down with a bang.

Llew woke, whimpered, and I scooped him up.

Morgan turned on me, scooping the herbs out of the mortar and flinging them into the pot without so much as glancing down. "Why did Arthur let him go? If my husband had done that to"— she struggled to say Malegant's name but could not—"anyone, he would have been arrested on the spot. Why not the same punishment for *him*?"

"We tried, Morgan. You were there. He escaped."

Morgan gave me a chiding sidelong glance. "Is that really the best you can do? Do you think me so dim-witted that that explanation will suffice? I'll go after him myself if I have to." She began pouring the amber liquid into two cups.

"No, don't. He's dangerous."

She snorted. "You think I don't know that? I've dealt with him before. I know how changeable his alliances are. He's in league with whoever benefits him."

"Much like you." The words slipped out before I realized I was even thinking them.

Her eyes widened, and she stopped pouring. "Is that what you think of me?"

"Does it really surprise you? You've always lived for yourself—you have said as much."

"Believe what you will." She paused as if thinking, then her mouth curved into a vindictive sneer. "You'd better enjoy holding that little boy because he's the last child who will ever fill your arms. Your bloodline dies with you. But mark my words—one day my child will be greater than even you. You may think I am concerned only with my own well-being, but you know nothing. Absolutely nothing."

I tipped one of the cups into Llew's tiny mouth, too stunned to respond. He gurgled and attempted to spit out the contents, but I wouldn't let him. When he finally swallowed, I put him back into bed with Camille, who woke only long enough to drink her own dose.

"I will stay with them," Morgan said. "Go back to your husband. I should be here, close to mine." I took a few steps toward the door before Morgan called after me. "Be on your guard. Evil spirits roam this night."

I rolled my eyes. Of course they did. It was the feast of the dead, the night when the veil between the worlds was the thinnest. But I was a trained priestess with one of Aggrivane's younger brothers as a guard. I had nothing to fear.

⁕

By the time Gareth and I emerged into the courtyard, the evening's drizzle had intensified to a light shower, but it wasn't stopping the revelers. The music had grown primal, fed by the deep vibrations of horns and punctuated by the rhythmic booms of drums. Around the central bonfire, a group of men and women chanted in a language ancient and dark. Although I did not understand the words, it felt somehow appropriate to invoke the ghosts of Samhain.

Even more people packed the courtyard now, so I no longer bothered to ask pardon for barging through groups or stepping on toes. Nor did they seem to care. Caught up in the ecstasy of the night, they only had eyes for one another and the spirits only they could see.

Past the painted woman decorating drunken couples with spirals and swirls, through the knots of undulating couples around the bonfires, and beyond the brawny twins hawking ale, I scurried, head bent to shield me from the rain. Then a hand shot out from a tangle of dancers, and I was caught up as they swirled through the crowd. Forced to keep up or be trampled, I was passed from one partner to another. The black eyes gazing back at me were eerily similar from one to the next.

When they finally let me go, the door to the great hall was in sight, but Gareth was not. I craned my neck, peering through the swirling mass of people to catch sight of his dark curls. Once I thought I saw him, but it turned out to be only the tanner. I was still looking for Gareth when I heard my name, spoken by a voice I recognized but could not immediately place. For a moment, I thought Gareth had caught up to me.

I turned instinctively and found myself looking up at a hooded man. When he angled his head to meet my gaze, the firelight flickered on his face, which was painted from temple to temple in red spirals. The effect was shocking, making him appear more demon than man, and obscured his identity as much as the Sacred King's had been at my first ceremony.

He leaned down so he was closer to my level. "Do you not recognize me?" He clucked his tongue disapprovingly.

I backed up, seeking escape, uncomfortable from his nearness and familiarity. Only a handful of people would have dared speak to me in such an informal way, but his build and voice did not match any of them.

"Do I know you?" I finally asked, frantically searching for the door that had been nearly within reach before he distracted me but now had vanished into thin air.

He chuckled. "Maybe this will jog your memory—'*As the dreamer dreams of solace, so I dream of you. Come with me now into the city made from earth and ashes, from which there is no escape.*'"

For a moment, I couldn't place his words. But then, with an icy chill, I realized he was quoting one of the notes, one of the ones no one else knew about.

"How? Why?" I stumbled back, unable to comprehend being face to face with the man who had stalked me for months. I edged back again but was met with cold, wet stone at my lower back. One glance down told me I had backed into the well. I struggled to keep my balance as he leaned into me.

"I told you I could get to you anytime, anywhere. And here we are." He cocked his head to the side. "Do you still not recognize me?"

He pulled back his hood, giving me a clear view of his decorated face. It took me a moment to see through the maze of markings, but when I did, a scream rose up in my throat. It was seized by panic, and I was able only to squeak out his name.

"Malegant."

He grinned mirthlessly. "That's right. And now you're coming with me."

He grabbed my wrists, preventing me from fighting back. I tried to kick my way free, but he avoided my blows just as he had avoided those in the hall. His other hand, clad in a glove, clamped over my mouth. Instinctively, I gasped, inhaling an astringent odor foreign to the leather that made me want to gag. But instead of letting me go, he pulled me close, spreading his fingers so they covered my nose as well.

My head tipped forward as I gasped for air, suddenly light-headed. The world spun around me as I fell, helpless, into his arms.

"That's it, my queen, just give in," he purred into my ear as he pulled me along.

To anyone with the presence of mind to pay us heed, we probably looked like every other drunken couple, one supporting the other as we danced ourselves into oblivion. I tried to speak, to cry out, to wrench my arms away, but I could not move. I was completely under his control. And I was slipping away, giving in despite my best efforts to fight whatever foul concoction was tempting my body to sleep.

My eyes began to close. The last thing I saw was him yanking off the glove and tossing it into the bonfire, where it was consumed by the flames.

Then there was nothing but darkness.

Waking was much slower than falling into the void. I was aware first of a rocking sensation and an occasional bump. Mind still addled, I mistook the rhythm for a cart or even a boat, but then I breathed in sour horse sweat. With a jolt, the events of the night came back to me. I struggled to open my eyes, heart pounding, breath heaving with the knowledge I was under Malegant's control.

My vision was hazy, marred by whatever drug Malegant had used on me and made worse by the steady rain. As we continued slowly, a blurred kaleidoscope of brown, green, and black marched with us. I tried to reach up and wipe away the rain clinging to my eyelashes, to clear my sight, but I found my hands were bound together and tied to the horse's saddle.

Then I felt it. Another heartbeat behind my own. The warmth of human contact. The familiar scent of wood smoke from the bonfires and just a slight remnant of the acerbic potion that beckoned me back to darkness even now. I fought back a wave of nausea as the realization of who was holding me upright dawned on me. Slowly, I raised my head, unable to make myself turn to look him in the face.

A low chuckle deep within his chest, a sound I felt rather than heard, was the only verbal acknowledgement he gave to my being awake, though his grip on me tightened.

There was almost no sound as we picked our way slowly down the slick, muddy track. We were still descending the steep path from the castle to the road below, so I couldn't have been unconscious long. We weren't so far away from the castle I couldn't escape. I just had to figure out how.

I breathed deeply, willing my mind to clear and fighting back a rising tide of panic. Being bound and still sluggish, escaping would not be easy, but I vowed he would not take me beyond Arthur's reach. I took stock of my situation. It was raining, so the road was wet. If our horse faltered, I would topple along with him and only gain Malegant's wrath for my efforts. He knew I was awake, so I had no element of surprise either. Nor did I have a weapon with which to wound. There was at least one horse ahead of us and one behind judging from the muddy squash made with every step of the animals' hooves. I had no way of knowing how many men were making the journey on foot. Malegant was too smart to leave me loosely guarded. He had seen me fight and knew my capabilities.

As I tried to think, the rain increased, sending streams of green paint into my eyes. So that was how he had slipped me past the tower guards. I was just a woman in a painted mask, a passed out reveler like so many others.

Inwardly, I cursed. How was this possible? Arthur had his best men, including an assassin, on Malegant's tracks, yet he'd walked out the main gate with me unconscious in his arms. It was a testament to the power of distraction. Chances were good no one was expecting him to hide in plain sight. What were the chances they were following us now?

I twisted around, straining to look past Malegant's broad shoulders for any sign we were being followed.

"No one is there. We're all alone, you and I, and my men will be of no aid to you," Malegant purred into my hair, his lips brushing my temple as he pulled me even tighter against him. I wriggled and turned my face away, trying to avoid his advances. His grip on my shoulders increased, fingertips digging bruises deep into my tense muscles. "Fighting only makes me want you more."

As if to prove his point, Malegant reined his horse to a stop and dropped the reins. His left arm slid to my waist, and he tipped me backward, pinning my arms between his body and mine as he leaned over me. I sucked in air and tried to squirm away, but he held me fast.

His lips came down on mine with surprising force, his voracious hunger forcing my lips apart until I gagged on his tongue. Summoning all my strength, I pitched forward against the solid wall of his chest and bit down hard on his tongue. He cried out and recoiled but not before I tore at his lower lip, drawing more blood.

He dragged the side of his hand across his gushing lip, yelling a string of epithets that would have made even Arthur blush. Before I could blink, the back of his hand hit me squarely in the jaw, sending me reeling, vision suddenly alight with stars and lightning. I was falling, the muddy ground quickly approaching my head, when his fingers wrapped around my calf, stopping my descent. Stinging pain spread across my scalp as he wrenched me back onto the horse by my hair. One of the gold combs that had held it in an intricate twist was lost in the mire. The strand of hair it had been responsible for fell over my face, sticking fast in the blood streaming from my nose and mouth.

His men had surrounded us, frantic to ensure I didn't escape. Their torchlight illuminated Malegant's face and his swollen lower lip. I saw myself reflected in his eyes—bloodied but far from broken.

Over his shoulder, the Tor was visible through a clearing. Its bonfires winking through the mists were an odd reminder of the feast we were supposed to be celebrating. But it also reminded me of the one weapon I possessed, one I doubted he would ever suspect.

Malegant yanked the black strands from my face, scrutinizing my eyes. He wanted me to cower and collapse, that much was clear. But he was dealing with a woman used to physical pain, trained to endure it. I would never give him the satisfaction of knowing how badly he had hurt me.

Instead, I laughed, a primal sound that stunned us both. Maybe it was the aftereffect of whatever floral essences he had used to render me unconscious or a side effect of his blow, but it was genuine. I had an idea of how I could escape.

"Bloody woman is crazy," one of Malegant's men said.

Malegant said nothing, just signaled for us to continue. His arms around me—certainly not weak before—became strong as two iron chains. There was no way I'd be able to budge until he wanted me to. But I didn't need to.

I waited until we had gone some distance and were out on the open road leading away from Cadbury before I relaxed against him. Let him think the fight had gone out of me or, better yet, that I had passed out from my wounds. I closed my eyes and breathed deeply, shutting out all sound, all sense of what was going on around me. I was aware of the energy of the night, of the feast, but as I searched deeper, I felt the familiar pulse of the Tor deep within the earth below us. I concentrated on matching my heartbeat to it, becoming one with it. As I inhaled, I drew it in, allowing the energy to pool in my fingers. Then I began to move them, slowly, subtly, drawing the mists toward me.

Once I was certain I had control, I opened my eyes. A short time later, we entered the forest. It had stopped raining but only recently. On either side, trees hugged the road so closely their dripping leaves still sent rills of freezing water down my back and between my breasts.

When we were sufficiently deep within their gnarled embrace, I let the force flow from my fingers. At first, only a ribbon of mist was visible here and there among the trees, not an unusual sight so near to dawn. But as we advanced, speeding toward our unknown destination, the fog grew subtly denser, obscuring the trees then crawling and whirling over the road like a sinister snake. It slithered upward, reaching from root to treetop until we could no longer see the coming dawn. Finally Malegant and his men slowed their horses, proceeding as though they feared the spirits hidden within the mists would accost them at any moment.

All the while, I worked the ropes binding my hands, ignoring the burn as they bit into my flesh. I nearly had enough slack when one of Malegant's men spoke up.

"My lord, there is evil magic here. Should we continue or take another route?"

Malegant tensed behind me. He stopped his horse, and the others followed suit. With one last burst of will, I brought the mists in so they surrounded us in a wall of white on all sides. I was just about to jump when Malegant seized my shoulder, forcing me to twist to face him.

He growled, low and menacing like a dog taunted past endurance. "What was your plan, priestess? To baffle us? Make us lose our way? Or did you simply hope we would turn tail and run in fright?" He clenched my fists, squeezing my fingers until I cried out. "You forget, woman, that I was married to two priestesses.

I know all of your tricks. And I also know what you require to perform them."

Malegant's smile was cruel. He nodded to the guard nearest us. "Break her fingers—each one of them."

◈◈◈

Pain shot through my hands as though shards of glass were flowing in my veins. I wanted to scream, but my sore, swollen jaw would not let me speak, much less cry out. Waves of nausea ebbed and flowed, but I sensed we weren't moving anymore. That must have meant I was wherever Malegant had intended to take me.

When I opened my eyes, I expected to be chained in a dark, dank cellar. But I was lying in a soft bed in a square room with a high timbered ceiling that met at a point in the center. Above me, candles flickered in a round iron chandelier. Slowly, mindful not to exacerbate the throbbing in my temples, I turned my head. A tall wooden chest swam into view, followed by a table and chair on one side of the bed and a small fireplace on the other. A breeze swayed the shutters on either side of the small window, carrying in the earthy, cave-like scent of moist rock and flowing water.

I tried to sit up, forgetting my injuries, and yelped as I unwisely pressed my weight onto my hands. I collapsed back onto the sheets, panting, blanketed in cold sweat, and fighting my rebelling stomach. My head began to ring.

"Now, that was not wise." Malegant clucked his tongue chidingly.

I jumped, unaware I wasn't alone. He must have been sitting somewhere outside my view.

He came toward me, his eyes reproachful. "Imogen worked so hard to set and bandage your fingers, and here you go trying to undo all her efforts."

Imogen? I recalled a flash of graying auburn hair and kind brown eyes amid the darkness. Perhaps I did have some memory of her.

Malegant grasped my upper arms and helped me to a sitting position, seating himself on the bed so his hip touched my leg. As I had on the horse, I tried to scrabble away, but every movement brought increased pain that threatened to hurl me back into the void of unconsciousness.

Once the dizziness passed, I looked at my hands. No wonder they felt five times their normal size. They were bound in reams of thick, strong cloth so bulky they resembled the heavy protective gloves worn by blacksmiths and bakers. Fascinated, I held up one hand and tried to move my fingers. The effort sent a jolt of pain through my hand, but my fingers remained immobile.

"Harming you was never in my plans; you made me do this when you tried to escape." Malegant carefully guided my hand back down to the bed. "Do not try to use them. Imogen is here to help you as you heal." He leaned toward me, weight forcing me onto my back once again. "Besides"—a spark of lust lit his eyes— "this way you can't fight back."

In a flash, he was kissing me just as hungrily as before. With a sickening chill, I knew what he intended to do. My lips went dry, my limbs began to shake, and my stomach, already unsteady, audibly voiced its willingness to void itself in any way it could. As he worked his belt loose, I tensed my muscles and prepared to fend him off, suddenly wishing I had paid more attention to my mother's lessons on hand-to-hand combat.

I forced my face to the side. "Please, no," I mumbled through my swollen jaw.

He pinioned my chin between his thumb and fingers, forcing my face back to his. He continued kissing me, smothering my breath with his lips. I knew better than to bite him again, even if my jaw would have let me, so I twisted my hips, hoping to gain some leverage to push him back. Wrenching an arm free, I aimed an elbow at the base of his neck and tried to bring my knee up between his legs while he was distracted.

But he was too strong, too quick. He caught my elbow and pinned both forearms behind my head, the weight of his body holding me down. I writhed beneath him, still seeking escape, but when his naked flesh touched mine, I quickly learned all I was doing was arousing him more.

I screamed silently as he thrust into me. Tears sprang from my eyes as he ripped me apart from the inside. I clenched my eyes shut as if that act alone could make him stop. I found myself fading away, no longer able to feel the pain or hear Malegant's grunts of pleasure. It was strangely like manipulating the elements, falling into the void between worlds. Only this time, instead of gaining power, it was being taken from me.

Something inside my mind shattered. The physical violation was one level of horror, but the truth of what he was doing did not lie solely in the act. He had taken my sovereignty, the right of every woman, every priestess—and especially the queen—to choose her lovers as she willed. Had he killed Arthur, taken my crown, and left me for dead, he couldn't have rendered me any more powerless. It was that thought, so much more damaging than my physical exhaustion, that made me stop struggling and simply endure what was being done.

Eventually I felt the sweet relief of his weight releasing me as he rolled off to one side.

Still panting, he kissed my cheek softly. "Thank you, wife. Let us see how quickly you can bear me a son."

I froze. *Wife.* I suddenly remembered the story of Malegant taking Fiona from her homestead to make her his wife. *He seeks to invoke ancient laws by which I am now his legal spouse.* But what about Fiona? Was he going to take two wives? And did he not know I was barren? Perhaps he didn't believe it. I closed my eyes and swallowed hard. *This was nothing like the attack I suffered as a child. Then I was a valuable commodity to be traded and bargained. Now I am owned. I am his property to do with as he pleases regardless of my will or commitment to the man who is his king.*

That was when I knew this nightmare was far from over.

Chapter Nine

Winter 501

As the days passed and Malegant's abuse continued, I began to dread the dark because I knew he would come. It wasn't uncommon for him to be out of his mind with drink, which only served to hamper his performance and prolong my torment. Sometimes when he couldn't satisfy himself sexually, he would beat me until my eyes were bloody and my body shredded by his fingernails and teeth.

Imogen helped me visit the latrine and conduct my business—a humbling experience to be unable to perform such basics without aid—then lifted me back into bed, stroking my hair and holding me as I sobbed and shook. She never spoke, only communicated with her eyes and a few simple gestures. I assumed she had been born mute, but I did not have the heart to ask, nor did I know how she would explain. Somehow, her silence comforted me.

Each morning, Imogen would help me wash, brush my hair, and feed me spoonfuls of pottage as though I were a child. We spent the interminably long days in each other's company, she knitting or spinning, me sleeping or staring out the window at the lake far below or the mountains towering above.

Each night, Imogen would again help with my ablutions and see me settled into bed before retiring to her own mat. Only when Malegant came, which he inevitably did, did she leave the room.

In time, as my wounds began to heal and I regained my strength, I grew restless and paced the length of the chamber, for there was little I could do without the use of my hands. One morning, Imogen surprised me by removing the bandages from my hands.

"What are you doing?" I asked, only to feel foolish because she could not reply.

Imogen fixed me with a determined stare. *It is time,* her eyes seemed to say. *Trust me.* Slowly, carefully, she moved the smallest finger of my right hand.

I sucked in air in anticipation of the pain, but it did not come. Only when she applied a slight pressure to my knuckle to make my finger bend did I want to scream. Still holding my gaze, she repeated her tortuous routine on each of my fingers. By the time we were finished, my brow was slick with sweat, and I was lightheaded.

Imogen patted my thigh, as if to tell me I had done well.

Every day for a week, we repeated this exercise once at dawn and once at dusk. After a few days, the pain was tolerable, though I didn't yet dare try to move my fingers on my own.

One week after starting to exercise my fingers, she gestured for me to try. Hesitantly, like a child attempting her first steps, I bent my right index finger. When it didn't hurt, I nearly whooped with joy. I tried my other fingers. They all worked. I couldn't help but laugh. Soon I was wiggling my fingers in front of me, a child discovering her hands once again.

The following day, Imogen produced a collection of small objects from a pouch at her waist: a small wooden block, a stylus, a rock, and a ball of yarn. She indicated each in turn, grasping it in her hand then handing it to me. After a few minutes, I understood. She wished me to get used to holding objects of various sizes and weights again.

Everything went smoothly until I tried to shift the rock from my right hand to my left. It hit the floor with a thud, a chip skittering across the wooden planks and under the bed.

Embarrassed, I bent to pick it up.

So did Imogen.

We knocked heads as we straightened.

I laughed, rubbing my forehead. She made a gargling sound that I could only assume was laughter and massaged her brow.

It was then I saw it, light as a shadow, delicate as a whisper. In the center of her forehead was the ghost of a waxing crescent moon, long ago faded into nothingness.

Tenderly, I traced its shape, a soft smile forming on my lips. "You are a priestess," I said softly. "Just like me."

In response, Imogen touched her thumb to my forehead, lips, and heart.

I embraced her, feeling at once the bond of sisterhood that joined all priestesses of Avalon. My mind raced. No wonder she had taken such good care of me. Her expertise was the only reason I was slowly regaining use of my hands.

"Thank you." It was not the first time I had spoken my gratitude since waking in this accursed place, but I felt it stronger now than ever before. "How—" I wasn't even sure what I wanted to ask. "How did you come to be here?"

A moment after the words escaped my lips, we heard approaching footsteps.

Imogen placed a finger to her lips as if to say, *Keep this between us. We will discuss it later.*

I shivered, knowing what would be expected of me. Malegant had his own ideas of how I should practice using my hands.

⚬⚬

The weather grew colder as each day passed until one melted into another like the ceaseless snow that covered the fortress with a thick white veil. One morning, when the snow was falling gently, I gathered up my courage and stuck my head out of the window. Looking up, I was pelted with thousands of icy feathers, but I saw enough to know we were on the uppermost floor of a castle made from a single wooden tower. In some ways, it resembled a granary more than a fortress. I twisted back around and braved a look down. Far below, the lake was churning with icy waves.

In the distance, I could just make out the edge of a thin bridge connecting the tower to some anchor on the far shore. The snow and ice made its rope railing look more like a giant cobweb. A fierce gust of wind rocked the castle, and I pulled my head in a little. The bridge was swaying. I couldn't help but imagine that anyone caught on it would feel much like an insect in a spider's snare.

Shivering, I climbed down off the ledge and tacked the fur lining tightly over the window. I sat in front of the fire and combed my hair with my fingers, relishing the heat. I had been here—I counted the full moons—three months, and this was the first time I'd dared think of escape. Why hadn't it occurred to me sooner? *You were in no condition,* my mind answered. *Only now are you strong enough.* Yes. I was finally strong enough to fight back. But how? There had to be a way out beyond the locked door. If Imogen could come and go, so could I.

I was still contemplating the possibilities when Imogen entered with our midday meal: freshly baked bread and bowls of hardy, dark stew. I ate my portion hungrily, especially grateful for the heat that made its way leisurely down my throat and into my stomach. My tongue tingled with hints of sage, rosemary, and wild onions mixed with the sweetness of parsnips, turnips, and something gamey—not venison, something wilder. "Imogen, this is wonderful. Did you cook it yourself?"

She nodded proudly.

After we had eaten our fill, she signaled it was time to begin my therapy for the day. We had progressed beyond holding simple objects to performing complex patterns. She showed me a set of movements, first placing the fingers of her left hand horizontally across her shinbone then touching certain points on the fingers of her right hand.

I copied her, pleased at both my dexterity and ability to recall the pattern she presented. After suffering so many blows at Malegant's hand, I had feared I would have lasting damage to my mind, but as each day passed, the likelihood of my fear coming true lessened.

Imogen clapped excitedly then touched the pads of two fingertips to the side of her nose, repeating the pattern she'd performed on her leg.

As I mimicked her movements, something tugged at the back of my mind. This exercise was familiar somehow, though its meaning was lost in the fog of my memory. Was it a game my mother had played with me? Or some kind of code Elaine and I had invented on one of our childhood adventures? No, it was neither of those. As we repeated the pattern over and over, the fog slowly lifted. Avalon. That was where I knew these movements from. She was a priestess, and so was I.

I repeated the pattern once more, very slowly, realization beginning to dawn. I could translate the gestures into words.

I can speak to you, but Malegant must not know.

Imogen was speaking to me through cossogam, sronogam, and basogam—the three types of signing Ogham. They were named for the body parts used to speak: the leg, nose, and palm. Written Ogham was taught early in our training, but only the priestesses who remained for advanced studies learned manual Ogham in preparation for the silence and isolation of the final days before consecration.

"How, how—" Now that we could communicate, I suddenly found myself speechless.

My son does not know I remember Ogham. He never pursued advanced studies, so he cannot sign, though he can write it.

I held up a hand to stop her frantic signing. "Wait. I must have misunderstood you. Did you say 'son'?"

She nodded. *Your captor is my son. For that I am deeply ashamed. Please forgive me.*

My legs turned to jelly, and I sank to the floor, unable to process what I had just learned. Not only could Imogen speak to me in her own way, but she was Malegant's mother. "But you helped me. . ."

Imogen sat in front of me, using nose Ogham so I would be sure to see her. *I wish you no harm. I myself am a prisoner here. If I could help you escape, I would. I do not condone the things my son does.*

"I need time to think about this."

I understand, she signed. *Just remember that in front of him, I am mute. If he finds out the truth, he will kill us both.*

"Or at least cut off our hands," I said, half in dark jest.

We were silent for a long while. I stared into the fire, trying to rearrange what I now knew of my world—the nature of the land where I was being held, Imogen's relationship with Malegant, and my ability to talk to her—with what little information I had gleaned during the months I was bedridden. Putting it all together was like trying to solve a riddle without all the clues. I needed to know more.

I turned to Imogen. "Where is Fiona? Why have I not seen her?"

She shook her head, eyes brimming with tears. *She is dead.*

I gasped. My eyes pricked. "Was it. . .was it. . .?" I could not bring myself to ask if my captor was to blame.

Imogen nodded.

Fiona had been such a sweet, innocent girl. She was so docile, there was no way she could have provoked him into deadly rage as I easily could. "What happened?

Imogen hesitated. *She knew too many of his secrets, as did I. He killed her and cut out my tongue.*

I clasped my hands over my mouth, horrified. "But you are his mother!"

She gestured for me to keep my voice down. *And he is a demon.*

⚜

Not long after my fingers healed, Malegant insisted I begin living with him on the main floor. "After all, you are not my prisoner. You are my wife."

And so my life developed into a new routine, one of serving, kneeling, and obeying Malegant's every whim. That very morning, I took on the duties of both wife and slave, although considering Malegant had made me his wife by kidnapping, I was willing to bet the two were one and the same in his mind. There were few others in the castle, so I assisted Imogen in preparing each meal. The thought crossed my mind that a quick end could be made to all of this with a simple "slip" of the wrong combination of herbs, but Imogen warned me against it.

I have thought of that as well, but so has he, she signed while carefully slicing carrots for the stew. *He will make you eat your portion first. Only once he sees you suffer no ill effects will he deign to eat.*

I shivered. So this man who held me captive was not only cruel and mad, he was clever, which made escaping his grasp that much more difficult. Maybe that was why Fiona had submitted. But I could not. I would not. The blood of queens sang in my veins. I could not let them down.

About two weeks later, in a lull between snowstorms, our little hideaway received its first visitors. From my vantage point in the kitchens, I could just make out two men, burly and wooly as bears, speaking with Malegant. Their unkempt appearance and guttural tongue were all I needed to place them as Picts. What they were doing so far south, however, was a mystery.

"My wife is very hospitable," he said. But then he caught sight of me, excused himself, and stalked in my direction. Without losing eye contact, he grabbed me by the throat, his fingers digging into my airway. "If you so much as make eye contact with my guests"—his breath was hot in my ear—"I will make certain you cannot walk, much less use those beautiful hands of yours. Do you understand me?"

I tried to speak, but all that came out was a strangled gurgle. I settled for nodding, but all that did was make the pain in my throat worse and rob me of what little breath I had left.

"When you serve us tonight, you will cover your face and answer to the name Fiona. While we eat, you will kneel in the corner until we have need of you."

Stars were beginning to dance before my eyes. I nodded again. Finally he let me go, and I bent over, coughing and my eyes streaming. When I looked up, he was gone.

⁂

Beneath the gauzy black veil, my face was covered in sweat. Every step I took was measured, every movement carefully carried out. I willed myself not to trip, my hands not to shake, as I placed the platter of lamb on the table and returned with a bowl of sauce.

Around the long table, Malegant and his guests paid me as little mind as they would a specter. All, that is, except for a woman I had not seen earlier. Her flaxen hair was loose, flowing down to her trim waist. She was dressed as though for battle, a long, menacing sword hanging at her side. Something was familiar about her, but I could not place what it was.

One of the men held up his cup, and I hurried to refill it.

"Why does your wife not show us her pretty face?" one of the men asked. "I do so enjoy a beautiful woman." He punctuated his statement with a sharp pinch to my backside.

I had to fight my instinct to smash the pitcher of ale over his head.

"Maybe she's not as pretty as he says," the woman scoffed. "Some men have to settle for less than the best."

Malegant pointed at her with a bone. "Like your husband?"

The men chuckled, and her cheeks reddened with rage.

"Watch your tongue, Lord Malegant." She toyed with her dagger under the guise of slicing a chunk off the shank before her. "Or you shall lose it."

Malegant sat back in his chair, a smug smile playing at his lips. "Aine, I'd love to see you try. Or do you not recall the outcome of our last tussle? I remember you pleading with me to spare your bloody carcass."

Aine was distracted from their exchange as I took away her used trencher and replaced it with a fresh one. She grabbed my wrist and removed the sapphire ring Arthur had given me from my finger. "Pretty bauble," she sang, looking right into my veiled eyes. "I think I'll keep it." She shoved me away.

"You never answered my question, my lord," insisted the man who had assaulted my backside.

"Her brother recently passed through the veil, and she doesn't wish others to witness her mourning," Malegant said dismissively. "But you did not come here to discuss our woes."

I retreated to the corner, adopting the submissive pose Imogen taught me—kneeling back on my heels, palms on the floor, head bent low to the ground. I wasn't sure how I was supposed to know when they needed me to serve, but if this was what Malegant wanted, I would do it.

As the night went on and the visitors fell under the spell of Malegant's thick, strong ale, they switched from the common tongue to the visitors' native language. I was fairly certain Malegant was aware I would be able to understand some of what was said, their tongue being not so different from my mother's native language, but he did not so much as cast a glance in my direction.

While I couldn't understand every word, I understood enough to follow the conversation.

"He's left Camelot in the hands of his second and has declared Cadbury his capital until such time as she returns," one of the Picts said.

Arthur. They were talking about Arthur. He was still looking for me.

"But surely he can't have many men left," Malegant protested. "How many of them would last for extended periods outdoors in the deep of winter?" There was irritation in his voice and perhaps the slightest hint of fear.

"Many of the knights have returned to Camelot, Cadbury, or been wounded," one of the Picts conceded. "But there are a few who continue to search."

"Let them come," Malegant said with sudden vigor.

"What makes you think they will come after you?" Aine asked.

"Arthur hates me already. I did kill one of his lords, a member of the Combrogi. I would think I was first on his list of suspects." Malegant sounded almost proud of his state of disgrace.

My stomach tightened. I had not known Uriens had died from his injuries. Tears welled in the backs of my eyes, and for once, I was grateful for the veil so no one would see me weep—ironically the very reason Malegant had given for its use.

The woman said something I did not understand. Everyone laughed.

The Picts pulled wineskins from their belts and passed them around. Everyone poured some of the cloudy brown liquid into their cups, and they toasted, but again I couldn't understand what they were cheering about. Slugging down the drink, Aine sauntered around the table to Malegant. Her eyes glowed with a lustful fire.

"Dear sister, do not be so bold in front of our guests," Malegant chided, this time in our native tongue, but his heart clearly wasn't in the rebuke.

"I am no sister of yours. Your mother always underestimated her control over her husbands' cocks." She traced a finger down his chest then began painting Malegant's face with the remnants of the jelly still on his plate from the final course. He pushed her away playfully. "Oh, but you are, sweet sister." He took her finger in his mouth and sucked off the jelly.

That was when I placed her. The woman sitting on Malegant's lap was the girl who had been painting the reveler's faces and bodies on Samhain. I froze, wondering if she knew full well who was sitting in the shadows beneath the veil. It couldn't be a coincidence that she had been there when I was taken and was also here now.

The Picts grinned. "You aren't the only ones who should have some fun tonight. What about them?" One indicated Imogen and me with a jerk of his thumb. "Are they for sale?" Malegant looked us over as if assessing our value. "The one in the veil is my wife, so no, she is not for the taking. But this one"—he indicated Aine—"would likely take you both, or you can share her with the other woman, if you like."

They studied Imogen carefully then each chose a companion. After one more slug of liquor, they each dragged a woman off toward the sleeping chambers.

Malegant was no less gentle with me. He tugged me to my feet and flung me over his shoulder. "Be grateful I think so kindly of you, wife, and know I will treat you far better than my guests. They have. . ." He paused in the middle of the hall, searching for the right word. "More brutal tastes."

⁘

A fortnight passed, each day a forgery of the last. Imogen came stumbling into the bedroom, bruised and bloody, the morning our guests were due to depart.

She signed frantically. *I have been through a lot in my life, but I cannot take being used as a whore any longer. Last night, those dogs abandoned Aine and both came at me at once.*

It was my turn to tend her injuries. I swabbed her bleeding thighs and gave her herbs against pain and disease.

"What was the shape of the tattoo on their right arms?" I asked, hoping to ferret out which of the tribes raised such brutes.

Tattoo? she asked, apparently dazed from pain. *Which one? They are so covered with them it would take close and careful study to tell one from another.*

So they were Highlanders then. That was even worse than I'd suspected. Malegant had kept me away from the majority of their discussions, but I'd gleaned enough to know they were negotiating some sort of bargain.

Imogen looked at me. *It is time. We must get out.*

"But how?"

She grasped my hand and smiled. *We will figure it out. Together.*

⁘

The next night, Malegant fell into bed next to me, deeper in his cups than I had ever seen him. He stank of that strange Pictish brew. They must have left the remainder of it with Malegant's sister. Whatever they had been bargaining for, her return had been payment.

"You must be happy to have your sister back," I said, trying to be pleasant when all I wanted was for him to pass out.

"My sister," he mumbled into the feather pillow, "is worthless. All of them are. First Leigh fails to kill Arthur, and now Aine can't even secure a simple exchange of lands. At least she was good for delivering the notes."

I sat up. That was a revelation. At least now I knew how he—or rather she—got in and out of Camelot to deliver me notes without being seen. I wanted so badly to ask him who Leigh was, but I was more afraid of sparking his temper by revealing too much interest in his motives.

Malegant turned his face toward me, head still glued to the pillow. "Aine claims I don't trust you and I never will. I should prove her wrong by explaining myself to you, not that I owe you even a drop of information." He narrowed his eyes at me. "But you have a strategic mind, so perhaps you will appreciate the brilliance of my plan. After all, it won't be long before the whole of Britain marvels at its intricacy, bowing before the brilliance of its new king."

I closed my eyes. So he *was* planning to overthrow Arthur. I'd suspected as much, but to have such a plan confirmed was another matter. But he had done more than prove me right; he given me another key to how his mind worked, another possible way too thwart him. His pride, which he so highly valued, could be turned against him.

"I would be honored to be the first to know." I swallowed hard, willing myself to say words I knew would please him. "As your wife, it is my right, is it not?"

He propped himself on one elbow and regarded me closely. "You are finally coming to understand. Good. Yes, it is time you know all."

"Who is Leigh?" I asked, bringing him back to his previous line of thought.

"One of my many half brothers. I used him to try to have Arthur killed, but then your spy or maid or whatever she really is interfered, so I had to change tack. Luckily, I have no shortage of half siblings who owe me their lives and therefore must do my bidding. I told you long ago how I was fostered for my own protection. When I returned, my mother had taken power, and I found I had a brood of younger brothers and sisters sired by the chieftains of the other six ancient tribes. But she was law-bound to none of them, so each made his own claim against me."

"What did you do?" I asked with mock concern, stroking his hair.

He shrugged. "What any man would do given the situation. If I was to take my rightful place as head of my tribe, I would have to kill each one of them. The eldest I killed with my bare hands, the entire village cheering us on. By the end of the year, my arms were bloody up to the elbows, my skin furrowed with scars. I was so crazed with blood and revenge I threatened even the babes. I remember pressing a dagger to the chest of a screaming toddler, threatening to cut out his heart. I think I would have done it too, had they not relented. In the end, the families I did not overthrow with steel paid me their loyalty in exchange for the lives of their youngest. Aine and Leigh were among them."

I lay in stunned silence, sifting through what he had just revealed. No wonder this man was so brutal—he'd always had to be. For him, brutality was a way, *the* way, to stay alive.

Malegant kissed my stomach, dragging his lower lip up to the cleft between my breasts. I thought he was going to begin his nightly work on me, but he laid his head on my breast instead.

"You and I have quite a history, you know," he drawled, tracing a finger over the muscles in my abdomen. "I was your mother's pupil. You were too young to remember, only able to wobble on fat baby legs. I remember three of your brothers and a sister. She was a lot like you, you know—same piercing green eyes and haughty attitude. She was already promised to another, but I vowed to myself that when you came of age, you would be mine."

I tried not to recoil from the thought of this man desiring me from childhood. There were taboos against such a thing for a reason. "Is that why you tried to have Arthur killed? Because he wed me and you did not?"

Malegant laughed. "It is so much more complex than that, but yes. You see, the man in whose house you lived, Lord Pellinor, sought to control all of the Summer Country. As I had no interest in his simpering daughter, I convinced him that if he arranged your marriage to me, I would cede some of my power. He was a useful tool, the old, pious fool. And your father wasn't much more formidable. All I had to do was remind him of my training with your mother, and he practically welcomed me like a son. Everything was arranged. I had already paid your right of purchase and price of virginity—what a farce that was."

His voice trailed off as his lips met mine, tenderly for once, and he began to move against me slowly, as though stoking his own pleasure.

"Your father owes me, Guinevere." He planted a line of kisses from one end of my collarbone to the other. "Were it not for that damned honor debt, you would have been my wife of the highest degree years ago. But then that fool Uriens told Arthur about you, and he swooped in and stole you from my grasp. But now the old man is dead. So"—he leered at me—"how do you think I should best extract payment from your father, from Arthur?" His hand closed around my throat.

"I can give you all the money owed you and then some, you know that." My voice shook, though I tried to temper it.

"But that's not really the issue, is it? No, your father did more than cheat me out of money. He cheated me out of my rightful wife. Then the king not only did the same—he sullied my name as well. This is revenge on many levels, Guinevere, a substantial righting of wrongs." He forced me onto my stomach, grabbed me roughly by the hair at the nape of my neck, and entered me with his usual force.

I cried out in pain. He twisted one hand in my hair and continued to pull, his other hand digging sharply into my right buttock. If only I could have associated pain and pleasure the way he did, I would have been in ecstasy.

"A son," he panted. "That will be the ultimate recompense. Then I will be the one with a legitimate heir." He bit my earlobe. "Arthur is a dead man, and I will get what is owed to me."

જ્જ્જ

The next morning, Malegant showed no sign of remembering his diatribe from the night before. The impending snowstorm that had driven away the Picts arrived, so we spent the day in close quarters, holed up against the cold and wind. I was on edge all day, waiting for Malegant to make some comment or show some sign of regretting what he'd said, but he treated me as though nothing had happened. The only difference was that he took Aine to bed that night.

I tried hard not to think about that. I still didn't know for sure that Aine was related to Malegant by blood, only that he thought she was and she vehemently denied it. Maybe she was right. But then again, this man broke every prohibition in our culture without a second thought. It made my skin scrawl to think he believed her to be his sister and yet saw nothing wrong with their relationship or, worse, carried on anyway. But I couldn't bring myself to ask Imogen the truth— I really didn't want to know.

Imogen interrupted my thoughts with a swift tap on my wrist.

Guinevere, I am afraid if we do not do something soon, he will tire of you. My son is like a cat with his prey. He toys with it until he grows bored. Then he goes in for the kill. I can already see the joy fading from his eyes.

"Then what do we do? We have to escape."

For a while, we were both silent, caught up in our thoughts. I twisted what I had learned around in my mind, trying to find some weakness, some chink in the armor of Malegant's plan we could use to our advantage. We were in a tower on an island surrounded by deadly cold water in a valley between mountains. The fortress was nearly impenetrable.

There was no way the two stout Picts would have crossed that string of a bridge that swayed in the wind outside the window, and neither could we. It was far too icy to try. There had to be another way in. And if there was, there was another way out.

"How did the Picts get into the castle?" I asked.

By boat, she signed after setting a mug of tea in front of me. *But it is heavily guarded.*

I brought the mug to my lips and breathed in the steam. It was earthy, heavy with the loam of the forest and berries forbidden to mortal lips. I breathed in again, trying to identify the scent. The distinctive smell of burning dried leaves—sage—was the first to assault my senses. Woody rosemary, marjoram, and thyme followed, chased by the sweeter aromas of mint and imported hyssop.

Imogen smiled. *I learned this blend from Argante when she was a young priestess. It opens the centers of the sight and will give us knowledge we seek. Let us drink in honor of our gods.* She held up her mug.

I let the warm liquid flow past my lips. On the whole, it had a pleasant taste, reminiscent of a salad of early spring greens, but once swallowed, it bit back with sharp spiciness that made me want to gag.

I closed my eyes and breathed deeply, allowing the liquid to flow through my veins. As it took effect, I relaxed for the first time in months. A second mouthful brought with it the sight—a vision of the tower burning while we rowed away to the safety of the far shore.

I opened my eyes.

What do the gods say?

"We set the tower on fire and escape in the boat. But how can that be? You said it was heavily guarded."

It is, but not at night. We don't have enough guards to keep watch at all hours.

I swallowed the dregs of my tea, tossing around the basic elements of our plan—fire, the boat. What else? How did it turn into action?

Fire, travel by water. . . I found myself invoking the goddesses associated with our quest—Ellen, the guardian of the ways; Nehalenni, patroness of travelers; and Brigid, the goddess of fire and forge.

That was when it hit me. Brigid. She was the key.

I grabbed Imogen's arm. "The feast of Brigid nears. On that night, the moon is full and will be eclipsed by the sun. That will afford us both distraction, as all cower inside against evil omens, and protection in the darkness. Once we have cleared the lake, we can invoke Brigid and burn this place to the ground."

She smiled. *Then we must make ready.*

Chapter Ten

Over the next several weeks, we took measures to be
certain we would be prepared for our journey. Imogen
sewed small pouches of herbs in our skirts so that we
would not be without aid if one of us became sick or injured. On
washing day, we smuggled warm cloaks and a change of clothes
out of the castle with the soiled linens, using a hollow tree stump
at the edge of the lake as a hiding place for our supplies. It was my
job to see that a certain amount of food was set aside, along with
a few wineskins. Finally, Imogen procured two small daggers—
purloined from the Picts, she said—as a means of protection and
for use in hunting.

When all was in place, we waited for the appointed hour.
Like everyone Druid-trained, Malegant would be using the feast
coupled with the eclipse, the time of greatest power, to perform
acts of divination. According to Imogen, his men—in whom he
had instilled sufficient misinformation—would be cowering in

terror and begging the gods to bring back the moon. That meant we only had to evade Aine to be clear to escape.

We made certain the day went like any other—serving at meals, sewing, and minding chores—while Malegant and his men sparred and negotiated matters of politics. Once night fell, we ate a quiet dinner, but I didn't fail to notice Malegant glancing expectantly out the window every few minutes, anticipating moonrise.

When he finally stood, I made to follow him to bed, but he held me at arm's length. "You are a priestess. You of all people should know I will sleep alone tonight, with only the bones for my company."

I lowered my eyes. "As you wish."

Imogen and I retired to the room we shared, and the tower went eerily silent. For a long time, all we could hear was the pop of the logs in the fire and the creak of the walls as they resisted the wind. We had just gathered our things and donned our cloaks when an eerie keening broke the silence. The hairs on the back of my neck stood on end. Beside me, Imogen stiffened.

We slowly inched along the darkened corridor toward the sound.

"That is old magic," I whispered. "Dark magic."

I felt it coiling around me, drawing me in like a rope. It was so seductive, so alive. It was the same power I'd tasted on the rare occasions I cursed our enemies, and part of me longed for more. When we reached Aine's door, the keening reached a feverish pitch. Without thinking, I put my hand on the door to peer inside.

Imogen pulled me back.

I could not see her signing in the dark, but somehow I knew

she was telling me to resist the temptation to watch. She shoved me past the door toward the staircase leading down to the dock.

Away from danger now, we lit a small oil lamp. Imogen was frantically weaving her fingers, a message that came in fits and starts, as though her hands could not keep up with her mind.

She was calling the Callieach. You had to step away, else she enter you by mistake. The Dark One is not particular about her vessel. That is magic no one in this land has practiced for centuries. She must have learned it in the Highlands.

"Is Aine truly yours?" I asked as we neared the door barred tight against intruders.

Imogen nodded. *Her father was my link to Icini gold. Though she never admits it. She believes herself a child of Eire.* She shrugged as if to say there was nothing she could do about it.

We struggled to lift the heavy beam from its catch. Above us, Aine's keening continued, though it was slowly morphing into a guttural chant. For a moment, I could not move. All I could do was listen, mesmerized by the sound of something my blood remembered though my mind knew it not.

I started from my trance as Imogen freed the beam with a thud that reverberated throughout the house. We both froze, hearts pounding. Aside from Aine's uninterrupted chanting, there was not a single sound.

We opened the door to a cold, clear night. Far above, in the black veil of night, the moon was turning a sickly shade of rose as the sun's shadow slid slowly across its surface. The wind buffeting the castle tore at our cloaks with icy fingers, as though determined to stop us from reaching the dock.

Somewhere, an animal's desperate screech punctuated the

silence, the cry of a soul that knows it's about to reach its end. It could have been deep in the woods across the water, but I had a sinking feeling it came from Aine's room as part of whatever arcane ritual she was performing.

We plucked our bundles from the tree stump and headed for the water. But when we drew near, it was clear the boat was not where we'd expected it. Where there should have been depth and shadow, we saw only a reflection of the waning light of the eclipse.

Imogen stamped her foot and cursed with her fingers.

"I don't understand. You said it was always moored here at night."

It is. She looked around. *He must have locked it up against the wind.* Her eyes grew wide. *Or he knows.*

We returned our packs to the stump in case we weren't successful in finding the boat, and I followed her back into the tower. There was only one place large enough to house a vessel.

Off to one side was a storage room used to house the provisions delivered monthly by a local fisherman whom Malegant paid handsomely for his discretion. Bags of grain sat next to sacks of sprouting onions and nuts, half eaten by the mice, while piles of firewood made an impassable fortress to the far end of the room. Above us hung rows of cheeses and bouquets of herbs. Barrels of salt fish and ale lined the opposite wall. But no boat.

Imogen stood with her hands on her hips, turning in circles as though the boat was there and had simply been rendered invisible.

"It's not here. Let's go. We can try again another night," I hissed. I had the increasingly terrible feeling we had been set up.

We could try the bridge, Imogen signed.

In my mind's eye, I recalled the thread of rope and wood

being tossed about in the wind. No, we should not dare try to cross it this night. Even if I could have used my powers to calm the wind, in her altered state, Aine was likely to sense the magic and raise the alarm. Silently, I shook my head and edged back into the main room without waiting for Imogen.

Aine's chanting had slowed into what could probably have been best described as crooning. She sounded as if she was singing a lullaby. Distracted by the sound, I didn't see Malegant until I ran into him, forehead knocking painfully into his chest.

"My love, why are you wearing your heavy cloak in the house?" he asked, fingering a fold of the material.

I was sweating, highly aware I had been caught. I shivered in fear. "I was cold. I—I can't get warm."

Malegant turned my face toward him with a finger at my chin. He scrutinized my face. "Your face *is* clammy, and you are deathly pale."

"What are you doing down here?" I asked.

"Aine called me. I might ask the same of you."

Aine's crooning drew my attention again, so it took me a moment to register his words.

"I—I don't know," I said, pretending to be dazed with fever.

He grasped my hands, and my shaking increased.

"Your hands are freezing. Let's get you into bed." He put an arm around me and guided me up the stairs to our room, calling for Imogen as we walked.

I would never know how she reached the room before us, but when he opened the door, there she was, as placid as though he had merely interrupted her knitting.

"I believe Guinevere is ill. Stay with her, will you?"

Heaviness filled my head as though I really were ill. Imogen helped me into bed, and I lay there, watching the candles blaze and illuminate Malegant's attempts to see the future in the patterns formed by sun-bleached bones of birds, oxen, and other animals I couldn't identify.

Aine soon stopped crooning, and I fell into an exhausted sleep, relieved neither she nor her brother appeared to suspect anything.

ഛലളൢ

That night, I dreamed of strange things. In my dreams, Aine was still chanting, though I could not see her. Her voice was all around me, coming from everywhere and nowhere. I was flying high above the tower and its island, then past the mountains and trees, then over open countryside. As I passed by, cairns burst open, the dead rising in their shrouds, some still carrying the weapons and finery with which they had been buried. They followed me to the sea, where I landed on a rocky beach. From the water came a cloud of ashes that slowly formed into a procession of souls.

"Find her!" they commanded. "Find her before *She* does."

Then the dream shifted. Merlin sat up in his bed, drenched in sweat. It was early morning. Without bothering to dress in more than a simple tunic, he ran, barefoot, to find Arthur. My husband was still in bed, and he looked up in alarm at Merlin's intrusion.

"Great magic, the like of which I've never seen, has woken our ancestors. They come with a grave warning." To my utter shock, Merlin went on to relay the exact contents of the earlier part of my dream.

"Who should we find, and who should we fear?" Arthur asked, confused.

Merlin leveled him with an impenetrable gaze. "I am not certain, but I think they are telling us to find Guinevere. And in answer to your other question—pray my suspicions are wrong."

My perspective shifted again, and I was in the throne room. Merlin was describing something to Arthur, Sobian, Lancelot, and Gawain.

"The auguries confirm it. This is the location of the magic I felt. It was ancient and dark, enough to drive the ancestors from their resting places with a warning. Whatever its source, it must be stopped. I beg you brave men, and woman, to join with me in finding this castle in the glass."

As they armed themselves to depart, I saw their destination. It was the very fortress in which I now slumbered.

Chapter Eleven

Spring 501

A few weeks later, as spring was beginning to paint the forest with its first blush of green, Malegant came to our morning meal dressed in his riding boots and traveling cloak.

"I am going out to begin collecting taxes in the nearby villages," he announced.

Imogen threw me a hopeful look behind his back.

"I am going with you," Aine pronounced.

"No, you are not. Someone needs to stay here to guard her." He gestured to me with his tankard of ale.

"But I'm bored."

"What do I care?" he asked around a mouthful of bread. "Besides, the fisherman should be here tomorrow with the next moon's supplies. Someone has to pay him."

Aine sat in a huff, her arms crossed like a petulant child's. "Isn't that the duty of your wife?" Suddenly she looked up. "You still don't trust her." It was a statement, not a question. "And you probably never will," she added more quietly.

After the dishes were cleared, Malegant led me upstairs to the room in which he'd first held me prisoner. "Please forgive me for this, but I can't have you getting any ideas about running away while I am gone."

He produced a length of thick chain with twin shackles affixed to one end. The other end was bolted tightly to the wall. He seized my hands and bound them in the iron manacles.

Immediately, fear formed a leaden lump in my stomach. My hands shook beneath his grasp, but I couldn't stop them. "What is the meaning of this? In the six moons I have been here, you never once chained me up. Have I done something to affront you?"

His face hardened. Before I could blink, he struck me full force across the cheek with the back of his hand. I stumbled back, knocking my head against the wall.

"You heard what I said. It was either this or break your hands again. Which would you prefer? Or maybe your feet too this time?" His voice was cruel as he raised an eyebrow and patted me twice on the cheek. "I didn't think so." He kissed me roughly and backed away. "Imogen will be instructed to treat you as before. She will bring your meals three times a day. There is a bit of sewing and a book for you to pass the time. The chain is long enough for you to reach the bed and the necessity pot but not to leave the room. I will return in a few days."

When he was nearly through the door, he turned. "Who knows, we may find another use for those chains when I return."

I glared at him, but he was already gone. I slid down the wall and sat on the floor, listening as he unmoored the boat and departed with the splashing of oars. No doubt he had a horse waiting on the other side of the lake to take him wherever he wished to go.

It was odd, but now that I was shackled with little freedom of movement, I finally felt like a prisoner. Maybe it was because I was free from the constant threat of beatings and rape, free from my fear of him. I hadn't realized it, but it was that fear, my fight for survival, that was keeping me sane. Before I realized what was happening, I began to sob, hysterical spasms over which I had no control. Curled up in a ball on the floor, I buried my head in my knees, clenched my fists in my hair, and wept.

For the first time, I realized the gravity of my situation. I was Malegant's prisoner, his "wife" of the lowest degree according to ancient tribal law. I had been violated and subjugated in the most horrible ways possible, robbed of all the dignity due to me as a queen and a priestess.

And what of rescue? Arthur surely would have sent all of the forces at his command to rescue me six months ago. They would have combed the forests and glens, rivers and mountain passes, for me. Six times the moon had waxed and waned, yet no one had found me. He'd probably even issued a reward so the people would be motivated to look or turn over any evidence they had. Briefly, I wondered how many false claims he fielded each pleading day, how many dark-haired daughters were passed off as imitations of the queen in the hopes of monetary gain. At the thought and the image in my mind's eye of Arthur's annoyance, I laughed as uncontrollably as I had cried.

The laughter buoyed my spirits a bit. I chewed on a morsel of a thought. If Arthur truly had issued a reward, I could use that to my advantage—if only I could get access to other people. Imogen had as little hope of escape as I, and Aine—well, I had the feeling she would rather see me dead than returned to Arthur, no matter the sum.

That left who? The guards? I hadn't had many interactions with them, but they were no ordinary mercenaries—of that much I was certain. It took a certain loyalty or compulsion to remain in an assignment as remote and joyless as this. So either they believed in Malegant so strongly they were willing to kill for him or he had some kind of leverage that made them obey his every whim. There might be an opening there, but it would take time and much effort, not to mention careful avoidance of their master, to feel them all out.

Exhausted, I eventually drifted off to sleep. When I woke, stiff and sore from my awkward position, the first thing I saw was that dinner had been set on a tray within arm's reach. Imogen must have had to return to the kitchens to prepare Aine's meal.

I stood and stretched, thanking the gods that at least Malegant had shown me the kindness of being able to move around. Munching on a leg of whatever poor bird adorned my plate, I went over to the window and looked out. The sun was sinking fast, turning the lake to a pool of blood, but the sound of the water lapping the shore was at least relaxing. I looked down. The dock was empty. We were all trapped here until Malegant returned.

I was about to give up hope and climb into bed when a new thought crossed my mind. Malegant had mentioned the fisherman was supposed to deliver supplies in the coming days. Perhaps if I could get free, he would recognize me or I could convince him I was being held under duress.

It was a weak plan, but it was more than I'd had a few hours before.

I fought against the shackles for a few moments, trying to slip my hands from their unyielding grasp. Somewhere deep in my mind, I knew this would do no good, but still I strained to make my hands narrow until my skin was raw and my wrists threatened to dislocate.

I decided to change tack. Holding my wrists up to the light, I inspected the locks on my manacles. They were the simplest type of barrel lock—not surprising since Malegant didn't know about the skill I had obtained from Isolde. Had Malegant been wiser, he would have bound my wrists together, but he'd allowed me the dexterity to sew. Fortuna had finally smiled on me.

I looked around the room. If I could find something thin enough, I could pick them. My sewing needle was too short and too delicate to do any good. There was nothing in the bed or within arm's reach that could help me. I considered asking Imogen to bring me something from the kitchen or barracks, but I didn't want to involve her in case I was caught. My eyes alighted on the bird on my plate. I said a silent prayer of thanks to its soul before I ripped the carcass apart and went to work with the wishbone. With a bit of luck, by morning, I would be free.

⁂

When the sun rose, my right hand was free but I was still struggling with the lock around my left.

I had gone through all of the smaller bones in the poor bird's body only to snap the last one off in the lock in my weariness and haste. Tears of frustration coursed down my cheeks as I realized my folly. Eventually, exhausted, I had fallen asleep again.

As soon as there was enough light in the room, I studied the jammed mechanism, trying to figure out how to fix it. At first I thought I could remove the bone with my fingernail, but the bone was just big enough to prevent me from getting underneath it.

From the hall, the telltale crunch of boots on rushes signaled someone was approaching. It was likely Imogen, but I put the other shackle around my right wrist, not quite locked, just in case Aine decided to pay me another unanticipated visit.

She had taken it upon herself to check on me last night even though Imogen was asleep on a pallet at my feet. Still awake and hiding my free hand beneath the blankets, I'd glared at Aine as she rounded the bed making sure everything was in proper order. Something in the glint in her eyes told me that had Imogen not been present, we would have come to blows. Ever since the night of her strange ritual, I'd had the sense she wanted my blood and would do whatever it took to get it. But she obviously wasn't keen on doing it in front of her mother. Thank the gods for Imogen.

The door opened, and Imogen waddled in, maneuvering the door with one hand while trying not to drop the tray she balanced on the other. As soon as she was within reach, I whisked the tray away, and she signed her thanks.

Have you made any progress? she asked.

"No. I can't pry the bone loose."

This will help. She pointed at the thin knife sitting next to a hunk of hard cheese on the plate. Aine would beat her at the very least if she knew Imogen had supplied me with a weapon, but still, she'd risked it to help me get free.

I kissed her and swallowed my breakfast as fast as possible.

Once Imogen had removed the dishes and gone to attend to Aine, I went back to work on the lock, trying to free the bone with the point of the knife. I was so engrossed in my work I was surprised to find the sun was high overhead when I looked up. Somewhere in the distance, the rhythmic slap of oars on the water's surface heralded the arrival of a boat, likely the one bearing the fisherman who could answer all our prayers. Slowly, the boat came into view, and equally slowly, I eased the tip of the blade beneath the bone. With an audible crack, the bone gave up its position in the lock and flew out, landing somewhere in the rushes.

It took all I had not to whoop with joy. But I had to restrain myself, for the fisherman was now on the docks, being warmly greeted by Aine and Imogen. He was wearing a hooded cloak, so I could not see his face, but from his build, I surmised he was young and, from Aine's body language, likely handsome. She was doing everything she could to entice him.

But even from this distance it was clear he was embarrassed by her advances. He scratched his chin nervously and shifted his weight from foot to foot. They spoke for a while—I couldn't hear their conversation—then he gestured toward the supply-laden boat. Aine indicated with a wave that she and Imogen would help unload it.

Before taking the first sack from the fisherman, Aine flipped her hair over her shoulder and brushed his hand. He smiled. She grinned back. They disappeared into the house several times, returning for another round of supplies, then eventually they remained in the main hall. Their voices drifted upward, indistinct but a reassuring sign of the stranger's continued presence.

All the while, I worked the lock, desperate to free myself while the man was still here. All my anxiety did was make my brow sweat and my hands grow clammy and slick. Several times I dropped the dagger, nearly missing my big toe once. Cursing and muttering prayers to every god I could think of, I kept jiggling the metal, looking for the sweet spot that would spell an end to my trouble. The release I felt when the lock clicked open was greater than any I'd experienced with a man.

Rubbing my wrist, I stood and pocketed the dagger. I was halfway across the room before I realized the tower had grown eerily silent. I rushed over to the window and breathed a sigh of relief that the boat was still tied to its mooring.

I crept over to the door. Praying it wouldn't squeak, I peered out. The hallway was deserted. So was Malegant's room. I didn't dare open Aine's door, so I crept down the stairs and into the main room. It was deserted as well.

Imogen was slicing parsnips in the kitchen.

"Where is Aine?" I really didn't want an answer, but I had to know before we could reinstate our escape plan.

She rolled her eyes and pointed at the ceiling. Then she made a gesture I'd never seen from a woman before. Apparently Aine was entertaining our guest with the friendship of the thighs, as my mother used to call it.

"Get your things and meet me back here."

Imogen pointed at a bundle at her feet. She was way ahead of me.

"You know what to do then?"

She nodded, signing the word for fire.

I raced back up the stairs on silent priestess feet and uncovered the bundle Imogen and I had made months before on our first escape attempt. I slung the bag over my shoulder and fastened my cloak about my shoulders. With one final deep breath, I said a prayer to Ellen to guide our path, and I stepped into the hall.

I immediately froze. Aine's door was ajar. I could have sworn it had been closed a moment ago when I raced past. I should have headed straight back to the kitchen, but I was compelled to peek inside. Making certain I made no noise, I crept up to the door. No movement disturbed the peace within. Hesitantly, I peered around the door. Aine lay supine on the bed, knees bent, one arm across her body, the other flung above her head. She wasn't moving.

"She's not dead," said a familiar male voice over my shoulder.

I jumped and grasped my thundering heart. It couldn't be who I thought it was. It just couldn't. Slowly, I turned.

Lancelot grinned at me. "She's only unconscious. A blow to the head will do that to a person."

I couldn't speak, only stare at him dumbly. How had he gotten in here?

"I was the fisherman," he explained as though reading my thoughts. "It's a long story, but we have not time for that now. We must get out of here." He reached for my arm.

"Wait. I have to do one thing first." I crept over to Aine's side, still fearful of waking her, and slipped my ring off her finger. I put it back onto mine where it belonged. "Now we can go."

Lancelot dragged me by the hand down the front stairs. Just as we were about to come into view, the main doors burst open.

Malegant strode in, an angry scowl on his face. "Aine! Imogen!"

Lancelot stopped so fast I smashed my nose into his back. We backed up a few steps, just far enough to stay in the shadows but close enough to watch the unexpected turn of events.

The head guardsman rushed in. "My lord, we were not expecting you so soon. Is all well?"

"My horse threw a shoe in the middle of the forest. I had to walk him back to town to have it fixed, but I wouldn't stay in their rat-infested inn for all the gold in Camelot," he said.

Imogen had entered the room now.

"Ah, good. Mother, some ale, please." She turned to fulfill his request, but he stopped her with a touch on the arm. "Why is the fisherman's boat still here?"

Imogen gave him a sly look and repeated the same gesture she had made for me.

Malegant rolled his eyes. "So that is where my sister is then?"

That was Lancelot's cue to turn. "Go! We have only minutes before he finds Aine."

"But Imogen—"

"Knows what she's doing. Come on." He dragged me toward the upper floor. "Change of plans."

Instead of going all the way to the top, where the sleeping rooms were located, he pulled me into a small alcove halfway in-between. I almost screamed. A man who looked passably like a slightly older version of Lancelot was standing there.

"Well met," Lancelot greeted him. "You are right on time."

The man shook Lancelot's hand and headed down the stairs.

"Who is that?" I hissed.

"Listen and learn," he answered with a chuckle.

Lancelot whisked aside a tapestry on the wall and opened a

hidden door leading out onto the rickety bridge. I stepped onto the landing, fighting a sudden wave of dizziness. Clouds were quickly filling the sky, and a sharp breeze buffeted the bridge, making it swing precariously. On either side, fog rose off the lake as the cold air hit its warm surface.

"Go on," Lancelot encouraged me.

I took a hesitant step onto the wood beams. Each was about the width of both my feet together, and only four beams made up the bridge, allowing me to easily grasp the ropes on either side.

"Why didn't we take the boat?" I asked, my voice shaking as I tested the next beam.

"The fisherman had to have it back for the ruse to work," Lancelot answered, sliding around me to take the lead. "I convinced him to let me take his place today. I told him if I didn't return in two hours to walk across the bridge and pretend he was the one who had made the delivery so he could get his boat back. It doesn't hurt that we resemble one another."

"And he agreed to that?"

"He agreed to my payment." Lancelot grabbed my right hand, leading me slowly onto the bridge proper.

Behind us, chaos erupted. Voices carried out the windows on the wind.

Aine clomped unsteadily down the stairs. "Who is this?"

"You should know, sweet sister. If rumor is true, you've been riding him all afternoon."

"He's not. . . I didn't. . ." Aine sounded confused.

I smiled, imagining her trying to reconcile the older man before her with the younger one in her memory.

"I'm sure you didn't, just like all the others," Malegant replied dryly. "Now if you don't mind, I am going to spend some time with my wife. We are not to be interrupted. Understood?"

"He's going to find out. We have to run," I pleaded with Lancelot, looking around wildly for a way to steady the bridge.

Lancelot shook his head. "We can't run. The bridge is too unpredictable. Can you calm the winds?"

"I think so." I closed my eyes, sent my consciousness upward into the clouds, and willed the air to be still.

"It's working," Lancelot said.

We took a few steps toward the middle of the bridge, and a primal roar stopped me in my tracks. It was Malegant. He must have found the unoccupied chains.

Below us, the fisherman's boat was a shadow in the mist. It was catching up to us. I could just make out two forms within. That meant Imogen and the fisherman had successfully escaped.

I shoved Lancelot forward. "Go! We have to get across before he cuts the ties and the whole bridge collapses."

Lancelot sniffed the air. "Or notices the fire. I can smell it already."

We walked as fast as the bridge allowed, the boat surpassing us easily. But then I noticed another shadow emerging from the fog. The mist parted and I saw Malegant had followed in his boat with two of his guards, both armed with bows.

Lancelot had noticed them too. He cursed. "I have no shield, so we have nothing to deflect their arrows if they can sight us through the mist."

"Yes, we do. Can you carry me across?"

He looked at me as if I was mad but answered like a dutiful champion, "Yes."

"I can direct the arrows away from us, but I can't walk and do that at the same time."

Without a question, Lancelot picked me up, one hand under my knees and the other at the middle of my back, shielding me with his body. "Do your best. I swear I will get us across."

I closed my eyes again and envisioned the wind curling around us as though we were encased in a protective bubble. Arrows whizzed by, closer than I was comfortable with.

Lancelot set me down. "Climb on my back. I want to have my sword free should we need it."

I did as he asked, but it was enough to break my concentration. An arrow grazed my left shoulder. I cursed.

Lancelot turned to tend to me but was knocked sideways against the ropes as the bridge shook. I fell flat on my face. Turning my head, I realized it wasn't just the bridge shaking. Around us, trees were shedding leaves like rain. Branches fell into the lake like boulders in an avalanche. Waves smashed into the prows of the boats. The entire earth was shaking.

The hairs on the back of my neck stood up, and a chill ran down my spine as a familiar keening filled the air. Aine was fighting back in her own way.

The ground rumbled again, and I struggled to my knees. Imogen's boat was just nearing shore, while Malegant's archers were fighting to keep their boat upright in the choppy waters. We had to make the most of our few moments of freedom.

I crawled toward the end of the bridge, afraid to stand lest another jolt send me tumbling over the edge. Lancelot clung to the ropes, carefully measuring each step.

Aine had to still be in the tower. Stopping for a moment, I closed my eyes and called on Brigid, the goddess of fire.

"Great goddess, protect me from my enemies, those who seek to use the elements against me. Consume them in your great forge," I prayed. I envisioned the flames Imogen had ignited in the storeroom growing stronger and stronger, the fires in the hearths hissing as they grew taller, raging out of their confines. I willed the entire tower to be engulfed.

The rumbling stopped as quickly as it had started. I got to my feet again and raced to the safety of land, Lancelot guarding my rear.

I almost kissed the ground, but a deep creaking behind us stopped me. The ground shook again, but this was more of a rolling thunder than the pervasive rumble from earlier. Across the lake, the entire tower was engulfed in flames and was quickly disintegrating. I could only hope Aine was still inside. As we watched, the upper floor fell inward, forcing the main walls out into the lake. They crashed with such force that a tidal wave carried Malegant's boat toward the shore.

Lancelot pulled my arm so tightly I thought my elbow would dislocate. We dashed into the woods just in time to avoid the crashing surf as the wave slammed into the shore, splintering Malegant's boat while propelling him and his men effortlessly onto dry land.

"It seems the gods wish us to be together. Why, they practically tossed me into your arms," Malegant said to me before drawing his sword and facing Lancelot. "So this is how it ends, is it? Brothers-in-arms in a fight to the death. I could, of course, take you prisoner and let my sister play with you, but watching you die will be so much more satisfying."

At his signal, the two guards, each with a loaded bow, advanced on me, Imogen, and the fisherman. I looked around wildly for some way to defend myself. The taller of the two, a middle-aged man with reddish hair sticking out beneath his helmet, took aim at me. I dove for the trees just as the arrow passed over my head. Scraped and bloody, I was safe for the moment, but hiding was no long-term strategy.

I grabbed the nearest branch I could find to use as a weapon and shot deeper into the woods. Once I stopped, I heard the clang of metal on metal as Malegant and Lancelot fought on the shore. The guards were venturing into the trees, so I had to keep moving. I made a slow arc that would lead me back to the shoreline. Imogen and the fisherman attacked one of the archers, so I made a mad dash in the opposite direction.

I had hardly moved before an arrow bit into my arm. I screamed in agony. It was the same side as the other arrow had hit, only this time it lodged in the muscle of my upper arm, rendering it useless for defense. The archer was already nocking another arrow, so I had no time to break this one off. I ran, trying to ignore the burning pain in my left shoulder, dodging between trees and praying his next bolt would find one of them instead of me.

As I passed a wide oak, I was wrenched sideways. A hand grasped my right arm. For one terrifying moment, I was afraid I had run straight into the archer, but when I looked up, I saw a face I recognized.

"Sobian." I hugged her, scarcely able to believe she was there.

"Lancelot and I found you together. He made me swear to stay here while he got you out, but he didn't say anything about not helping you escape." She handed me a sword. "Here, you'll need this. Oh, turn around."

I bit my lower lip, trying to make as little noise as possible as she broke the shaft of the arrow.

Not far away, Malegant and Lancelot battled on, grunting and puffing as they both tired. They were ankle-deep in muddy sand churned into mush by their boots. I was certain that as long as Lancelot didn't make a major mistake, he would prevail. He had more training and a more refined technique than Malegant, who fought as he did everything else—all passion and force with little strategy to back it up.

"Do you trust me?" I asked Sobian.

"Of course, though I doubt you would say the same."

I smiled at her despite myself. "Then don't try to stop me." I swallowed hard, asked the goddess Morrigan for protection, and stepped out into the open. "Malegant! I am here. Stop this battle. It is I you want."

Malegant turned, surprised by the sound of my voice. That was the advantage Lancelot needed. He shoved his sword into Malegant's gut, easily piercing through his armor. Malegant staggered backward and fell, his head landing just shy of the water's edge. Blood pooled in the muck, a trickle escaping his lips as he struggled to hang on to life.

I knelt next to him. His eyes had lost their menace, replaced by fear that revealed the boy he must once have been.

"It is over, Malegant. All of this planning, all of the pain, all of the terror. It is over, and you never truly got what you wanted. I am not your wife, nor ever will I be in any true sense of the word. For every bruise you gave me, for every bone you broke and every time you defiled me, I call upon Ceridwen to take equal vengeance. And not just for myself. In Fiona's name and all of your wives', for every woman you have ever harmed, I curse you. May your soul never find rest."

I could have gone on, but the light went out from behind Malegant's eyes. The hand grasping his wound fell limply to his side. He was dead.

But we were not out of danger yet. I stood, expecting to see joy on Lancelot's face, but instead he held stock-still, frozen by something I hadn't seen. I followed his gaze to see the redheaded guard holding Imogen by the neck. She was weeping for her dead children, heedless of the blade at her throat.

"Let her go," Lancelot called.

"Drop your weapons, and maybe I will."

Lancelot and I both flung our swords to the ground.

"We have done as you asked. Now please, return her to us," Lancelot said.

The guard sneered. "You just killed my lord. He thought that she"—he indicated me with the tip of his dagger—"was worth pursuing. So now I want her for myself—to reap whatever value she brings. That is what I offer. This woman's life for hers."

"I do not know the woman you hold hostage. Her life means nothing to me," Lancelot bluffed. Unseen by the guard, Lancelot was working a dagger loose from the back of his belt.

"So we are at an impasse then."

"It appears so."

I passed behind Lancelot, our heads together in what I hoped the guard took as consultation about his demand.

Lancelot whispered, "I'm going to lunge at him. As soon as I'm clear, aim for his head." He passed the dagger to me.

I flipped the blade around so it was in my palm. "I'm not good at this."

But it didn't matter. Before either of us could move, Sobian and the fisherman tackled the guard and sent him sprawling face-first in the mud, his own dagger sticking out of his back.

Chapter Twelve

For a few moments, none of us moved. In the dying daylight, we stood like statues on a shore ruined by destruction. Leaves and branches littered the shore as though a powerful storm had blown through. The shoreline was in tatters thanks to the tidal wave and Lancelot and Malegant's battle. Three bodies littered the ground. Across the water, the ruins of the tower were smoldering, sending plumes of smoke into the dusky sky. If anyone found this place in the next year or two, they might wonder what had taken place, but they would never guess the devastation was all from the rescue of the queen.

The fisherman stirred. "Please allow me to offer you shelter for the night."

I eyed the man who was so much an older version of Lancelot with suspicion. "How do we know this isn't a trap?"

"Because it isn't," Lancelot stated.

I turned to him. "How do you know?"

"Sobian and I spent many weeks with this man before putting my plan into action. Diarmad is no traitor to the crown."

The fisherman bowed. "My queen."

"You—you know who I am?"

"Indeed. I have pled my case before you many times. I have always found you and the high king to be both fair and wise. When this good knight sought my help in discovering your location, the least I could do was aid him in whatever way I could."

But I wasn't ready to trust him yet. "You are well-spoken for a common fisherman."

"I am anything but common, my lady. But it is a tale best told with a cup in hand in front of a warming fire. Please, will you accept my hospitality?"

Lancelot regarded me pleadingly. "Guinevere, we need to remove the arrow from your shoulder. Be reasonable."

He was right. My shoulder pulsed with pain, and all of us needed rest.

A short walk later, we approached a small round house fashioned of branches and mud, much like most of our ancestors would have used. From the shadows, a small brown goat bleated.

"That's Ceana. She provides milk and cheese. She's a sweet girl." Diarmad petted the goat as one would a prized hound.

When we stepped inside, my eyes took a moment to adjust, but soon I found we were in a one-room hut with a hard-packed dirt floor. A large fire pit dominated the center of the room. Hanging over it from a long chain was a cauldron of something that smelled divine. On one side was a small oven, likely used for baking bread, while opposite was a small mattress and pillow. A few pegs in the wall held a cloak and three tunics. The only other items in the room were several fishing staffs and nets. He lived as simply as a Druid—or perhaps a Christian hermit.

I couldn't help but wonder how a man of such simple means had found his way to Camelot's court. And more importantly, how he'd become involved in rescuing me. I threw him a sidelong glance. Lancelot may have trusted him, but I didn't.

We need to see to your wound, Imogen signed, as if I could forget the throbbing of an arrow in my shoulder.

"Diarmad, this is Imogen. She cannot speak, but I can understand her hand language and can translate for her."

Diarmad gave Imogen a small bow and touched his thumb to his forehead, lips, and heart. "I know a priestess when I see one. I do not have much, but everything I have is yours."

He laid out four blankets side by side and withdrew so I could undress.

I lay down on one and steeled myself for the painful procedure to come, draining the flagon of mead Diarmad placed by my side. "Lancelot, how did you come to know and trust this man?"

He stood over me. "I suppose that is a good tale to distract you. Brace yourself. This will hurt." He began to draw out the arrow.

I cried out, grasping for something to squeeze. Sobian handed me a wadded-up cloth. I would have rather bitten on leather, but given the circumstances, this would have to do.

"The worst is yet to come, I'm afraid." Something in Lancelot's voice told me he'd done this many times on the battlefield. He knelt beside me.

Nothing could have prepared me for the searing pain that shot from my shoulder straight to my head as the arrow emerged. I screamed but heard my own voice as if from far away, white dots dancing like snowflakes before my eyes. All I wanted was to pass out. Maybe when I woke, the whole business would be over. But no, I was a warrior, a battle queen, some small voice insisted above the shrill ringing in my head. If I couldn't be present for this, I did not deserve to lead others into the same peril.

I was just coming back to full consciousness when my shoulder exploded again, this time accompanied by a splash of something wet. Someone was blowing on the wound in an attempt to allay my pain.

"It's wine," Lancelot explained. "It will clean your wound before Imogen stitches you up."

I was panting like a woman in labor. I turned my head to the side. "That story you were going to use to distract me?"

"Oh yes. It begins many years ago, when I was a young warrior just come from Brittany. I was a lone fighter for hire in those days, anxious to test my blade and build my reputation. I had fought my fair share of battles in order to secure passage to Britain but nothing like those I would face on this isle."

I cried out as Imogen's needle bit into my flesh. Sobian sat next to me and held my hand, while Diarmad busied himself at the cookfire.

"I made my way up north to the land of Angus in the southern Highlands. There I found much work among the warring chieftains. It was there I first met Diarmad."

"You may not expect it, but many a nobleman in Bernicia—where I'm from—has interests up yon way," Diarmad interjected.

"He was recruiting warriors for his army back here. I became one of them."

"Only after you defeated half of the tribes—enough to earn the name Angus. Still hold lands up there, do ye?" Diarmad gestured with his bottle of brew.

I sucked air as Imogen drew the sutures tight. "May I have some of that, please?" I pointed at the bottle.

"Where are my manners?" Diarmad fussed around for another mug.

I gestured to him impatiently, and he came over. I took the bottle without asking and took one long swallow, then another, and one more for good measure. Wiping my mouth with the back of my hand, I said, "Continue."

Lancelot was so surprised by my unwomanly behavior that it took him a moment to find his train of thought. "After I joined Diarmad in Bernicia, people began noticing the resemblance between us. Quite by accident, we came to realize we were related through my mother's line. I grew up in the sacred grove of the Forest of Broceliande—our version of Avalon—and was raised by the Lady of the Lake, so my parents were but shadows in my memory."

Diarmad picked up the tale. "A woman came to court, claiming to know great things about my past and future. She said I would fall from the heights, never to rise, but that my most trusted man, one of my own blood, would rise higher than I could ever dream. I was intrigued for I knew of no relations still living. This seer wanted a hefty sum for the rest of her knowledge, so I sent her away, but she took a liking to Lancelot and promised him if he did a favor for her, she would reveal to him his true parentage."

Diarmad's voice was coming from far away now. I missed what the nature of the woman's favor was as the pain and drink overtook me simultaneously and I passed out. Apparently neither man noticed, for Lancelot was still talking when I opened my eyes again.

"I followed her most willingly, and she led me to a modest holding where an old woman lay dying. Aoileann was her name, though most called her Eileen or Helen. 'My son,' she said as she embraced me. No one had ever called me that. She told me she was pleased to see me in the employ of my uncle—her brother—and knew I would forever be safe with him. I spent only one evening with her but was able to be present when she passed through the veil." Lancelot cleared his throat then did not continue.

I twisted around and immediately regretted it as my pain flared anew. But I got a glance at the dark green poultice covering my wounded shoulder. "Imogen, what is that? It smells like a midden heap next to a latrine in the heat."

She circled around so I could see her gestures. *Priestess, you know the answer. It will speed your recovery and keep infection away.* She helped me to my feet.

Leaning on her arm, I took a few unsteady steps toward a rug near the fire around which all the others sat.

"Eat," Diarmad insisted, shoving a bowl of fish stew in my direction along with a mug of ale. "This is when the tale takes a dark turn. One day, a young man came to court asking for my strongest warrior. I thought he was going to challenge him to a duel, but he instead relayed a message from King Lot. Lot was planning to challenge Arthur for the throne and desired the strongest and most powerful warriors to join him. This boy here"—he clapped Lancelot's shoulder—"had the sense to refuse. However, I did not. That is how I lost everything."

I looked up from my bowl. That was it. That was why I knew the man's face. I had seen it in my vision while I lay dying in Dyfed. As he explained the repercussions of his actions, my suspicions deepened. If he had committed treachery once, what was to stop him from doing it again, especially now that he had me in his grasp, weakened and nearly alone?

"Arthur condemned me along with Lot and Uriens. I fled Bernicia in shame and settled here because I had built up some measure of respect with Lord Malegant, who always promised he could get me back into court. I suppose he would have had his plans succeeded."

My hackles rose. "So you knew what he was going to do?"

Diarmad was quick to defend his honor. "No, I speak only in hindsight. All I knew was he held this castle in the lake as one of his many fortresses. He mainly used it as a retreat, a place to hide mistresses. I supplied what he needed when he needed it. You see, when I lost my title and my wealth, I still retained many of my connections. I can get anyone just about anything they need."

He cleared his throat noisily. "Last summer, on one of his journeys through the area, he advised me he would be wintering here with a few guests. I assumed he was spending the time with his wife and friends, so I didn't question what he needed. I didn't give the arrangement another thought until these two found me." He gestured at Lancelot and Sobian. "When Lancelot told me his suspicions, my blood went cold. To abduct the queen was most serious indeed, and I was aiding him, albeit unknowingly."

"How did you find each other?" I translated for Imogen, who was held rapt by the story.

Lancelot and Diarmad exchanged glances. "I think that a tale for another time. Our queen is injured and no doubt exhausted, so we should let her sleep."

I hadn't realized it until Lancelot said it, but I was bone weary. At his words, my entire body sagged. I put my half-eaten bowl aside and let Imogen guide me to the pallet. Two moments later, I was in a deep, dreamless sleep.

ঞেও ৩৯৩

I woke with a start, uncertain where I was and fearful of reprisal from Malegant. Then, slowly, the events of the previous day returned to me. They were not a dream. The biting pain in my shoulder was proof.

I stood slowly, my legs wobbly from all I had endured. As I moved, every joint hurt, every bruise cried out for attention, but it was nothing compared to what I had endured at Malegant's hand. Imogen, who had been helping Sobian divide up their supplies for the journey home, helped me dress.

Before I could ask where Lancelot had gone, the steady clomp of hooves broke the silence, and I froze, fearing we had been discovered.

Peace, Imogen signed. *'Tis only Lancelot.*

"You're up early," I said by way of greeting as he entered.

"I wanted to be at the village before dawn in case any of Malegant's spies remain. The last thing we need is to alert them of our plans or our method of travel."

"Lancelot, I know you want to use this steed to carry me back to Camelot, but I cannot ask Imogen to walk that distance. I would like her and Sobian to go on ahead of us and be the messengers of good tidings to Arthur. We can follow."

"But there is only one horse. Sobian sold hers in order to be able to stay in town while we formulated a plan to rescue you. You cannot expect to walk all that way. You are wounded and, forgive me, not in your strongest form."

"That has never stopped me before. I will not ride while someone I owe my life to walks."

Not long after, we were saddling the horse and giving Imogen instructions. She didn't want to ride on ahead of us and was still protesting through a series of emphatic gestures, but we insisted.

"Arthur needs to be told we are well," Lancelot insisted. "I set out with Arthur, Merlin, Kay, and Sobian after Merlin told us of his horrifying nightmare. We were split up during a storm, so the others likely don't even know Sobian and I are alive, much less that we found Guinevere. She and I will be traveling slowly and resting frequently. The sooner Arthur can be made aware, the sooner he can send guards to accompany us the rest of the way."

"Take this." I slipped the gold-and-sapphire ring off my finger. "Arthur gave me this and will recognize it. It is my signal to him that I am alive and have truly sent you."

But I cannot speak to him, she signed, her eyes huge with fear and anxiety. *How will I pass on your message?*

"I can understand you," Sobian spoke up.

"You can?"

Sobian grinned. "I understand all manner of hand signals. I was a spy, remember? Do you think I never impersonated a priestess? I had to be authentic or risk being found out."

I stared at her incredulously. Was there no end to this woman's abilities?

"Well then," I said to Imogen, "it sounds like Sobian will be your translator and guide." I hugged her. "I know you are scared, and you have already done more for me than I could ever ask of a dozen people, but I need you to do this one last favor for me. When this is all over, I promise you can retire in any way you like. You are welcome at court if you choose, but if not, name your desire and we will fulfill it."

She nodded. *The journey will give me time to grieve my children in peace. I will do as you wish.*

Lancelot secured her pack, which was loaded with all the provisions she would need should she somehow be separated from Sobian. "You know the directions?"

Imogen nodded.

"Good. May the gods guide your path."

I squeezed Imogen's hand. "Thank you for all you have done."

She smiled. *Don't thank me yet. We both still have a long journey ahead.*

·ֵ಄಄಄·

After saying farewell to Diarmad, Lancelot and I headed east, our backs to the progress of the sun. It was about noon on a cold but pleasant day. We would not get far before nightfall, but at least it would put distance between us and the ruined tower. I wanted to be as far from there as quickly as possible.

Our first two days of travel passed without incident, the air growing colder as we neared higher ground. We were fortunate to find shelter in farmsteads, but soon we would not be so lucky. The snow-covered hills of Dartmoor had to be crossed before we reached the safety of the southern terminus of Fosse Way and the road back to Cadbury.

On the third day, we set out to conquer the passes. Had we been on horseback, the journey would only have taken two days at most, but on foot, we faced a trip of at least three times that length.

"What do you feel?" Lancelot asked.

Eyes closed, I searched the energy of the earth and sky. "Nothing. We will have good weather for at least the next two days. Beyond that, I cannot say." I opened my eyes. "This isn't an exact skill, you know."

He laughed. "But a helpful one. I wish I'd had you on my past journeys. You would have saved me many cold, wet nights."

We walked in silence for a while, the ground underfoot sloping steadily upward and the vegetation scarce. Soon there was no path, only wide crags and fissures in the rock, which Lancelot navigated as though he was following a map.

"How do you know this area so well?" I asked.

"I don't. But I traveled it once before, looking for you." He smiled. "Arthur has done everything in his power to try to find you. When you were discovered missing and Gareth was found dead—"

My hand flew to my mouth. "Gareth is dead?"

"Yes. I suppose you would not know. The Samhain revelers said he was stabbed in a fight, right in the middle of the crowd. But it was a mortal wound; no one could have saved him."

"But Gareth was guarding me. There was no fight. Surely I would have known. Unless. . ." The words needed not be spoken. I was certain to the marrow of my bones that Malegant had done this. That was how he'd ensured I was alone and ripe for the picking.

Lancelot cleared his throat. "As soon as we realized you were gone, Arthur launched the biggest search party the country has ever seen. Men and women from all over Britain looked for you in every part of the country. We knew whoever had taken you couldn't have gotten far, but we decided to search everywhere. Merchants and trading caravans had their wagons inspected at every major crossing, and every boat that sailed from our ports was searched before being allowed to weigh anchor. He really did all he could."

I tried to fight the pain welling up inside me. All those resources, all those plans, and yet. . . my mind flashed through months of torment, submission, and pain. Tears overflowed before I could stop them. When I could speak, my voice was strained. "Why was this place so difficult to find? Why did it take so long?"

Why didn't you find me sooner? Why didn't Arthur come for me himself? Those were the questions I really wanted to ask.

Lancelot stopped. He picked up a stick and sketched a crude map in the snow. "Cadbury is that stone over there." He pointed at a rock sticking out of the snow about three arms' lengths away. "This area is open plain, and these are the mountains we are in now." He gestured to each with his stick. "You were here." He drew a circle surrounded by a wavy-lined lake and mountains like spear points. "We were not even aware this area was habitable. That is why no one looked there."

He looked at me, his soft, caring blue eyes seeking forgiveness. I nodded, relieved to be able to genuinely give it.

He took my arm, and we continued walking as he spoke. "It was only after Merlin's dream that we had specific guidance on where to look. He used some kind of crystal to guide us—until the storm. Worst storm I've ever seen, and I've been trapped in many. It was two nights after the eclipse. We had just made it through the narrowest pass in these hills when the sky darkened far too fast for a normal sunset. The air took on the tang of metal, and the wind blew fiercely then suddenly stopped. We knew we had to seek shelter and fast, but there was nowhere to hide. Before we could make a plan, the rain fell in large, heavy drops. We made it to the outskirts of the forest before the hail came too. Lightning flashed all around us, chasing us wherever we went. That's when Sobian and I became separated from the rest."

I thought back. Two days after the eclipse. What exactly had Aine's dark power shown her? Was it possible she could have known? That she could have directed the storm to keep them away? She was certainly in control of powers that should only have belonged to a trained priestess. But if that was the case, then why had Malegant left me alone? Perhaps he had not known help was coming or Aine had not realized her plan was not completely successful.

The path became so slippery with ice Lancelot and I had to hold on to one another to stay upright.

After a while, he looked at the sky. "We should find a place to spend the night."

Eventually, we came upon a cave. After ensuring it wasn't currently occupied by a slumbering bear, Lancelot rousted the bats from its roof. I will never forget their squeaking and the ghostly shiver of their wings as they winged past me to find a new place to haunt. Warrior or no, I cowered in fear until I was certain they were gone. We spent the night slumbering amid our fur-lined cloaks with only a tiny fire to keep us warm. In the still, small hours of the night, Lancelot embraced me in his sleep, his touch igniting the wound in my shoulder. I recoiled, his touch and the sudden pain bringing back vivid memories of Malegant. A small cry escaped my lips as I scrambled to my feet, shaking and desperate to be more than an arm's length away from him.

"What is it?" He looked up, still partially asleep, confused.

I couldn't speak. I tried to catch my breath, which was coming in ragged gasps, but could not. I doubled over. My chest was caving in. I couldn't breathe. It was as though fear was smothering me.

"Guinevere? Are you ill?"

I couldn't stop shaking. My mind kept replaying the same memories—Malegant breaking my fingers, beating me, raping me, tearing my flesh to ribbons. Tears made hot rivers down my cheeks in the cold night air.

I must have looked to him like a feral beast because Lancelot spoke to me in the same soothing tone he used on unbroken colts. "Everything is fine. I mean you no harm. You are safe, Guinevere."

My heart was pounding in my head, but at the sound of my name, the rushing thoughts slowed a little. I could understand where I was but not yet why.

He must have noticed the effect because he tried again. "Guinevere, look at me. No one will harm you."

I met his eyes, and my heart began to slow.

"That's it. It's me, Lancelot—your champion. I am sworn to the Goddess in all her names to protect you, remember? I am here to take you home."

Slowly, my chest muscles relaxed, and I gasped in a few deep breaths. I was beginning to remember who I was, where, and why.

Lancelot reached out his hand. "Come to me, Guinevere. You will be safe. I swear it."

Hesitantly, I took a small step forward. My arm moved without conscious command to him. When our fingertips touched, I did not flinch but rather relaxed into his warmth.

Lancelot held my hand gently and slowly led me back to where we had bedded down. "I will not hurt you, but we will be warmer if we are close together. If you do not wish to touch, at least let us share our cloaks."

I allowed him to cover us both, our bodies nearly touching. Soon my eyelids grew heavy again, and darkness descended to take all the memories away.

§

The next morning, we woke to a light snowfall. After breaking our fast on a brace of squirrels caught in Lancelot's traps, we set out on what we hoped would be the last leg of our journey through the mountains. After that, we should have been able to take the Roman roads back to Cadbury. We walked in tense silence for a while, trying not to slip on the uneven, rocky terrain. Neither of us acknowledged what had taken place last night.

Finally, Lancelot said, "Guinevere, I know this is beyond the bounds of my role as your champion, but what did Male—"

I whirled on him. "Do not say his name. He is dead. It is over."

"But Arthur must be told. Do you wish to tell him yourself what happened, or shall I relay it? Which would be easier for you?"

I stopped. "Why need he know? Is it not bad enough that one of us is haunted by the memories? Why should I so burden him?" I didn't want to tell him anything, say anything. If I voiced my experiences, there would be no denying them. They would be real and irrefutable. I couldn't do it. I just couldn't.

"You need to tell someone. You'll never be free until you do. I swear on all the gods and the Lady of the Lake who raised me that I will repeat what you tell me only to the king."

I fought him for a while, but eventually, as the sky grew lighter and the sun traversed the sky behind a bank of darkening clouds that began to shed tiny flakes, I told him everything, starting with caring for Camille and Llew all the way through learning Imogen's identity and our plans to escape. As much as I wanted to edit my experience and keep the worst from him, I forced the words through my lips. By the time my story was complete, I could barely stand. Reliving it was nearly as bad as going through it the first time.

The snow was falling harder, piling up around our ankles and hampering our progress. On Lancelot's advice, we had each taken a stout stick from a pine tree to use as a walking staff. I was grateful for the support.

We rounded a bend, and I gasped in wonder. Before us, the land plummeted to a deep chasm with only a small ledge hugging the eastern face of the foothills. The hills dropped off sharply to a void of rock and ice, small scrub trees growing defiantly here and there from fissures in its smooth face. Far below, a gray-and-white-capped river flowed, its roaring current only the slightest whisper to our ears. On the far side, the sun was beginning to set behind foothills identical to the ones we had just traversed, where trees promised to lead to level land if one only kept walking long enough. Directly ahead, across the gorge, the ledge widened to accommodate a small stand of fir trees and a tiny cabin.

"There." Lancelot pointed at the house. "That is where we will rest this night."

"Will we have to cross the chasm?" I asked tremulously, memories of the crude bridge at the tower still far too fresh in my mind.

"No, if we keep to the ledge, it should take us there."

"Good." My teeth chattered as much with fear as cold.

Lancelot led the way, testing each step with his staff before making it, clearly uncertain whether or not to trust his sight as to which parts of the snow-packed ground were solid and which were not. We were purposefully silent, knowing what the slightest noise could do at this elevation when the snows were heavy and their pack unreliable.

The cabin was in sight when the rumbling began. Instinctively, we looked up then at each other. We hadn't made a sound. But someone had.

"Someone else is here," I said, spine prickling, ears fully alert like a hound.

It came again—a regular crunch, crunch, crunch—growing steadily closer, but because of the echoes of the gorge, I couldn't tell if it was in front of or behind us. I drew my sword.

The mountain grumbled again, shaking the ground beneath us.

Lancelot picked up a rock and threw it across the path ahead. It bounced off a tree trunk, clattering to the ground. Not a moment later, an arrow whizzed past us and lodged in the earth where the rock had fallen.

"It's a trap," I whispered.

Lancelot nodded, looking around. "There are likely men behind us, so we cannot turn back, but I don't see a viable way around either."

We charged forward, running at top speed to evade any additional archers, and narrowly missed a rope strung across the pass. Once over it, Lancelot tripped it as we hugged the trees on opposite sides of the trail. A net rose out of the snow, closing over nothing. Lancelot cut it down and slung the mesh over his shoulder.

The sound drew out our attackers. They emerged from the trees—the archer, another man, and a golden-haired woman—confident in their trap. Lancelot was able to dispatch the archer before the others assumed a defensive stance.

My mouth dropped open as I found myself facing Aine—who I'd thought was dead—and more surprisingly, Diarmad.

They took advantage of our shock by charging. Aine came at me as though to tackle me but then shoved me to the right, nearly sending me skittering over the ledge. Thanks be to the goddess Druantia I caught a bowed branch of pine in time to stop my slide. I scrambled to my feet, and Aine swung at my head with her wicked axe. I ducked and weaved so that I was behind her. She turned before I could land a blow, but I was now too close for her massive weapon to be of much use. She turned it and slammed the pole into my ribs, knocking me back, but I was inside her guard again before she could swing.

In my peripheral vision, I saw Lancelot struggling with Diarmad, each knowing the other's fighting techniques, skills, and weaknesses.

I decided to try to distract Aine to break her concentration. "How did you get ahead of us, Aine? Why follow us all this way?"

She panted, "I know these mountains better than your knight. You killed my brother, so I will take your life. But not before ransoming you for all your puny hide is worth."

So she didn't plan to kill me, at least not yet. That certainly changed the tenor of this fight. I relaxed a little, working to disarm her. Out of the corner of my eye, I saw Lancelot bring Diarmad to his knees and ensnare him in the net he had salvaged.

Aine must have seen it too, for she turned and, with a feral war cry, swung at Lancelot. He dove out of the way but not quite in time. Her axe bit into his thigh. Lancelot crumpled, momentarily defenseless. Struggling to regain his footing, he threw a handful of snow at Aine, hoping to blind her, but she avoided it and raised her axe to deliver the fatal blow.

I screamed and lunged for her, but Diarmad wriggled his way out of the net and came at Lancelot at the same time. In a split-second decision, I changed the arc of my blade and swung at Diarmad instead, ripping a hole in his gut. His blade too made deadly contact, but not with Lancelot. His final act was to save Lancelot by driving his sword into Aine's throat. She gurgled in surprise, dropped her axe, and fell, her blood staining the snow a bright crimson.

Diarmad collapsed into Lancelot's arms. Lancelot could only stare at him, shocked.

I ran to Diarmad's side and knelt next to him. "Oh, Diarmad, I am so sorry. I thought you were going to kill Lancelot."

He smiled ruefully. "I was. But when your blow landed, I knew I could not let that viper live."

I held his wound, watching helplessly as life drained out of him.

Lancelot slowly recovered from his shock. "Why join with her, Diarmad?"

"She traced you to me. Said she would make it worth me turning on you. It was either die by her hand or yours, and after so many years of living on nothing, I'm afraid her promises of riches outweighed my loyalty, even to you." He groaned. "I am so sorry, my friend. . ."

Lancelot bowed his head. "All things are forgiven in the end." He looked at me.

I placed a hand on Diarmad's brow. "May the Lady guide you home, and in her arms may you find rest. Drink from her cauldron and be reborn without sorrow or stain. Go in peace."

Diarmad smiled and covered my hand, red now from his blood, with his own. "Forgive me." He breathed one last time and closed his eyes, still for eternity.

The mountain rumbled again, and Lancelot looked up. "We will get no additional warning. Come. We must hurry or the avalanche will bury us along with our enemies."

◈◈◈

Cold, bloodied, and limping, we reached the cabin just before sundown. It must have been a hunting lodge for it was well stocked with preserves, blankets, and a store of firewood. Although what anyone would have hunted up here eluded me. We had seen signs of a few bears but were at too high an elevation for deer or boars. Squirrels and fox were everywhere, but there were easier places to lay traps for them.

But as the sun sank lower, the wolves began to howl, and I understood. I shivered as their mournful cries turned my blood to ice.

"They are the banshees of the animal world," Lancelot said. "That's the one thing I never got used to when traveling on the open roads. I know their habits, but that doesn't stop something inside me from cringing when I hear them. But we'll be safe in here."

Lancelot insisted on examining me before allowing me to tend to him. He sewed a few new stitches in my shoulder blade and pronounced two of my ribs broken from the butt of Aine's axe, but that was the extent of my injures.

Finally he let me see to his thigh, which was still trickling blood. He had removed his breeches out of necessity, and strangely, I was acutely aware that the hem of his tunic was the only thing preserving his modesty. Much to my horror, the thought made my cheeks burn as I bathed the wound. His fingers dug into my shoulders, and I blew on the gash, only too aware of the intimacy of the gesture.

"You never did tell me how you came to find Diarmad on this journey," I prompted. "Perhaps telling me of it will help distract you from the pain." And me from my embarrassment.

"Where did I leave off?" he asked as I repeated the procedure with water, seeking to see just how badly injured he was. "Ah yes, Sobian and I were separated from the rest of the group in unfamiliar land. We headed north because that's what I've always done when I am lost. It's something I remember the Lady of the Lake telling me. 'Whenever you have lost your way, follow the North Star home.'"

He stopped talking and flinched as I probed his wound with my fingers. "It is not nearly as deep as it should be. Your movement must have taken some of the force out of her swing. Don't walk for a while, and there shouldn't be any lasting damage." I met his eyes briefly, seeing relief in them, and poured honey into the wound to clean and bind it before stitching him up.

Lancelot continued through gritted teeth. "After walking for what felt like days, we came upon Diarmad's house, much as you and I came upon this place. At first, he was wary of me. But once I recognized him and recounted our past history—something no one else could have known—he began to trust me. One day, Sobian returned from town with word of activity in the tower. We watched it for several weeks before we saw you. When Diarmad told us he was due to deliver supplies, Sobian saw our way in. It was her idea to have us switch places. I believe you know the rest."

"She is a master of intrigue," I credited, slathering the stitched skin with a liberal coating of Imogen's stinky salve before I covered it with clean cloth. "This shows no signs of infection. But you need to lay off the heroics," I joked with a wag of my finger.

He grabbed my finger and twisted. "Only if you promise not to get yourself kidnapped again."

I writhed in mock pain and protest. When I looked up, our faces were less than a hand span apart. We froze, staring at one another for a long time. Finally, I dropped my eyes.

"We should sleep," I muttered.

He cleared his throat. "Yes, indeed."

We retired to opposite sides of the bed, backs to one another. I sent my consciousness down into the earth, intent on thanking all the gods who had saved my life today. But I sensed something else, something looming and oppressive. I sat up suddenly.

"Lancelot?"

"Mmmm?" He was already partially asleep.

"We need to stay here. A snowstorm is coming."

Large flakes fell from the sky for the next three days, and it was three more before we could leave the cabin. I was grateful for the extra time to rest and recover from our injuries.

But soon enough, the sun broke through the clouds, turning the forest into a wonderland of glittering snow and shining ice, a frozen paradise into which we ventured, full of hope that we would soon be home. Our progress was slow. Lancelot was still limping and leaning on a stripped pine branch for support. We took turns carrying the heavy pack of supplies, and I had to stop often to give both him and my shoulder a rest. Another two days passed before we finally came upon the old Roman road leading to Isca. We could follow it for the remainder of our journey.

"There is a village just up ahead," Lancelot said, weariness in every aspect of his demeanor. His shoulders slumped, his eyes were heavy, and his gait was sluggish. "I know this area. We will be safe here."

We must have looked like a couple of outlaws when we stumbled into the village. I combed my fingers through my hair, but it was hopelessly tangled. At least we'd been able to wash in an icy pond earlier in the morning, so I didn't think we smelled worse than anyone else who'd been on the road. But our clothes were dirty and torn from multiple fights, and bruises blossomed all over our bodies.

I pulled the hood of my cloak farther down over my forehead as we passed a small Christian church, uncertain whether someone of my faith would be welcome in this town. I had heard stories of how well the missionaries were doing in the south, and I had no desire to suffer persecution on top of everything else. Just in case, I pulled a few withered juniper berries off a bush as we passed and squeezed them until I had just a few drops of juice on my fingers. I touched my forehead then wiped my fingertips on my skirt. This juice was nearly the same color as the ink in my tattoo, so touching it would enable me "smudge" the tattoo if needed, making it appear to be drawn on rather than permanent. It was a trick all priestesses of Avalon learned in case we ventured into unfriendly territory, but I hoped my precaution would prove unnecessary.

We stopped at the mouth of an alley where two buildings opposed each other and a wooden fence forced a dead end beyond them. The one to our right, if the sour smell was any indication, was a stable—and not a very clean one. To our left was what I could only guess was an inn. Music and raucous laughter flowed out of its open door while men and women played games of chance in the street, shouting over the din from inside. At the far end of the lane, a group of youths used the fence to practice knife throwing, a crude target having been drawn on its surface.

We pushed past patrons in various states of inebriation. All glared in response, but no one was bothered enough to make a scene. The air inside the inn was thick with wood smoke, scents of food—some new, some several days old—and strongest of all, stale ale. Men and women of all ages, shapes, and sizes crowded every table and corner, laughing, joking, or conducting business in hushed conversation. Serving women and children darted in and out of the crowd, providing mugs of thick dark brown ale or golden mead alongside loaves of bread, steaming bowls of stew, or joints of meat. In exchange, coins of all values, from gold and silver to the most meager metal, changed hands—and not just for food. At quite a few tables, men were buying companionship for the evening.

As one of the serving maids passed us, my stomach rumbled audibly. We found an empty place to sit at the end of a long table. The top was laden with burning lumps of candle wax. No one bothered to remove a candle when it burned out—they simply stacked a new one on top of the pool of wax made by the last one. The benches were covered in furs and hides, a welcome comfort after days on the road.

A burley man sidled up to us. "What will it be then?"

"Two mugs of ale and two joints of that boar on the spit. We would also like a room for the evening," Lancelot requested.

The barkeep glared at Lancelot. "One room?" He looked from Lancelot to me. "It's a shame, but our only private room is in use. You'll have to sleep in the common room tonight or seek shelter somewhere else."

He started to walk away, but Lancelot put a firm hand on the man's arm. "Tell me, who is your distinguished guest? Unless it is the high king himself"—Lancelot surveyed the room—"and I doubt he would stay here, you will ask that person to remove himself from those quarters. Unless you would like me to remove him myself."

"Who are you to demand such things?"

"Lancelot du Lac, High King Arthur's Master of the Horse and member of the Combrogi."

The innkeeper snorted. "And I'm the queen."

I turned to him. "Actually, I am."

The innkeeper scowled at me but inspected me closely. Then he roared with laughter. "Tonight the queen, tomorrow the unruly slave girl, isn't that how it goes for your lot?"

I smiled inwardly at his assumption that I was a prostitute playing a role to satisfy the fantasy of my customer. It was probably safer than admitting my true identity as we were still in Malegant's lands. If he wished to believe it, then I would not correct him. Playing along, I merely dropped my eyes to the floor.

The innkeeper cackled again. "Hey, boys, you have to come see this one." He motioned to two young men who were obviously his sons. "And bring them two wet ones and a piece of the piggy."

"Why did you not tell him who you are?" Lancelot whispered to me once the innkeeper had gone.

"We can't have them know who I am, can we?" I looked around, but no one was paying us any heed. "You are safe because everyone knows Arthur's knights go where they please. But the same is not true for me. Until we're back in Cadbury, I trust no one. Neither should you. Pretend to be my customer. They are entertained by it. The more enthralled they are, the less likely they are to be suspicious."

"You are a devious one, you know that?"

I gave him a coy smile. "I've been around Sobian too long."

The innkeeper's boys arrived. They were tall like their father but not yet fully grown. They kept a close watch on us while they set down our trenchers and the rest of our meal.

"Look," the older one said, "she even has the queen's marque." He pointed at my forehead.

"The marque is fake," I said in a sultry whisper only he and his brother could hear, looking up at then through my eyelashes. "This man told me he wanted to be with the queen, so I've done my best to fulfill his wish."

I curled myself around Lancelot, hip touching him suggestively, one arm around him while running my other hand inside the collar of his shirt and playing with his chest hair. I expected the surprised look on his face, but I wasn't prepared for the shock of pleasure that ran up my arm from my fingertips. I did my best to recover by aiming the smoldering I felt Lancelot's way.

"If you say I'm the queen, I am the queen," I purred. "As long as the price is right, I'll be whoever you want me to be."

When I looked back at the boys, both of their mouths were hanging open.

I fixed them with a longing stare, dropping my voice once again. "Are you boys interested in tomorrow night?"

They both stuttered, their words incomprehensible.

The older one recovered first. "But the marque—if it's not real, how did you get it?"

"Like this." I brought my thumb to my lips and licked it seductively, sucking just enough to hold their attention. I brought it to my forehead and down in an arc. The "ink" of my tattoo smeared just as I'd hoped it would. Thank the gods for juniper berry juice.

"Oh." The younger boy sounded disappointed. "Well then, we'll leave you to your meal."

"But I may be back around later to ask about your price," the older added quietly.

I winked at him.

As soon as they were lost in the crowd, I breathed a sigh of relief.

"You know you're going to have to keep up the ruse of being a whore for the rest of the evening, right?"

I gave Lancelot a lingering sidelong glance. "Does that make you uncomfortable, my noble knight?" I couldn't be sure if it was the play of the light from the fire pits or if he blushed.

Before I had a chance to tuck in to my meal, the innkeeper returned. "Your room will be ready shortly, sir."

From somewhere above, a racket rose above the din. It sounded like a herd of bulls were running through the upstairs rooms. A few moments later, the barkeep's sons emerged, each carrying one end of an unruly minor noble. The younger had him under the arms and his brother was fending off kicking feet.

"I will not be treated in this manner. I am a descendant of a Damnonii chieftain as well as a Roman general. I will not stand for this."

"No, but you'll lie down for it," someone in the crowd yelled, garnering raucous laughter.

"If you have a problem with our treatment of you, take it up with the member of the Combrogi who is in our midst."

Lancelot waved at the indignant upstart. He leaned over to me. "Sometimes I'm so glad I accepted this position."

"But not when a crazed noble's half sister is aiming a sword at your gut."

"You jest. That is the best part."

I found myself unable to look away from his smile. Even with the bruises discoloring his right eye and the cut across his other cheek, his looks and charm were enough to make any woman melt. I tore into the hunk of meat in front of me and continued to watch him. "You're enjoying yourself, aren't you?"

He swallowed a mouthful of food. "It's not often I get to spend the evening with a woman of questionable virtue."

"Then you must not spend much time at court."

He laughed. "Point taken."

We finished the rest of our meal while making idle conversation with the patrons around us. A toothless old woman was trying to keep up, but her poor hearing made her repeat nearly every word.

"Cadbury, did you say? Have you met the king's new wife?" she asked a rugged, road-weary man who appeared to be a merchant of some sort. "They say she's a beauty, striking as one of the fey."

My heart froze.

"No. She did not accompany him into town."

The woman's reply was lost in the din of voices.

I grabbed Lancelot's hand to get his attention. "What did she mean 'the king's new wife'? Surely the old crone was mistaken."

Lancelot's face clouded. "I wish she were. This is something best discussed in private. Follow me, and don't forget your role."

"Oh, I haven't," I said, sliding a hand around his waist as he rose. I was surprised at how comfortable I was playing the harlot with him.

Lancelot tossed a handful of coins to the innkeeper as we passed. He acknowledged the largess with a nod to Lancelot and a knowing grin at me. I smiled back and slid my hand down to Lancelot's backside as we ascended the stairs. A few muted hoots floated up from the more observant patrons.

I collapsed on the bed almost immediately once we were alone, exhausted from keeping up the pretense and hollow from the possibility of Arthur's betrayal. New wife? What could that possibly mean? I glanced at Lancelot, both hoping and dreading he would pick up the thread of our conversation, but he was busy rummaging in our bag for the supplies he'd need to clean his leg.

I stood and busied myself by fetching a ewer of water and a basin, which I placed on the floor next to him. I curled up on his other side, tucking my legs into my skirt and hugging them. A cold weight had settled in my chest, like at the onset of catarrh, but this was no illness. It was the weight of betrayal.

"The old woman wasn't wrong," Lancelot said in low voice, as if loath to speak the words. He peeled back his bandage as he continued. "After six moons of searching with only your golden comb to tell us you were taken via the main road into town, the other lords and some of the Combrogi were ready to declare you dead. Arthur did not wish to give up the search, but in the face of your disappearance and the arguments that even if you did return, you would not bear him any heirs, he invoked the ancient laws allowing him to take a second wife. She has no title beyond royal wife and will never be equal to you in stature, but she has already brought him one son, sired before you and he were wed."

I turned around so quickly the stitches in my shoulder pulled. I grimaced. "How does he—how does anyone know the child is his?"

Lancelot chuckled darkly. "One look at him and there is no denying his paternity."

Kneeling, I took the pot of salve from Lancelot, suddenly needing to occupy my hands. "Arthur did mention having another life planned before he became king." My hands trembled as I spread the thick ointment on his thigh. "I suppose now he has everything he ever wanted." Despite my best efforts to breathe and appear calm, my voice betrayed me, shaking with every word.

Lancelot stopped me by placing a hand on mine, which was perilously close to his manhood. "You do not need to continue to act the part here. Not when it is only us. Unless"—his voice grew husky—"unless you wish to do so."

I looked up at him, realizing only then how my hands had transgressed. For a moment, I considered his offer but quickly rejected it. It would be a long time before I could lie with a man after what Malegant had done. Besides, I would not betray Arthur even if he had done so to me.

Laughter bubbled out of me from some deep, hidden place, quickly turning to sobs as the full weight of what Lancelot had said hit me. I laid my head on his knees and wept. With one hand, he stroked my hair as I cried; with the other, he finished bandaging his wound. As soon as he was finished, he slipped an arm under my knees and carried me to the bed.

I clung to him, feeling awash and adrift. He was the rock keeping me from drowning in the darkness. When finally no more tears would come, I curled up in a ball within the warmth of his arms.

"What am I now?" I asked in a voice that sounded small and fragile even to my own ears.

He brushed a stray lock of hair from my face. "You are who you've always been—our queen. She is nothing to you."

"But he has pledged himself to me. What of that?"

"So have I. No matter what, I will not leave you." Lancelot kissed me gently on the forehead, as a mother does her child. It was oddly reassuring. "I cannot lessen the sting of betrayal you must feel, but know this: no one—and I mean no one—will deny you your true role now that you are safe. If they do, they will have to face me."

I smiled into his chest, mood lightened by degrees despite the overwhelming heaviness threatening to engulf me. This man had not only rescued me from my tormentor and defended my life, now he was promising to help me through a terrible transition back to my life with Arthur. Merlin's fears be damned. Choosing Lancelot as my champion was the wisest thing I had ever done.

ଊୄ ୄଊ

The sun was setting two nights later when we approached Cadbury. The fortress could be seen from a long way off, silhouetted against a red sky. After six months of fearing I'd never see home again, I practically ran toward the gatehouse, heedless of the steep climb up the terraced side of the hill. At some point my energy would give out and I would collapse, that much was certain, but right now, all I wanted was to be within its sheltering walls and see Arthur again.

Lancelot struggled to keep pace with me as we ascended the hill. "Guinevere, slow down. You will injure yourself even more."

"I don't care. I'm home. I'm free. It's over!"

"There is one thing you should know before—"

Lancelot never got to finish his sentence. The guards in the towers spotted us and raised the cry, "Lancelot has returned with the queen."

Soon the cry was taken up by the other guards and the townspeople. Before we knew it, we were being ushered inside on a wave of people, some of whom I recognized, others who were strangers, but all were equally joyful. I smiled and waved to them all, so relived to be home, to be safe.

"Make way for the queen," they cried one after another until the doors of the great hall opened.

I was prepared to run into Arthur's arms, but what I saw stopped me cold. Morgan stood next to Arthur, her sly, catlike smile in full effect. Her hands rested on the shoulders of a boy of about four years who was watching me curiously. Arthur was sitting in his usual place, an uncomfortable expression on his face.

"Morgan—I—you are the last person I expected to welcome me home." My voice sounded false even to my own ears.

"Welcome to *our* home," she corrected, looking up at Arthur with affection.

It took me a moment to process this. Morgan was in the place of the queen—in my place. What had Lancelot said? Arthur had married someone he'd known before he met me. But that woman couldn't possibly be Morgan. She had been in Avalon—at least until the incident with the poison. . . then I remembered the vision I'd had as I looked into Merlin's eyes at Corbenic when he told me of Morgan's fate. It was this exact scene. Morgan had been standing with her hand on her son's—their son's—shoulder.

Arthur finally stood, arms outstretched, and came to meet me. "Guinevere! The gods be praised. I thought we would never see you again."

As he embraced me, I was wooden, unable to return his affection in such an odd situation.

It was Morgan who finally drew us apart. "Nor did I." Her voice was tinged with regret. "We are blessed beyond measure. Is not that right, husband?"

Years of living with her had attuned me to the subtle sarcasm Arthur probably missed. Her use of the word husband, the one which should have been rightfully only mine, stunned me more than if she had delivered a swift blow to my head. Suddenly, it all made sense. He had married Morgan. He had known her before, perhaps during the time she went missing after her banishment from Avalon.

I looked at the boy. It was as Lancelot had said. No one who saw him could deny he was a younger version of the king right down to that particular shade of straw-blond hair and the cleft in his chin. He had Morgan's bright blue eyes, watchful and unnerving. He smiled at me innocently.

My heart and mind shattered. Here in front of me was the life I had always wished to live. Arthur with his heir, a handsome boy who favored him so strongly, but the woman playing the role of wife and mother was my worst enemy. Suddenly I recalled the day in Argante's hut when she had quizzed Morgan and me on elements of the law. *A man takes a second wife*, she had said. She'd known even back then when we were merely girls this day would come to pass. The world tilted. I grabbed Lancelot for support to steady myself.

"Guinevere?" Arthur asked, holding out a hand to me. "Are you unwell?"

I stepped back and began to cry uncontrollably, rage tinting the edges of my vision red. "How dare you ask me that? You have no idea what misery I have felt! Now I return to find you married to *her*."

"Calm down," Arthur said. "I can explain. I did not know about Mordred"—he indicated the boy—"but Morgan was pregnant before you and I wed."

My whole body was shaking. "Of course. If you had known, you wouldn't have married me." It was a statement, not a question.

In a flash, the sight showed me an alternate life, one in which I thought I was marrying Aggrivane but was given to Malegant instead. One in which Morgan was queen and I lived the life of a slave only to die at Malegant's hand. When my sight cleared, I looked at the family in front of me.

I wheeled on Morgan. "I suppose I am to be grateful to you for consoling my husband in my absence or for saving me from my captor, the murderer who was to be my husband."

Morgan looked at Arthur, forehead wrinkled. "I do not understand what she is saying. Do you?"

Arthur shook his head and took my hand. "You have had a great shock. Perhaps you should lie down, then we can discuss this."

My heartbeat quickened into a deafening pounding, and my eyes clouded over with black and white spots as anger overtook me. "No. I do not want to lie down or be calm." I jerked my hand out of his grasp. "I want to hear you say it, Arthur Pendragon! *I* am your wife, not her. You chose me, remember?"

Arthur regarded me warily, as if I were a beast about to strike. "Yes, you are my wife. But so is Morgan now. I assure you we can sort this all out later."

"I don't want to talk about it later." I flexed my fingers, itching to attack. "You!" I yelled at Morgan. "You are nothing but a manipulative, backstabbing whore. You always do what you can to ruin my happiness. I will kill you for this."

I lunged at her and knocked her to the ground, intent on tearing at her eyes. Morgan fought me, but she was no match for a woman who had been tormented as I had. I was about to punch her in the face when Lancelot pulled me off and wrenched my arms behind me.

Arthur helped a stunned, bleeding Morgan to her feet. "What has happened to make her this way?" he asked Lancelot. "This is not the woman I married."

"She has been through a great deal—" Lancelot began.

"I am your wife," I yelled amid hiccupping tears. "Do not speak of me as though I am not here in front of you. You wish to know what has happened to me? I will tell you. I was kidnapped, raped repeatedly, and beaten nearly to death by one of your men while you faithlessly took this woman to your bed. Lancelot and Sobian saved me. But now I see I may have been better off dying at Malegant's hand."

I wrenched free of Lancelot's grip to scratch wildly at my own skin, which suddenly pricked painfully. I fell to my knees as my sight clouded with memories of Malegant, and my time in his tower mingled with Morgan's triumphant expression at Arthur's side. I held my head and screamed. It was all too much.

From somewhere far away, Arthur called for Grainne and ordered her to take me to Avalon—now.

As Lancelot dragged me from the room, I looked at Arthur through strands of wild, tangled hair. "What did I do to deserve this?" My voice was small now, all the fight gone out of me.

"Nothing," he answered, concerned.

"And everything," Morgan added.

The last thing I remembered was hearing Mordred ask in a small, scared voice, "What is wrong with that lady?"

"She is ill," Arthur answered kindly.

"She is a madwoman," Morgan clarified.

When the darkness came, I welcomed it.

PART THREE

Outlier

Chapter Thirteen

Summer 501

When I opened my eyes, I was in my old priestess's chambers in Avalon. Around me, grayish stone walls gleamed in the summer sunlight. I blinked, taking in the room that was both familiar and foreign. Little had changed even though dozens of women must have called this room home since I was last here. A tall wardrobe stood open against one wall, a handful of blue robes and cloaks visible on pegs inside. A small table with a jug and wash basin, mirror, and comb was on one side of the bed, another table with a tray of bread and a steaming cup of tea on the opposite side.

Warm, sweet breezes wafted in from the eastern window through which I could see the holy Tor, but I had no desire to be out in them. I pulled the fur blanket closer, seeking warmth I feared I would never feel again. I was still shaking, my mind racing with hundreds of terrible thoughts. What if Arthur didn't accept me back at court? Was that the real reason I was here? Would I never return home? What if Morgan was right and I was a mad-woman? Would the whole of Britain come to hate me? I curled up in a ball, trying to fight the sensation that my skin was peeling off, that some feral version of me was slowly emerging from it, red and raw and wounded beyond repair.

The only memories I had of the journey were fragmented. The rocking of a cart, Imogen's kind touch reassuring me every-thing would be well, the bitter taste of some brew I now knew to be drugged, and the darkness of a mind that could take no more pain.

I lay in bed, breathing deeply for a long time, willing the shards of my mind to coalesce, but the harder I tried, the more they fractured.

"You should have stayed with me," Malegant's voice said. "I could have spared you all this."

I sat up, looking around, but I was alone. Malegant and Aine were dead, but they were haunting me, their voices the only dis-ruptions in my waking nightmare.

"You caused this," I said quietly, answering the imaginary voice.

"We did not," Aine responded. "Where is your husband, your mate, your support? Is he not supposed to see you through times like this?"

"Stop!" I yelled, tears springing from my eyes yet again. "Leave me alone!" I pulled at my hair, trying to get the voices to quiet.

Viviane appeared in the doorway, pausing before rushing to my side. "Guinevere, be still. Be at peace. You are in Avalon. You're safe." She sat next to me on the bed, one arm wrapped pro-tectively around me.

"No, I am not. I will never be whole again," I sobbed.

She let me cry and rocked me like a babe, stroking my hair and cooing softly. "May the Lady grant you peace. May she bring you all the love your heart needs, and may you heal in time."

Once my tears dried up, she helped me drink the tea. Normally I would have fought the effects of the herbs, but today I embraced them. Rather than making my eyelids heavy as I'd expected, they washed over me like an ocean wave, leaving an eerie feeling of peace in their wake. I felt like myself again if only for a short time.

ഐ ഐ

After a few days of the herbs, the voices faded and the shaking stopped. I still felt raw, as if I was walking around without my skin, but at least I could get out of bed. The pain and betrayal were still there, but my mind was clearer now. I could think about my situation more rationally. Grainne took on the role of my personal attendant, and I was grateful for her constant presence.

We were walking through the flourishing herb garden one morning when I asked her, "Do you think Arthur hates me?"

She smiled at me, her golden hair catching the sun. "No. I think you surprised him. He really never thought he'd see you again—even after Imogen showed him your ring and offered him a small shred of hope. Then you showed up like an avenging ghost, all vitriol and fury. They grieved for you, mourned for you, truly." She took my hand. "Lancelot, too. Just when our lives were beginning to feel normal, you came back. It will take time for everyone to adjust."

I stopped and pulled a weed from between two stems of bright green lovage. "He didn't even wait a full year, Grainne."

"He didn't have to," she said gently. "Under the law, he could have married Morgan at any time, but he never thought her worthy of being the king's wife—she was an orphan, after all. But when you were thought dead, Morgan told him the truth about Mordred."

We stopped on the porch to Viviane's rooms. "But how did he know her? That is one thing I cannot understand."

"That is a conversation you should have with Viviane, not me. She has answers beyond my ken. I only know what Morgan told the rest of court, and that I have relayed to you."

I hugged her. "Thank you for your constant support and friendship."

She smiled at me. "From your first moment in Avalon to our last breath. You know that."

I knocked on Viviane's door as Grainne meandered off to help the others, who were preparing the island for midsummer. Unlike Argante, who as Lady of the Lake had lived in a crude hut fashioned from saplings much like Diarmad's home, Viviane retained the stone quarters she had occupied as Argante's second. These days, that role was filled by her daughter, Ailis, the girl I had rescued from peril in a tree many years before.

I was expecting Ailis to answer the door, but when it opened, I found myself looking at Nimue, the daughter of my maid, Octavia. Nimue had been sent here to escape my father's wrath five years earlier, and though she was only eleven, she was tall and thin, her haunting green eyes betraying an intelligence far beyond her years. "Guinevere, come in."

I watched her as I made my way inside. She was dark haired like her mother but had the pale skin of her father. I had no doubt that beneath the placid surface she so carefully cultivated bubbled the temper she had displayed upon being told she was to leave her mother's home. I looked forward to getting to know her better while I was here. I leaned down so Viviane could embrace me.

"Welcome, daughter." She gestured for me to sit in a wicker chair across from her. "Nimue, you may go."

The girl gave a slight curtsey before bouncing off.

"She shows exceptional promise. Ailis and I have been giving her special lessons. She craves knowledge like no one I've ever known," Viviane explained as she poured hot water into two cups and added different herbs to each one. "But enough about Nimue. How are you today?"

"I am feeling better, thank you." I studied her face, the same blue eyes that had first captivated me when she came to Northgallis after I started showing signs of the sight. They were framed by a few more wrinkles now, but they were no less kind. Her brown hair was pulled back in a complicated knot that left only the locks in the very back trailing down to her waist. She had been Lady of the Lake for many years now, but I would never get used to seeing the triple moon symbol of the high priestess on her brow.

"What troubles you?" She had been studying me too and clearly saw in my expression something she didn't like.

I cleared my throat, trying to summon the courage to ask her the same question I had posed to Grainne. But this was more difficult for I knew Viviane would give me an honest answer. I had to be certain I was prepared to hear what she had to say.

I took several sips of tea and waited for the numbing warmth to flow through my veins before I spoke. "Viviane, I need to know. How did Arthur and Morgan know one another?" I bowed my head and stared deep into my cup as though I could divine the answer from the leaves within.

"You are in an awful hurry to have answers," Viviane noted. "Would it not be better to heal from the abuse you've suffered then face the changes in your home?"

I shook my head. "I want to know it all. That way I can piece it together in my own time."

"You have always been a headstrong girl." Viviane took a deep breath. "Do you remember when the Kingmaker appeared in the sky? Merlin told us it meant a great king would soon assume power. That king was Arthur. He was the Sacred King." She watched me, waiting for her words to sink in.

When they did, it was like a punch in the gut. I stared at Viviane, unbelieving. "You knew all along. You knew and never told me. Do the manipulations of Avalon run so deep?"

I never saw Viviane lash out, but suddenly, there was a crack and my left cheek stung.

"I may be your friend, Guinevere, but I am still Lady of the Lake." Viviane's tone was stern with warning like a disapproving mother's. "I deserve your respect, as does this sacred place. As you well know, Avalon does not mettle in the affairs of kingdoms or people. We joined together whom the gods indicated, and their will took its course. If you wish to be mad at someone, let it be your husband or Morgan. It was not I who betrayed your trust."

Chided, I sank back in my chair, weighing her words. She was right. What was more, Merlin had tried to tell me. Years ago, at Corbenic, he'd told me I had seen the king in Avalon, but

I couldn't wrest the memory from my mind. Maybe some part of me had known all along and was just unwilling to admit it. Because if Arthur was the Sacred King. . . "Morgan was the Virgin Queen. That is how they met."

"Yes." Viviane examined her own cup.

I went through the course of events in my memory. "But Morgan was not with child after Beltane. When was Mordred conceived?"

Viviane looked up. "You should really discuss this with your husband. He can tell you from experience. I can only relate hearsay."

I stood. "I don't care if what you know is third- or fourth-hand. I only want to know the truth."

"Guinevere, sit. I do not appreciate your tone."

I genuflected before her, touching my thumb to my forehead, lips, and heart. "Forgive me, Lady. I forgot my place."

She lifted my chin with her hand and bid me rise. Once I was seated again, she reluctantly continued. "From what we can tell, they reunited after Morgan was banished from the isle. I'm sure you know about that?"

"Yes. Merlin told me."

"The reason we couldn't find her is that she was following Uther's army. Somehow, she had gotten wind that Arthur was a soldier and went in search of him. From what I can tell, once they found each other, they were inseparable. Until—"

"Until Uriens directed Arthur's attention my way," I finished for her. I rubbed my fingers on either side of my nose. "So Arthur gets his first love as well as his queen, and I get nothing. That is fair."

Viviane stroked my leg. "The Goddess never promised to be fair. Only to lead you on the path she sees fit."

"Apparently she plays favorites," I grumbled.

"Perhaps, but she sees the world in its totality. We only see our small part of it." Viviane glanced outside, and I followed her gaze to where Imogen was happily weeding in the garden, speaking in Ogham with the soon-to-be-consecrated girls. "Take Imogen, for example. She has lived a life of power and pain no one here could have predicted. Yet the Goddess chose you to bring her back to us, to give her a few years of happiness in this life. Compared to her, you are the favored one."

I stared into my nearly empty cup, aware Viviane was watching me.

"How would you like to take up your life of priestesshood again?" she asked. "It will help you heal."

I nodded. "It would be good to have a purpose while I'm here."

"Good. You can begin by assisting me at the sunset ritual tonight. Tomorrow you can help Imogen with the gardens and perhaps sit in on a lesson. You remember the schedule?"

"Yes. My time here will be part of me always. Thank you, Viviane, for giving me a second chance. I doubt few others would."

Viviane placed a hand on mine. "We all have need of mercy, including Arthur and Morgan. You would do well to remember that."

☙❧

Viviane was right. The physical labor did me good, as much, I daresay, as the rhythm of morning and evening ritual. Weeks passed, then months, and my physical wounds healed, yet I found I could not let go of my spiritual demons. Anger, pain, and resentment haunted me, a trinity of oppression I battled every day. I disarmed them by evening only to awaken to them freshly formed in the morning.

As I worked, turning the earth, planting seeds, and tending to growing sprouts, I had much time to think. Merlin had informed me about Morgan at Corbenic, but I was too thick to heed his cautions. He told me the Goddess had warned about division between sisters, and what did I do? Physically attack one of my own. Had Morgan not already been banished from Avalon, I likely would have suffered the same fate for attacking my sworn sister. But instead, I had been granted clemency.

That was what was on my mind as I approached Merlin and a group of young students one early autumn morning. He was seated on the stump of a fallen oak that had been sheared off by lightning during a recent storm, gesticulating grandly as he spun some tale that captivated the girls. They sat at his feet in the grass, some as young as ten, others much closer to legal womanhood. They looked up at him adoringly, lovesick expressions on each face.

As I approached, I heard the end of the story. "So Deirdre, foretold from birth to bring about so much destruction, took her own life by throwing herself out of a chariot and onto the rocks below."

"Her story is so sad," lamented one girl.

"But so romantic," crooned another.

"Too bad she wasn't a priestess. She could have made that terrible Conchobar leave her alone," added a third.

Merlin smiled and nodded in acknowledgement when he caught sight of me, then he returned his attention to the students. "Nimue, what do you think?"

"I feel sorry for her. When she finally finds happiness, Conchobar has to come along and ruin it—to the point where she kills herself rather than face her fate. It's not fair."

Merlin leaned toward her. "No, it is not. But Deirdre isn't all to be pitied. Remember, she manipulated Naoise into eloping with her. If she hadn't interfered, the tragic events would not have happened."

"Is this your way of telling us to mind our own business?" Nimue asked tartly. "Because I doubt that will happen around here."

The girls giggled.

Merlin chuckled, spreading his arms wide. "All right, that is enough for today. You may go."

Some of the girls cheered and scampered away while others hung around in groups, sneaking shy looks at Merlin when they thought he wasn't watching. Nimue hung back, waiting to catch Merlin's attention. I couldn't hear what she said to him, but her adoration was plain. She only stopped talking when another girl elbowed her aside, complaining loudly that Nimue had taken up enough of Merlin's time.

I shook my head. That easily could have been Morgan and me. Some things never changed.

When the girls finally straggled away, I greeted Merlin with a small bow. "She's sweet on you, you know."

Merlin smiled as he watched Nimue walk away. "I do. Jealous too. I daresay poor Branwen will pay for her boldness."

"Merlin, I know it has been many years since you were my teacher, but do you think you could indulge me in one more lesson?"

"Of course. What do you wish to know?" He took me gently by the elbow and led me down to the lake where we could walk among the reeds and grasses as we talked.

"How do you ward against jealousy?"

He smiled, running a hand through his now-short hair, which was still bright orange in the soft light despite a sprinkling of silver. "That is the age-old question, is it not? I assume you speak of Morgan."

I nodded. "I have dealt with my painful memories and am beginning to recover from Malegant's abuse, but in all of my time here, I have yet to find a way to let go of my blinding hatred toward Morgan and Arthur or at least get control of it."

"It is the undoing of many a life, many a nation, and something even I have not yet mastered." Merlin stopped, turning to face me. "If I may be frank, you have always been selfish, Guinevere."

I glowered at him, not wanting to hear this speech yet again.

"You are a woman now, not a child. You must learn that even though you are queen, many things do not concern you at all. When you return to your husband, try to remember he did not intend to hurt you. In fact, his actions were not about you. He was thinking of the future of the realm and of his own heart. What would you have done in his place? Would you have waited for him if you believed him dead and knew Aggrivane could be yours? Be honest."

I studied his eyes for a long time, mulling over the question. "No."

"Then how can you ask the same of him?"

I looked away, defeated. He was right. I was being completely unreasonable. "But it is *Morgan*," I whined, hanging on him as I had as a child.

He laughed. "I would have been disappointed if that wasn't your response." He placed a gentle hand on my shoulder. "I know the two of you have a natural dislike of one another. It is only because you are so much alike." I started to object, but he silenced me with a look. "You will learn to live together because you must. But it will take time. You will need to look beyond your personal feelings and learn to sacrifice for the good of those you love. That is the true measure of a queen."

Chapter Fourteen

Winter 502

rthur was alone when I found him upon my return to Camelot. I needed to see him, but I was not yet ready to face Morgan. He was sitting in the circular meeting room overlooking the city and staring out the window. He appeared so deep in thought he did not hear me enter.

"Arthur."

It took him a moment to respond, and when he did, he was like one waking from a dream. Slowly, he turned, and a smile like dawn broke on his face. He stood, hurrying to embrace me.

This was the reception I had expected and so badly needed when I first returned to him in Cadbury. I let myself melt into his arms, remembering how safe and secure I had felt there before everything changed. I would not think of Morgan, only of him. Repair my relationship with my husband first, then worry about her.

"Guinevere." He breathed my name the way he had on our wedding night. "It is so good to have you back."

He held me at arm's length, looking me over as though searching for any outward signs I had changed, for anything that might still betoken the crazed woman who had entered his court six moons earlier. My bruises, cuts, and broken bones had healed of course, but if he could have seen within my heart, he would have beheld the interweaving scars and stitches threatening to burst at the slightest tug. Arthur gestured for me to sit with him, which I did, unsure of how to speak with him now.

"Lancelot has told me everything. You need not ever speak of it. If that bastard who hurt you wasn't already dead, I'd kill him myself." He clenched his fist in frustration that he could not avenge me. Then he asked, "How are you?" His sapphire eyes were full of concern.

I dropped my eyes to my lap. "I am better. Thank you. It is . . . strange . . . being back here again with everything so different." I looked at him, wondering if he would acknowledge the living ghost who would forever haunt our love.

"Guinevere," he whispered, shaking his head. "I owe you so much, an explanation words cannot begin to express." He looked down, unable to meet my gaze.

"Why, Arthur? Can we start there?"

When he finally met my gaze, his eyes were shining with unshed tears. "I thought you were dead. No one could find you. We searched everywhere—every fortress, every cave, every seaport—and there was not even a trace. I had my suspicions your disappearance was somehow linked to Malegant—"

I flinched at his name.

"But we couldn't find him, much less connect him to a crime we couldn't prove had been committed. There were whispers you could have abandoned me for another man, gone back to Avalon, or worse, taken your own life."

I gaped at the foolishness of those ideas, and Arthur put a hand on mine.

"You must believe I paid no heed to any of this. But I will not lie to you. As time went on, my hope dimmed. Then those in my council began to speak of remarriage. I didn't think it right, but even the priests said that given the circumstances, God would understand if I wed another."

I was silent for a moment, wondering when Arthur, a devotee of Mithras, had started listening to Christian priests. "What now then? Surely you will not stay married to both of us?" I laced my hands together in my lap to conceal their shaking.

Arthur would not meet my eyes. "Many others have already asked me the same, and Morgan has requested I divorce you. But I will not do it. You are queen. That is an honor that cannot be conferred onto more than one woman at a time, and you have done nothing to cause me to revoke it. The people would be outraged if I put you away."

"Oh, I'm glad to know the people would be upset because you certainly don't look as though you would be."

Arthur shot me a contemptuous look.

I couldn't fight my frustration any longer. "Why can you not divorce *her*? Why must it be me? After all, as you pointed out, I was married to you first, and I am queen." I sounded like a petulant child, but I didn't care. He had to understand how ridiculous this whole situation was.

"Morgan has brought me a son, a child I never expected. I cannot ignore that."

Pain twisted my heart. Yet again I was being condemned because my children had died and I could bear no more despite my best efforts to encourage life within my womb. Would I ever escape that horrid curse? I swallowed hard, summoning the courage to ask a question I had to voice yet dreaded hearing the answer. "Forget everyone else. What does your heart tell you?"

Arthur's gaze pierced my very soul. "I love you both. I know it isn't what you want to hear, but it is the truth. When I met Morgan in Avalon, she was the Goddess, and I never thought to see her again. I had almost forgotten her when she appeared in camp and told me she had given up everything to be with me. From that moment on, I was hers."

Arthur stood and made a slow circuit of the room as he spoke. "If Uther hadn't died, if I had remained simply Lord Ector's son, we would have wed—and quite happily. No one looks into the lineage of a soldier's wife. But then I found out I was no mere soldier but the son of the high king, and everything changed. From being free to marry her, I was now forbidden—all because she couldn't tell me the names of her kin." He shook his head. "It tore my heart in two to know we would never be together."

He stopped in front of me and bent so we were at eye level. "Now, as things have changed and I am free to be with the one I love, I understand what I did to you when I asked you to marry me, that I put you in much the same tragic circumstance, and for that I am sorry. I would not wish such agony on a Saxon."

I smiled at him because it was the right thing, the polite thing, to do, but I was certain it didn't reach my eyes.

"I couldn't leave Morgan to the wiles of fate, so when Uriens expressed interest in her, I realized his would be a safe household for her to be in, one where I could be sure she would not be ill-treated."

"And one that afforded her frequent visits to court."

"Yes, that too." Arthur sounded guilty.

"So where does that leave us?"

Arthur did not answer. Whether he had none or simply chose not to respond, his silence unnerved me more than if he had yelled. The familiar panic I had felt since leaving Malegant's tower was returning, coiling around my heart. If it squeezed tight, I would lose my composure again.

I stood, seeking air at one of the windows. My eyes fell on the statues surrounding us. In my absence, the stone images depicting Arthur and me as high king and high queen had been installed. "Will she have her own statue too? What a great legacy for future generations. 'Look at King Arthur and his brood of wives,' they'll say. 'He really must have been someone grand.'"

Arthur stood too. "Guinevere, please don't be this way."

"What way is that? Hurt? Outraged? Indignant? How would you have me react?" I ran a fluttering hand through my hair. "Think about how you would have felt if the situation were reversed. What if you had been captured in war with the Saxons, brutally abused, then managed to escape only to return home to find me married to Aggrivane?"

Arthur's jaw tensed, but he said nothing.

"That is how I felt seeing you with Morgan. What's worse is she has given you the one thing I never will—a son. And she can continue providing you heirs. So as much as you may contend that I am and always will be queen, I know she means more to you for that alone."

Arthur seized my shoulders hard. "You are my wife, and I still love you. But Morgan is my wife too, and I love her as well. This is how things are. Unless you wish to divorce me and forfeit your power as queen, you will both have to find a way to accept it." There was no malice in his words, just the starkness of truth.

So this was my new world. Little more than a year ago, we had been celebrating Arthur's latest victory over the Saxons. We had been happy. Now I had to share my life—though it was not of my own choosing, I had fought so hard to build and sustain this life—with the one person I hated more than all others. When would the Goddess stop testing me?

꧁ ꧂

Living with Morgan meant more than simply vying for Arthur's attention. The servants, especially the newer ones, had grown used to answering to Morgan while I was away, and they were uncertain which one of us now held sway. Some made their loyalty clear. Octavia and Sobian, who was still acting the role of my maid, would never take orders from Morgan again, while another small cadre of women were devoted to Morgan. Though their words showed they understood I was queen, their actions proclaimed Morgan their mistress. When we appealed to Arthur, each wishing to have him side with us, he held up his hands and told us to work it out without him, locking us in his study until we came to an agreement.

Glaring at one another across the table, we tried to find a compromise.

Morgan was quick to try to preserve her newfound power. "I

have been running this household for more than a year, Guinevere. Why can you not simply let things be?"

I snorted, pacing the length of the small room. "Would you
have allowed me to walk into your home with Uriens and take
over without a fight? I think not. You have little experience in running a house this large. I have been doing so for five years."

"Four. You were away for the last year, remember?" She
arched an eyebrow and took on an imperious tone. "Your time is
mostly spent in matters of judgment and diplomacy. The best you
can hope for is to employ talented stewards and maids to oversee
things for you. You should leave the household matters to me. I
have the time to personally oversee such things."

I settled myself on the corner of the table and looked down
my nose at her. "What then do you propose would be my duties?"

"Besides being a thorn in my side?"

"I could say the same about you."

"You would oversee your own personal maids, of course,"
Morgan drawled as though she were doing me a favor. She was
quiet for a moment, then she sat up as though she had an idea.
"You could handle the guests and their servants as well."

Though I was not happy with that being my only area of
power among our hundreds of servants, Morgan was trying, and
she had a point about the time I spent with Arthur in my role as
queen. "Fine, let's start there."

By spring, however, it became apparent that while Morgan
was excellent at getting the servants to do as she pleased and
ensuring the quality of their work, she was ill-equipped for the
record-keeping and handling of finances that came with being
in charge of so many people, especially on a feasting schedule as

unpredictable as Camelot's. So we found ourselves back in that same small room negotiating our duties once again.

"Camelot will be broke before the end of summer with you running things." I glanced over a list of supplies and costs for the previous month the head kitchen maid had provided to me. "Though I daresay the merchants will miss you. Who pays this much for oysters? We live on a bay. They should be nearly free, especially to the king. And where are you importing our wine from—Rome? This bill is unacceptable. Gaul gives us a much better rate, and the product is fresh, unlike the bottle of vinegar we served to the Breton ambassador last week."

"You wish to be in charge of the finances? Take them." Morgan spat the words but was unable to completely mask the relief in her voice. "But then let me oversee provisions for our guests. At the moment, their poor maids know not who to listen to for you tell them one thing while I have trained our staff for another, so they get mixed messages. Lady Ettarre has written Arthur to express how shocked she was at the incompetence of our maids." She leveled me with an icy stare. "It's almost as though you are trying to make me look bad."

I rubbed my tired eyes then glared at her. "Yes, Morgan, you've found me out. Are you happy?" I snapped, voice heavily laced with sarcasm. "Do what you like. I have much bigger problems than whether or not Lord Pelles's wife is happy with the way her servants behave while they are here. The Saxons are threatening Bernicia and the Midlands again. Arthur is preparing for battles on both fronts. When *will* this war be over?" I sighed.

Our domestic squabbles at an end, at least for now—I had no doubt Morgan would continue to push the boundaries of her power as royal wife—I fell into bed, much in need of the surety I could find only in Arthur's arms. He held me for a while, but when he thought I was asleep, he carefully untangled himself from my arms and rose.

He was headed for Morgan's room—that was certain. I didn't bother to try to stop him. He had been playing this game for months now, sometimes even returning to our bed before dawn in the hopes I would think he'd never left. Did the fool really believe I couldn't feel the bed shift when relieved of his weight or hear the creak of the door when he returned?

When I'd first returned, Arthur patiently waited as I found my way back into his arms after Malegant's brutality. For a while, I'd believed I might serve as his wife in every way again. Once we were sharing a bed, it was as though nothing had changed. During those blessed weeks, under the cover of darkness, I was able to convince myself Morgan didn't exist. But then I woke in the middle of the night to find Arthur gone. That was when my ears became attuned to the signs of his departure.

Arthur still spent some nights with me, though they were decreasing steadily in number. I wondered if there was any logic to his choice of companion for the night or if he simply decided on a whim.

One night, I worked up the courage to question him about it. "Tell me, husband, how do you decide between me and Morgan each evening? It must be nice having your choice of women." Admittedly, that wasn't the kindest way of asking, but I wanted him to know I felt slighted by his actions.

Arthur paused in the middle of removing his tunic. For a long moment, he looked at me as though I was daft. "How can you ask me such a thing? It is my duty to act as husband to both of you." He stood and headed for the door. A few paces from it, he looked back over his shoulder. "You are fortunate I respect you, Guinevere. Most men would have beaten you for even inquiring."

So there it was. Our marriage had deteriorated to the point where my husband wanted to hit me for questioning his motives. That was a far cry from the affection and honesty of our early years together. I had gained nothing by my curiosity. In fact, I had practically driven him into Morgan's arms. Now I would never know his reasons. Maybe Morgan didn't ask such questions. Maybe she didn't challenge him at all. Whatever the truth, it was clear she had found a way to satisfy him that I would never match.

Chapter Fifteen

Summer 503

ord reached us of Pellinor's death on a stormy night just after Beltane. The weather prevented us from trying to arrive in time for the funerary rites, but despite all that had happened between us, I wanted to be there for Elaine as she mourned her father's passing. So as soon as the weather cleared and the roads were dry, Arthur, Kay, Lancelot, Sobian, Octavia, and I headed south to the kingdom of Dyfed and Caer Corbenic, where we had first met. As she did not know the family, Morgan remained behind at Camelot to oversee affairs in our absence.

But the pleasant weather was only a tease. For most of the trip, heavy rains hindered our progress, mucking up the horses' hooves and flinging mud onto cloaks and armor. We had to turn back several times when flood waters made the old Roman main roads impassable. The deluge had spotted the flat land with makeshift lakes and ruined entire tracks of grain and vegetables.

Occasionally we encountered the victims of nature's wrath: hollow-eyed children and starving men thin as rods. We did what we could to alleviate their suffering, but all the gold in the country would not be enough to repair these shattered lives.

The result of this detour was that we had to keep to the roads that hugged the Saxon border, land long ago conquered and settled by the northern invaders. Sometimes we even crossed over into their territory, putting us in much closer proximity to our enemy than any of us were comfortable being. Signs of their growing influence were everywhere, from their strange round huts to the harsh language spoken in the towns and pale faces with nearly white hair peering at us as we passed.

We were in grave danger if anyone recognized us, so we took precautions. We had stopped flying the royal standard of Pendragon several days prior and had stripped ourselves of all jewels. We sent our valuables on separately to Corbenic for safekeeping. Weapons were hidden with care, and we all dressed simply, hoping to appear as innocuous any other riding party. We simply wished to pass through in peace.

The sun was just beginning to slip below the horizon, coloring the dappled clouds a joyous mixture of peach and gold, when we arrived at a village near the convergence of the former kingdoms of Kent and Sussex. The areas were now one realm ruled through an alliance of two Saxon brothers, Alle and Octha, both kings who our spies told us were allied in dreams of a united Saxon empire. We considered trying to push on through the night to escape into less threatening territory, but it soon became clear both men and horses were exhausted.

We accepted the kindness of a local lord who took pity on our fatigued party and lodged us in the safety of his residence for the night. It was nothing like the fortifications we were used to, but his compound reminded me of my parents' descriptions of their childhood homes. The main building was a large rectangular structure of wood cemented with hardened mud and fortified by a ring of sharp spiked logs sunk into the ground with their points reaching skyward, mortally threatening anyone foolish enough to try to hurdle them. A second spine of points encircled the first and sheltered a set of less important buildings. As we passed through, I spied a storage area, blacksmith, stable, granary, and a handful of other necessities. A wooden gate with heavy iron hinges and a massive bar stood open at the south end of the wall, ready to admit citizens and travelers until nightfall.

Sobian and I had just settled onto our shabby pallets on the floor of the main room, near the central fire with the other women, when a disturbance outside put the servants on alert. Three of them spilled into the courtyard, and I could just make out the silhouette of a hooded woman in the torchlight outside. She was speaking excitedly in the guttural language I had heard as we passed through other towns, urgency apparent in her body language. The servants appeared at a loss to help her, but one slipped back inside and whispered to the lady of the house.

She glided over to us. "Our visitor seeks the services of a midwife. The woman who usually fills this role for us is old and gravely ill. Can any of you be of assistance? She says it is urgent."

I nodded. "I will help her. I have been well trained in the womanly arts."

Sobian made to stop me. "Your husband will never allow you to go unattended, and none of the men will go into the room with you." We had agreed not to refer to Arthur or me by our real names lest we be identified by our enemies. "I am coming with you."

I wanted to protest, but she was right. Delivering a child in danger by myself would be difficult, and I had no way of knowing how capable the Saxon woman would be of helping. "Then you may be my assistant."

We gathered supplies and followed the Saxon woman into the night, trailed by Kay as our guardian. As we moved away from the fortress, down a lonely road in the light of a half moon, I watched the Saxon's round hips swinging in time with the bounce of tight golden curls as she walked, back straight as an iron rod. She appeared to be acting as a maid, but her clothes were not the rags or simple homespun of most servants. I began to wonder what was going on.

She saw me watching her and pursed her full lips in annoyance. "No one knows we are here, and you will keep that secret," she commanded in heavily-accented broken English.

"Of course. May I know the woman's condition?"

"Waters flowed early morning, baby not come. She grows weary. I fear she will die." She fixed me in a piercing blue stare that left no room for argument. "That cannot happen."

"I give you my word as a priestess I will do all I can to keep her and the child alive," I swore, showing her the faint blue tattoo on my brow.

There was no cultural equivalent of my status in her world. She regarded me warily and nodded, but something in her expression told me she was not convinced.

The secluded hovel we approached stood out in sharp contrast to the fine clothing the Saxon woman wore. Even from the outside, I could tell it had only one room. Two tiny unglazed windows, a door, and a smoking chimney provided the only ventilation.

I pieced together the most likely scenario. This woman and likely the other who labored inside were obviously nobility. My best guess was the pregnant one had gotten herself with child by someone she should not have—a lover or perhaps the son of an enemy but certainly not her husband—and they had retreated here for the length of her confinement for her own safety. There was nothing around for miles, no neighbors to witness the woman's shame. It was not the first time such a thing had happened and certainly wouldn't be the last.

The woman's strangled cries reached me even before the brawny Saxon guard opened the door to admit us. He watched warily but backed off at a signal from the woman who had recruited us.

I stopped her before we crossed the threshold. "Wait. What is your name?"

Her body went rigid, and I knew she would not answer me.

"I must be able to call to you with instructions amid the chaos we will encounter inside, so please give me a name. It need not be your real one." I added with a wry smile, "Unless you would rather me call you 'girl.'"

My implied insult had the desired effect. The Saxon woman's face puckered in annoyance. "Udele," she said flatly as she swept through the doorway.

"I am Corinna," I lied, taking my mother's name. It was how everyone outside our party knew me on this journey.

A wave of heat hit me as soon as we entered the room. It was even tinier than it appeared from the outside. A fire blazed in a pit built into one wall, smoke struggling up the narrow chimney. Not four feet away, a small, pale woman who bore a striking resemblance to Udele writhed in her mean bed, two serving women alternating between trying to hold her down and trying to give her strength as the contractions rolled through her body.

Udele rushed over to one side of the bed and held the young woman's hand, speaking quietly to her in their native tongue. The intimacy of the moment confirmed my suspicion they were more than maid and mistress. From their resemblance, I guessed them to be sisters. Sobian set the towels, basin, and bottles of herbs we had brought with us on a small wooden table next to the bed, and I moved to the woman's feet to examine her. As I probed her belly and peered between her thighs, Udele called the girl Mayda, which I assumed had to be her real name. In her weakened, pain-crazed state, no woman would have been able to respond to a false name.

"Mayda," I called to the beautiful young girl in the bed, and Udele shot me a dirty look. I ignored her and continued. "Mayda, your body is ready, but your baby cannot be born as it is. I can try to turn it, but it will be painful for you."

Udele translated what I had said, and the sweat-soaked woman nodded weakly, saying something I did not understand.

"Do what you must," Udele barked.

My training in Avalon took over, and I lost all connection to what was going on around me as I manipulated her womb, inside and out. I was vaguely aware of Sobian at my side mopping up the blood streaming from between Mayda's thighs, Mayda's screams, and Udele's agitation as she tried to keep her sister calm, but they barely registered. All of my attention was focused on the stubborn babe who was determined not to be born. As the hours dragged on and Mayda's strength failed, it seemed increasingly likely she would die too. Finally, I was able to slip my hand around the baby and turn its head toward the birth canal.

I rinsed my arms in the basin and stroked Mayda's head. It was time for her to summon all her strength and push her child into the world. I didn't need to tell her, for now that the baby was in place, her body was eager to be rid of it. Mayda cried out as a spasm rippled through her belly.

Udele and I helped Mayda sit up, and she braced herself against the waiting arms of her servants. As she bore down, barely stopping to take a breath between pushes, the top of the baby's head came into view. Mayda screamed again, and I guided the child out, head, right shoulder, left, then the rest came easily in a rush of viscous fluid.

"You have a son," I told Mayda, and Udele translated.

Sobian took the child, still attached to his mother, and quickly cleaned him. He was a sickly shade of violet but needed no prodding to take his first breath. His throaty wail filled the house just as clearly as his mother's had. I breathed a sigh of relief and glanced at Mayda. She was crying but whether out of happiness, exhaustion, or something else, I did not know. Sobian wrapped the baby in a clean towel and placed him on the table.

"I know who they are," she whispered in my ear, followed by a quick explanation.

I had been trying to place why Mayda's name sounded familiar and understand why this elaborate ruse had been necessary. Sobian put the pieces together for me.

They were royal daughters in their society. The younger of the two southern Saxon rulers, Octha, was engaged to the younger sister of his brother's wife. Mayda's name had been mentioned as

Octha's betrothed in our spies' report, as had her sister's, because the union of these two royal families represented a formidable threat to our southeast kingdoms. Arthur would be quite interested to learn how I had chanced upon them under such unusual circumstances.

Once Mayda delivered the afterbirth, Udele picked up her dagger and made for the child, but I stopped her. "Burnish the blade in the fire first so the wound will not get infected," I instructed.

"Matters not," Udele muttered, but she did as I asked anyway.

I helped her cut the cord and turned to lay the now pink baby in his mother's arms, but Mayda was sleeping. "He will need to eat soon, so you will have to wake her."

Udele shrugged and held the gurgling, fidgeting boy as Sobian and I cleaned up. Mostly she regarded it with a look of disdain. I had a cursory knowledge of the language thanks to Arthur, and I thought I heard her tell the child it would have been better had he not been born. A shiver ran down my spine. I remembered Udele's quick move with the knife and wondered if she'd had a more sinister intent than to cut the cord.

When I looked at her, she was watching me intently. "Will she live?" she asked with a jerk of her head toward her sister.

I carefully examined Mayda, trying not to wake her. The blood had ceased flowing, and her body was quickly returning to normal with no signs of infection or complications. "Yes, but she will need much rest."

Udele nodded and gestured to one of the serving women, who handed me a heavy purse of coins. "For your trouble."

It would have been an insult not to accept, so I took the purse, thinking of how we could use the money to help the destitute citizens we encountered on the road, not to mention pay our host for his hospitality. But then another thought occurred to me. "Also for our silence?"

Udele's smile was wicked. "Of course. Now go, Queen Guinevere."

I raised my eyebrows. "You know who I am?"

She shrugged and gestured toward my forehead. "Was guess. Others with mark stay with farmers, not crowned men. They have no slaves." She cocked her head in Sobian's direction.

"Not many *Aethelings* bear their children in hovels," I countered, praying Sobian's theory was accurate.

Udele—or Elga, as she was truly called—nearly dropped the baby in surprise. "How you know?"

"When you said your sister's name, it triggered a memory," I said carefully, not wanting to reveal Sobian as my source of information, or worse, provoke Elga's wrath. All she needed to do was call her guard, and we would have a bloody fight on our hands. I pressed on before she had a chance to react. "Elga, I mean you no harm. It is in each of our best interests to keep what has transpired tonight a secret. I swear to you I will do so if you will promise the same."

I hoped she would listen to me, knowing we were at a dangerous impasse. On one hand, she knew who I was and where our whole party was staying. If she but breathed my name, we would all be dead before dawn, and her people would have free reign over the country. But on the other, I knew her and her secret. All I needed to do was let it slip to our host where they were housed, and both Octha and Alle would be on their doorstep before they could flee. The brothers would undoubtedly kill their wives, whose family would seek revenge, sparking civil war and weakening them to the point where our forces could overtake them if they weren't killed by their own.

Elga gulped, mouth still open. "Why you help if you knew who we are? We are enemies." Her tone betrayed she truly did not understand. Clearly, she would not have done the same if the roles were reversed.

"I have taken vows to harm no one without cause," I explained. "You gave me no provocation, only asked for my help. So I gave it."

"Now I am indebted to you," she said bitterly, more to herself than to me.

I shook my head. "No. If you keep my presence in the area a secret and let me pass through unharmed, there is no debt. I am not here for political reasons, and I will not harm or disturb a single one of your people. Know that unless you attack us, I am your ally."

The baby began to cry hungrily, and Elga looked at him as though she had forgotten his existence. The familiar hard look returned to her features. "You say nothing of this." Then she cocked an eyebrow and added, "No proof anyhow."

I shivered again, sensing the menace in her words. "It will be as though this night never happened."

"Yes. I swear you not be harmed, Queen Guinevere."

I backed slowly out of the room, listening to the child wail. As soon as Sobian and I were safely on the other side of the door, I breathed a sigh of relief. I signaled to Kay it was time to depart and he shoved off with a final glance at his stone-faced counterpart.

We had walked only a short distance when the crying became an ear-splitting screech, was muffled, then suddenly stopped. That was not the sound of a suckling babe. The silence was too complete. I began to shake and sank to my knees as Elga's warning rang in my ears—"no proof anyhow." I turned and threw the pouch at the closed door, where it exploded in a shower of silver coins. I could not accept money tainted by the shadow of death no matter how noble my intentions for it.

I turned to the side of the path and retched, grieving for the murdered child and the naive mother who had never gotten to hold him.

☙ ❧

I told no one what had transpired with Elga and her sister. It appeared she was true to her word as well for we continued on into Dyfed in peace as though nothing had ever taken place. Now Caer Corbenic stretched out before us like the peak of a mountain on the horizon. It was strange to view it from afar, sprawling on the top of a cliff overlooking the sea. It was so much more imposing now despite the fact that this time, I approached its gates a free woman. Somehow the specter of the past still loomed, surrounding me in a chill as damp and pervasive as the mist and spray of the waves breaking on the rocky shore below.

I took a deep breath, willing this to be a peaceful reunion. The last time I had seen Elaine—six years earlier—was at the feast where Arthur proposed to me rather than to her as we had both expected. For as long as I lived, I would never forget the depth of sorrow etched into her features that night, a macabre combination of disappointment and jealousy. I had what she wanted, and she, in not being chosen, had failed to meet her mother's high expectations yet again. Combined with the heartbreak she had suffered when Isolde fled to Ireland with Elaine's betrothed, a roguish Pict named Galen—an act Elaine wrongly believed I had also played a part in—I feared she would never forgive me.

Elaine was waiting for us at the entrance to the great hall, dressed in black and clearly in mourning for her father. Despite the grief etched into her features, Elaine had grown into a beautiful woman. The intervening years had rounded her once-childish body into womanly curves and transformed the plump plains of her face into soft, delicate features.

No word of a wedding or birth had reached us at Camelot, so I was surprised to see she held the hand of a small boy, maybe five years old, with curly blond hair and eyes so clear and icy blue he looked more fey than human. He was unquestionably hers so closely did he resemble his mother, but the eyes were a gift from someone else.

"Guinevere, thank you for coming," Elaine said before remembering herself and dropping into a low curtsy. "I mean, my queen."

As Elaine repeated her obeisance to Arthur, not daring to look him in the eye, the sparkling emerald she wore at her throat—the gift Arthur had given her at that ill-fated dinner—drooped low, brushing the neckline of her gown.

Arthur touched Elaine's hand and bid her rise. "My lady, I wish our visit were under more joyful circumstances. Your father was a great man, one of the best in the realm. I only regret we could not be present at his funerary rites."

Elaine's smile was tinged with sadness. "I have no doubt he

knew of your great respect for him." Only now did she dare meet Arthur's eyes. "My lord, before you retire, may I present to you my son, Galahad. It is my dream he may one day be a member of your Combrogi and be of great service to Camelot."

Arthur bowed with exaggerated formality to the boy. "Galahad, I am pleased to meet you." He laid the hollow of his palm on the boy's forehead. "Remember you carry the blessing of your high king with you always. I look forward to the day I can welcome you to my court."

Elaine blushed like a flower in full bloom at the compliment.

Galahad responded by bowing to his king. "It is my honor, my lord."

Elaine had trained him well.

"I must help Lancelot with horses," Arthur excused himself. "May Lord Galahad accompany me?"

One look at her son's hopeful expression and Elaine consented. Galahad took Arthur's hand and walked to the stables at his side. They reminded me so much of the son I had lost and the father Arthur was to Mordred—and could have been to my own son—it took all the strength I possessed not to cry.

Sensing my pain, Elaine put an arm around me and led me inside. "I think we both grieve," she said gently as we took seats near the fire.

"Indeed. I mourn your father's loss yet find you blessed with a child."

Elaine's cheeks colored. "Yes, he was quite unexpected." She twisted a large enameled ring on the middle finger of her left hand. "But he is the child my father always knew I would have, the child of the prophecy, and my father lived to see him born and proclaim him his heir." There was a note of pride in her voice.

My lips parted in surprise. "Galahad is your father's heir? What about your older brothers? Will they not contest losing their lands and title to a child?"

Elaine's lips twisted into a cheerless smile. "They can try, but the people of our tribe, I daresay all of Dyfed, are well aware of the prophecy and have voiced their agreement he should be chieftain when he comes of age. Besides, my mother has declared herself ruler until that time, and none of my brothers will dare stand against her."

"I wouldn't either," I muttered, remembering Lyonesse's cruelty all too clearly.

Elaine was silent for a while as if contemplating something. Then she reached behind her and unclasped her necklace. She held it out to me, the large emerald winking in the sunlight.

"What's this?" I asked.

"A peace offering. Arthur should have given it to you that night."

"Elaine, I cannot accept this. It was his gift to you."

Elaine laid her hand over mine and gave it a gentle squeeze, letting the jewel fall into my palm. "Now I am giving it to you. I never apologized for accusing you of being complicit in Galen's betrayal or for not speaking to you all these years. I had no right—"

I slipped my hand out from under hers and held up a finger to silence her. "Elaine, you were heartbroken. I understand why you said what you did, but I've long forgotten it."

"But I—I am truly sorry. I want you to know I bear you no ill will."

I shook my head. "Let us not speak of it. There is nothing to forgive."

Elaine bit her lip as though she doubted my sincerity, but she kept her council.

"Your boy is quite fine, Elaine," I said.

"Thank you." She glanced over her shoulder as if to make certain it was just us in the room. "I was hoping to talk to you about his future."

She looked at me with wide, expectant eyes, the way she had since we were children and she had something to say but wished I could read her mind so she would not have to give it voice.

"What is it, Elaine?"

She dropped her gaze to her lap and twisted her skirt nervously. After a long pause, she spoke, voice shaking as the words spilled over one another. "May I be so bold as to ask to come live at court with you and the king? I—I fear remaining at court with my mother." Elaine rolled up the sleeve of her gown as she spoke, revealing a ring of purple bruises just below her right elbow. "She did not dare touch me while I was pregnant for fear of hurting my child, but now she does as she wills. I know she will never harm him, blessed by heaven as he is, but I am another matter. Normally I would offer my sufferings up to God as I have always done, but I cannot—not anymore."

She finally raised her eyes to meet mine. There was fear behind them mingled with sorrow. I looked closer at the bruises, seeing them clearly now. They were imprints from where Lyonesse's fingers had dug into Elaine's arm as though Lyonesse had pulled on her as she sought to flee.

I swallowed hard, remembering the day Lyonesse had

slapped her grieving daughter, blaming her for Galen's misdeeds, and another day when Isolde showed me the crossing welts on her back after a whipping from Lyonesse in retribution for speaking against her.

There was no question in my mind, nor did I need to consult Arthur. "You and your son are always welcome at Camelot. I would be happy to have you as a lady of my court."

"Please do not tell my mother this was my idea."

"Of course not. My invitation was part of my reason for paying you a personal visit." I said it as gravely as I could muster, nodding for emphasis. In that moment, we were once again co-conspirators in a secret plot, just as in our youth, and I could easily let the years slip away and imagine our lives had yet to unfold before us.

Changeable as ever, when Elaine looked at me again, her expression was somber. "I know you must be wondering who my husband is, but please know I cannot tell you. We are wed in the eyes of God, but though he is a just and upright man, he wishes not to acknowledge me, and my mother has forbidden me to name him on pain of death. Suffice it to say that though he is a nobleman, he has not the lineage my mother would prefer and therefore is not to be mentioned."

I nodded, feeling the long-forgotten, but somehow familiar, twinge of unwanted complicity that came with Corbenic's web of lies and ever-changing ruses. "We shall put it about that your husband is an emissary who spends much of his time abroad. That way no one will ask too many questions."

Elaine bit her lip again. "He is one of Arthur's knights. That much is safe to say."

My stomach dropped. Who? I desperately wanted to ask. Did

she mean one of the Combrogi or any of Arthur's fighting men? If so, there were hundreds.

"Oh, Elaine, I do not believe that is a wise thing to say even if it is true. You have no understanding of the perils of life at court. Friendly though they may appear, everyone is looking for an advantage, and if they find one, you will be undone—have no doubt. Court gossip can turn the smallest grain of sand into a valuable pearl. By dangling such a bit of information in front of them, you will be inviting the wolves to your door."

"The Lord commands us not to lie. I will tell the truth to the extent I am able and still uphold my vows to my husband and mother. They are the only ones who know the truth, and I am certain they will not reveal it." She squared her shoulders and looked down her nose at me with an unyielding gaze.

It would have been easier to bid a statue come to life than to sway her now. I just wished she knew the peril she could be creating for herself and her son, especially if his father chose not to acknowledge him too. Selfishly, I was glad the scandalmongers would have a new subject upon our return.

Before I had a chance to reply, a maid poked her head in and curtsied. "Forgive me for interrupting, but Lady Lyonesse is ready to receive you."

"We have been summoned," I muttered. "Some things never change."

I made to follow, but Elaine stopped me with a brief embrace. "Thank you. I cannot speak for my son, but I know your kindness has saved my life."

༄ৡ৹

Arthur and I decided to hold a pleading day at Corbenic to give the southern people a chance to speak with us without having to traverse the country to reach Camelot. Notices were sent by messenger to the surrounding kingdoms, and a week later, residents from Dyfed, Dyfnaint, and the Summer Country presented their cases to us.

I had forgotten how boring pleading day could be. After doing this for six years, each complaint sounded like the last. One chieftain had raided another's cattle, a merchant had swindled someone in the market, a farmer's daughter had proved herself to be of questionable virtue. I barely heard most of the requests as they came through. Even Arthur was meting out justice by rote. I was ashamed to admit it, but by noontime, I was playing a mental game to see if I could guess the punishment Arthur would give out as soon as the crime was described.

But my boredom was not meant to last. Not long after we resumed our afternoon session, a clamor arose in the hall. A woman was shouting at our men in a guttural tongue that sounded vaguely familiar.

Arthur must have understood them because he chuckled. "Guards, stand down and let the woman enter."

I leaned over and whispered in his ear, "What did she say to them?"

"She called them dogs and told them to let her go or she would personally ensure Freya would remove their testicles and feed them to them."

"A Saxon then?"

Arthur looked up as the doors opened, the woman still struggling to shake off the guards. "Not just any Saxon."

The woman finally wrenched herself free only to trip and land on her knees at our feet, an obsequious posture I doubt she ever intended. It was only when she raised her chin to us that I recognized her.

"Mayda!" I exclaimed.

"Ja."

Arthur arched an eyebrow. "Have you met?"

I realized only then that I had never told him of my encounter with the princesses on our way to the Summer Country.

Mayda saved me from having to explain. "Ja. Your queen provided me a great service. I will be forever in her debt—a deficit I hope to repay in part today."

I was startled by how well she spoke our tongue, much better than her elder sister.

"Mayda, why have you come here? Who else knows you are here?" Arthur asked.

"I come to give you warning. My husband brings an army to overthrow the mountain. He and his brother have allied to win a victory they say will make them dominant forevermore."

Arthur tensed and brought a fist up to his lips. "What mountain?"

"They called it Bay-don."

"Badon." Arthur slammed his fist on his thigh and cursed. "Who sent you here? Why are you telling us?"

Mayda cowered in fear. "They do not know. They cannot know. If they know, if *she* knows"—Mayda gave me a look that I could only assume meant her sister—"I am dead." Her eyes were wild and scared like a trapped bunny's.

She looked to me for reassurance, but I had none to give. I

was still too shocked to be certain whether she was telling the truth or not.

Arthur spoke to me as he considered the frightened girl at his feet. "If she is telling the truth, then they intend to take the fort above Aque Sullis. If they do, they will control the Sabrina Estuary and split the country in two." He turned back to Mayda. "How long do we have?"

She scrunched up her nose as she calculated. "They were still planning when I left them. But they must know I am gone by now. If they suspect, they will move all the faster. I would guess a week, no more."

Arthur gritted his teeth. "Then we have no choice but to trust you and prepare for battle."

◈◈◈

Orders flew like birds as we made ready to depart. The remaining petitioners were politely turned away without even the slightest hint of what was afoot. We couldn't afford to lose the element of surprise. If the Saxons found out we had been warned, all our efforts could be for naught. They were unlikely to give up their campaign, but Mayda's betrayal would definitely incite them to anger. The last thing we needed them to do was take it out on the countryside, torching farmsteads, murdering peasants, and slaughtering cattle simply because they could. They had done it before under Vortigern, and the whole of the country had taken many years to recover from such devastation. It was for this reason, if not for Mayda's safety, that secrecy was paramount.

As chests were packed and mounts readied, people became

aware our party was leaving unexpectedly. To quell the rumors, we loosed a story that Arthur's uncle, Lord Mark, was ill and requested Arthur's presence at his bedside. It just so happened the same route would also naturally take us toward Aque Sullis.

The fastest couriers and most trusted knights awaited Arthur's command, standing shoulder to shoulder with the members of our household who had made the journey with us. To anyone on the outside, it would appear that before taking his unexpected leave, the king desired to honor those most loyal to him during his first years on the throne. But in reality, we were quietly making ready for war.

As Arthur called each man before him, he placed a small purse in the man's palm as though he was bestowing a commendation upon him. But the purse really held only enough coin to supplement rations, refresh mounts on long journeys, and if necessary, tempt the lord to whom the messenger was sent to obey Arthur's royal request.

"Bedivere, take the men and go ahead of us to help prepare the fort. Gather as many provisions as you can behind the innermost walls and secure an unobtrusive supply line. Ask the garrison commander about their defense strategy. They will have a secret way to keep the fort supplied while under siege. Kay, I want you to shore up the defenses. I have not visited this fort before and do not know its state of readiness. Whatever you do, do not raise alarm among the people. I don't want them knowing anything is amiss until it is time to send them away. The less time they have to talk, the better."

Kay and Bedivere bowed to Arthur and returned to their places.

Two boys stepped forward next. The older appeared to be a seasoned rider judging by his muscled physique and sun-darkened skin. The other could have seen no more than fourteen summers. The poor lad was unable to stop smiling nervously and wiping his palms on his breeches.

Arthur addressed the youngest first. "Daniel, I am told you are from Rheged, so you know it and its ruler well, is that right? The freckled boy cleared his throat. "Yes, sire. My cousin is a knight in his army. I know routes traveled only by the deer and can be at Lord Owain's door upon the next sunrise. Well, after the one tomorrow," he babbled.

Arthur's patience held surprisingly firm. "Good. Ride on ahead to ask Lord Owain's assistance in defending the fort and return word to me. Catch us on the road if you can. Do you understand?"

"Yes, sire."

Arthur turned to the other boy. "Owen, they say you know how to cross the country in half the time of other men. Do you swear to me now this is true?"

Owen bowed his head. "Yes, my king. Mountain passes, river roads—I will take whatever courses enable me to best fulfill your command."

"Good. You will have perhaps the longest journey of all. You will go to Pelles in the Summer Country and ask him to join his army to Cadwallion's in the Midlands. Then you will march with them on Mount Badon from the northeast, but do not approach the hill unless you see the signal. If you do well, I will bring you into my court and ensure you are trained as a future Combrogi."

Order after order followed, sending men in all directions, including one to fetch Morgan, for we were sure to be in need of her healing skills. But before Arthur let them leave to fulfill their tasks, he made them swear the same oath of loyalty each of the Combrogi and allied kings and queens had pledged.

He preceded the oath with, "Remember, your word binds you under pain of death. If you do as you are asked, you will be greatly rewarded, but if you betray my trust, your duplicity will resound for generations, and yours will not be the only blood spilled in atonement."

With that threat spurring them to action, the room quickly emptied, leaving me, Arthur, and Mayda, who sat unnoticed, impassively watching the proceedings. I motioned her over to us, and she sat on the step below the dais.

"I am sure you have had plenty of time to contemplate your fate," Arthur said gently.

Her light blue eyes were sincere when she looked at Arthur. "You are a good king. I wish my husband was so, but all he and his brother think of is power and land. All they want is to rule the whole of the island, and they will do what they must to feed their ambition."

She shifted her gaze to me. "I knew what I was doing when I made the decision to come to you today. I knew I was as good as dead no matter the outcome. If they caught me, if I was lucky, I'd only be badly beaten. But more likely, I would be killed outright for I abandoned my husband, betrayed my ruler—my *Aetheling*—and shamed my family. But after the kindness you showed me when I was in peril, I could not stand by while they destroyed your kingdom. I want to live in Britain as much as anyone, but not if it means doing so at the price of another's blood. A title and a throne are not worth so great a sacrifice."

"You show a compassion not often displayed by your people, especially by one so young," Arthur remarked. "You have nothing to fear from us. Consider whatever obligation you feel paid in full."

"I give you thanks, but it will not be settled until the last of my blood has drained from my body. My sister will be sure of that."

I took both of her hands in mine. "Mayda, you have in effect given up your life, at least as you knew it, to help us. In turn, we wish to help keep you safe. We could provide you with a holding in an obscure village. That is one option, but you would still live in constant fear." I glanced at Arthur. "What we propose instead will require even more sacrifice from you. There is a convent in Bernicia which has taken in women of your race before, those who sought refuge after the battle of York. I can arrange safe passage for you if you are willing to spend the remainder of your days there."

Mayda's mouth was open, but no words came out. She stood and paced from one end of the stair to the other and back again, slowly finding her voice. "I can never leave? Even if those who hunt me are dead? So I am to be imprisoned for my kindness?" She looked at me to confirm her suspicion, left hand fluttering near her mouth.

I chose my words carefully, not wishing to alarm her further. "Think about your options. If you continue running, you will be looking over your shoulder until the day you find a knife buried in your back. Yes, a convent can resemble a prison cell, but you would not be alone there. You would have sisters who speak your language, will teach you a trade, and will help you learn their ways. I cannot offer you much, but this is a guarantee of safety, a home, and warm food to fill your belly."

"But I know nothing of this god. Why would they take such as me?"

"The sisters would rather see those who have no other options slowly come to love their god than die in the streets. They act only out of compassion. I doubt you will get the same offer from your sister."

Mayda shot me an evil look, making her look like a younger version of Elga, but I could see her resolve melting. She knew she had no other choice.

"Ja, ja, I will go," she said at last. "But please make certain no one knows of this, or it will all be for nothing."

"You have our word," Arthur said. "There is a sister at a nearby convent who will accompany you along with one of my guard."

Mayda's eyes grew wide. "What if this sister betrays me?"

"She will do no such thing. She is foresworn not to." Arthur handed her a small roll of paper. "This will guarantee your safe passage. But you cannot be known by your given name lest your true identity be discovered. What name do you wish me to inscribe here?"

"Call me Udele. I know it was what my sister bade you call her before you discovered who we were, but it was my mother's name, and it is the only way I can take my family with me."

Arthur wrote her name as she requested and called for one of the waiting women. "Take this lady to the convent and see she is safely on her way before returning."

CHAPTER SIXTEEN

Just over a week later, we were standing atop the outer palisade of the fort of Mount Badon, watching as Arthur's men hid a circular ditch around the perimeter of the fort with dried grass and bracken. Alle and Octha were experienced campaign leaders, so we had no hope of fooling them outright with this most rudimentary of defenses, but by felling the grass fifty handspans on either side, we could at least hope to fool them into charging into it. Those unfortunate enough to do so would be greeted by a grave of sharp wooden spikes. Because the ditch was asymmetrical, the remaining troops would be wary of where they placed their tread, leaving them vulnerable to our archers and slingers who would launch their missiles from the wall on which we now stood.

Arthur paced, running a hand through his golden hair as though he was afraid he was forgetting something. "Will you read the stones again?"

"Arthur, I have told you I must see the size and composition of the army to be able to give you a definite outcome. For now, the best I can do is conjecture, and based on that, the stones say the same thing as they have from the beginning. Your strategy of coming at them from all sides will lead us to victory, but only if we ensure the tower is well guarded. The reasons are not clear, but we will need adequate defenses behind the second wall."

"That means they will certainly breech the boundary wall," Arthur mumbled.

"Did you really expect they would not? The best we can hope for is to slow them down long enough for the rest of our plan to be in place. Failing that, we are well supplied, and they are far from home, so there is always the chance we can starve them into submission, pick them off one by one as they forage for food."

Arthur stopped beside me and looked out over the town of Aque Sullis. "Pray it does not come to that. Even if we succeed in cutting off their shipments, they can always turn to plunder. Even with Gawain and Bedivere's efforts to relocate the people, I am certain most of the populace will stay in their homes. If the Saxons starve, the people are as doomed as fattened calves. Yet if we send in a reserve unit to defend the town, we tip our hand."

I raised his hand and rested my cheek in its warm, calloused hollow. "The Morrigan is with us. I swear she will give us her backing."

For a long time, we stood motionless save for our breathing, watching the setting sun burnish the horizon in brilliant amber. Mark's and Constantine's troops from Dyfneint and Cornwall were already here, as were Pelles's from the Summer Country. Morgan had arrived only a few hours earlier with her guard and the armies from Gwynedd and Dyfed were due to arrive soon. At least we had that in our favor. When those from distant lands would appear was anyone's guess, as was the location of our enemy.

Snatches of conversation crossed the distance to my ears as Lancelot and Bors instructed the men at the gatehouses to watch for any sign of the incoming army.

"They will come at us from the northeast via Fosse Way, which passes right below the fort. By this, they will hope to cut off our food supply and any defenses we may summon from the east," Lancelot said. "Be on your guard for you know not when they will arrive."

As I watched the town of Aque Sullis bolt its doors and shutter its windows to the oncoming war, I thought how odd it was to see such a thriving town so utterly deserted. When Viviane and I traveled from Northgallis to Avalon so many years ago, we had spent the night in this town, taking in the healing waters of the shrine. Nearly a decade later, the cries of the street vendors hawking their wares still rang in my memory and the thought of the warm spiced flatbread we ate caused my mouth to water. But when I made myself look at the town as it was now, the bustle of activity was replaced with the void of uncertainty, its exotic aroma supplanted by the stink of fear.

Thinking of my last time in the area and the new life it had brought to me, my mind drifted to Mayda. I wondered how she was faring on her own journey to a fate she'd never anticipated.

I glanced at Arthur. "You were not so surprised when Mayda interrupted our audience, husband. Tell me, how do you know one of the Saxons' highest-ranking women?"

Arthur's eyes gleamed with mirth despite the gravity we were facing. "I could ask you the same question. I was surprised that she came—that I did not expect. But I recognized her voice. She was there when I fought alongside your father at York. Her younger brother had been taken prisoner, and she begged me to spare his life, a request I daresay we may all regret as he is a powerful leader in the Saxon army. I heard no such tearful pleading from her sister, who I have little doubt would have regarded her brother as a hero had he died by my sword."

"She is cruel. That is for certain," I agreed.

"And what is the service Mayda wished to thank you for?"

I crossed my arms, hugging my shoulders, and turned away from him. "When we were lodging in Saxon territory on our way to Dyfed, Elga came to the door disguised as a peasant, asking for a midwife. I delivered Mayda's baby, a boy who lived only a few hours—much like our own. But unlike our child, Mayda's was murdered, killed by Elga's hand as soon as I was out the door." I shivered at the memory.

To my great disappointment, Arthur did not look appalled or even surprised. "Such is the fate of many an unwanted heir." He saw my expression and hastened to explain. "I may well have suffered the same misfortune without Merlin's wisdom. He alone understood the danger my life posed and so sent me away from my parents. Mayda's son was not so lucky."

I was about to reply when Gawain and Bedivere passed through the gates, shouting a hearty greeting. They were trailed by a cluster of fifty or so men, women, and children, all of whom I presumed chose to seek refuge in the fort rather than flee or take their chances in their own homes.

We met them in the courtyard just as the night fires were being lit. Arthur gave instructions to the families as to where they could stay and take refreshment and where to gather at sunrise so they could be secreted away to safety. It was only when they had departed that I noticed the dozen or so women who remained behind. They were all clad in warrior's breeches and armed from their copper-belted swords to the daggers in their boots and the deadly pins in their hair. It was clear before I even reached Arthur's side that they had come to fight.

I heard Sobian's accented voice before I picked her out in the dancing flames of torchlight. As usual, she was at Arthur's side, joking with him and touching him in a familiar manner that suggested a sordid past between them. Funny how after all we had been through together, her flirting no longer bothered me.

"Did you really believe we would pass up a chance to fight, Arthur Pendragon?" Sobian laughed. "We're women of blood and iron, of that you can be sure. Where else in all the land will you find a group of warriors who have learned from experience to defend themselves in any situation? Land, sea, river"—she gestured around her—"hill fort, it makes no difference. Flesh is cleaved the same way, and blood runs just as quickly. Please, let us provide service to you. After all, it is the least we can do for your kindness in helping set me and my lasses into an honest life."

Bors returned from the wall just in time to hear the last part of Sobian's request. "Arthur, you are not considering this preposterous proposal, are you? Who lets a woman fight? The lot of you should be off at dawn with the others so you will be safe."

Sobian snorted. "Safe from whom? There is no guarantee those who flee this place will make it to safety. For all we know, the Saxons could be out there right now, surrounding us and voiding our best laid plans—"

"'Our'?" Bors mocked. "This is our fight, not yours, *woman*. Get back to the hearth where you belong."

Sobian had a long dagger at Bors's throat before he'd even finished speaking. "Say aught like that again, I will have not only your head but your stones as well."

"Stop it, you two." I stepped between them, forcing Sobian to lower her weapon. "Save your hatred for the Saxons. We need all the fighters we can get inside the keep, remember? I say let them fight if they wish." I turned to Bors. "As to your question of who lets a woman fight—I do. I will be on the ramparts with you, and there is nothing you can do to stop it. You can thank me once the battle is over."

❧❦❧

Dawn broke a misty gray in the valley below, shrouding the village and road from view. In the courtyard behind the second palisade, a press of women, children, elders, and others who would or could not defend the fort shuffled from foot to foot, waiting on Arthur's orders.

Deep within the hillside ran a system of tunnels which led in and out of the fort through the thick forest behind it. Originally constructed to ferry troops in and out of the garrison, it would now be used to move innocents to safety without alerting the Saxons. Elaine had come with us from Corbenic for this very purpose.

At the center of the throng, Elaine wrung her hands, fretting.

"Guinevere, I do not think I can do this alone. I am not familiar with the area. What if I get us all lost or killed?"

I placed my hands on her shoulders, forcing her to stand still. "We are not sending you off without a guard, you goose. If you fear losing your way, let one of the locals guide you out. It is only a little more than a day's hike from here to Cardiff. Once you emerge from the caves, just follow Fosse Way northwest, and you will eventually see the port. All you need do is stay strong for them until you can get them safe housing across the estuary in Dyfed. And if anyone can do that, it is you. It is your land, after all. I have faith in you."

Elaine smiled softly and took a deep breath. "If you believe I can do it, then I know I can."

I squeezed her shoulders and signaled to Arthur, who handed Elaine a green flag raised high on a pole.

He raised his voice above the din. "Everyone who is leaving should follow the Lady Elaine and her green banner. She will lead you to safety across the channel."

The line moved slowly, inching single file through the doors of the keep and down into the darkness of the underground passages. When most of the crowd had disappeared, Arthur approached a score of women who stood, unmoving, near the gate. Octavia was among them.

"You should hurry if you wish to keep up with the others," he urged.

"We're not going," said a black-haired woman wearing the apron and cap of a baker or cook. She crossed her massive arms, which could have rivalled most of the Combrogi's and, I had a feeling, wielded a deadly iron pan. "If they get to stay and defend this fort"—she rolled her eyes at Sobian and her band of female pirates—"so do we. I have cooked for these men for twenty years. I am not going to abandon them now. Besides, who do you think will tend the soup pot and change bandages while you are giving orders? Mouths don't fill themselves, and you've got no camp women to assist you here."

Arthur could not argue with her, so the women stayed behind under Morgan's command, tending to the necessities of the fort while the rest of us waited on the ramparts, watching the fog slowly thin. I was grateful Elaine and her party would have some natural camouflage to bring good fortune to the beginning of their journey.

⁖⁖⁖

It was nearly midmorning when shouts arose from the watchtowers. The valley below was becoming clear, but I had to rub my eyes at what I saw. Peeking out of the mists were the tips of hundreds of tents, smoke from the cook fires competing with the fog to obscure the enemy army from sight. Their temporary camp stretched as far as I could see, eventually melting into the trees on the horizon.

There had to be nearly a thousand men camped in front of us—more than twice our number. How could they have made camp since nightfall without arousing any suspicion? Men could be ordered to be silent, but no matter how well-trained the animals, they whinnied and stamped as they willed, yet the guards who watched swore they'd heard nary a sound. It was as though they were phantoms from a previous war, there to reenact a battle long since decided. I shivered, wondering what magic they could have wrought to go unnoticed.

The warriors looked so small from my vantage point, as though I was a god looking down upon the earth and could crush them under my thumb. But it would not be nearly so easy—that much I knew. As the view became clearer, I watched those closest to the outer palisade as they went about their business, clearly preparing for their first maneuver. Bushy-bearded men mended leather armor and sharpened spears of varying lengths while boys with long poles poked at the piles of grass and bracken, trying to determine the boundaries of the trenches. Several armored women were practicing attack and defense. On the outskirts of the camp, the ring of axes signaled the felling of trees for firewood and, I feared, the building of siege weapons.

Not wanting to waste precious time, I took up my board of Holy Stones and arranged an accurate ratio of their troops to ours, accounting for the spears, swords, and stone hurlers I had seen plus the handful of archers they likely kept well out of view.

I closed my eyes and tried to imagine the scene from their perspective. Even without the sight, it was not difficult to imagine how impressive the fortress must appear to an army used to battle in open fields. Directly before them was the span of broken grass, trampled as though under a hundred hooves. Beyond lay a ring of bright green grass, a seemingly innocent lot that put any fortunate enough to cross the chasm directly in the sights of our archers atop a long wall of sharp, thick wooden stakes that stuck out of the ground like hundreds of angry styluses. Three gatehouses flanked the main entry, with two more at intervals on either side to guard the indirect approaches. Beyond, the massive triangular hill dominated the landscape, its steep grassy slopes a formidable challenge for even the most experienced of climbers. From this vantage point, the thin silhouette of the fort itself rose like a rearing horse, surrounded by yet another ring of spiked timber.

I left the stones on our side alone, indicating we would not change tack, and waited to see their response. Finally, I opened my eyes.

"We still have a few days," I told Arthur and Lancelot, who stood in the main gatehouse, sizing up their opponents. "They need to locate and fill in the ditch wide enough to get their men across then make their way through the outer fence. By then, our archers and slingers should have depleted their front ranks to almost nothing. The stones say it will buy us enough time for the outer flanks to be in place. . .but just barely."

"How did the Saxons get here so quickly?" asked Arthur.

It was Lancelot who responded, pointing at the edge of the camp where some of the horses were being turned loose. "They traveled on horseback and carried provisions in wagons, but they do not intend to fight mounted. Those are tough-bred pack animals only. It appears the Saxons have no intention of leaving with them, so you can be certain they will fight to the death."

"But they will certainly die. There is no way an army on foot can take a fort such as this. That is why it was built. To even try is suicide," I protested.

Lancelot shook his head. "I have seen enough of war to know there is nothing stronger than a force determined their cause is in the right. And according to Mayda, they believe this victory is their destiny, so they will fight all the harder. We must prepare for a long, bloody fight."

"No, not yet," Arthur said. "I may be able to buy us some additional time. Is there one bridge left intact?"

Lancelot wrinkled his brow. "*Oui,* the western gate." He indicated it with his finger.

Arthur stormed off in that direction with me following closely at his heels.

"Arthur, please, no. Why sacrifice yourself when we can wait?" I grasped at his arm.

He shook me off. "Did you not hear me? I can weaken their leaders and stall them through a single action. All of their work will have to cease until the matter is settled. I indulge you in most things, but I will not in this. Kay!" he called, then added to me, "Either come with me or stay behind, but I will challenge them either way."

⚬⚬ ⚬⚬

The gates creaked, and we rode single file across the bridge, Arthur in the lead. Kay and I followed, Lancelot bringing up the rear. Morgan had chosen to stay within the safety of the walls, preparing for any wounds that would need to be tended once the fighting began. We each bore a sprig of mistletoe, a sign of truce to Briton and Saxon alike, which hung in the rafters of every fort throughout the island for healing and as a signal of peace. Above us, on the wall, our warriors gathered to watch, their weapons lowered according to Arthur's command.

We stopped about thirty paces past where the grass had been trampled down. A clamor arose from the edges of the encampment as the warriors noticed our approach. As Arthur had predicted, all work ceased, and those at the forges and saws gathered in their tribal camps to gawk.

"Alle, Octha!" Arthur bellowed. "Come forth. We bear Freya's sign of peace, so I swear no harm will come to you."

The front line of Saxons picked up their spears and round shields, forming a defensive wall against any treachery we might attempt. They muttered and jeered in their own tongue, sure we could not understand them, but I needed no translator to know they were calling for our deaths. Slaying us would have been easy enough for them, but I wagered they feared the wrath of their gods, especially since Arthur had invoked their goddess of war. From somewhere in the crowd, a rhythmic banging erupted, and as those in front took up the motion, someone began chanting. Soon the whole of the camp was likely to surge and engulf us.

Then a low horn broke through the clamor, followed by total silence. The crowd slowly parted, and two men emerged followed by Elga and a man who had to be her champion.

The two men were brothers, both tall, nearly the same height as Arthur. They had muscular arms and broad frames that made it clear they could give a threatened buck a challenge before felling him. Alle, clearly the elder by several years, had a mane of white-gold hair twisted in odd knots and braids reaching nearly to the center of his back. His beard was decorated with golden baubles and twisted into a series of spikes that made him appear more demon than human. Octha, on the other hand, was shorter. His long flaxen hair, worn loose at his shoulders, nearly matched the hide armor protecting his chest from ribcage to clavicle. His skin was smoother and less weather-worn than his brother's save a jagged scar winding from his left temple to his nose, just skirting his eye socket.

Alle stepped to the front and addressed us in his language, which Arthur translated for the rest of us.

"You come here, to our camp, bearing a token of peace. Are we to take it as your surrender?"

Arthur chuckled darkly. "No. I come to challenge you by right of honor, as *Aethelings*, to single combat to the death. You cannot refuse without disgracing yourselves—that much I know."

"You mock our gods by wearing their tokens of truce yet demanding violence!" Octha yelled.

"I do no such thing," Arthur countered. "I bear the seed of peace only as a signal I mean no treachery. I seek to avoid the clash of armies and the loss of countless lives. How much bloodshed follows is in your hands."

Octha growled, but Alle remained impassive. The brothers conferred in hushed tones that were more like a series of grunts.

Alle turned back to us. "We accept, but as there are two of us and only one of you, I will fight you alone with my brother as witness. Name your terms."

"We fight now, on the grass with its edge and the hidden ditch as our bounds. Two spears and a shield for each. As I have challenged you, you may strike first. The victor claims the fort but must swear he will not harm the others here present."

Elga eyed me suspiciously as Alle weighed Arthur's stated terms. I doubted she liked these odds any more than I did.

"Agreed."

Arthur dismounted and removed his mail armor, leaving only the leather undersheath so the two would be evenly matched. According to tradition, I had the right to inspect Alle for any weapons or hidden trickery that did not abide by the terms of the agreement. Elga did the same for Arthur, making a show of running her hands across his body and checking under his armor and in his boots.

"Kay, why are we letting him do this?" I whispered, biting my thumbnail.

Kay placed a reassuring hand on my shoulder. "His choice of weapons was no accident. He knows what he is doing. I promise you he will live."

The two kings took their places on the grass, careful to keep the invisible gorge at their sides. Arthur chose to begin with a single spear and shield, while Alle took up spears in both hands, shield slung over his left arm.

The banging and chanting began again as the two faced off. Alle circled Arthur, testing him, trying to force him to turn his back on the fort. He struck with one spear at Arthur's shield and hooked his other behind it, yanking forward to try to dislodge the defense. Arthur leaned back, narrowly avoiding the second blade, and pushed outward, using Alle's own motion to unbalance him. The Saxon stumbled back, and Arthur swung his own weapon, piercing Alle's thigh.

The crowd grumbled and redoubled their clanging.

Alle snarled and came at Arthur again, this time using his shield as a battering ram to force Arthur back. Arthur dug in his heels, trying not to slip, but his boots skidded along the grass against his will. Alle was pushing Arthur nearer to the center of the field, and Arthur could not attack since all of his effort was put into halting the assault. But without warning, Arthur bent double, sending Alle tumbling over his back.

I expected the Saxon to sprawl onto the ground, but he was a better trained warrior than I'd anticipated. He recovered by rolling to a halt, spears held close to his body to keep them in hand. His shield had shattered as he hit the ground, and Arthur stabbed down at him, but Alle evaded and was quickly back on his feet. He punched his spear toward Arthur's shield, aiming for a vulnerable area at the base of his armor, but Arthur anticipated him and raised his shield at the last moment so the tip of the spear lodged in the boss at its center. With a wrenching motion, Arthur relieved him of his now useless weapon.

Arthur retrieved his unused spear from Kay so that he now held two and turned once again to face Alle. Alle twirled his remaining spear expertly, deflecting Arthur's jabs with movements similar to a swordsman. Only once did he breech Arthur's defense and slice his side, right beneath where his armor ended. Had Arthur retained the chain mail, he would have been uninjured.

Arthur hissed and instinctively stepped back, going on the defensive until the pain, writ clear on his face, abated.

The two were perilously close to the ditch now, avoiding its edges by sheer luck. Alle changed tack, turning his spear sideways to use the pole like a staff. Arthur mirrored him, holding his spears double to provide extra strength. Their dance reminded me oddly of the battle between the Oak King and the Holly King on Beltane, only this quest for power was very real. They were tiring, both bleeding, arms dropping lower and lower as the strain of the long battle fatigued them. Once, Arthur's foot slipped as he found the edge of the ditch, but he was able to save himself and step away. But that gave him an advantage Alle did not have. Rallying, Arthur guided Alle to where the ground gave way and forced him onto his back, pinning both his shoulders to the earth with his spears. Alle's screams silenced the chants of his followers.

Arthur kicked aside Alle's remaining weapon and turned to Octha. "I will let him live if you will retreat this instant, never to harass my people again."

Octha's face split into a menacing grin. "You know I will do no such thing."

In stony silence, Arthur removed his spears from Alle's limp arms and rolled him into the pit. Alle's screams echoed up and over the field as his body was impaled on the stakes. While Octha stood motionless, Arthur limped over to his horse, and Kay gave him a boost into the saddle.

"It is done. And you have lost. Return to your home," Arthur panted.

"By right of blood vengeance, we shall vindicate my brother and slay you all!" Octha called after us as Elga's guard gave chase.

"Burn the bridge!" Arthur yelled to the guards as we crossed.

A shower of oil followed in our wake, then with the tickle of a torch, the whole thing was ablaze.

"Now what do we do?" Kay asked.

Arthur passed a hand across his fatigued face. "Pray the gods speed Owain and the others to our aid."

Chapter Seventeen

It was no use telling Arthur he had made the Saxons' hostility worse. That he realized as much was evident by his silence as Morgan cleaned and dressed his wounds.

Spurred on by rage and grief, by nightfall, the Saxons had the trench revealed and a wide swath of it filled. Our archers rained down arrows and hurled stones on those who crossed, but Octha's army was so large it felt as though for every man we killed, two more appeared.

It took little battle training to know they would set the gatehouse and outer palisade ablaze at the first opportunity. So while Arthur slept, I slipped away to the first unoccupied place I could find—a deserted granary at the base of the keep. It was dark and still inside, the only light seeping in between slats in the wooden walls. I sat where the gap was largest—the only place I had a clear view of the stars—and prayed.

I rarely used the gifts afforded to me as a priestess, but Arthur needed to sleep and to heal, and we needed more time to allow our backup troops to take their positions.

Lady Morrigan, hear me, I prayed silently. *My husband, a devotee of the soldiers' god Mithras, has been rash, and I could not stop him. I fear our pride will cost us not only this fort but our very lives and the future of this isle you hold so dear. Do not abandon us, Great Mother, but hear my desperate cries for aid. I ask you to give us the time we need to turn this enemy from your shores. Aid me now, Great Lady, by bringing the elements under my command.*

I sent my consciousness down into the earth, closed my eyes, and raised my arms high. The wind whistled in response. Concentrating on the blackness behind my eyelids, I waved my arms, willing storm clouds toward me, pulling them on the howling wind until the stars were blotted out. Channeling all my guilt and rage, I twitched my finger and imagined a spark rising upward to charge the clouds. I brought my arms down hard, and rain pelted the roof, followed by a bolt of lightning and the answering peal of thunder.

I had done what I could. The Saxons would be unable to set anything alight tonight, and no one would dare battle in the muck and mire quickly taking shape in the grass below the hill. I started to rise, but a wave of dizziness forced me back to my knees. It had been so long since I'd done anything of the kind I had forgotten what a toll it took. I lay down on my forearms as another wave hit me, and I closed my eyes in a vain attempt to steady the spinning room.

The crack of thunder woke me from what I'd thought was a dreamless sleep. I stood cautiously, testing my legs. Finding them steady, I rushed back to Arthur's side, images emerging from the fog of sleep with every step.

In the dream, which was beginning to feel more like a vision, I'd stood at the entrance to the subterranean passage leading out of the fort. At first I saw the dark, uneven walls of the tunnel that had swallowed Elaine and the residents of Aque Sullis only hours before. Then there were figures within, only shadows, but instead of moving away, they were coming toward me. We had made arrangements to have food and supplies ferried in through the passage if the siege was drawn out, but it had been only a day since the Saxons made camp, so why anyone would be using the tunnels to get into the castle made no sense. Unless—yes. As they came toward me, I saw the glint of steel in the low light.

"Arthur, Arthur!" I shook his shoulder, but he did not wake. Damn that sleeping draught Morgan had given him.

I spun around, trying to remember where Lancelot or Kay were lodging. I knew not, so I wandered the empty halls searching for someone, anyone, who would listen to my fears. In the dining hall, I found Octavia curled up by the fire, and I gently roused her.

"Octavia, we have to find some of the men. I believe we are in danger here."

When she'd gathered Kay and Gawain, they listened to my story with somber expressions. While others would have laughed at the imaginings of a silly, frightened woman, these men had enough respect for the sight to take me seriously.

When I was finished, Kay sighed. "It is possible. Similar things have been done in Rome and other places, though I would hardly credit these barbarians with being cunning enough to conceive such a plan."

"You saw them today. Alle and Octha are hardly backward fools. There is strategy behind all they do, and that makes them a double threat."

"We should take a look just to be certain," Gawain decided.

The rain had slowed to a drizzle by the time they reemerged from the tunnel.

"We have been halfway down and saw no signs of recent occupation, but it is hard to tell what footprints were made by those fleeing yesterday," Kay said. "If you have any reason for concern, we should seal it up. But we don't want to wake the entire barracks with our hammering. I will stand guard until the morning."

I went back to Arthur's room and climbed into bed next to him, wondering as I listened to his breath if I was a fool. The tunnel was our only method of escape if things went badly. Tearing down a wall would only slow our egress. But if I was right. . . I shuddered and drew closer to Arthur, willing sleep to carry away my fears, founded or no.

The rain had done its job. Three days later, we were still at an impasse, the Saxons prowling impatiently outside the castle, our guards trading shifts with equal unease behind the safety of the wall.

Not only were the timbers soaked and the ground turned to mud, the ditch had filled with water during the storm, washing away much of the debris the Saxons had used to fill it.

So as dawn broke on the first clear day, I rejoiced that I had not only bought us time but set them back a bit as well. Or so I thought.

By midmorning, knots of Saxons were placing long, wide pallets of tightly nailed planks over the gorge. Though they tried to defend with their shields, our arrows and stones found targets while men and women emerged from their protective cover to cross the bridge. But the number of Saxons successful was still small compared to their total.

From the gatehouse, Arthur yelled, "What are you waiting for, you fools? Burn them down."

But his command went unheeded as a second Saxon battalion split down the middle and a great rumbling like an earthquake shook the ground. The sound of grating wheels and creaking wood reached us before the thing emerged from cover, but Arthur knew well enough what it was.

"Fall back!" he commanded, and all but those expressly required to stay with the gate retreated up the hill to the safety of the second palisade.

I caught only a glimpse of the battering ram before Arthur grabbed my hand and pulled me along to safety. It was little more than a pointed tree trunk suspended by rope over a wheeled base, much like the bottom of a cart. A crude roof had been built over the top and covered in hides, ostensibly to protect it from fire.

It crashed into the gate before I'd reached the base of the hill, and its reverberating boom knocked me off my feet. Again it came, but this time I was ready. By the time I reached the second palisade, the archers had killed most of the warriors keeping its pendulum in motion, and as the second group took up position, the archers let fall a cauldron of oil, which quickly caught fire and killed everyone around it. But it was not enough to save the wall, for what damage the ram had begun, the fire finished, incinerating the guards who had sought to stop the Saxons' progress.

"Light the signal fires!" Arthur commanded.

As Saxons streamed across the trench into the courtyard at the base of the hill, archers fanned out along the last remaining wall. Some fired on the advancing Saxons while others let fly a volley of flaming arrows, one group toward Lansdown Hill to the west and the other toward Dean Hill in the south. At the summit of each hill, large bonfires flared to life in response.

"Now we must pray the kings will do as we have asked," Arthur said to himself.

I scanned the countryside for signs of hope. At first there was nothing, but then I saw them, small as ants—the northern troops riding at full speed to cut off the Saxons' left flank.

"Arthur, they're coming!" I shouted, but my voice was drowned out by screams within the keep.

I raced inside, sword drawn, to find the tower in chaos. People were running through the halls, some bleeding, some seeking to escape injury. Others lay dead, crumpled where they had stood. How was that possible? The Saxons hadn't yet gained the terraces. How could our people already be fighting for their lives? I fought my way through the fleeing servants to find Sobian battling a Saxon woman wielding a war hammer. That was when I understood. I had been right. They had been here all along.

"There are about fifty of them," Sobian said between slashes. "Hid in the cellar, as far as I can tell."

Together, we dispatched the woman, and I took her armor, not having had time to don any. We followed sounds of distress to the kitchen, where a pair of Saxons were menacing three of the servants. It was a cramped space, but one servant was holding her own with a frying pan while another made do with the spit from the fire and the third wielded a knife resembling a small sword. Taking a cue from one of the maids, I grabbed a wooden serving tray and tossed it to Sobian to use as a shield.

Amid the maids' clamor, the Saxons failed to hear us approach.

Sobian had one's throat cut before the other could react, and as soon as he dropped his defense, I ran him through.

One of the maids whimpered.

"Will you be all right?" I asked, and she nodded, obviously horrified by the violence she had witnessed.

The keep was once again quiet by the time Sobian and I made it to the ground floor, doing our best not to look at the corpses we passed and praying they were no one we knew.

But near the front door, Sobian stopped short. Sprawled on the floor was one of her girls, a long slash down the front of her chest. Sobian knelt next to her and cradled her head.

"I will find the bastard who did this to you, Bonnie, and rip out his entrails. I swear it to you." She kissed the younger girl's forehead and stepped over her body, determined to continue.

Outside, the tumult was deafening. Some of the Saxons had gained the hill and were using makeshift ladders to try to scale the walls surrounding the keep while stones and arrows flew in every direction. Sobian darted off, and I ducked into a gatehouse for safety. Leaning against the wall to catch my breath, I had an unobstructed view of the fighting far below. The Saxon numbers were dwindling. Owain's army had nearly dispatched a third of them, and Pelles's contingent was pushing the remainder ever closer to the foot of the hill. Soon there would be nowhere for them to run.

I needed to find Arthur. He was still weak from the duel with Alle and no doubt by now had undone any healing that had taken place. I had to get to him before he injured himself beyond saving. I searched from one gatehouse to another to no avail. I would have to enter the fray.

I descended into the open courtyard. Immediately I found

myself trapped in the middle of a melee in which weapons were being wielded indiscriminately. The Saxon in front of me stank of burning flesh, his right arm raw with oozing blisters. Unfortunately, he appeared to be left-handed. We grappled, parrying and thrusting like the dozens of fighters around us. Try as I might, I could not disarm him while hemmed in by bodies. He pushed me back, and I stumbled, saved from falling only by the back of the warrior behind me. The Saxon's sword came within a hairsbreadth of my head, slicing off a hunk of my hair and part of my ear before I could bat it away. Ignoring the pain, I aimed a blow at his ribcage, but I needn't have bothered. A large stone whizzed over my shoulder and hit him square in the forehead. The Saxon's eyes widened, and he fell backward, dead.

Stunned, I turned to see Octavia holding a sling, another stone at the ready.

"Your mother always said I was a good shot," she yelled triumphantly.

I started to laugh, but then the warrior behind her raised his arm. I understood what he intended to do and flung myself at Octavia as the bearded bastard let his weapon fly. I was too slow. His javelin caught Octavia in the lower back as I pulled her down—one moment too late.

I gasped in horror as my heart broke into a thousand pieces and the war around me faded away. Amid all the screaming and bloodshed, I no longer cared if I lived or died. Yet again, I was holding someone who meant everything to me as she slipped away.

I'd never thought of Octavia as a servant but as a second mother. Now I was watching the light slowly drain from her eyes. She was there in my earliest memories, holding me on her knee in the warm spring sunlight, helping me struggle into my first set of armor, weeping as I left for Avalon, comforting me after my mother's death, and soothing my uncertain heart during my first days of marriage. Whether I'd prattled on about a new toy, a pretty dress, my infatuation with Aggrivane, or complained about my husband, she was always there with a kind word and a patient ear. She was listening, always listening, but soon her ears would hear no more.

I wanted desperately for the last thing she heard to be my love for her, but I could not form the words. Horror constricted my throat, and she was in too much pain to speak, so I simply interlaced my fingers with hers and lay with her in silence on the hard dusty ground as her life drained away, our eyes betraying emotions our tongues could not express.

I found my voice only after she had gone, and I recited the traditional prayer for those who died in battle. "May the Goddess grant you rest, daughter who has died in her service. Her blessing be forever on you."

With shaking hands, I closed Octavia's eyes and laid my head on her silent chest. Cold slowly seeped from the earth into my bones, leaving me numb and hollow and wishing for death myself.

⋆⊙⊙⋆

I could not recall what happened after or how the battle finally ended. I was told Sobian guarded me as Octavia died and Lancelot avenged Octavia's loss, two acts for which I would be forever grateful.

My next memory was of walking among the dead. There were so many, more than I could have imagined in my worst nightmares, all bloody and broken from all manner of injuries. It was not uncommon to see limbs hacked off or twisted in grotesque contortions or men holding in their own guts from gaping wounds. Others were severely burned and howling in pain. I helped those I could to the infirmary, where Morgan quickly took over. But for those less fortunate, whose wounds had not killed them but would not heal, the only thing I could do was whisper a blessing, obtain permission with a nod, grunt, or whisper, and give them the Goddess's final mercy—a quick death.

Numb with shock, I carried out my duty as a priestess by saying a final prayer over each of the bodies I encountered, Saxon and Briton alike. With the help of the other women, I washed and dressed them in makeshift shrouds with equal dignity for whether friend or foe, all were children of the same great gods. We burned the bodies of the Saxons, as was their custom, and buried our men on the site of the battle, their bones an eternal reminder of the horrors that had taken place here. After we departed, this fort would never be used again.

After two sleepless days, priestesses from Avalon arrived to continue the rites of the dead, relieving me to tend to Octavia. I could not bring myself to bury her with the fallen warriors, much less dump her body into the ditch with the nameless dead once we ran out of burial space.

Nearly faint with exhaustion, I walked down to Aque Sullis to secure permission from the priests to bury her in their cemetery just outside of town. As she was a Roman and this was as close to Roman soil as we could be, they were more than happy to oblige my request. I doubted my title and the sizable donation I made to their shrine hurt our cause.

In the following days, news trickled in from returning Combrogi who had pursued the fleeing Saxons. All told, fewer than one hundred Saxons escaped alive, Octha and Elga among them. Although they were now well within their territory and likely so shaken by their losses it would be a long time before they raised a sword against us again, I could not help but remember the fury on the *Aethelings'* faces as Arthur and I fled into the sanctuary of the hill fort. I feared we would yet pay for the wounds inflicted on their pride.

Chapter Eighteen

One month passed, then two as we recovered at Cadbury. Slowly, bones mended and wounds healed, at least those that could be seen. Those inside our minds and hearts would take longer to cure. I took small comfort in knowing that mine were not the only haunted eyes ringed with shadows. Sleep eluded us all, and when it deigned to appear, it was accompanied by vivid nightmares that forced us to relive our strife. I wondered often how Arthur lived with the memories of more than a dozen battles.

Our court tarried at Cadbury in this convalescent state until we could wait no longer, seeking a normality I doubted would ever come. Soon the snows would begin to fall. We needed to make ready for Camelot if our slow-moving party was going to make the long journey back home before the roads became impassable.

But Arthur felt we could not leave without honoring those who had made our victory over the Saxons possible. So he declared a weeklong feast to mark our triumph. He sent a sizeable donation to Aque Sullis so the townspeople, who were not untouched by the battle, could join in the celebration as well.

"Are you certain we can afford to be so generous after so costly a war?" I asked, not wishing to imply ingratitude but also mindful of practical matters.

Arthur shrugged off my concerns. "A few years of peace and bountiful harvests will more than recoup our losses."

"But bountiful harvests are not guaranteed."

"No, but the goodwill of our people goes a long way toward making them possible. Trust me."

So I did. Kings and lords, nobles of every clan and rank, Druids, priestesses, Christians, warriors and their families all descended upon Cadbury with the speed of a flock in flight—or a plague of locusts, as our fretful host referred to them.

The first two days honored those who had given their lives in service to their king and country as well as those who had acted heroically in battle. The Combrogi met for the affair in Cadbury's cavernous great hall, which was decorated with the standards of kingdoms and tribes who had contributed men or funds to the battle of Mount Badon. Rather than sitting in the far end of the room, Arthur had asked that a platform be built in the center of the room so everyone present would be able to see us and we them.

So as the festivities began, Arthur, Morgan, and I were surrounded by the Combrogi, their wives and children, and our own families, as well as Merlin and Viviane, who led an ancient prayer for the dead.

"Hail spirits of our ancestors, those of blood, bone, and spirit. We invoke you from beyond the seventh wave. Join with our fallen brothers and sisters who wait just beyond the veil. Be their guardians and protectors as they make their final journey to lands of golden sun, perfumed breezes, calm seas, and verdant meadows. May peace and joy be upon them for they died noble deaths. May those whom Ceridwen chooses rise again from her cauldron hale and whole to be reborn and defend our children's children and maintain the peace bought with their blood in this lifetime."

Grieving families were invited to come forward and receive our royal condolences. Each family brought with them a small token of the one who had passed—many times a ring, a dagger, or some other personal possession. We collected them in baskets that would later be taken in solemn procession to a nearby sacred pond and offered to the gods with prayers for mercy upon the departed. In exchange, we gave them their soldiers' pensions, and to the poor, we gave a set amount of additional funds to help them weather the financial strain of their loss.

Some wives, now completely bereft of income, begged us to help them find work lest they turn to crime to feed their families. Arthur found each of them positions in the sculleries, dining halls, or sleeping chambers of Camelot or one of the noble houses. Those who expressed an interest in or talent for a trade were employed in shops. Regardless of their status in society, no one would scorn a war widow, for to do so was to call down the ire of the gods.

Before they departed, we asked the names of their preferred tribal and personal gods and blessed each of them in those names. "Be at peace. For though you grieve, your loved one lives on. A long draught from Ceridwen's cauldron heals all infirmities and makes all men new. In due time, they will be reborn. You who grieve suffer far more than they. In the holy names of your gods, we bless you and pray you will come to know that this is but one turn in the cycle of life."

Of all of them—widows, families, and in a few cases, even orphans—the ones who will remain with me forever are Nimue and Peredur, Octavia's children, now orphans. I had seen Nimue only a year before, but now her ethereal green eyes shed silent tears onto the blue robes of a priestess. She held the hand of her brother, who stood beside her like a statue, the image of stoic grief.

Even though he had been at court since the tournament where Arthur and I met, Peredur would always be to me the boy who had shed no tears as I bid him farewell before leaving for Avalon. I still remembered the sweet smell of his hair—like fresh clover—as he pressed his wooden dog into my hand, telling me the creature was magic. I never saw Peredur's father again after I departed for Avalon. He had been killed in service to Uther's army by the Saxons. And now Peredur was here, mourning the loss of his other parent at their merciless hands.

It was Peredur who roused me from my reflections. With great solemnity, he presented us with Octavia's memorial, a necklace of coins from her native Rome.

"My mother wore this around her neck when she fled from Rome. It was all she had in the world when she joined your family," Peredur whispered. "It is only right she should have it on her journey to the next life."

I took the necklace, not pausing to examine the coins. I didn't want to think about her life before I knew her, how she must have suffered as a lone woman, hardly more than a child, traveling any way she could—by caravan, boat, or on foot—to put as much distance as possible between herself and her native land, where her whole family had been killed by the invading Visigoths. She had told me the story many times, but in the naïveté of my youth, I thought it a tale of grand adventure rather than grim reality.

I took Peredur's hand. "Your mother was so much more than a servant to me. She was my nursemaid, my teacher, and my closest confidante. Losing her was like losing my mother all over again. My heart will never heal from that wound. There is little I can do to comfort you now except tell you this—she died peacefully." I tried to choke back my emotions, but the tears broke free any-way, and my voice faltered. "In—in my arms. She did not speak, but her eyes said volumes. They shined with love, love for both of you, for the life she was leaving. She spent her entire life caring for me, and she died defending me. You should be proud."

Nimue's head snapped up.

I was startled to see not grief in her haunting eyes but pure, cold hatred.

"Proud? We should be proud she died doing her duty—defending her mistress? She never had a choice to follow you. She did as she was bid and died in bondage."

"What are you saying?" I stammered.

Her green eyes narrowed, hard as chips of ice. "Do you really not know? My mother was a slave." She scoffed at my shocked reaction. "Yes, a slave. Your father didn't welcome her with open arms out of some sense of charity. He bought her on the docks. She may not have told you, but the boat that brought her to Gwyn-edd was a slave ship. She was captured in Gaul. The friendship you hold so dear was nothing more than duty, pure and simple."

"Nimue," Arthur said gently but firmly, "I saw Octavia's love for Guinevere firsthand. It was no sense of duty. Who told you such lies? Surely she did not admit this to you herself. No mother would debase herself so to her children."

"The Lady herself told me, and she speaks the truth."

Arthur shook his head. "Even the Lady of the Lake can be mistaken."

Nimue's gaze flickered between Arthur, Peredur, and me as she weighed the plausibility of Arthur's words.

Peredur squeezed his sister's hand. "Does it really matter, little rose? Our mother is dead either way. We are here to mourn her with our friends, and I for one would rather the focus of her legacy be on the good she has done."

"She died a hero and a free woman. As high queen, I declare that here and now. Whatever the truth, I release Octavia from all bondage. If not for her bravery, you would be mourning me at this moment. I will forever be in her debt and therefore in yours. Name your price. What is it I can do to help ease your loss?"

Peredur and Nimue looked at one another. I doubted they would ask for monetary compensation for they both had fruitful lives, he as part of Arthur's army and a Combrogi-in-training and she as a daughter of Avalon.

"Erect a memorial stone here and at Camelot in her honor," Peredur declared. "They will ensure she is remembered as she should be. That is all we ask of you."

"It will be done," Arthur and I said in unison.

Peredur and Nimue melted back into the crowd, though I caught Nimue watching Merlin closely as he sang a eulogy for the dead. Having their song proclaimed at the royal court by the Archdruid and chief bard of Britain was the highest honor that could be bestowed upon any subject. His song would be taught to all other bards and repeated in halls and hovels throughout the kingdom so the legacy of those heroes would remain as long as memory prevailed. No one would forget those who had fallen in the battle of Mount Badon.

The following day, we gathered in the great hall with the members of the Combrogi and Mount Badon's remaining men. We formed a smaller group, more intimate than the grieving rite, because Arthur wanted to bestow his honors on those who'd experienced the battle away from the prying eyes of courtiers and others intent only on spreading gossip.

Clustered among the sea of men were Sobian and her remaining women. As usual, though they certainly didn't blend in, they were right at home. Also as usual, Gawain was flirting with Sobian, who looked on the verge of punching him. Fortunately, before things could escalate any further, Arthur began his speech from the same dais we had occupied the day before.

"I would have preferred to hold these honors in our council chambers at Camelot, in the sight of my ancestors, but under the circumstances, this is the best alternative." His smile was a beam of light warming the entire room. "First, I would like to thank all of you for your service to your king and country. As we noted yesterday, there is no greater sacrifice than to give one's life for one's country. But you, all of you, risked your lives and survived to fight another day. And for that, I will hold you forever in my heart."

He reached down to me, and I grasped his hand. He pulled me up next to him as though I weighed no more than a feather.

"First, I wish to acknowledge my wife, the first battle queen in several generations to lead her people in times of conflict. If not for her bravery and skill, the fight would have been over before it had begun." He took my hand and kissed it. "My love, you have my eternal gratitude and, I daresay, the respect of everyone in this room."

Morgan glared at me—a sure sign I'd gained no respect from her—but the Combrogi's cheer was deafening. Arthur spun me around, and they smiled at me. Lancelot jumped up and placed a ring of leaves on my head.

"They aren't laurel, but this was the best I could do this time of year," he whispered before kissing my cheek and hopping back down. I prayed no one else could see the blush his act had produced.

"Gentlemen, gentlemen, calm down. There's more celebration yet to be had. The second person I wish to honor is Aggrivane." He sought out my former lover in the crowd. "Please come forth and receive your due."

Aggrivane hesitated only a moment before being propelled forward by the shouting men. He scrambled onto the dais with surprising grace.

"My friend," Arthur addressed him with the ease of a comrade-in-arms, "I really should arrest you for treason for you disobeyed a direct order. But you are Lot's son, so I should not be surprised."

A low chuckle rumbled through the assembly.

"If not for your wisdom, hundreds of Saxons would have escaped," Arthur added. "Tell me, how did you think of pursuing the ships before the overland riders?"

"Call it learning from past mistakes." He gave Sobian a barely perceptible nod. "There have been other battles where I was not as well advised, nor our men as fortunate. Luckily, the gods gave me a second chance."

"Indeed!" Arthur boomed. "For your creative tactics, you may take your place with your father, reporting directly to him. I name you now Second Council of Strategy."

The men erupted into cheers again as Aggrivane expressed his thanks.

"Settle down," Arthur chided. "There are many others among you who deserve our praise. Sobian, known formerly as the Scourge of the Sidhe, please come forth."

Sobian wound through the throng of men followed by the five other women who had survived through Badon with her.

Despite my initial misgivings about her and her place at court, she had saved my life twice now—first in rescuing me from Malegant and again in this battle—and over time I had grown to care for her. "Thank you," I whispered in her chestnut hair as we embraced. "I owe you my life."

She pulled back as if stung. "You owe me nothing. I swore my allegiance to you. I did nothing more than any of these men would do in similar circumstances."

Arthur had listened to our exchange, though I was fairly certain the rest of the room had not heard it. "Oh, but you did. Your actions were anything but commonplace. These men here"—he gestured to the room at large—"are paid to use their bravery and skill against any enemies to the crown. You and your fellow female warriors are different. You volunteered to be in harm's way. You offered your swords, spears, and lives when you saw a need. If that isn't the true definition of bravery, I don't know what is."

Sobian nodded, standing even taller now.

Arthur continued. "As if that were not enough, your battalion took on all comers. Some of your women are not here to celebrate with us, but we honor them the same. I am told that among the dozen of you, you killed nearly thirty Saxons. Is that true?"

"Well, I didn't stop to count them," she said with a sly smile and glittering black eyes. "If I had, you'd be talking to a corpse."

I laughed along with several of the men. That was the fiery spirit I had come to admire in this pirate-spy-turned-heroine.

"Indeed, you are right," Arthur admitted. "But that was not your only service to the crown. You stood guard over the queen as she nursed a dying friend. You are the reason we are here today rather than mourning her. As we all know now, you are more than the maid you appeared to be. There is little I can do to repay such a service, but I will try. I offer you a boon. Name what it is you wish, and it shall be granted."

A few gasps broke the silence, but no one seemed to know what to say. For a king to offer a boon was almost unheard of except for in legend.

Sobian, normally so cool and collected, was clearly stunned. She stood perfectly still, oblivious to the waiting crowd. Her lips were parted as though she intended to speak, but no words formed. Then she blinked, and her face took on a quizzical expression as though she were weighing her options, deciding if her request was likely to be granted. The crowd shifted, waiting impatiently to hear what she demanded.

Finally, Sobian fixed Arthur in a resolute gaze. "I wish to become a member of the Combrogi."

The room went completely silent. Sobian's girls looked between one another in utter shock. Then the yelling began.

"A woman cannot be part of the Combrogi!" asserted a deep voice I thought I recognized as Bors's.

"Indeed," another agreed. "Does the word not mean 'fellow countrymen?'"

"You're going to quibble over the word's origin?" Lancelot challenged. "Does your name not mean 'exotic'? Then why are you Bor-ing?" He chuckled at his own quip, which infuriated Bors all the more.

"It *cannot* be done! It shall not be done, not while I live," Bors roared, emerging from the crowd and jamming his dagger into the wood at Sobian's feet with a violence that made the dais visibly shake.

Sobian did not even flinch. In one fluid movement, she grasped the dagger and jumped down, knocking Bors onto his back. She landed in a crouch on his chest, dagger at his throat. "Shall I kill you now so I can claim what is mine?"

Arthur motioned for her to stand down. "There is no need for that. Sobian has made her request, and under the terms I freely laid forth, I must grant it. If any of you"—he narrowed his gaze on Bors—"feel so strongly against this, you are welcome to relinquish your position." He turned to Sobian. "You. Up here. Kneel."

She obeyed.

"Repeat after me. 'I, Sobian of—where *are* you from?—do swear now—"

"I know the rest." She returned his smile and took one of our hands in each of hers. When she touched Arthur, something passed between them I couldn't quite read. "I, Sobian, daughter of Grendel the Dark One of Ulster, do swear now special allegiance to my king, queen, and country. I swear also to uphold my fellow Combrogi, to defend and honor them in all things, and to keep close to my heart the confidence of my lord and lady. Should I fail them or break these vows, may the wrath of the gods be visited upon me."

Arthur helped her to her feet, and we embraced her in turn. "Welcome, fellow countrywoman."

ꙮ ꙮ

Slowly, families began to depart from Cadbury, returning at long last to their homes to enjoy our newly won peace. We said our farewells to those not accompanying us to Camelot and packed our own caravan for the long journey home. At the last minute, I noticed Merlin was not in his customary position next to Arthur. I found him and my husband with Viviane, Nimue, Morgan, and the other priestesses.

I placed a hand on his forearm. "Merlin, why are you not with our party? We are nearly ready to depart."

Merlin turned, expression just the slightest bit wistful. "As I have just told Arthur and Morgan, I am not coming with you."

"What? I—"

He held up a hand to silence me. "Badon was my final battle as Arthur's advisor. I have seen what may yet come, and I wish no part in it. I have seen too much death in my years as counselor to kings." He slid his arm around Nimue's waist and pulled her to him. "Now that peace has come at long last, I wish to devote my remaining days to teaching and being with those I love. Arthur has already given his consent."

Over his shoulder, Viviane flinched, her gaze resting jealously on Nimue. Inwardly, I sighed. If even the Lady of the Lake could be supplanted, I couldn't feel too bad about Arthur's affection for Morgan.

I hugged him. "If that is what you wish, far be it from me to oppose you. We will miss you though. Who will keep us out of trouble?"

Merlin laughed, running a hand through his graying hair. "One is coming who will more than make up for my absence, I assure you." He bent down, lips grazing my cheek. To everyone else, it probably looked as though he was kissing me farewell, but his voice was stern in my ear. "Have a care whom you take into your confidence. Not everyone at court wishes to see your star continue to ascend. Remember the prophecy."

I remembered it all too well. The first part had already come true when Arthur took the throne. The second appeared to be happening now with Viviane in power in Avalon as Lady of the Lake. I repeated the third and final part to myself silently. *The day will come when sister shall oppose sister, both in this sacred place and without. Loyalties will be tested and betrayed, so heed my warning. That which is birthed in jealousy shall not give life but infect all who draw near. Therefore, act with love and not out of spite. Only then shall you escape the fate the stars foretell.*

I shivered. Merlin was right. I must keep my own counsel and keep careful watch over my actions lest those words come to pass.

PART FOUR

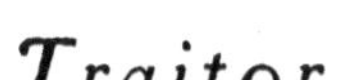

Traitor

Chapter Nineteen

Spring 504

Elaine was driving me mad. She paced constantly, running her hands through her hair, fiddling with her dress, unable to concentrate on her sewing or even sit still for a meal.

She'd been this way all winter. Then, I'd thought it was the effects of being cooped up inside with little to occupy her mind, but now the sun was bright, the breezes cool, and we were supposed to be enjoying simply being alive.

"Dear heart, what troubles you so?" I asked from my blanket beneath a pink dogwood. "Elaine, did you hear me?"

A little ways away, Elaine was picking at her fingernails as though determined to rid them of their cuticles once and for all. She looked at me, perplexed. "What do you mean?"

"This." I put a hand over hers to stop her from peeling off more skin. "Your agitation must have a source. Out with it so the rest of us can live in peace."

She searched my eyes as if trying to decide whether or not to trust me, then she glanced away. "I shouldn't say."

I knelt behind her, took her hair in my hands, and began twisting it into a golden braid just as I had done when we were children. "Of course you should." I adopted a mock stern tone. "Your queen commands it."

She sighed and nodded toward the training yard where roughly twenty of Arthur's men were sparring in pairs and small groups. "I thought I would enjoy being closer to my husband at court, but now I find it brings me nothing but distress. During the day I try to think of ways to be pleasing to him, to get him to pay attention to me, while at night I watch him dazzle all manner of women, talking with them, flirting with them, even with you. I am not certain it is all frivolous either." She turned to look at me, her long tresses slipping out of my hands. "If that was not enough, I dream of him at night. Being at court is best for my son, and I would rather be here with his father than anywhere else in the world, but I cannot stand it."

I couldn't help but feel sympathy for her. "Sweet girl, you deserve none of this. Why do you not ask him for a divorce?"

Elaine twisted around. "It doesn't work that way in my faith. Our marriage was consummated—everyone knows that because of Galahad. I would not trade his life for anything, but as a result, I am bound to my husband whether he admits it or no. To leave him now would be a mortal sin, though I doubt there is a greater hell than to love someone whose heart will forever belong to others. How do you do it, Guinevere—live with Morgan and Arthur, especially with Mordred always under foot?"

I bit my lower lip. That was a good question. How did I manage? Oddly, Mordred had never been sore spot for me. Even though he was a reminder of my failing as a wife and mother, I could not bear him any ill will, innocent as he was in the machinations of his parents. In fact, I enjoyed helping to raise him, showering him with all the affection I could never give to my own deceased children. Now, as he grew, he came to me for advice often, which was balm to my heart.

His mother was a different story. She tolerated my tenderness to her son as long as he followed the rules she laid out and behaved as she taught him, but she made no effort to hide her disdain for me. Because of that, when I first returned from Avalon, I had expected constant discord between us, and there was for a time, but we'd learned to tolerate one another. I had accepted Arthur's preference for Morgan's bed over mine, though a small part of me resented her for it.

Finally, I answered, "I have no idea. Some days I want to kill her just as much as I did in Avalon. We still hate each other, but we've developed a sort of truce. I still loathe sharing Arthur with her, but I have no choice."

Elaine gave a small, wry laugh. "Neither do I. I see my husband with other women every day. I know he is in love with someone else. I can see it in his whole demeanor. He looks upon others with a softness I will never know." She choked back hurt and rage-filled tears, clenching her hands at her sides. "I am determined to find out who his mistress is—if for no other reason than to relish the look on her face when I tell her he is already mine."

I twisted to face her. In that moment, she looked so much like Lyonesse it was frightening. "Why will you not tell me who he is? I will tell no one. I promise. But at least I could counsel him to be more discreet. Or perhaps I can convince Arthur to send him somewhere on a diplomatic mission. Then you could live here in peace."

She shook her head. "I must take that secret to my grave. But mark my words, she *will* regret crossing me."

Without knowing why, I shivered. Something in the tone of Elaine's threat cut to my very core. I never wanted to be on the receiving end of her wrath.

I placed gentle hands on her shoulders, looking her squarely in the eye. "You cannot go on like this. If you will not allow me to spirit him away, then we must find something for you to do—something to distract you from him. What makes you happiest?"

She answered almost instantly. "Drawing and prayer. You know that."

I nodded. "Well then, you shall be Galahad and Mordred's tutor. It will give you a chance to spend more time with your son. You can teach them each day after they go to the stable yard for their lessons. Art lessons will be a nice addition to what they already learn from the Ollamh Arthur employs."

"Do you really think they will want to learn art? Aren't boys more interested in swords and punching each other?"

I laughed. "Yes, but they are of an age you can convince them to do anything if you put it to them in terms of their future career as knights. I'll remind them that scouting will be an essential part of their training and tell them the story of Tristan and how his accurate maps won the battle of Caledon Wood for us."

Elaine grasped my hand. "Thank you, Guinevere. You've always known just what I needed even before I did."

I smiled at her, pleased to see her mood lifted. "Well, there is one more thing, something I wasn't going to mention yet, but I could use your help. You must swear you will keep it secret at least for now."

Elaine placed a finger to her lips and leaned in close. "I swear it. Tell me."

I took a deep breath. Just because I was not happy with it did not change the facts. "Arthur is thinking of becoming a Christian."

Elaine squealed in delight. "Oh, do you know what this means?" She clasped her hands at her breast and looked up to the sky as if in prayer. "A Christian king of Britain. I never thought I'd see the day. God be praised."

I lowered her hands to her sides. "Do not get too excited yet. He is just exploring the idea. He says the war changed him, and he's met with Father Dafydd a few times. But you know how priests are. Arthur could use someone to help him understand what being a Christian really means, how it is lived out in daily affairs."

Elaine's eyes widened like the gibbous moon. "Truly? You wish me to counsel the king?"

"Given your love for Christ and your Church, I can think of no one better to guide him."

Elaine threw her arms around me. "You will never know what a gift you have given me this day."

⁕

Elaine's new position tutoring the boys turned out to be a boon for me as well because it gave me a chance to see Lancelot every day when he brought Galahad and Mordred to her chambers. In the aftermath of the war, I had found myself craving his companionship. Arthur was distant, seeking comfort of his own in Morgan's arms and leaving me to deal with my own trauma all alone.

As he had promised that night in the inn, Lancelot was there for me no matter when I needed him. At first, he'd merely listened as I confided my fears, holding me when the panic was overwhelming and letting me cry when the guilt surfaced. Sometimes I fell asleep in his arms. When I woke in terror in the dark of night, it was not Arthur I sought but my champion.

One night, months after we had returned to Camelot, I slipped into Lancelot's doorway, breathless and sweating, heart still pounding from the vivid nightmare in which Elga had succeeded in killing both of us at Badon. I was so happy we were both alive I didn't even greet him. I ran over to where he lay drenched in moonlight and kissed him, waking him from a sound sleep. He never tried to push me away, merely smiled into my kiss and drew me to him. Peeling away my sticky shift, I bit his neck, letting him know I no longer wished our relationship to be chaste. He responded by tangling a hand in the hair at the nape of my neck and pulling me on top of him. His face was buried in my breasts as I moved against him, welcoming his touch as though I was starving without him. And maybe I was. It had been ages since Arthur had touched me.

When we had finally sated our hunger, he laced his fingers in mine and smiled. "I knew you cared for me. Finally, so do you."

That was how it had begun, but that certainly wasn't the last of it. Every day, Lancelot sought me out once the boys were safely in Elaine's care. Arthur and Morgan, who claimed she wanted to convert with her husband—I didn't believe that for a moment— were taking their catechism lessons at that time, so we had no fear of being caught, which often made us reckless. Once, he didn't even pull me into a room—he grabbed my hand as I came around the corner, pushed me up against the wall, and took me right there in the hallway.

We grew bolder as time wore on, and no one gave indication of suspecting our forbidden trysts. On Beltane, I found him waiting in my chambers after dinner. It wasn't long before we were intertwined on the bed, gasping as we searched each other's bodies. Forgetting myself, I cried out under his probing tongue.

Lancelot clasped a hand over my mouth. "I am flattered, but do you wish all of Camelot to know what we're up to?"

I felt my face, already pink from exertion, flush. "Many couples will do the same tonight. Perhaps I was not heard?"

But Lady Fortuna was not with us. Not long after, Arthur called my name from the other side of the door. "Guinevere, are you unwell?"

Damn. Of all the people to be nearby. Admonishing Lancelot to hide, I hastened to don my tunic.

Bracing myself for what may come, I opened the door and placed a hand on my middle back. I prayed my moan could have been mistaken for pain. "There is no need to worry. I simply wrenched my back."

Arthur grimaced in sympathy. "Do you need any help?"

I shook my head. "I will manage. Thank you."

"At least allow me to massage your back."

Seeing no way around it, I opened the door farther so he could pass through, and I scanned the room. Lancelot was nowhere in sight.

"Where does it pain you?" Arthur asked once I was facedown on the bed.

I indicated a muscle below my right shoulder blade that had a history of giving me trouble.

"Ah, that one again." He kneaded my back with long, soothing motions.

It wasn't long before I realized he had intentions beyond relieving my sore muscle. His breathing grew ragged, his arousal evident.

I could not do this with the possibility of Lancelot somewhere in the same room. Carefully, I turned onto my side. "Arthur, I do not think that is wise. What if we make the muscle worse?"

"A bit of loosening up may be just what you need." He kissed my neck, trailing his tongue across my shoulders.

I pretended to give in, trying desperately to think of ways to resist without offending him.

There was a knock at the door.

"Go away," Arthur muttered but went to answer it anyway.

It was Lancelot. He must have escaped out the window or crept out while Arthur's attention was on me. "My lord, I am sorry to call on you at this late hour, but you were seen entering this room, and Morgan is looking for you."

"Can't it wait?" Arthur asked through gritted teeth.

"I think not."

Arthur paused, and I sensed him soften. *Thank the gods. Tonight was one night I wanted you to choose Morgan over me.*

"Of course." Arthur gestured to me over his shoulder. "The queen has injured her back. See she wants for nothing."

Lancelot bit back a smile, bowed to Arthur, and stepped into the room.

"How did you escape?" I asked, incredulous, as soon as the door was closed again.

He grinned and nodded toward the window. "Magic. Now, where were we?"

Chapter Twenty

Summer 507

A pleasant breeze blew in off the bay as we sat in Camelot's council chambers. Gawain and Peredur were debating how best to use the Combrogi's skill in peacetime. Peredur was arguing that since each kingdom was represented on the council by a lord and a knight, they should establish a school to train future members who may not be able to afford to travel to Camelot to serve Arthur directly. Gawain, on the other hand, felt their skills would be best used as a traveling band of soldiers policing the countryside in cooperation with the local kings and lords.

"We have here two intriguing yet contrasting proposals. What say the rest of you?" Arthur inquired of the group.

"If we bring Peredur's vision to life, I would like to travel to each school to ensure they have adequate horsemen to train the cavalry steeds as well as inspect their methods," Lancelot requested.

"What about women?" Constantine jested. "We already have one here. Why not recruit more?"

Sobian faced him down, picking at her fingernails with her dagger. "Afraid I have bigger berries than you? Oh wait, I saw yours just last week." She made a clucking sound with her tongue. "I'm afraid my twig is longer too."

"Enough," Arthur called. "Gawain, I am intrigued by the potential of your plan to keep the Combrogi going through future generations. But it comes at a large financial cost. How would you recommend paying for it? Am I to ask the kings of each territory to shoulder the burden, which means raising taxes, or do you have another source of funding in mind?"

"We amassed considerable fortune from the Saxons—" Gawain began.

But I didn't hear the rest of what he said for in the courtyard below, a ruckus was brewing. I stood and went over to the window, straining to see what interruption awaited us.

"Make way," a young deacon called. "This man of God is here to see the king."

Around them, the crowd of people parted, a few dropping to their knees and crossing themselves as a priest blessed them.

"It is so good to see how the true faith has spread," the priest mused loudly.

I shivered. I knew that voice. Father Marius had returned at long last from his sojourn in Rome. This could mean only one thing—trouble was sure to follow.

I slipped silently around to Arthur's side and whispered, "We have visitors."

Arthur cocked an eyebrow.

"Father Marius has returned. He and his followers are asking after you."

Arthur nodded almost imperceptibly, never taking his eyes from Gawain. "You make a valid point, Gawain," he said as though I hadn't spoken.

A few moments later the priest in question made his entrance. All discussion ceased immediately, and half the room got to its feet, some with weapons drawn to defend us against whoever threatened our peace.

"My king, I am so pleased to hear about your conversion," Father Marius said by way of greeting. "The Bishop of Rome sends his blessings." He extended his arms as though he would embrace Arthur.

"Father Marius," Arthur acknowledged coolly.

"Bishop," he corrected. "His Holiness saw fit to elevate this humble servant of God." He held out his hand as though he expected Arthur to show deference.

To his credit, Arthur didn't move.

At least that explained why I hadn't immediately recognized Marius. Gone was the shoulder-length golden hair shaved in the Celtic style. Instead he wore his hair short and cropped into a circular tonsure that left the top of his head completely bald. He also wore a short hooded mantle over his signature crimson robes.

"*Bishop* Marius," Arthur amended, "I thank you for your kind words. I will gladly speak with you later, once our meeting has adjourned. Will you and your"—he looked the deacon up and down, unsure what to make of him—"boy take some refreshments until then? Kay, will you please escort our guests to the audience chamber and see they are comfortable?"

Kay obeyed, trying his best to usher the two men out of the room, but Marius would not be swayed. "My lord, I mean no disrespect, but I think it fitting that I stay."

His appearance may have changed, but his personality certainly had not.

Arthur pressed his lips together and took a deep breath before answering, fighting to keep calm in front of his men. "And why is that?"

Bishop Marius was itching to take a seat. "I bring news from across the Continent that may well influence your decision-making."

Constantine spoke up. "We have had a long day and are no closer to reaching a decision, my lord. Perhaps we should break for a while so you can speak with your guests. We can resume tonight after the evening meal if you are in a hurry to decide."

I wanted to hit him for speaking up. The last thing I wanted was a private audience with this hateful man who had apparently only prospered as the years passed.

"You are a wise man. We shall all meet back here after we have supped. You may go," Arthur dismissed the group.

Kay and Lancelot lingered behind in their role as our protectors, but once the rest of the Combrogi dispersed, we gathered in the small antechamber off the round meeting room. At an order from Arthur, servants set out goblets of wine and the platters of breads and cheese intended for the Combrogi. Bishop Marius seated himself with royal flair on a stool near the window, a location which guaranteed all eyes would be on him. Arthur and I stood around him, uncertain how to proceed.

Arthur was not afraid to speak first. "Please tell me, Father—or what should I call you now?"

"'Your Excellency' is the proper term, but as we are no strangers, you may call me Bishop Marius if you like," he answered with a smug smile while his deacon hurried like a frightened slave to pour him some wine.

"Your Excellency, what news is so important that you saw fit to interrupt an official gathering of the council?" The slight twitch in Arthur's jaw as he ground his teeth did not escape my notice.

"Must we rush our time together?" Bishop Marius said languidly, picking up the goblet and swirling it in lazy circles. "I have not even been introduced to this lad"—he indicated Lancelot—"or had a chance to greet your lovely wife." His voice was as sweet as nectar, but the way he narrowed his eyes at me left no illusions that his views on me had softened over time.

"I would say it is wonderful to see you, *Your Excellency*, but it is a sin to lie to a priest, is it not?"

Arthur shot me a look that would have chided me to tears had I been a child. But I was not, and I had not forgotten that this man was the main reason why I had been torn away from the love of my life and kicked out of my father's house, something for which I would never forgive him.

Father Marius clucked his tongue. "Such temper, my queen. Do you remember what happened when last you loosed your wicked tongue on me?"

"Do *you* remember what you said when last we met?" I countered. "You said I was cursed and compared me to Lilith, the mother of all demons, if I remember correctly."

"You exaggerate, my dear." He looked at Arthur. "I was merely trying to explain a possible reason she had not yet borne you an heir."

Arthur wasn't buying his story. "You forget, *Your Excellency,* that I know what transpired between you and my wife before we met."

"Are you certain? Who is to say she is telling you the truth?" Bishop Marius asked before he sipped his wine, his manner as blithe as though we were on a summer outing.

I opened my mouth to respond, but Arthur was faster. "I trust my wife."

"At least one of them," Marius said disapprovingly.

Arthur refused to acknowledge the dig. "Guinevere has given me a thousand reasons to believe every word she says. You, however, are relatively unknown to me and have yet to gain my trust. I do not care what rank or title you hold over me in the eyes of the Church. In this world, *I* am still high king, and *you* are my subject, so I suggest you remember that."

Marius appeared not to have heard Arthur's threat. He smiled. "Well then, perhaps now is the time to begin earning your trust. That news I mentioned? I thought you would be interested to know that Clovis of the Franks is winning his war against the Visigoths in southern Gaul."

"What has this to do with us?" I asked.

"Patience, my queen. Clovis won the support of the Gallo-Romanic aristocracy by virtue of his choice to embrace the Christian faith. It is their money funding his war and their men who are sacrificing their lives to rid the Continent of the savage unbelievers."

Arthur was watching Marius with keen interest. "So you are saying my new faith could have political advantages as well?"

Marius took another swig of wine. "Certainly. The Romans

and the Franks—Clovis's group at least—now consider you a strategic ally, provided of course you don't make any bold moves against them. I am willing to bet you have quite a few Gallic supporters as well, although they tend to be a quieter lot."

I wrinkled my brow. "You are a man of God, so how are you getting your intelligence?" I was trying to ascertain if his words were all lies to gain favor in Arthur's eyes or if his information was genuine.

He smiled, apparently guessing my motive. "During my time in Rome, I met many dignitaries. As a result, I now have friends in monasteries and palaces from Byzantium to Gaul. You could do worse than to have someone in my position at your side."

"I already have a strategic advisor, Bishop Marius. I have no need for another," Arthur said, but I could see he was chewing on the idea that damned priest had just fed him. "And I do not seek to usurp him. I am simply giving you the benefit of what I know. My greatest concern is and always will be in spiritual matters."

"I already have a spiritual advisor as well."

"Oh, that is right. I have heard of this young priest. What is his name?" The bishop feigned ignorance.

"Father Dafydd," I supplied.

Marius snapped his fingers. "Yes! His reputation has reached even the ears of Rome." He turned to his deacon. "Timothy, would you be so kind as to fetch Father Dafydd? I would like to meet him and express my gratitude for all he has done."

I stopped listening as Marius and my husband debated some matter of the Christian faith, something about a heretic called Pelagius and whether or not perfection was possible without grace from their god. They held opposing views, which each expressed passionately. They were giving me a headache.

I was grateful when Timothy returned with Father Dafydd in his wake.

Arthur greeted Dafydd with a warm smile and a manly embrace. Then he turned to the bishop. "Bishop Marius, may I present to you Father Dafydd of Dyfed, personal confessor to myself and certain members of my court. His humble example is much of what attracted me to Christianity."

Father Dafydd bowed, eyes wide and cheeks flushed, as though astonished to have someone of Marius's rank in his presence.

Marius bid him to rise. "Word of your excellent care of our king reached me even in Rome. I wish to thank you for carefully shepherding him into the fold."

Father Dafydd looked down humbly. "I only answered his questions and guided him as he sought me out. The rest was the work of God."

"Ah, but it has found a willing instrument in you."

"You are too kind."

"Not at all. In fact, I must confess I have an ulterior motive for calling you here. His Holiness has expressed a deep desire to see this land converted." Bishop Marius looked at me pointedly before returning his attention to Father Dafydd. "You did so well with our king that he wishes to see your work continue in other parts of the isle."

"But who will fill my role with the king, Lady Morgan, and Lady Elaine?"

"I am sure we will find someone."

Someone like you?

"Wait." Arthur put out a hand to halt the conversation. "You cannot simply replace Father Dafydd. If I wish him to remain, he will do so."

"I'm afraid he can. He is my superior, and I am answerable first to him," Father Dafydd said.

Arthur spluttered, unused to anyone contradicting his will.

"Where will you send me?" Father Dafydd asked with more calm than I felt.

I narrowed my eyes at the bishop. Something wasn't right with this situation. Marius did nothing without personal gain, so wherever he was assigning our beloved priest would surely benefit him. I hoped he was sincere in his compliments and the younger priest would be rewarded accordingly, but past experience encouraged doubt to gnaw at my stomach. No doubt Bishop Marius was also aware Father Dafydd had not insisted I convert along with my husband and was, therefore, a failure in his eyes.

Bishop Marius stroked his chin where the shadow of whiskers had begun to appear with the advancing day. "I was thinking you would be perfect to preach to the Highlanders."

My mouth fell open. The Highlanders were notorious for their intolerance for missionaries. Sending Father Dafydd into their lands was akin to a death sentence. "Not even you could be so cruel!"

"Cruel? No, I am giving this man the greatest opportunity a Christian can have—the chance to preach to a pagan people. If he can successfully convert them, it will cement his place in history, like our revered Patrick. If not and he loses his life in the process, he will achieve the crown of martyrdom, which is the ultimate goal of all Christian souls. There is no greater sacrifice than to lay down one's life for one's faith."

"Nothing we can say will change your mind, will it?" I said, finally understanding the strategy of Marius's visit. He meant to take over as Arthur's advisor. The man was brilliant—evil but brilliant.

"I am afraid not."

Father Dafydd bowed his head humbly. "When do I depart, Your Excellency?"

"I think it best for the transition to happen quickly. You will have tomorrow to say your good-byes."

I looked at Father Dafydd, unable to believe this kind man would soon be gone forever, likely to be replaced by Bishop Marius. Tears filled my eyes, and I blinked them back, determined not to let that vile man see how deeply he had affected me.

"Would that all men had your grace, your tolerance, and your fortitude," I said to Father Dafydd quietly as I escorted him from the room.

"But if they did, there would be no need for people like you and me," he answered with a soft smile. "Every wife has a duty to guide her husband to the side of right. I am afraid you are doubly pressed in this regard as a priestess and as a queen living amid religious turmoil. Promise me one thing."

"Anything."

"Do not allow Bishop Marius to gain control of the king. Remember that you are as powerful as he, and do not let him intimidate either of you. I must listen to him, but you are under no such obligation."

I nodded. "I swear I will do everything in my power to do as you have asked." I paused, trying to decide whether or not to ask the question weighing on my mind. "Are you frightened of your new assignment?"

Father Dafydd smiled once more, lit from within. "'The Lord is my shepherd, and so I shall not fear.' When I became a priest, I made a vow to do whatever God willed of me, just as you did when you became a priestess. We may not always like what they say to us, but we must follow where they lead." He placed a hand on my shoulder. "May your gods bless you and give you strength."

I bowed my head to hide the tears seeping from my eyes. "The same to you."

He squeezed my hand once and disappeared around the corner.

I never saw him again.

CHAPTER TWENTY-ONE

Spring 514

Arthur shook me awake. "Guinevere!"

"What?" I mumbled, refusing to open my eyes or shift from my comfortable position.

"I have had the most incredible dream! Wake up! I must tell you about it."

"Go tell Morgan about it. She's your favorite wife, is she not?" I grumbled.

"You don't understand. Please, just listen."

Arthur's voice was so animated I couldn't ignore it, as much as I wanted to. I rolled onto my back and opened my eyes. It was still dark, probably a few hours before dawn. The room around us was quiet save for Arthur's ragged breathing. I said a silent prayer of gratitude, invoking the goddess Arianrhod, who watched over all couples engaged in lusty affairs, that this was one of the rare nights Lancelot wasn't with me.

I turned toward Arthur. His eyes were more alive than I'd

seen them in ages, sparkling in the moonlight like faceted jewels. I couldn't resist teasing him. "What? Did you dream that Marius allowed you to keep us both?"

If he heard me, he didn't react. "I have seen her, Guinevere!"

"Who?" I propped my head on one arm so I could regard him closely.

"The Blessed Virgin. She came to me in a dream." His eyes unfocused as he recalled the vision he had seen. "She wishes me to undertake a quest."

I wrinkled my forehead, suspicious of his dream. "What kind of quest?"

Arthur drew me upright, palms on both of my shoulders, and looked me straight in the eye. "She wishes me to find the Holy Grail, the cup which touched the holy lips of Jesus Christ and held His Precious Blood." Arthur's whole expression was alight with fervor. "This is why I came to you first. You, too, have dreamed of it."

I tried to keep my face neutral, though I had little doubt Arthur's fertile imagination had something to do with this. He had spent too much time with Bishop Marius lately, who, with Merlin and Father Dafydd gone, had become his advisor in all things. "Arthur, slow down. Tell me exactly what you dreamed."

His eyes took on that dreamy expression again. "The Virgin Mary appeared to me. She was dressed all in blue, like the robes I've seen you wear. Her long brown hair was loose and uncovered, spilling over her shoulders, and she was suffused with light. It should have blinded me, but it did not. Behind her, the world was split in two, ringed in a circle, onto which her crucified Son was bound. In the top half of the circle, there was happiness and light. Camelot prospered, and the land was fertile. She touched the circle, and it spun so that Our Lord was crushed beneath it. There below, storm clouds raged and lightning flashed. Sickness, death, and decay were everywhere. Camelot lay in ruins at the hands of our enemies."

I recognized the image Arthur described. She was not the Virgin Mary but the goddess Fortuna with her wheel of fate. She directed all things, positive and negative, and her whims determined whether we prospered or fell to ruin. But now was not the time to contradict him. "Go on."

"The Blessed Mother held out a cup—at least I think it was a cup. It could have been a bowl or cauldron too. The light coming from it was so bright it was difficult to gaze upon it for too long or look directly at it. Above the cup was a shining white host, the symbol of our Lord here on earth."

Host or full moon? The Grail—holy to Christians and Druids alike—was, for my faith, the repository of all inspiration as well as the tool the goddess Ceridwen used to bestow rebirth upon those destined to live again. Its shifting appearance was no surprise to me for, as Arthur accurately recalled, I had seen it in my dreams since I was a child. Once it was a golden chalice. Then a drinking horn. The next time an iron or bronze cauldron. Once, it was even a stone. We could argue all day over the identity of the woman, but one thing was for certain—Arthur had indeed seen the Grail.

"Did the woman say anything to you?"

He nodded. "Once I had taken in the scene, she regarded me placidly and said, 'My son, you have served me well, but now I have a greater request of you. You are to seek out this holy object, not for yourself or for a select few but for all. It is a gift for all my people and a sign of my heavenly blessing. With it, you shall know peace and everlasting contentment. But take care not to betray the promises you have made to me, for doing so will cause this gift to vanish and your reign of peace to come to an end.' Then she held the cup to my lips, and I drank of it. It was at once the sweetest and most bitter liquid I have ever tasted. It was as though blood and starlight had combined."

I knew the taste well. Once imbibed, it could never be forgotten. The night in Avalon when I found out about Mona's dreams and Morgan's lack of lineage, I had dreamed I drank from the Grail. The shock of bitterness awoke me, and from that moment on, my life changed. I wondered if the same would now be true for Arthur.

"When she drew the cup away, I felt an acute sense of loss, like some vital part of me went with it. I knew in my heart I would not be at peace until the Grail is found. She left me with these parting words, 'Go now, son of the high dragon, and do as I have commanded. I am with you always.'

Arthur grasped my shoulders, his blazing blue eyes locked on mine. "Do you see, Guinevere? This is my destiny. All the battles and trials that have come before, even my conversion, were preparation to make me ready for this heavenly quest. Turning away the Saxons may have been the first step on the road to peace, but finding the Grail will cement it for all time. My legacy to this land, *our* legacy to this land, is to retrieve the Grail and preserve the peace in Camelot forever." He fell silent then, most likely contemplating his dream once again.

I blinked, trying to comprehend this sudden obsession that had overtaken my husband. Was he drunk or ill? He had been sober when I retired for the night, and it was not like him to drink once supper was ended unless there was a great feast. I felt his forehead. Though his cheeks were rosy with excitement, he showed no signs of fever. Maybe he was in his right mind. If Fortuna had truly come to him, I was not one to stand in her way.

"Grainne recently returned from Avalon with rumors that the Grail Maidens have abandoned their post beneath the Tor and moved their holy treasure somewhere in our land. I didn't think anything of it when she told me because Avalon is full of such whisperings, born of moon madness or too many nights of fasting, but what you say confirms her report."

He embraced me. "You believe me?"

"I cannot confirm if it is your destiny, but yes, I believe you are under divine orders to find the Grail." I was so grateful he had come to me first rather than Morgan or that damned bishop, either of whom might have manipulated his experience to suit their own needs.

Arthur kissed me deeply. "Then you will support me as I raise the quest?"

I shifted my position so I was sitting in his lap, legs wrapped around him. "I will do you one better—I will help you. We ride together, side by side, just as we swore to one another we would be in all things."

⚬⚬

Arthur sent for the Combrogi before dawn colored the eastern sky, and soon Camelot was abuzz with rumors of the unprecedented voyage to come. The kitchens were set to full staff to prepare rations for the men. Only the stables, forges, and armory buzzed with more activity as horses were shod and groomed and men prepared for unknown battles by mending shields and armor and sharpening blades. I spent most of my time in the armory, directing the flow of weapons and men, while Lancelot held sway in the stables. As my champion, he normally would not have left my side, but Arthur had agreed to allow him to join them on the quest since he was the most widely traveled and might be of assistance.

Mordred, newly returned from his five-year fostership with Lot, had been asking every day for the last week to accompany his father, little dismayed even though Arthur always forbade it. Mordred was not quite seventeen, the age at which he would qualify, but I doubted Arthur would have let him go—and put his only heir in danger—at any age.

Morgan, Grainne, and I were preparing poultices, draughts, and other herbal remedies the men may need on their quest when Arthur burst in.

He grabbed my hands. "The Combrogi are nearly all here. I need to know where to begin looking. My dream told me nothing. The Grail could be in the north country or Brittany or just around the bend for all I know."

I looked at him, wondering what he wanted from me, as I kept one eye on the bubbling brownish-green concoction simmering at my side.

Arthur huffed, impatience rising along with the color in his face. "You have the sight. Isn't there anything you can tell me?"

I snorted, slightly offended. "Arthur, I'm not your personal oracle. Besides, I cannot foretell the future. I can only see what is happening at this very moment. If you want the future, ask your other wife."

Morgan looked up then. "What does he want?"

I regarded her over my shoulder. "For us to tell him where to find the Grail."

Morgan went back to the herbs she was grinding with her pestle. "I'd suggest starting in Avalon."

Arthur threw up his hands and stomped out of the room, muttering something about women being no help. Morgan and I laughed in a rare moment of camaraderie that reminded me of our better days in Avalon.

"You know," Grainne said, "I think there is something we can do to help the Combrogi."

I strained the simmering liquid into a vial and set it on a shelf to cool. "What is that?"

"Tomorrow is the time of equal day and night. If the three of us join forces, I am willing to bet the gods will enlighten us. Our gifts may be different, but if this truly is Fortuna's command, she cannot ignore our invocations."

"Yes," Morgan said. "I like this idea very much."

I stared at her, weighing Grainne's idea. "But you are Christian now. Isn't such a thing against your faith?"

"Normally, yes, but it is the Grail we seek, holy to both faiths. I'm sure God wouldn't mind me breaking one little rule in this special circumstance."

"Even so, we do not know the exact time of balance. We would need that information to tap into the magic of the day," I said.

Morgan's smile was sly. "Ah, but we know someone who can tell us."

"Who? Merlin is not here, and Marius is not versed in the stars," I noted.

"No, you witless woman. Your beloved, Aggrivane."

I glared at her, crossing my arms defensively. "He is not my lover."

"Not anymore, but that doesn't mean he cannot be of use."

I mulled over the options in my head, trying to decide how best to approach Aggrivane. We had barely spoken since I returned from Avalon years ago because his son had died from the fever he'd contracted just before Malegant kidnapped me. But on the other hand, when Aggrivane found out the nature of the mission Arthur was sending us on, he would be eager to help. Aggrivane had always dreamed of finding one of the thirteen holy hallows of Britain, and the Grail superseded them all. No doubt his Christian wife would urge him on even more.

"I will ask him. If you are right, then the Combrogi will leave as soon as Arthur tells them what we've found." I put down the wooden spoon I was using to stir a thick burgundy gooseberry paste. "Grainne, can you take over here? I must be sure to be packed before our ritual."

"You need not rush. You will not be going with them," said Morgan as I removed the apron covering my tunic.

My head snapped up. "How do you know?"

She tapped the center of her forehead, indicating she'd seen it with second sight. "Trust me."

Her laughter trailed behind me as I ran into the night, intent on finding Aggrivane.

⚬⚬⚬

The appointed day and hour had come.

Thin shafts of sunlight occasionally pierced through the low, milky clouds as we picked our way through the moss-covered rocks where the earth met the sea far below Camelot. Only a few hours before, high tide had submerged this whole area in shoulder-deep saltwater all the way to the base of the cliff on which the fortress rested. But now it had retreated, leaving behind gleaming tide pools in the pockmarked stone. Waves still lapped at the outer banks, so we stayed farther inland, but we ventured out far enough that the hiss and gurgle of the surf could be easily heard.

"Here," Grainne called our small party to a halt. "This is the place."

We sat on the soft moss in a loose semicircle, three small pools between us. We joined hands, eyes closed and breathing deeply to attune ourselves to the energy around us. That was more difficult than it seemed in this place of shifting sea and land, both grasping and conceding power with each roll of the waves. Add to that the warring of day and night in the sky above us, and it took us some time to find the place of calm deep within where all acts of magic have their origin.

"Lady Danu, Lord Lir, rulers of this sacred place, we do you homage. We come in peace to implore your aid. The Lady Fortuna has commanded our king to seek the hallowed Grail, one of the treasures of Avalon. In this time of equilibrium, we ask you to help us, your priestesses, as we seek the location of this sacred vessel so that he may fulfill her holy will."

The wind rose in response, whispering in its secret tongue, lifting the sleeves and collars of our blue robes. Along with the sweep of the water and the cries of the gulls, the wind lulled me into a trance. Everything went silent as though the entire world had ceased to exist. For a few splendid moments, all the elements, night and day, summer and winter, were in balance.

Morgan, Grainne, and I blinked at each other in wonder.

When a ray of light spilled its glimmering liquid gold onto the pool in front of me, I knew it was time. Squeezing my sisters' hands, I leaned forward to gaze into the water. A starfish clung to one side, scarcely noticing a small crab scuttling over him to reach the safety of shore. Rings of green algae floated on the surface, and if I stared past them, the stones and shells at the base of the pool became visible.

But then a white-gray mist clouded the surface, and I lost all sense of the mortal world. I was flying on the brown and white wings of an osprey, viewing a far-off landscape through its masked eyes. Below, a procession of women wound through a narrow valley between two dense thickets of wood, following a thin ribbon of silver water as it sought the faraway sea.

Their blue crescents marked them as priestesses, and their silver-gray robes and belts of dangling silver charms singled them out as keepers of the Grail. They chanted as they walked, eyes closed, feet effortlessly skirting rocks, fallen branches, and even the delicate buds of lavender snow flowers.

At the head of the nine women, one carried a thurible of glass and copper that glowed as if with its own light, providing amber illumination and scenting the air with a heady smoke through holes in its spiraling metal finial. Behind her followed two women acting as guards, each carrying a fearsome silver sickle. Next came my childhood friend, Rowena, her long dark hair caught in twin braids that bounced as she walked. She carried a tall silver amphora that I instinctively understood contained waters from the red-and-white spring. Two more guards came after her, then a veiled woman swathed in golden robes. She could be none other than the Grail Maiden. Her sacred charge also was veiled, so I could not see what form the Grail took within her hands. Another pair of guards brought up the rear.

Magic radiated from them like a shield, preventing me from drawing too near. I cried out, hoping to catch Rowena's attention, but she paid me no heed. They were following a voice only they could hear and gave no indication of their destination.

Frustrated, I soared high, trying to use my avian senses to tell me where we might be and in what direction they were headed. The air currents were a tailwind pushing me along. This time of year, they usually came from the south and east. The women were walking against the flow of the river, so that must mean they were traveling north.

But to where? Banking upward again, I scanned the horizon for some familiar landmark. After following them for what felt like hours, I saw it—a wide circle of tall thin monoliths surrounded by a white chalk ditch. Inside the large circle were two smaller ones. That had to be the ancient Sanctuary of the Stars. I expected them to head toward it and camp there, but they passed it by.

By then, I was losing my connection with the bird, slowly regaining my human consciousness. I had learned all I was going to know. I opened my eyes to find Morgan and Grainne blinking at me as if they too had just awoken from a dream.

We thanked the God and Goddess in turn but did not share our experiences. Those were for Arthur alone to know.

"Shall we tell him?" Morgan asked.

Grainne and I nodded. "Let's go then."

⁓ ❧ ❧ ⁓

We found Arthur assembled with the Combrogi in the meeting chamber. He was standing atop the table to be better heard over the clamoring crowd. He must have just told them what the quest was to be for they were cheering and whistling, pagan and Christian alike, as we wound through the throng to his side. Lancelot helped me climb onto the table, where I came face to face with a beaming Bishop Marius.

Not one to lose the opportunity to pontificate in front of a crowd, Bishop Marius held out his arms as though welcoming the adulation of the crowd until they finally quieted. "My brothers and sisters, we have been blessed by God to not only have a Christian couple to lead our land"—he nodded at Arthur and Morgan, ignoring me completely—"but now our king has been favored by heaven to be the instrument of the greatest miracle of our age. As you embark upon this perilous journey, I beg you to consider the well-being of your souls and shrive yourself of any sins before you depart. Only in that way will any and all of you be worthy to behold such a sight as the Holy Grail. Were it in my power, I would accompany you myself. But as my duties keep me here, go forth with my blessing and that of the Father, Son,"—he made the sign of the cross over the gathered soldiers—"and Holy Ghost."

Some of the men crossed themselves while others made the sign of Avalon and a few stared awkwardly at the ground.

"Thank you, bishop. We go with joy in our hearts knowing we have your benediction," Arthur said to Marius with a pleased smile. He turned back to the assembly. "Some of you may have noticed I have yet to mention where we are going. That is because I do not know myself. But I have asked three of our strongest seeresses for their guidance—"

"I must strenuously object," Marius interrupted. "It is highly improper to consult pagan oracles when you have been entrusted with a Christian mission."

"Jealous they have knowledge you do not?" came a female voice from deep within the crowd. It was one of Sobian's girls.

"Yes," someone else agreed. "Let them speak."

Morgan and Grainne looked at me hesitantly before joining us atop the table.

I cleared my throat. "Know that what we see is not writ in stone but shifts with the actions of men. The most we can do is advise you as best we know."

"See?" Marius yelled. "Even they admit their information is fickle at best."

I ignored him. "The Grail has indeed left Avalon. I have seen its procession. Earlier today, they passed the Sanctuary of the Stars on the great chalk plain. Head south, and you shall meet them. But beware. They are heavily armed, so if you desire the Grail for yourself or have any ill intent, better you stay behind than face their blades."

"Indeed," Grainne continued, "not all who undertake this journey will return. For some of you, this will be your final task— I have seen your souls march to the Otherworld. But fear not, for all who set out do so under the aegis of the Goddess."

Morgan stepped forward. "Of you, only three shall find the vessel. One will prove unworthy and return before glimpsing its glory. But when it is brought to Camelot, all those honored by the great King Arthur shall behold it. So have I seen, and so shall it be."

The crowd was silent, stunned as though the threefold Goddess had appeared before them and spoken words of prophecy. Even Marius was speechless, contemplating the implications of our words.

Arthur was the first to find his voice. "Choose your groups and your destinations. Stay out of Saxon lands for we do not wish to start a war on this mission of peace. Eat, drink, and say your farewells for we leave at dawn."

Once the four of us climbed off the table, everyone began talking at once, making it nearly impossible to hear any one person, but Morgan's voice still found me. "Arthur, be careful. Not just for my sake but for your son's."

"Mordred is nearly a man. He will be fine."

Morgan rubbed her belly. "Not Mordred. Your new son." Her smile was more luminous than I'd ever seen it.

"You are with child?"

"I am. You will have another heir by midwinter. Hurry home." She kissed Arthur softly.

Arthur hugged her tightly. "This is the best possible news you could have sent me off with. I will return with the Grail for our son—or daughter."

"Benedictio Dei," Marius blessed them with a joyful grin. He apparently approved of this second marriage even more now that it had been graced with new life.

Arthur caught sight of me, and his expression changed. He was unable to hide the flash of pity that came before his joy transformed into sobriety. Anger, hurt, and jealousy warred within me. After all this time, he still felt pity for me. I had finally accepted I would never bear him another child, but now Morgan was going to publicly prove once and for all that it was I who was barren, not Arthur.

"This changes everything," Arthur said.

I took a deep breath, willing myself to be calm and collected before answering. "Indeed it does. A baby will turn the whole castle upside down." I forced a smile.

Arthur's face clouded over. "No, I mean you cannot accompany me on the quest. Morgan will need a midwife. You must stay here and look after her."

"No." I would not let Morgan take away yet another opportunity. "Grainne is just as qualified as I am. That is no cause for concern." Every muscle in my body tensed as I fought for control over myself, my voice growing more strained.

Arthur took my hand and patted it. I was sure he meant the gesture to be comforting, but in my current mood, it was patronizing.

"I know Grainne is your friend, but after how badly your childbirth ended, I cannot trust her with the life of Morgan and my child. Plus, someone must see to Camelot while I am away. You are my queen—only you"—he looked me deep in the eyes to ensure I understood his double meaning—"have the authority to pass judgment in my absence. You are the only one I trust with this power."

I nodded, understanding what he was trying to convey. Morgan may have been his royal wife and mother to his child—soon to be children—but I was queen. That was something Morgan could never take away from me.

"Camelot will be safe in my keeping. This do I swear to you. Return to me hale and whole, husband." I kissed him then looked at Morgan, who was reveling in the well wishes of those who had heard her announcement. "For you have more to live for than ever before."

Chapter Twenty-Two

Summer 514

Arthur wrote to Morgan and me as often as he could, keeping us abreast of their progress and obstacles in finding the Grail. By the time they reached the Sanctuary of the Stars, the Grail maidens had long since moved on, and they were having trouble tracking their movements.

Arthur wrote, *"Despite the setbacks we encounter, I have great faith that the Holy Ghost will direct us to the Grail in the end. As each moment of our lives has led us to this point, each step we take brings us closer to our destined prize. Its acquisition will assure Camelot's safety and prosperity as well as fix our legacy in the annals of time. Have no fear for me, for my passion for this great quest does not wane with time but rather grows as I see signs of God's divine hand all around us. I beg you to keep me, the Combrogi, and this divine mission in your prayers. I send my love to both of you and to my son."*

When I read the letter aloud to Morgan and Mordred, he grumbled, "As his son, I should be by his side, not here with the women."

But as much as he complained, Mordred was making good use of his time stuck in Camelot. He'd proclaimed himself Lord of Camelot in his father's absence and my champion while Lancelot was away. He more than proved himself worthy of the jobs, displaying a subtle cunning he could have learned only from Lot and—despite his age and general attitude of superiority—a wisdom no doubt born of Ana's influence.

Elaine was as taken with his progress as though he were her own son, which I supposed was only natural given that Galahad was off with Arthur and his men. Now that the boys were too old for her art lessons, she clung to me like spider silk, and her constant vacillations in mood grated on my nerves. Between Morgan's gloating over her advancing pregnancy and Elaine's ever-shifting joy at her son's good fortune and despair that he would never return, I was surrounded by madwomen. I was liable to lock Elaine in the dungeon if I couldn't find something useful for her to do.

One sticky summer afternoon when the clouds hung low in the sky, teasing us with the prospect of a storm, the Irish emissary and I were discussing the finer points of a new treaty with King Illan mac Dúnlainge of Leinster. I was trying to convince him that a proposal of marriage between Mordred and his lord's daughter was only one option to securing peace in our lands when one of Arthur's scouts was announced.

"Forgive me," I said to the emissary, who, to my great annoyance, appeared relieved to be given leave of my argument. "Send him in."

The scout was still breathing hard when he sank to one knee before me. "My lady, I come in advance of a party in need of your help. Lancelot and several others were most grievously wounded in Rheged battling a man who called himself the Grail Sentinel. I beg you make ready for their party."

My hand flew to my mouth. For a moment, I could not speak. Fear coursed through me, panic riding in its wake. Lancelot, the man who had saved me countless times, the one whom I considered invincible, was wounded, and badly enough to be transported here. What of Arthur? Had they been together? My knees shook. But then, just as quickly, my experience on the fields of battle and my training as a priestess overrode my emotions.

"The king? How many injured? What is the extent of their wounds?" I found myself asking when all I wanted to do was collapse and cry.

"The king is well, I assure you. He is off in another land, following a lead in pursuit of the holy relic. Eight wounded in all. Most are in need of stitches and bone-setting, but I fear Lancelot suffered the worst. He took a blade in the side, and we cannot fully staunch the bleeding."

"How much time before they arrive?"

The scout thought for a moment. "A day at most."

"Thank you for giving us time to prepare." I asked for Mordred to be sent to me. Once he arrived, I said, "See that our guest is well attended. Also, please find your mother. I have need of her assistance." I nearly choked on the last sentence.

Mordred's face lit up at his new responsibility. "Yes, my lady." He turned to the scout. "Come, sir. Follow me."

I found Elaine in the chapel, on her knees. "Elaine, raise your prayers to God as you work. We must prepare the barracks to receive a number of wounded."

By nightfall, we had converted the barracks into an infirmary, just in time for the soldiers to arrive. Morgan set up a station for mixing herbs and dressing wounds while Elaine ensured supplies were at the ready and water was boiling in the cauldron over the fire. Grainne and I prepared a room in the castle, which was warmer and drier, for those requiring our constant attention.

The carts pulled into the gates of Camelot in the small hours of night, desperate shouts and whinnying of horses breaking the silence of the slumbering castle. Mordred stumbled from the entrance hall and began seeing to the horses without being asked, relieving the men to carry the wounded into the barracks.

The cart bearing Lancelot was in the middle of the pack. Before I even saw his face, I knew he was near to dying. His clothes and the sacks beneath him were pools of black, and even from a distance, the stench of infection made bile rise in my throat. Next to him in the cart were the spoils of his hard-won victory—the armor and head of the knight he had killed.

I wrinkled my nose at the rotting head and told the nearest guard, "Spike that up with the others and take his mail to the armory to see what we can learn from its construction. You two"—I gestured to Gareth and Owain, his guards on the journey here—"get him into the castle. Morgan will show you where to go."

I watched them go, conflicted about whether to attend to him immediately or assess the others first.

"Go, be with him," Grainne said as if reading my thoughts, as if she knew exactly what we were to each other. She squeezed my arm. "You and Morgan are his best hope. I have Elaine to help with the others. Go." She shoved me gently toward the doors.

Morgan was already removing Lancelot's clothing when I arrived. I grabbed a rag and soaked in it hot water, then I applied it to an area around his wound where his clothing adhered to his skin.

"It's a wonder he has not died of blood loss," Morgan said.

Lancelot looked to have been beaten within an inch of his life. His eyes were swollen, painted with purple and black bruises. His lower lip was split and puffy, a long gash running from the left side up an inflamed cheekbone. As my eyes traveled lower, his injuries only worsened. His skin was pale and clammy, a sure sign of inflection if the stench from the wound between his ribs wasn't indication enough. One shoulder stuck out at an odd angle, and he appeared to have taken several crushing blows to the chest. But those would have to wait.

The cloth around his wound finally gave way, and we were able to see the full extent of the damage. The skin around it had already begun to fester, the sickly yellow-green bile the source of the stench. The men had done their best to pack the wound with moss and spider silk, and it was likely the reason why he was still alive now, but it was also the source of the infection.

"We're going to have to cut this skin away," Morgan said. "We need to cleanse the wound first though. Give him some poppy juice to ensure he feels nothing and does not wake."

While she doused his wound with vinegar, I forced Lancelot's mouth open and poured in a carefully measured dose of ruby syrup. Too little and he could stir, crazed with hallucinations. Too much and he might die.

"Be strong, my champion. For me. For the Goddess who raised you and the one who chose you as her own," I whispered in his ear.

We set about the gruesome task of cleaning and debriding the wound. I was thankful for my years of training in Avalon, and even what I had seen at Caledon Wood and Badon, for without it, I surely would not have made it through the surgery. Once we could see the wound clearly, we found the source of the bleeding.

"It looks like he received the bite of an axe. We will have to close it off with heat," Morgan said. "Take that poker out of the fire and bring it to me."

I looked at her uncertainly. I'd never heard of such a method except in conjunction with amputation, which was external, not internal.

"Do you wish him to live or no?" She snapped her fingers at me. "The Greeks did this with much success. I learned it from the healer of Uther's army, a Saracen woman. Have no fear."

She placed the glowing tip of the poker into Lancelot's wound. His flesh sizzled, giving off a smell not unlike meat over a spit. Morgan rinsed the wound once again—this time with boiled, cooled sea water—and inspected it.

"That should stop it." She handed the poker back to me and motioned for a second one, which she placed on the external wound. With a puff of smoke and another sickening whiff of burning flesh, it closed. "If he was likely not to move this area, I would dress the wound as is, but given he will likely tear it open again, I think it best to reinforce it with stitches. Would you like to do the honors?"

I knelt at Lancelot's side and carefully sewed his wound. "Where did you learn all of this? It goes well beyond our training in Avalon."

"One does not spend years as a camp woman without learning a thing or two." Her smile was wry. "Or did you believe I spent all of my time whoring? Of course you did. A battleground where the injured are from multiple lands is the best school a healer could ever ask for, if not the toughest."

After I finished sewing and bandaging Lancelot's wound, we set his broken bones and cleansed his remaining wounds.

Muttering as she worked, Morgan gave vent to her innermost feelings about her profession. "I've told Arthur a thousand times to bring a priestess with him on every mission for we could save lives if they were tended earlier, but he does not listen."

Finally, we lifted the calfskin shades to let in fresh air and cleaned up the space so it resembled more a sick room than a surgery tent. I placed sweet-smelling herbs in vases and on hot coals and cool cloths on Lancelot's forehead and neck to bring his fever down.

"Do you remember how to make a healing beer?" Morgan asked me.

"Yes."

"When he is conscious and can tolerate water from the sacred springs, give him a thick beer of honey, mugwart, oats, and nettles. He will not like the taste, but he has lost a lot of blood, and it will do wonders to help him regain his strength. Then, and only then, allow him to try some bread. We don't need him suffering stomach ills on top of everything else."

I nodded, relieved to see her go. I began the process of brewing the ale, and once it could be left unattended, I sank to the floor next to Lancelot's unconscious form and prayed. My mind could scarcely form words, but I trusted that my patrons, Rhiannon and Lugh, as well as the Morrigan, patroness of those wounded in battle, and Brigid, the great healer, would know the cries of my heart without words.

Sometime in the midst of my prayers, I must have fallen asleep for I walked in the land between worlds with Lancelot, battling a giant dressed in black, the man whose cruel eyes had stared at me from Lancelot's side in the cart. I saw how hard Lancelot had fought and how he received every wound we'd tended, but what I did not know was why.

The knight had just sliced into Lancelot's side with a fierce-looking axe on a long pole when I awoke with a start to a soft rapping on the door. I grunted something that was supposed to resemble "enter," and Elaine peeked around the door. I sat up, motioning for her to come in.

She handed me a cup of wine, which I gratefully drained. "I thought you could use some relief. I have already slept a little. Morgan is abed, and Grainne is watching over those in the barracks. Get some sleep. I will stand vigil." Elaine's eyes misted over, and her face became wistful.

Her expression reminded me of her youthful crush on Lancelot and her fancy that he would become her husband. Oh, how our lives had taken paths we could never have foreseen.

I stood and kissed her cheek. "He is in the hands of his gods. We have done all we can."

Elaine smiled sadly and fingered the enameled ring on her left hand. "Indeed. I will pray for him."

I returned her joyless smile. "That is all we can do. If he wakes, please come find me. Oh!" I suddenly remembered the beginnings of the beer. I covered it tightly. "Be sure no one disturbs this."

Elaine nodded, sitting on a stool at Lancelot's side.

As I slipped out, Elaine took Lancelot's hand and kissed it. Silent tears rolled down her cheeks. Was it possible? Could Elaine still harbor feelings for Lancelot? Surely he could not be her mysterious husband—or could he? I shook my head. No, he certainly would not have engaged in an affair with me were that the case. Yet the memory of Elaine's grief lingered in my mind, as did the seed of doubt.

⁂

One week passed, then two. Lancelot did not improve. I began to fear he would never wake. My days were spent in constant vigil at his side, trading off with Morgan or Elaine only to sleep or perform necessary duties. By the time the full moon came around, we were all at our wits' end.

Morgan wanted to give him wolfsbane to try to draw his spirit back, but I was hesitant.

She wheeled on me when I expressed my concern. "So it was all right for Isolde to use the same drug on you when you were far less injured, but you take issue with me using it to save a dying man?"

I couldn't answer her because she was right in calling out my hypocrisy. But I couldn't let go of the story Merlin had told me about her poisoning Rowena so long ago in Avalon.

"How do you know you won't kill him?" I asked.

She glared at me. "You know I do not know. I am only doing as we were both trained. And as I have far more experience in these dire situations than you, I do not think you are in a place to judge."

I decided to lay my fears on the table. "What about Rowena? You made a mistake once, and she nearly died."

"*You*"—she pointed at me—"were not there. How dare you judge me based on what you did not see for yourself?" She shook her head. "Is that it? Are you afraid I will poison him on purpose? To what end? I have nothing to gain if Lancelot dies. He is Arthur's dearest friend. I would do nothing to hurt him. Why do you always insist on finding me guilty before even asking my side? I may not like you, but I am not out to destroy everyone I meet."

She was right. "What did happen that day?" I asked in a small voice.

Morgan gave a sarcastic laugh. "Twenty years on and now you wish to know." She turned away from me as she prepared the elixir. "I will tell you this—it was not I who added the offending herb to my brew but another who wished to take my place as second. I will not name her, as I have never found proof, but if I ever do, I will kill her with my bare hands in public for all to see. *That* is the real reason why I left Avalon. I could not remain there knowing there was one willing to kill to take my place."

She gave Lancelot the wolfsbane, and we continued our cycle of vigil, tending wounds, and sleep.

A few days later, as I was trudging back from a particularly difficult pleading day, during which I'd lost my patience with the petitioners more than once, Owain and I crossed paths.

"You look like death visited you then changed her mind," he joked.

I glared at him but said nothing.

"Are you hungry?" He was already steering me toward the kitchens.

"Famished," I answered as I sank down on a bench.

He set a cut of meat in front of me on a thick trencher of bread along with a mug of heady ale.

We chewed in silence before I finally asked him, "What happened to Lancelot?"

Owain looked up. "I was wondering when someone was going to ask. Nasty situation that. We were heading into a valley near the border of Rheged and Powys when we encountered him." Owain gestured out the window to where the knight's head now decayed on a pike. "Did you know the villagers are calling him the Black Knight since his entire armor was dark? Anyway, he called himself the Grail Sentinel and declared that anyone who sought it must defeat him first. None of us know if he had any official position or was simply a local loon capitalizing on the quest, but we had to face him in case he was really the final guardian." Owain took a long draught from his cup. "Whoever he was, he was well trained. He insisted on challenging each of us to single combat. You've seen what he did to Lancelot. The others in the infirmary are the ones who managed to escape. Some were not so lucky."

I stared into my cup. "I wish I had known how all would suffer." I looked at him. "I had the chance to stop this, to talk Arthur out of this madness, and I did not."

Owain scrutinized me. "Who said this would be easy? A quest commanded by a god or goddess never is. Think about the old tales. These situations are sent to test our strength and our faith. If we pass, the rewards will be great."

"If" was the word ringing in my head as I finished my meal. I was just about to thank Owain for his company and insight when Elaine found us. Her eyes were red-rimmed, and tear stains marred her face. My heart stopped. Surely she was here to tell us Lancelot was dead. I placed shaking hands on her shoulders, looking deep into her eyes.

"Lancelot is awake," she whispered.

"Oh, thank the gods." I hugged Elaine.

I started to release her, but she stopped me by holding up two small vials. She must have taken them from the store in Lancelot's room.

"May I borrow these?" she asked. "If I am correct, they are chamomile and comfrey. I would like to use them on my nervous stomach and sore knees."

I squinted at them, making sure she had properly identified them. "Yes, but be certain not to ingest the comfrey. It is poisonous."

Leaving Elaine, I rushed to the sick room. I was so relieved to see Lancelot conscious that I fell to my knees at his side.

"How do you feel?" I asked, grasping his hands. It took all my willpower not to kiss him lest someone walk in at the wrong moment.

"I'm in pain. A lot of it. And I'm having trouble recalling how I came to be in Camelot. I remember the knight and his armor, but that is all. I don't remember drawing my sword or being attacked." Lancelot looked down at his mending body. "But obviously I was." Looking at me, he added. "Thank you for saving me, Guinevere."

I put a hand on his shoulder. "You remember who you are, where you are, and who I am, so you will be well. It will just take time." I handed him a cup of healing beer.

He started to shrug then winced. "If you believe so, it must be true." His tone was slightly flirtatious, so I knew he would be just fine.

"I will stay here with you as long as you like. But when you feel up to getting out of bed, let me know. Morgan has given me detailed instructions on how to continue your treatment."

He puffed out a small laugh, all his broken ribs would allow. "Follow it or face the consequences, yes?"

"Something like that." I chuckled. "Finish your beer."

◦◦◦

Again the moon waxed and waned, and we had no word from Arthur nor any of the other questing knights. Lancelot was improving, eating a steady diet of liver and whatever greens we could find to help him regain his strength. Each day, we walked with him around the grounds, going a little farther each time.

By spring, Mordred's seventeenth year was drawing near, the time he would be considered a man according to his father's tribe. But Arthur had not yet returned, so Lot stood in at Mordred's manhood ritual. Morgan, as his mother, was not allowed to witness the ritual for it symbolized Mordred breaking free of his need of her and coming into his own. However, as priestesses, Grainne and I watched over him as he meditated deep in the woods the night before he was set loose to kill or be killed by whatever beast the Hag decreed.

In silence, we approached him, Grainne dressed all in white with flowers entwined in her hair, acting as the Virgin Goddess who armed him for the hunt. She gave him a spear and a sling with a single stone. I was the Mother Goddess. My red dress reflected the blood with which I now painted him, blood kept from the stag Arthur had killed in Avalon, reconstituted for this very purpose. His absent mother represented the Crone and the wisdom he had gained at her skirts. Together, we handed him off to Lot and the other men, who would council him until nightfall, when his hunt would commence.

The following day, we haunted the forest, trying to sneak a look at the young warrior and making noise to throw off his senses. It was great fun for adults but, I was sure, not amusing to Mordred, who could not return to this camp until he had proof of his kill.

Lancelot and I walked and talked as we usually did but were so engrossed in our conversation we failed to notice when we became separated from the others.

Thunder rumbled in the distance. It was the first thing that drew our attention away from each other.

"A storm is coming," I said stupidly as heavy drops of rain began to fall.

We raced back toward the castle, but the rain was coming down so hard we both knew we would not make it before the storm broke in earnest. With a deafening crack, lightning struck a tree not one hundred paces in front of us. I screamed and practically jumped into Lancelot's arms.

Once my heart had slowed to its normal rhythm, I looked around to get my bearings. Even through the rainy haze, I knew where we were. I grabbed Lancelot's arm and tugged.

"Come on," I yelled over the rolling thunder. "I know where we can take shelter."

I led him to a small hut deep in the woods. It was made of

bent saplings, just as Diarmad's had been, but this made his house look like a castle. I pushed on a clump of branches, and they gave way, allowing us entry into the tiny dwelling.

The hut was a single room, barely wider than Lancelot was tall. The floor was bare earth, and a circle of rocks served as a fire pit. Overhead, a few ancient clumps of herbs hung from the roof, long past their prime.

Lancelot immediately went to the only furniture in the room—a small chest. He pulled out a moth-eaten blanket and threw it at me playfully. I caught it and dried my hair while he kindled a small fire.

"It's a hunter's cabin, meant to be a retreat while they wait for game or need a place to spend the night," I said by way of apology for the mean surroundings, dumping my wet cloak in one corner. "Not nearly as nice as the one we found in the mountains."

Outside, lightning lit up the sky, and thunder shook the ground.

"It is fine, I assure you," Lancelot said. "I've bedded down in worse places."

I peered through the branches. "I hope Mordred won his hunt already. I cannot imagine fighting a wild animal in weather like this."

Lancelot stood behind me. "He is fine. The animals have better senses than we do. They would have disappeared into their dens, burrows, and caves long before the storm rolled in."

I felt simpleminded in the wake of such a logical explanation. "You know this from experience, I suspect?" I turned, not realizing until it was too late that I was now trapped in the cage of his arms.

Lancelot's face was only inches from mine. "I have spent quite a bit of time in the wild." He backed up, turning away. "Some of it with you," he added with a small laugh.

I sat next to the fire and traced random patterns in the dirt to distract myself from his nearness, his smell, and the heat beginning to course through my veins. He wasn't ready yet, I told myself. He still needed time to heal.

Lancelot sat down opposite me, the small orange flames between us. For a while, we simply listened to the storm. Eventually he pulled off his wet shirt and discarded it next to my soaked cloak.

He said my name between booms of thunder. "Can I tell you something?"

I had to move closer to hear him. "Anything."

"Sometimes—" He swallowed and tried again. "Sometimes I feel like I will be forever haunted by a memory I do not have. Of the Black Knight who almost stole my life."

I gazed at him, unused to a man being so open about his feelings. Perhaps it was his Breton ancestry that made him be so candid with me. I gave him a small half smile. "I understand, in a way. I too was haunted—but by what I *did* remember. If Avalon taught me one thing, it is that until you admit what you've experienced, you cannot move on."

Lancelot stoked the fire and added more wood until it was a respectable size. "But how can I if I cannot remember it?"

"I can help you."

"How?"

"We have a ritual of remembrance in Avalon. I went through it myself before I returned to Camelot. All you have to do is trust me." I stood.

He took my hands. "I have pledged my life to you. Say the word, and it is done."

I plucked a handful of herbs from the clusters above. Sage and wild lettuce. They were dusty and bone dry, but they would do. I rearranged the stones so that, when placed on top of them, the herbs would smoke but not be consumed by the flames until they had given off their full fragrance.

"Do you have a water skin?"

Lancelot unhooked it from his belt. We each took a drink, then I poured a generous amount on the fire. I inhaled deeply. It was hickory wood. This was a good start.

I cast the herbs into the steam and fire. "Move over."

He moved against one wall so I could sit in front of him, water skin in my lap.

"Now breathe deeply."

We both inhaled.

"Close your eyes. Listen the rhythm of the rain." Once his breathing slowed, I took his hand and placed it on my chest. His breath caught, but I ignored it. "Now concentrate on matching your heartbeat to mine."

I poured another handful of water over the stones, and they hissed, sending hot white smoke into the air.

"Open your eyes and look into the steam. Tell me what you see."

His heartbeat increased along with his breathing. "The Black Knight is coming at me, swinging his terrible axe. I am defending myself but only just. He slams into me, knocking me to the ground. But that is not enough for him. He bangs my head into the ground, punching me about the face and chest while I am immobile. But I rally, pushing him off, struggling to my feet. I slash out with my sword, getting in a few good blows before he is on me again. I force him back, knocking off his helmet, and he stares at me with those crazed black eyes." Lancelot's voice caught.

His body trembled against my back. I poured more water onto the rocks.

"Then what? What happens next?" I prompted.

"He wraps his hands around my neck, trying to suffocate me. I'm choking, but then I get a grip on his hair and yank his head back. Turning my head, I bite his fingers, forcing him to release me. We come at each other again, breathing heavily. He swings his axe, catching me in the side. I am down, done for. But my companions are not. They rush the knight and finally bring him down as I fade in and out of consciousness. They help me up and put a sword in my hand, holding down the dying knight.

"'Take your honor for this victory is yours,' they say to me. Suddenly, I am full of strength. I know what I must do. I raise the blade and bring it down through the flesh and corded muscle of his neck, through the bone and nerves, until it rolls to the side in a river of blood and he is no more."

"Good, now there is one more thing you must do so this new knowledge does not haunt you." I patiently recounted the steps of closing one's mind to a memory, the very same steps Viviane had taught me so many years before when I first arrived in Avalon.

Silence descended on us, comforting as a blanket. We sat in it until a peal of thunder startled us out of our reverie. I glanced over my shoulder at Lancelot. His skin was covered in sweat, face pale as chalk, eyes still haunted. I started to get up, but he held me fast.

"Thank you." His voice was husky, as though he'd just awoken from a deep sleep. "You truly are a goddess."

I ducked my head, embarrassed, and plucked at my tunic, which was clinging to my skin in the heat from the rainwater, fire, and steam. "I am not. I am a priestess, and it is my sworn duty to use what I know to give relief to those who are suffering whenever I can."

Lancelot brushed a piece of hair from my cheek. "There is something else, something I haven't told you." He shifted so I could face him. "After the battle, when I was unconscious, I saw the place where the Grail is kept. I was allowed to venture inside but only so far. When I tried to move forward, it was as though an invisible barrier held me back. But I could see beyond. There, on a pedestal, was the Grail. But it was veiled. Nearby was a beautiful woman with eyes like leaves after the rain and ink-black hair. She had your face."

I gasped.

Lancelot put a finger to my lips. "I heard her voice, or rather your voice, in my head. 'Son of the Lake, your soul is torn. You cannot serve the Grail and the queen, for she is Sovereignty, singularly demanding of your attention. You must make a choice.'"

He leaned into me, his breath warm on my lips. "I chose you. I will never behold the Grail in its true form because of that, but I am at peace. I have been yours from the moment I set eyes on you at the tournament."

I learned in and kissed him, my fingers tangling in his black curls, tightening, pulling, wanting. Needing. Our tongues touched, seeking the deepest recesses of one another.

I gently pushed him onto his back, mindful of his still-mending wounds, and pulled off my tunic, baring my breasts in the firelight. Leaning over him, I ran my tongue over his chest and stomach, stopping only when his trousers got in the way. Running my fingers slowly up his thighs, I groaned when I felt his arousal. He lifted his hips, and I peeled off his trousers. I'd intended to take him into my mouth, but he guided my hips over his. I closed my eyes and brought him into me.

I raised my arms and brought the energy of the storm into my body, every nerve tingling as I moved against him, grinding my hips in time with the vibration of the thunder all around us.

Lancelot sat up and lowered his head to my breasts, tongue flicking, tantalizing, teasing. I arched my back, crying out as pleasure built in my limbs. I moved my hips faster, seeking release. He moaned and kissed my neck, gripping my shoulders as his breathing grew ragged. I closed my eyes and grasped his shoulder blades. Waves of pleasure washed through me, and I dug my nails into his back and tossed my head back with a primal scream. Moments later, Lancelot groaned, and a spasm shook him as a surge of warmth filled my loins.

We collapsed in a heap next to the fire, panting, slowly returning to our senses.

I gazed at him, amazed at how happy I felt. This man was once again my lover, and I had no shame in it. For what felt like hours, we lay in each other's arms, caught up in our own thoughts, his fingertips tracing lazy circles on my upper arms.

"We should probably go," Lancelot finally murmured. "The worst of the storm has ended, and the others will be wondering what happened to us."

"Mmm. . . hmm," I replied but made no move to get up. Then I remembered Mordred and my duty to him.

After hastily donning our clothes, we stepped out into the

rain. It was still coming down hard, but I relished it, letting it wash the sweat and smell of desire off of me.

Lot and Grainne were waiting beneath the canopy of an ash tree when we reached the place Mordred had departed the morning before.

"We were caught in the storm. Found a hunter's hut," I explained before anyone could ask.

"We were too," Lot said, holding up his dripping sleeve as proof. "But we were not so lucky. This is the best cover we could find."

"It helps to know these woods." I rubbed my hands together. "Any sign of Mordred?"

"Not yet."

The rain slowly dissipated, then the sun broke through, giving the remaining drops an Otherworldly quality, like golden showers of faerie dust. I laughed and ducked out from beneath the leaves, spinning in the rain like a giddy young girl. It wasn't long before Grainne joined me. We held hands and skipped in circles, reveling in the joy of the moment.

"Look!" Lancelot cried, pointing toward the west.

At first I thought he was directing our attention to the vivid rainbow stretching across the sky, but then a figure caught my eye. Mordred stood at the edge of the wood, scratched and bloody, a large boar slung over his shoulders. He flung his burden to the ground and flashed a triumphant grin.

Lot was the first to reach him. "Congratulations, son. You are now a man of the tribe."

Mordred wrenched a tusk from the boar and used it to slit open the beast's belly. I painted Mordred's face and chest with the blood, confirming the veracity of his kill.

Then, while Lancelot and Lot spoke words of welcome into the tribe of men, Grainne and I removed the beast's entrails, seeking to divine Mordred's future in them. I plunged my hands into the hot, steaming mess, and my sight clouded over. Mordred was before me, fully grown. His face was painted in wild symbols with woad and chalk, hair limed for battle. Behind him was a vast army of Picts, Irish, and Saxons, and next to him stood Elga in all her ferocious glory. I could not see whom he opposed, but whoever it was stood little chance of victory over this army.

I came back to myself with a start and looked at the proud boy being kindly harassed by Lot and Lancelot. What was to come to turn him into such a hardened warrior? I shook my head, seeking to clear it, and washed my hands and arms clean.

"The gods have foretold you will be a great warrior," I told Mordred, keeping the particulars to myself. There was no need to burden him at such a young age with knowledge that may or may not come to pass. "Receive the blessing of Sovereignty." I kissed his forehead, lips, and heart.

Grainne took up his spear and sling along with a sword specially commissioned by Arthur for this occasion. "Be armed by the Goddess and live to uphold her ways."

Lancelot and Lot cheered, lifting Mordred onto their shoulders.

"Now, son. . ." Lot chuckled. "Let's find you a woman and finish making you man!"

Chapter Twenty-Three

Winter 515

The Grail party was secreted into the castle under cover of darkness and heavy guard. We couldn't let everyone know they had found the Grail until we knew for certain. It wasn't that I didn't believe what I had seen or that the mysterious object really was the Grail, but if word leaked out uncontrolled or, the gods forbid it, if we were duped, there would be chaos in Camelot. We could not afford to take that chance.

The next morning, in the silent moments before dawn, the Combrogi gathered in the secret labyrinth at the center of the castle. No one spoke or even shuffled their feet. We were all waiting, holding our breath for what was to come. In the shadows and bushes around us, crickets sang their hymns to the dawn, and a warm, briny breeze blew in off the ocean.

Arthur arranged us carefully in the center of the labyrinth around the apple tree from Avalon. He was at the northernmost point with Galahad. Morgan and I were on either side of them, then Marius next to Morgan, Peredur next to me, and the rest of the questing knights around the circle. Lancelot chose the southern point, opposite Arthur, and Elaine stood behind Galahad, beaming. The Grail women stood on either side of our circle, the ones with the intimidating scythes guarding the only door against uninvited guests.

As golden dawn crested the horizon, Arthur spoke. "We are here to witness an event not only of our generation but of an epoch. This treasure has been hidden from human eyes for over five hundred years save to a chosen trained few." He nodded to the Grail guardians, who inclined their heads as one in acknowledgement. "For the first time, secular eyes will fall upon a sacred vessel some believe was an ancient gift from the gods, others the cup touched by Christ Himself before His death. Whatever the truth, we know it is a holy relic deserving of our respect and veneration." He let his words sink in then stepped aside, allowing me to take his place at the fore. "As the representative of Sovereignty herself, our queen has the honor of unveiling it to you."

To my left, Bishop Marius cleared his throat loudly. We'd had quite a row the night before over who would oversee the Grail ritual. He believed that as a consecrated representative of Christ on earth, he should be the one to preside. I'd reminded Marius that I too was consecrated, which he refused to acknowledge as valid. The argument grew heated, the entire Grail party taking sides and no one knowing for certain how to settle the argument. Peredur and Galahad were firmly in Marius's camp, while the Grail women sided with me. To my astonishment, Morgan made no move to assert her own authority and actually sided with me.

Finally, it was put to the Grail Maiden to decide for she was the only one among us who knew the true nature of the vessel. She took my hands and read the lines on my palms before doing the same with Marius, who was loathe to hold still for such a pagan practice.

She looked up and made her proclamation. "Ours is the final generation in which men and women will seek the Grail with equality. It will pass through the hearts, minds, and hands of many men in years to come. Therefore, it is only right that Sovereignty herself reveal it to the world. This has been our queen's destiny from the moment she was born. The dreams she had as a child are realized in this very moment."

I stepped forward, quite unsure how to begin. There was no precedence for this, no well-taught ritual of Avalon. But as the fates would have it, the Grail guardians knew what to do, or at the very least, they were excellent at making up pageantry on the spot.

The Grail Maiden stood in front of me, her back to the crowd. She held the Grail out to me, and I took it with shaking hands. She reached up and removed her veil. I gasped, recognizing Mona's deep black eyes immediately. Her hair was gray now, but there was no mistaking her face. So her dreams, though they were of the ancient past, had led her to the Grail too.

She touched my forehead, lips, and heart, in effect transferring her power to me. We bowed to each other, then she slid the veil from her shoulders and placed it over my hair. Immediately, silver light and comforting warmth filled me as they had the day I chose my champion. I was no longer the queen but the Goddess.

Mona backed away, melting into the throng of maidens, while a blonde-haired woman glided toward me with the thurible. She walked sunwise around me and my precious charge three times, enveloping us in haze of sweet smoke that reminded me of honeysuckle. She then circled the knights, purifying all present.

Rowena approached and poured ice-cold water over my hands. She then dipped an evergreen sprig into the pitcher and used it to shower all present. She waved her hand over the water, and it shimmered, changing before my eyes. Stepping to one side, she motioned for me to remove the golden cloth from over the Grail.

I took a deep breath, remembering the many forms it had taken in my dreams. Slowly, I drew the cloth away.

A gasp went up from the crowd, but no one spoke.

I looked down. In my hands was a bronze cauldron about the size of a large winter squash. It was decorated with intricate scrollwork, much like the pattern on the robes worn by the Lady of the Lake. As I gazed at it, I found I could read it, but it shifted as soon as I understood its meaning. It was not something I would ever be able to put into words, for it was the wisdom of the ages, meant to be held only in the soul, not transmitted through human senses.

On the sides of the vessel were four golden seals, each representing one of the elements. I turned it in my hands so I could see each in turn. Nearest to me was the seal of earth, depicting mountains, trees, and a pointed buck. As I looked at it, I was enveloped by the scent of pine and freshly turned earth. The next was air, an ethereal design that brought to mind clouds and invisible summer breezes. As I watched, it ruffled the edge of my veil. Next was the seal of fire, which glowed a rose-colored hue and was hot to the touch. Finally, a seal depicting waves and streams. It was cold, like melting snow, and smelled of briny seas.

Rowena poured water from her vessel into the Grail. She then took my free hand and one of Marius's and joined them together over the Grail. Even in my altered state, my stomach clenched at his touch. He scowled at me as we each silently blessed the vessel and its contents in our own way before releasing our grasp.

An inner voice told me to drink, so I did. A sweet honeyed mead filled my mouth, more pleasant than anything I had ever tasted. It had to have been the drink of the gods, the potion of Ceridwen that gave new life to the dead. It coursed through my veins, warming and healing every part of me. My once-broken fingers reset without pain and old battle wounds mended, though their scars remained. Even my womb glowed with warmth, and I knew that had I consumed this drink when I was younger, I could have borne children again. But alas, I was growing too old for such things.

As the tingling subsided, I was granted a single vision—a blond woman of the north, a Votadini from the tattoo on her left shoulder blade, sneered in the heat of battle. But she was not my enemy. I knew not her name but was certain that she, and perhaps her people, were part of the life I had yet to live.

All of this took place in the space of a breath, a single heartbeat. Looking up, I passed the Grail to Morgan, who also appeared surprised when she drank. For a moment, her eyes clouded over, then she handed the cauldron to Marius, a wrinkle in her brow indicating she was contemplating her own vision.

As Marius touched it, the Grail changed. It became a chalice of finely wrought gold, more perfect and beautiful than any of our goldsmiths could have created. Marius drank from it, tilted his head up as though seeing something no one else could, then reluctantly passed the cup on.

As it moved down the line, the Grail changed back to the cauldron or became a bone drinking horn or a plain pottery cup depending on who held it. Only for Peredur, Galahad, Arthur, Elaine, and Camille did it take the form it had for Marius. Based on the serenity or puzzlement on each face as the cup passed on, I surmised everyone was granted some sort of insight upon drinking.

Only when it reached Lancelot did the pattern change. The Grail again became veiled. Just as he'd predicted, he could not see it, nor did he drink from it. All because he'd chosen me. He met my eyes with a soft smile as he passed it on untouched.

Once all had drunk from it, the Grail returned to Mona's possession.

"You are a blessed few, the only people who shall consume from this vessel. Now it must be held in a sacred place where all can venerate it but none can touch it. My sisters and I shall continue to stand guard for as long as the Lady wills it, but it needs a lifelong protector and champion. Who shall fill this role?" she asked the assembly.

Galahad stepped forward. "I shall. God has told me it is His will."

"And I." Peredur stood next to Galahad, smiling at him. "You will need an attendant."

As one, they knelt before Marius.

"Bishop, we ask you to take us into holy orders straight away and instruct us in the ways of Holy Mother Church," Galahad said.

Marius's face lit up. "As God wills it, my children." He made the sign of cross over them both. "I am humbled by such a task."

I highly doubted it.

"There is one more among you who has been called by the Grail," Mona stated.

Everyone looked around, mumbling.

Finally, Camille squeezed Aggrivane's hand and went to Marius. She fell on her knees before him, face nearly touching the ground. "Your Excellency, when I drank from the cup, I felt the same urge that came upon me many years ago when I first received the body and blood of Christ. For many years, I longed to become a bride of Christ, but that path was denied me by my family. Instead, on pain of death, I married a kind, loving man." She glanced over her shoulder at Aggrivane, who stood in stunned silence, pain chiseled into every feature. "I bore him a son and heir who died many years ago. I have done my duty to him and to my husband."

She mouthed "I'm sorry" to Aggrivane before continuing. "I ask you to release me from my marriage vows that I may take the veil and become the first Christian woman in charge of the Grail's protection."

The courtyard erupted in a melee of voices, some praising her, others filled with derision. A few vowed to defend the insult to Aggrivane's honor. I said nothing, as stunned as Aggrivane, who still hadn't moved.

"Silence. Let the bishop speak," Arthur shouted.

Marius regarded Camille curiously. "What you ask of me is no small task, my child. It is true you have fulfilled your duties to your child, but what of those to your husband? They continue on even though your womb bears no more fruit."

Camille shook her head. "I bore the one child only. Before then, and since, my husband has allowed me to live as a bride of

Christ as I have asked of him. He is away in foreign lands much of the time, so I am not denying my duties to him in asking such a thing."

Marius didn't appear to know what to make of this. "Are you saying you no longer have relations with your husband?"

I winced. This was not a conversation they should have been having in the company of others, even the Combrogi. Before Camille even answered, I was mortified for Aggrivane. I had to do something to stop this madwoman from bringing further embarrassment upon her husband and her house.

I put out a hand. "Please, let us continue this conversation in private where such delicate matters can be discussed openly without fear of what may come of them." I motioned Lot to take his son back inside.

Camille turned on me, still on her knees but looking for all the world as though she would bite me. "No! I have sinned before God in breaking a private pledge of virginity by marrying and bearing a child, and I will confess it before the whole court."

"Your sin is one thing, but do you not care for the ruin you bring upon your husband in the process?"

Camille stood, coming nose to nose with me. "You would care more about saving face for Aggrivane than what is right before God, you who never stopped loving my husband." She pulled the dagger out of my belt.

On all sides, Combrogi drew their swords in my defense.

Camille backed up, blade raised in her gloved hands to show she meant no one harm. She turned back to Marius and began sawing off locks of her hair. "No, Your Excellency, I have not had relations with my husband these fifteen years. I am a privately sworn holy woman now. See?" She held up a chunk of her hair. "This is proof of my devotion to Christ and to the cup which bore His blood. Whether you accept me or no, I am His slave. I am only asking you to make it official before all."

Marius was silent, clearly thinking as he watched the impassioned woman hack off her hair. "There is precedent for what you ask, though it is rarely used. If you were, as you claim, vowed to Christ in your heart before you married and did not wish to enter into such a union, then I doubt your marriage was ever valid in the eyes of God. The better question then is to ask this—does your husband give consent?"

All eyes turned to Aggrivane, who was nearly at the door, his father dragging him by the shoulder. Aggrivane faced the assembly, skin pale and clammy, clearly uncertain as to what to say. He cleared his throat. "Camille, if you wish to devote the remainder of your life to God, I grant you permission."

The crowd buzzed again, but Bishop Marius silenced them by raising his hand. He took the dagger from Camille and returned it to me. He spoke to Camille. "That being so, I declare your marriage dissolved in the eyes of God. You may enter the order whom I council. But be forewarned. Any more rash acts such as this"—he gestured to her shorn hair—"no matter how piously intended or induced, will result in disciplinary action. A servant of God, especially one who wishes to guard the Grail, must be meek and mild, not given to flights of recklessness."

"Thank you, Your Excellency." Camille kissed his hand then the hem of his robe.

"It is decided then," the Grail Maiden declared.

Elaine stepped out of the crowd in the silence that followed.

"I—I have something to confess." Her voice was timid at first but gained confidence with every word. "I know I shall not attain heaven with this secret on my soul, so I wish all of you to bear witness to my shriving." She walked over to her son and clasped his hands. She swallowed hard before continuing. "Galahad, all your life you have asked me who your father is, and I have refused to answer you. Today, as you prepare to enter the service of the Church, I tell you to look upon him." She pointed at Lancelot. "He is the most honored of the king's knights, his master of the horse and the queen's champion, Lancelot du Lac."

I grasped Arthur's arm, legs suddenly weak, head buzzing. Lancelot was married. My mind whirled. That meant we were doubly complicit in our affair, each betraying not only a spouse but a dear friend.

After a few moments of stunned silence, Galahad went to Lancelot and kneeled before him. "Father." He looked up at Lancelot, all the years of wondering plain in his eyes along with his admiration. "Do you claim me as your son?"

Lancelot raised his son to his feet and embraced him. "I always have. It is I who ensured that you have had all you desire. Go with my blessing into a life of service to your god." He turned a steely gaze on Elaine. "You, however, I do not accept. I have never loved you, nor will I ever. You lured me into your bed then into marriage by trickery. I never agreed to be your husband, nor do I call myself that now. Here and now, with public witness, I disavow all knowledge of you, woman."

Elaine crumpled in pain, face contorting as tears streamed down her face. She wailed as the crowd broke anew into a confused buzz of conversation, some condemning Lancelot, others

Elaine. I rushed to Elaine and put my arms around her, holding her up as she shook in the deepest of heartache.

"You are my husband!" Elaine shrieked.

"Actually, if he indeed entered marriage against his will, then just as with Camille, the marriage is not valid," Marius interrupted, quieting the whole room. "However, it also means our Grail champion was not conceived within the bounds of a sanctified marriage." He paused, holding Galahad's future, all of our futures, in the balance. "But that is the sin of his parents, no transgression of his. If God is willing to look beyond and bless him with the Grail, then none among us may judge."

Galahad breathed a visible sigh of relief.

Arthur took hold of the situation then, before anyone else could make more proclamations, inspired by the Grail or not. "We have all had an unforgettable morning. I beg you please do not start rumors about what has taken place here today. I do not swear you to secrecy but beg you be truthful and discreet in what you choose to disclose. Go now and return to your lives, forever changed by your encounter with the Grail."

Elaine was still wailing as I dragged her away from the labyrinth.

ജ2 2ഓ

"Her husband?" I rounded on Lancelot later that night when he found me in one of the deserted towers. "All these years and you couldn't have told me you were married?"

Lancelot reached out to me. "But I am not, not in any meaningful way. You heard the bishop."

I sat on the floor then, face buried in my hands. "How did this happen?"

Lancelot sat next to me. He took a few deep breaths before replying. "When Arthur left Corbenic to marry you, he needed someone to guard against Isolde's wrath and the revenge of the Irish. He found me and offered me the position." He brushed the hair out of my face. "I accepted only because I knew you to be from that house and thought I would see you again. I did not yet know you were engaged to Arthur. My first night there, Pellinor feasted me until I was deep in my cups. That is when his daughter came to me in the dark of night. Inebriated, I thought her to be you. So Galahad was conceived. It was only the next morning I discovered my mistake and Elaine told me of your upcoming wedding.

"The following month, she learned she was with child. I told her I wanted nothing to do with the child but would pay for its rearing until adulthood. That was not good enough for her pious family, who sought to undo her sin. Under pain of exposing me to Arthur—and thus to you—as a philanderer worthy of neither trust nor honor, much less the king's esteem, they forced us to the church, where we were wed. I never told anyone because to me, there was no marriage. I do not believe in her god, nor did I vow myself to her. You are the only woman to whom I have ever pledged my heart or soul."

I looked at him then. "Truly?"

"Truly." He tried to slip an arm around me, but I shrugged him off.

"I need time to think, Lancelot. I cannot simply rush back into your arms after a revelation such as this."

He bowed his head. "As you wish, my queen."

Chapter Twenty-Four

Construction began on a chapel to house the Grail almost immediately after our ritual. Galahad, being its champion, selected an island just off the coast, within sight of Camelot on clear days. Arthur, to my surprise, had architectural ambitions like his father, so when Galahad was free from his priestly studies, the two spent most of their time closeted away, working on designs. Marius even contacted some of his friends in Rome and paid for safe passage for two of them to Britain so Arthur's dream could be executed with the latest advances in Roman engineering.

I had seen Arthur's final plans. They called for an inner sanctuary with a gleaming red cupola supported by six tall stone pillars. A walled chapel and living area would surround this sanctuary, with a defensive wall three times taller than a man encircling that. The outer wall wasn't just protection against would-be thieves. It was also defense against the crashing waves, especially during storms. The whole structure would be accessible only by a narrow causeway created by natural rock and sand deposits. At high tide, it would be completely inaccessible, except by boat, making it the perfect place to house such a treasure.

With my husband occupied and my champion at least temporarily disgraced, I returned to Avalon with Mona and Rowena. I needed time and space to sort out the tangled knot of my life, and I could think of nowhere better.

I invited Morgan to accompany us, if only to make amends with Viviane, but she just laughed, saying, "Avalon abandoned me. Why should I return, especially now? I am a Christian woman, remember?"

"You are as Christian as the Saxons," I scoffed. "We both know you put on a show only to assure Arthur's continuing affection. And perhaps to gain favor with Bishop Marius."

"What I do is my business alone, Guinevere. Go back to the isle if you must. But I will remain here with *my* husband. You can tell Viviane I will never return."

But when we reached Avalon, I could tell Viviane nothing. She lay ill in her chamber, growing weaker by the day, according to Ailis, who was acting as her guard. She allowed me to see Viviane only because of our long friendship.

Viviane's skin was gray, her lips and fingers tinted lavender. Her eyes were closed as if in deep slumber, but the rise and fall of her chest was barely perceptible. A small vein slowly pulsing in her neck was the only other sign she still lived.

"She is unconscious now but had quite a time before. She started feeling ill just after the new moon, and at first we thought she had a normal illness. But then about a week ago, the convulsions began. Slowly, she became paralyzed and now. . ." Ailis's voice shook, "I believe she is nearing the veil."

"Poisoning?"

Ailis nodded. "That is what we suspect. But we have checked her belongings, and Nimue personally tests her food, so we cannot find a source."

I tossed and turned in my bed for the next two nights, turning Ailis's account of Viviane's mysterious illness over and over in my mind. There had to be something we were all missing. We were a community of trained healers, after all. But then again, we were trained to give life; only a rare few knew how to take it.

Restless, I finally decided to get up and walk the labyrinth, as I often did at home when wrestling with weighty issues. Around and around I trod, allowing my feet to trace the pathways of their own accord, freeing my mind to think on Viviane, Morgan, Lancelot, and Elaine—all of the distractions I had come here to escape. So deep was I in my thoughts I barely noticed when I reached the top of the Tor. Only Merlin's distraught voice made me pause before I was seen.

"Surely the Goddess will release her soon. Viviane has served her well. Why prolong her sojourn here?"

"Is there anything we can do bring her peace?" a female voice asked.

"Are you suggesting we hasten her death?" Merlin's voice was sharp.

"No." The woman laughed nervously. "I simply wish to see her death be as painless as possible. Provided we cannot find a cure, that is," she hastily added.

I shifted my position behind the stone separating us. If I

angled my body just the right way, I had a slightly obstructed view of the couple. Long dark hair came into view first, then blue priestess robes. Finally, the lone candle flickering between them illuminated bright green eyes. It was Nimue.

Merlin sighed and laid a hand on her shoulder. "Perhaps it will be my time soon as well. I have taught you everything I know, my daughters are grown, and Arthur has no need of me anymore. With Viviane dead, what will be left for me?"

Daughters? I had long suspected Ailis but was not aware of any other children of the Archdruid.

Nimue seized Merlin's chin, forcing him to face her. Her eyes were hard with malice. "You should know the answer. Me." She kissed him hard, letting her lips reflect her anger at his neglect to factor her into his life's worth.

I backed away slowly. Something in Nimue's disposition frightened me, but it also inspired a thought. Racing back down the Tor, I prayed that for Viviane's sake, I was right.

When I reached Viviane's chambers, I woke Ailis with a shake.

"What is it?" She raised herself onto one arm and squinted at the window. "It is not even dawn yet. Go back to sleep."

"Ailis." I shook her again to make sure she didn't go back to sleep. "Who prepares Viviane's meals?"

"Nimue. Why?"

I tugged on her arm. "Come with me."

I lit a candle and dragged her out into the night. We paused on the threshold to Nimue's room, just long enough to ensure it was still unoccupied. I began throwing open chests and drawers.

"What are you looking for?" Ailis asked, shocked at my actions.

"Proof of Nimue's guilt. I have heard a secret conversation tonight that leads me to suspect her." But there was nothing to be found. "The kitchens."

Ailis likely thought me mad as she followed me, but when I opened a small bag of rye hidden deep in the pantry, we were assaulted by the stench of fish.

"Oh," Ailis exclaimed. "This is ergot. Rotten rye. Deadly. Such a thing should be destroyed." She looked at me as her thoughts fell in line with mine. "You don't think. . ."

I nodded.

One of the young acolytes, a girl of perhaps ten summers, appeared to begin the day's baking. If she was surprised by our presence, she said nothing, merely knelt and made the sign of Avalon in deference to Ailis, who was acting Lady during Viviane's illness.

"Does Nimue prepare the Lady's bread with this?" She held up the offending bag.

"Yes, Lady," the girl replied. "She says it is special but not to touch it. She threatened to curse me and anyone who ate of it if I did."

Ailis looked at me. "We must find Nimue."

But we were too late. By the time Nimue was dragged, kicking and screaming, from the forest, even graver news than the likelihood of Nimue's guilt reached us.

"Merlin is dead," one of the young priestesses told us, her hand fluttering around her mouth. "They say his body is still warm. Nimue is covered in his blood."

⚬⚬⚬

Viviane slowly recovered as the ergot left her system, but she was likely to have lasting damage to her nerves. Two weeks later, she was well enough to be carried to the Tor. Rowena, Ailis, and I trudged up the labyrinth behind her, just as I had done so many times in my years as a priestess in Avalon, but tonight our purpose was far grimmer than any ritual. Tonight we would see justice done for Merlin's murderess.

Nimue knelt before the altar stone, barefoot, hands bound, and head lowered as if to shield herself from the intense heat of the fire burning on the other side of the stone.

Slowly, Druids and priestesses formed a circle of alternating white and blue robes around her. I stood to Nimue's left, unable to read her face thanks to a thick strand of raven hair that had fallen loose of its knot during her struggle with those who had brought her here.

Viviane and the new Archdruid, who took the title Myrdin—an imposing man of middle years with a full beard as white as clouds—stood before her.

"Nimue, priestess of Avalon, you stand accused of murder, a most unholy crime on this isle and across this land," Myrdin declared in his deep baritone. "It is said you killed the Archdruid of Britain by bloody means in the hopes of gaining his power. Also, you are accused of conspiring to kill the Lady of the Lake and take her office. What say you to these charges?"

Nimue raised her head, her hard eyes glinting like fresh-cut emeralds. "I did as you say, and I would do so again."

"You admit your wrongdoing then," Myrdin said. "When Merlin's body was found, he was pierced through the wrists with wooden stakes, had suffered a blow to the head, and his throat was slashed. You said as you were apprehended that you were defending yourself. Tell us, what manner of crime requires such lengths?"

"I arranged to meet him as we have been doing for many years. It is no secret we were lovers." She cast a gloating glance toward Viviane. Then she pointed at me. "If you wish to know what we talked about, ask her. After all, she was there."

"You knew I could hear you? How?"

Nimue tapped her tattooed brow. "But what you don't know is what happened after you left." Her eyes filled with tears, and her voice quavered. "Merlin turned on me, and I feared he would do me harm, so I picked up a stone and swung it at him to deter him. I caught him on the head."

"But he was not found on the Tor, and that does not account for the way his arms were pinioned or his cut throat," I reminded her.

She turned her malice on me. "Ah, the queen speaks. Tell me, am I being tried in Avalon's or Camelot's court?"

"Both." The steel in my voice surprised even me. "You will answer us."

Nimue laughed, a strange, unhinged sound. "And if I don't? You will kill me anyway. Why not let Merlin's death remain a mystery? It is more exciting this way."

One of the Druids approached Nimue. She raised her arms, and thunder and lightning filled the sky. The Druid jumped back, much to Nimue's delight.

She cackled madly. "Do you see? I have his power within me! All that he was, I am now!"

Viviane stopped the show in the heavens with a wave. "You

know nothing more than that which I taught you, which any woman here can do. You are not as powerful as you think."

"No? I breathed in his last breath, and have consumed his blood. I can do all he could and more!" Nimue was crazed now, eyes wide, practically foaming at the mouth as she struggled against her bonds.

"So that is why you killed him," Myrdin said. "In that case, I think we can safely assume you pinioned his arms to keep him still while you slit his throat, a quick but intimate death."

"As you say." Nimue rocked back and forth, consumed by what she saw as her own genius.

"And as to your attempt to poison me?" Viviane asked.

"I tried to wait, but you wouldn't die. Why wouldn't you just die?" Tears sprang to Nimue's eyes and rolled down her cheeks. "Then we could have been together, and I wouldn't have had to do this."

Myrdin cleared his throat. "You have confessed to crimes against the Archdruid and Lady of the Lake. Now you must face the consequences."

Viviane spoke. "Your actions are an affront to the Goddess and God and a betrayal of your vows. As such, you shall suffer the threefold death, never to rejoin our community. Do you understand?"

Nimue did not reply but held Viviane's gaze. Two priestesses helped Nimue to her feet and stripped her of her blue robes until she stood shivering in only her shift.

Viviane slowly approached the fire and withdrew an iron poker tipped with a small flat square. She carried it to over to Nimue, hands shaking.

"I would not do this for anything in the world," she said with a ragged breath. "But you have dishonored this holy mark and no longer deserve to bear it. Do you understand?"

Two Druids stepped forward, each bracing one of Nimue's arms. She held herself defiantly tall and proud, glaring at Viviane. "Do what you must," she answered, voice devoid of all emotion.

"So be it then," Viviane said quietly, raising the brand.

I looked away, unable to watch. The white-hot metal met Nimue's forehead with an audible hiss. When I looked back, tiny tendrils of smoke danced skyward as the crescent was burned off her brow. To her credit, Nimue did not cry out, though her eyes streamed with tears and her face contorted in silent agony. When the Druids released her, Nimue fell to the ground, clutching her head and making animalistic grunting sounds. For a long while, she lay on the ground, dazed.

When she finally stirred and climbed unsteadily back to her knees, the Archdruid approached her. When he stood next to Viviane, they drew blades simultaneously and pointed them at her.

"The blade is naked against her. Never again shall she be one of ours," they said in unison.

Slowly, each member of the circle came forward, touched their blade to her throat, and repeated the words. When they returned to their place in the circle, they turned their back toward her, signifying her excommunication.

I was the last to do so because as queen, I had one final duty to perform. I placed my hand on Nimue's shoulder, forcing myself to look at the angry red and black weeping wound between her eyes. I took a deep breath, remembering the willful young girl who had grown up in my father's hall.

"I am so glad your mother did not live to see this. Under other circumstances, you would face your temporal punishment outside the mists, on unhallowed ground, like other criminals, but you have committed no ordinary crime. You have spilt blood consecrated to the gods in a holy place. Therefore, to maintain balance, like must happen to you.

"I will show you one final act of mercy. I will allow you to choose the manner of your death. But it will be a death which you approach willingly in recompense for your actions, not one wrought by human hands. Should you refuse, wild beasts will be unleashed to tear you to pieces. If you do not wish this fate, you may choose to be buried alive in a cairn, submerge yourself in the mist and marshes, walk willingly into the flames on the next holy day, or cast yourself from the top of Chalice Hill, but know if you survive, we will leave you for dead. You have the night to think it over. We will return for you at dawn."

I drew my dagger and repeated the ritual of excommunication, but instead of sheathing it, I laid it on the ground before her. "You have one other choice. You may take your own life this night."

I looked into Nimue's haunting eyes to make sure she understood. What I saw was not the fear I had witnessed in the eyes of countless criminals condemned to death nor the contrition of one afraid to meet death. It was the stark, shocking lucidity of the truly insane, the ones who have given themselves over to the dark forces that tempt them away from everyday life.

Just when I thought I would get no reaction from her, she smiled. A wicked grin split her marred features, and she laughed, a manic, high-pitched cackle.

"You have no idea what you have begun this day. My blood will haunt this land forever. Never again will you know peace."

It was a curse, one proving how truly dangerous Nimue was. Around me, the priestesses and Druids chanted as those left to guard her took up their positions.

⸻ ⸻

At dawn, I returned with Viviane and Myrdin. Nimue had made her choice—but not without struggle with whatever dark forces possessed her. Her fragile body, covered with self-inflicted scratches trailing the length of her arms, legs, and chest, lay in a pool of blood. Deep gashes marred her wrists and elbows.

As a criminal and an oath breaker, she would have no funeral. Her body was loaded onto a stretcher and placed in a boat bound for the outside world. We committed her body to the bogs on the other side of the mists just as had been done to outlaws in ages past.

CHAPTER TWENTY-FIVE

Summer 518

Outside the mists, the Grail was true to its promise of peace until our own men began to turn on us. The rumors began with rumblings from the countryside of bands of marauders terrorizing farmers and herders, destroying crops and livestock. Then one of Arthur's men was brought before us, accused of inciting a riot in a village by killing the local lord's heirs and carrying off his eldest daughter to become his wife.

I would never forget the intensity in his eyes as he strove to justify his actions, pupils dilated, blue-green irises burning with the passion of the depraved.

"What would you have me do, sit around and whittle figurines out of wood? I am a fighter. I know nothing else. When the opportunity for combat doesn't arise naturally, I make one." He pointed a stubby finger at Arthur. "You made me this way. I am only doing what you've trained me to do."

The warrior's words hit Arthur hard. He sent the man to work in the gold mines of Gwynedd, hoping a sense of purpose would rehabilitate him.

That night, Arthur ran a hand over his tired face and through his graying hair. "I wish Merlin was here to tell me what to do. He was wise. He would know how to handle this."

I wanted to remind him that he was the one who had told Merlin he could go and replaced him with Bishop Marius, but I did not. I stroked his shoulders instead. "You too are wise. You learned from him. You have his wisdom inside you."

My words calmed Arthur for a while, but there was one thing we weren't prepared for—a charge against Arthur's own kin.

The next full moon, only three days after Beltane, we heard cases as we did every month, but there was something different about this gathering. The crowd was agitated, restless as if they were waiting for something. Many of them didn't come forward, so I began to wonder why they were there, what it was they were present to witness. I didn't have to wait long.

One of Arthur's underlords from Strathclyde, a man called Ceredig, approached our thrones with a hooded woman at his side. He bowed before us, expression somber.

"My king and queen, Lady Morgan, I am sorry to have to lay this before you, but I must do my daughter justice. I charge your son, Lord Mordred, with the rape of my daughter, Caitlin."

I inhaled sharply. That was a most grievous charge. If Mordred was found guilty, the official penalty would only involve a fine, but it would also make legal any retribution the girl's family wished to make against Mordred, including murder.

I looked at Mordred, who appeared as stunned as I was. He was holding onto Morgan's arm as though he would fall without her support, and his mouth was open in silent horror.

Arthur's whole body was taut, but he responded as he would have if the person in question were a stranger. "What grounds have you for this charge?"

"Three days ago, on Beltane eve, my daughter attended the fires with her friends. Your son and his companions met them late in the night, when they were already deep in their cups. Your son took a particular liking to my daughter. They danced together, and soon he took her off to a secluded area. I have several witnesses who will testify to this. After that—" Lord Ceredig became flustered, apparently not wishing to speak of sexual details about his daughter.

Arthur held up a hand. "Let us hear from your daughter."

Caitlin lowered her hood, revealing two bruised eyes, several scratches, and what appeared to be a bite mark on her cheek. When she lifted her arms, there were bruises on both wrists, and the longer I looked, I realized they matched the ones on her neck. This woman had definitely been abused. The question was, by whom?

"We went off into the woods, as all couples do on Beltane," she spoke in a small, shaky voice. "Mordred kissed me and touched my body, to which I had no objection, but when he began to remove his trousers, I knew what he intended was different from what I wanted. I told him no, but he wouldn't listen. He tried to hold me down, and I fought against him, scratching at his hands and face, screaming with all my might, but he was too strong. It was then he—he overpowered me." She looked down, clearly ashamed.

I grasped the arms of my chair, digging my nails into the wood and fighting the panic that followed her testimony. It was so much like my own experience with Malegant that the memories, so long ago locked away, threatened to come rushing back.

"What did you do then?" Arthur asked in his most tender voice.

"Eventually, I stopped struggling." She looked up, eyes pleading. "I just wanted it to be over. When it was, he stumbled away as though nothing had happened. I lay on the ground, sobbing. That is how one of my friends found me."

"Is your friend here?"

Caitlin nodded and pointed at a plain girl with hair the color of dirty dishwater. She was standing with two others of the same age who must have been their other companions.

Arthur motioned the girl forward. "You may return to your father," he said to Caitlin.

Caitlin's friend curtsied awkwardly in front of us.

"What is your name?"

"Ellen."

"Ellen, what is your account of that night?"

"What Caitlin says is true. We met the boys and danced, and she went away. Not long after, we heard screaming, but it took us a while to find her. By then, the deed was done. I found the poor thing crying and shivering. She was bleeding, especially from—" She motioned to the place between her thighs.

Arthur turned his attention to the other two girls. "Do you support her testimony?"

"We do, my lord," they answered in near unison.

"Thank you, Ellen." Arthur motioned Mordred forward, his face stricken. "What say you to these charges?"

Mordred looked as though he had no idea what to say. "I didn't rape her if that is what you are asking. What she said is accurate up to the point of me leading her into the forest."

"What happened then?"

"I—" He looked at Caitlin. "I don't remember. The next thing I recall is meeting up with my friends at a dockside tavern."

"You lie!" Lord Ceredig yelled.

Caitlin clung to her father as though her life depended on it.

"Son, if you cannot recall, how can you be certain you did not do what you are accused of?" Arthur asked.

"Because I would never do that!" Mordred's voice cracked. He looked at his mother. "You raised me better than that." He turned back to Arthur. "I have sworn a vow to you to respect all of your people. I couldn't, wouldn't do this." He was desperately pleading now.

"Are any of your friends from that night here?"

Mordred looked around. "Yes, Naill."

Arthur gestured for him. "What say you?"

Naill stood confidently before Arthur. "They are all correct about the attraction and going off. What happened then, I cannot say. I was with a girl of my own—consensually, mind you. We had agreed to meet at the Paps of Anu—that was the tavern—if we split up. Mordred came in shortly after I did."

"Did he say anything that would lead you to believe he'd forced himself on that girl?"

"No, sire. He said he had lain with a girl, but it sounded like she was agreeable."

"Did he have any marks on him indicating he had been in a fight?"

"No, only those consistent with the heat of passion." Naill grinned.

Caitlin found her voice and used it to shout at Mordred. "Then what are those scrapes on his knuckles? I gave him those."

Mordred held up his left hand. "These are from archery practice yesterday. Ask Lancelot. He was there."

Arthur and I inspected his hand.

"He is telling the truth," I said. "His wounds are too recent to have been received on Beltane."

"He could have reinjured himself!" Caitlin's father yelled.

"Silence, all of you! I've heard enough. Does anyone else have anything else to add?" Arthur asked.

The room became eerily silent.

"My wife and I will discuss this in private and return with our judgment. Lancelot, guard Mordred. Kay, Bedivere, Bors, make sure the crowd remains peaceful."

He and I went to a small antechamber reserved for this and other private matters.

Arthur leaned heavily against the closed door. "You were trained as a judge. What do you think?" Even though we were alone, his voice was barely a whisper.

"I don't know. I want to believe Mordred, but because he cannot remember, either one of them could be telling the truth. It's clear she was abused and probably even raped, but the question is was Mordred the perpetrator? Her family could just be accusing him to try to extort money from us."

"On the other hand, even if he is innocent, if we let him go without punishment, it will appear the law does not apply to him because he is my son."

"Arthur, we cannot punish an innocent man."

"I know, Guinevere. I know." He banged his fist against the wall. "Three decades on the throne, and this is the most difficult decision I've ever had to make."

When we returned to the great hall, the crowd was growing

restless. All eyes were on us as we took our seats. Arthur spoke. "We cannot determine whether or not a crime has been committed by the man accused. However, since it is possible, Mordred, you will pay this family the full body price and honor price as prescribed by law."

"This is outrageous!" Caitlin's father roared. "The crown is simply going to pay away his offenses? I demand stronger punishment."

"Lord Ceredig, we have ruled. You cannot bring suit again," I reminded him. I chose not to remind him there were now other legal ways for him to exact revenge.

"However, given the shame this charge has brought upon the throne, I hereby strip Lord Mordred of his membership in the Combrogi, and all the rights and privileges that accompany it, for a year and a day. At that time, we will consider reinstatement," Arthur added.

"What?" Mordred attempted to surge toward us, but Lancelot held him fast. "This is ridiculous! You are practically disowning me over a crime I did not commit." He pointed at both of us. "You will pay for this! Mark my words."

"Lancelot, Kay, lock him up until he regains his senses." Arthur addressed the crowd now. "This pleading day has ended. If you have concerns that have not been addressed, please take them up with your local lord or return next month."

⚬⚬

Mordred didn't speak to any of us unless he had to, which was to be expected. What I hadn't anticipated was Morgan's added hostility toward us. If it had only been me, I wouldn't have been as surprised, but her anger at Arthur was unprecedented. Granted, Mordred was her son, but what else could we have done?

After Mordred's threats, Lancelot and I decided it was best we end our relationship. Though we had reconciled after my return from Avalon, things were never the same between us again. Couple that with the possibility of Elaine, unstable ever since she had been publicly humiliated by Lancelot, finding out, and there was no sense in continuing.

In Lancelot's mind, that meant leaving Camelot. A few weeks after Mordred's censure, he was packed and prepared to be away. We met at the edge of a swampy clearing leading away from Camelot. It was nearly midnight—Lancelot wished to leave under cover of darkness to avoid questions from the Combrogi, whom he was abandoning.

"Where will you go?" I asked.

"I'm not sure. Maybe back to Brittany, perhaps to the Goddodin. I still have some lands there."

I vaguely remembered Malegant or Diarmad making reference to that. "So this is good-bye then."

He smiled in the way that broke hearts every time he neared a woman. "Not yet. We still have a few moments more." He leaned toward me.

I put up a hand. "Lancelot, you know my position on that—"

"That's not what I'm suggesting." He put his arms around my waist and pulled me to him. "I simply want to hold you one last time."

I sank into his warmth, my head on his chest, and listened to his heartbeat. Around us, the forest continued its chirps and clicks, oblivious to our presence. We hugged each other closer, loathe to part. But finally the moment came.

Lancelot was the first to pull back. "You know I have loved you from the moment I saw you at the tournament, and I will always love you, simply from afar."

Tears welled in my eyes. "I love you too. It may have taken me longer to realize it, but I do. I do not know how I would have survived these years with Morgan were it not for you. You will be in my heart always."

I rose onto my tiptoes and kissed him, long and deep.

That was when I heard a crack in the trees. I started to step away but was too slow. We were still in each other's arms when Mordred and Aggrivane leapt into view, weapons drawn. Instinctively, Lancelot pushed me behind him and drew his own blade.

Elaine emerged from behind Mordred and Aggrivane, clapping slowly. "Isn't that touching? You're still defending the trollop after all these years. And those declarations of love? Almost as good as a bard's song." She pretended to wipe her eyes.

"Elaine, what are you talking about? Did you follow us?" I squinted at her in the moonlight.

"Oh, yes. He's been following you for some time now." She indicated Aggrivane and circled us as she spoke. "You know, I've suspected for years that my husband—do not bother to protest, Lancelot—was unfaithful to me. Then Mordred mentioned he thought Guinevere to be unfaithful as well. I couldn't imagine the two of you together, but it was worth investigating. Turns out I was right."

I turned my attention to Aggrivane. "And what are you doing here?"

"Having my worst nightmare confirmed. Not that I haven't known for years what was going on." The dejection in his voice and disappointment in his eyes tore my heart in two. They asked the question, "Why him instead of me?"

I had no answer.

Mordred cleared his throat. "We are not here for a reunion. Let's get on with it." He leveled his sword at us. "In the name of High King Arthur, you are both under arrest on suspicion of adultery and treason."

As Mordred approached me, Lancelot slashed at him, tearing into his arm. Three guards appeared from the trees. I had no weapon nor any will to resist, so I allowed one to bind my hands while the others assisted in capturing Lancelot. He laid one low before Aggrivane finally disarmed him. Lancelot continued to struggle as he was bound.

Aggrivane's expression was full of disdain. "Believe me, I take much pleasure in doing this." He brought the butt of his sword down on Lancelot's head, knocking him out. "Carry him," he ordered the two Combrogi who remained unharmed.

They each grabbed him under an armpit and dragged him forward, feet scraping the ground, head lolling to one side.

"Elaine, take care of our injured friend," Mordred called as he led the way into the woods.

"Where are you taking us?" I demanded, finally terrified.

Mordred looked back over his shoulder. "He is going to the prison. You are going to face the king."

Chapter Twenty-Six

A week later, Kay led me, bound in iron shackles, before Arthur in his council chambers. I had been in here countless times over the years, but this was the first time I'd ever felt threatened in this room.

Around the table stood my friends, the Combrogi. But today their faces were anything but welcoming. Bors, Accolon, and Gawain regarded me with disgust, while Bedivere, Sobian, and Lot gave me looks of pity and concern. Even the statues of Arthur's ancestors seemed to scowl at me from their stone perches. With a start, I noticed someone had covered my statue with a black cloth. That was the true measure of the trouble I was in.

A special area had been set up at the head of the table. Arthur sat in his usual place, with Marius on his left and Morgan on his right. The empty chair on the other side was presumably reserved for Kay. Three additional chairs off to the left were occupied by my accusers: Elaine, Mordred, and Aggrivane. I looked around, searching for my place, but there was none. I was to stand then, as one already condemned.

"Where is Lancelot?" I asked Kay in a whisper.

"He is being held in a safe place."

I barely had time to comprehend his words before the court scribe read out the charges against me.

"Guinevere, Queen of Camelot, you stand accused of treason by way of an adulterous affair with your champion, Lancelot du Lac. What say you?"

I looked at them each in turn, amazed that people I knew so well could so quickly become strangers.

"I am guilty of no crime," I said in a loud, clear voice so the entire assembly would be sure to hear.

"How can you say such a thing when we have witnesses who have already attested to seeing you in his embrace?" Marius asked, his voice as full of disgust as the day he condemned me before my father.

"So the witnesses have already spoken? Am I not to be part of my own trial? Is this how Camelot is governed now?"

"You were there," Marius spit. "You know what they have told us."

"Do I? For all I know, they may have told you they caught me fornicating with the devil himself. Would you like to hear my side, or have you already sent the headsman to sharpen his axe?"

"Guinevere, that is enough." Arthur addressed me for the first time. "Tell me what happened. And if anyone interrupts"— his cold stare threw daggers at Marius—"I will have him or her removed from this room."

I swallowed, fighting to control the panic and nerves at war within me. "Badon changed me, as I'm sure it changed many of you." I looked into each face in turn, seeing a few nods, a few expressions of agreement. "Before then, I was able to live with Morgan being my husband's second wife. When he abandoned me for her after the war, I had no one. So I sought out companionship." I fixed Marius in a cold stare. "But not in the way you would imply. A few days ago, when we were 'discovered,' as you say, we were saying our farewells, queen to champion. Nothing improper took place."

"Maybe not that night," Mordred interjected. "But it had on plenty of previous occasions."

"What proof have you of this?" Arthur asked.

Aggrivane spoke up. "I saw the two of you once, many years ago, in the stairwell outside Elaine's chambers. Lancelot had just given charge of his students to her. You were kissing, your hands all over one another. When I realized you were not aware of my presence, I followed you. I did not stay long, but I saw enough to know you had carnal knowledge of one another up against the wall."

I tried hard not to react, at least not visibly, but my whole body began to shake. I heard my heartbeat drumming in my ears. I remembered that day well. It was our most reckless moment, and now it was being used to condemn us. I stared at Aggrivane, wanting to ask why he had kept it a secret for so long. But I dared not.

"Do you still claim innocence?" Marius asked.

I forced myself to hold my head high and remain defiant in the face of this farce. "I never claimed innocence, only that I am guilty of no crime, and that I maintain."

Marius rested his elbows on the arms of his chair and steepled his hands at his lips. "How do you reason that?"

"The law allows a man to take more than one wife—this we know. It used to allow a woman the privilege, too."

"But that no longer applies due to questions of paternity."

"Exactly. Given that I cannot bear children, that law does not pertain to me."

"You are saying you should be allowed to have an affair simply because no issue can come from it?" Marius scoffed.

"In these circumstances, yes." I turned to Arthur. "You put me away mentally and emotionally long ago, just as the nobles had advised you to do when it became clear I was barren. But I stayed with you. I prayed. I begged the gods to prove them wrong. But they did not hear my prayers. Then when I came back from being held by Malegant, I found you had indeed replaced me. You forced me to learn to live with Morgan as my near equal and constant competitor for your affection. Even this I did in fidelity until you abandoned me in my darkest hours after the war. Only then did I waver."

"So you are blaming your sin on him?" Marius laughed. "You are even more a fool than I anticipated."

I ignored him, focusing all of my attention on making Arthur understand my plight. "What else was I to do but love the man who offered me everything you denied me? I have not the resolve or the fear of the gods to keep me pure like your Christian nuns. You must have suspected something. By your silence, you gave your permission, Arthur Pendragon, but now in my hour of need, you remove it. Merciful and just ruler indeed!"

Arthur's eyes flashed dangerously, but there was a softness in his expression that told me my words had done their work. "I will not deny I am partially to blame for the situation we find ourselves in today. But I will not allow your offense to go unpunished either. You are a judge. You know the fines your kin must pay for this offense. I also banish you from Camelot. You are hereby stripped of your title of queen and sent back to Northgallis to live out the remainder of your days."

My stomach seized at his pronouncement, and I feared I would vomit in front of the whole court. My head swam as the Combrogi erupted into deafening argument around me, shouting at Arthur, Marius, and me. I fought to steady myself, having nothing to brace my body against.

Kay started to rise to escort me out, but Marius stopped him by placing himself between Kay and Arthur.

"High King of Camelot," he said in his best sermon voice so it would carry over the uproar.

Arthur rose to meet Marius's challenge.

"You have addressed the charge of adultery, but what of treason? By betraying you, she betrayed the crown. Surely you will not let that go unpunished? In order to keep your Combrogi together"—with a sweep of his hand, Marius took in the entire room—"you must show you govern the land by one law, not a separate rule for yourself and another for your people, just as you showed them with your son. They need to know that the supreme law which governs your heart is the law of Christ, which forbids adultery—here the method of her treason— under pain of death."

The Combrogi erupted again, several rising from their seats.

"Sit down and be silent, or I will throw you out!" Arthur bellowed.

"Think of her eternal soul, Arthur," Marius continued, unaffected by the outburst. "She is already in the depths of sin by her pagan profession. Would you damn her soul to eternal fire by letting her treachery go unpunished as well?"

"This is ridiculous," Aggrivane shouted. "No one wishes for her death."

"He goes too far," Mordred said at the same time.

The clamor started up again, with Combrogi lining up to take sides with either Marius or me. As ludicrous as the whole situation was, it was oddly comforting to know most of the knights stood behind me, even those who were party to bringing me here.

Arthur huffed, weighing his options.

"There are alternatives, my lord," Kay reminded him. "She could be tested by fire or water."

Morgan snorted. "She's a priestess. She could cheat that even with the king's blood fresh on her hands." She sneered at me, clearly enjoying the opportunity to be rid of me once and for all.

"A better option would be judicial combat," Aggrivane offered. "It is used only as a last resort, and I would say we are there."

"She is a battle queen," Constantine reminded him. "She will win that as well. It does nothing to serve justice."

"Are you trying to kill me?" I cried, fighting through the ringing in my head. I tried to remain stoic but was rapidly losing control. "Bishop Marius, you claim that in your faith, adultery is punishable by death, but did your Christ not stay the hand that would have stoned the Magdalene? Why do you not show me the same mercy?"

All eyes turned to Marius, awaiting his response.

"The Magdalene was a repentant prostitute. I see no signs

of repentance in you." A sly smile split his face. "If, however, you are willing to publicly confess your sins—all of them—convert to Christianity, and live out your days in a convent, I think you could be allowed to live."

So that was it then. Just as in my father's court, it came down to my faith. Marius hated the Avalonian priestesshood so much he was willing to make my life the price of his agenda.

I took a deep breath. "I made vows many years ago that I have no intention of breaking"—I looked at Morgan—"unlike some. I do not see what my faith and the charge of treason have to do with one another, but under no circumstances will I break the oaths I've made to my gods."

"They relate," Marius sneered back, "because your king, whom you offend with your treason, is a Christian man. By adopting his religion, you show faith in him and make slight recompense for your offenses. I will give you one more chance to change your mind."

I stood still and silent, willing the power of priestesshood to flow through me.

"Very well then. Arthur, her fate is in your hands. How would you treat any other traitor to your crown?"

"I need time to think this through. Kay, take her to the prison and be sure she is well guarded. I will rule at dawn."

Lot rushed forward to kneel before Arthur. "Once, you spared my life when I was far more deserving of your vengeance than she. I venture to say you've never once regretted it. Please, show her the same mercy. If you must have some outlet for your wrath, take my life instead. It is yours to do with as you please."

My heart broke at Lot's selfless gesture. He would have been my father-in-law had I married Aggrivane. I knew he wished that was how things had turned out, but I'd had no idea the depths of his affection for me.

"Thank you," was all I had a chance to say as I was led away by Kay and two guards.

⁂

I was imprisoned in one of Camelot's cellars that had been converted to hold criminals awaiting trial or those considered too dangerous to house in normal rooms. I shivered as I tried to keep my mind off the deliberation going on upstairs and keep some small shred of control over my sanity.

When the door to my cell opened the next morning, I was certain they had come to lead me to my death. But it was Sobian, not Kay, who greeted me. One look at her horrified face told me something was very, very wrong.

"What is it? What has happened?"

She shook her head, unlocking my shackles in silence. "See for yourself."

I expected her to lead me back into the castle, but instead we walked across the grounds to the edge of the river, not far from where it emptied into the bay. A small knot of people stood on the bank, their backs toward us.

"Arthur?" I asked tentatively.

He turned, holding out an arm as though asking me to pass beside him.

As I approached, the crowd parted, and I caught sight of a small boat that had been dragged onto shore beneath a willow.

When I was close enough to see there was a body within, I dropped to my knees in the sand.

"Oh, no. No, no, no, no," I cried, tears choking me.

Inside lay Elaine, clad in a white dress with a garland of flowers in her hair and her head resting against a small pillow, surrounded by all of her favorite flowers: lilies, daisies, roses, and buttercups. She was pale, and her eyes were open, staring forever at the heaven she'd always longed for.

The men lifted her ashore, but I already knew it was too late to save her. I had seen enough dead bodies to know when the soul was gone. When they put her in my arms, her skin was ice cold.

"Oh, Elaine, dear heart, what have you done?" I asked her as I gently closed her eyes.

"These were in her hands," Sobian said, holding out a roll of parchment and a spike-shaped flower with clusters of purple bells.

The flower was comfrey, but it was untouched. It was merely a symbol. She wanted us to know, even before we opened the missive, she had taken her own life. From out of the depths of my memory, I recalled the day she had borrowed the vial of comfrey from the room Lancelot was being treated in. I had told her not to ingest it because it was poisonous. Vaguely, I wondered if that was when she'd first gotten the idea.

I rocked her in my arms like a baby. "Sweet girl, why?"

"Guilt," Arthur said. He handed the small parchment to me.

I wanted to ask him to read it to me, but I could not speak.

"Sobian, will you stay with Guinevere while we take Elaine up to the castle? We will lay her out in the council room along with the contents of the boat. If this is how she wanted to die, then this is how she will be buried—and in holy ground. I care not how her life ended. She is still a child of Christ."

Numbly, I trudged behind Arthur back to the castle. I couldn't feel my feet nor even the rest of my body. All I could do was weep and wonder why my oldest friend had chosen to take her life and if Arthur was right. *Please, Goddess, do not let this be over me.*

They wouldn't let me stay with her body, but Sobian was allowed to sit in my cell with me while I read Elaine's final words.

I go to meet my Maker without the Sacraments but not without making my final confession. I do so publicly so those involved may know the heaviness of my heart. Maybe because of this they will not judge me for what I have done but let me go in peace.

They say "I love you" is supposed to be a blessing, but for me, it has been nothing short of a curse. The ones I love the most are the ones who have hurt me the deepest. I, in turn, have done nothing but hurt them.

Guinevere, I never meant for your life to be in danger when I condemned you in front of Arthur. I simply wished to have revenge for the betrayal I felt. As I cannot have your death on my conscience, I will cause my own, praying that Arthur will consider your wrongs avenged. Our Lord said, "There is no greater love than to lay down one's life for one's friends." This I do for you out of deepest love.

*By the time you read this, I will be at peace, and I wish
the same for you.*

Pray for my tormented soul.

Elaine of Corbenic,
Daughter of Pellinor and Lyonesse, wife of Lancelot du
Lac, mother of Galahad—chosen one of the Grail

I handed the note to Sobian without a word and motioned
for her to leave me.

"Arthur said he will take another night to consider your case
in light of Elaine's death," Sobian said.

I nodded, but I didn't really hear her. I was too numb, too
broken to care about my own fate.

With nowhere to sit but on the earthen floor, I picked a corner and hunched my knees up in front of me. A single thought
chased itself around my mind—I was indirectly responsible for
Elaine's death.

Images of her flashed through my mind, like the portraits
she'd so loved to draw. Elaine as a young girl, picking daisies under
the summer sun; covered in mud when we returned from exploring the moors; her joy upon hearing one of Isolde's fanciful Irish
stories— dear, long-departed Isolde, who had also taken her own
life, I recalled with deep sadness—Elaine's love-struck expression
when she first saw Galen; the single tear dripping down her cheek
when Arthur proposed to me; her face shining with pride over
Galahad; and finally, her stricken expression when Marius suggested I should die for my crimes.

The dam within me broke, and I wept for my friend. Somewhere in midst of the pain, a thought struck me—depending on Arthur's decision, our separation might be brief.

◦◦◦

Once I had cried myself dry and the shock of Elaine's suicide started to wear off, I was once again acutely aware of my own situation.

Arthur is merciful. You've seen him judge hundreds of people. He is nothing if not reasonable. He won't harm you. You have nothing to fear. That was what I told myself. But the more I tried to pray and remain calm, the more panic shot through my veins.

You are going to die. You have betrayed your king and country. Your affair caused your best friend to die. You will meet the Goddess on the morn, and she will not be merciful. Those thoughts were much louder than my feeble attempts to calm myself.

My breathing grew shallow and short until I was hyperventilating. In this state, I understood Nimue's insane rantings in a whole new light. I understood why she'd rocked back and forth because I was doing the same. This was ten times worse than the fear I had felt in the cave with Lancelot or even while in the grip of Malegant's torture. At least in those situations, I'd had some small means of fighting back. Now I was completely helpless. My fate was in the hands of someone whom I had hurt badly.

I bit my knuckles to keep from screaming.

That was how Aggrivane found me, weeping on the floor like a child and making small whimpering noises around my fist. At first, I didn't even recognize him. Of all things, it was his scent, clean like the woods after a rain, that brought me back to my senses.

He was sitting next to me and holding my head against his chest, which spasmed occasionally. I realized he was crying. No, not crying—bawling. I touched a hesitant finger to his neck and found rivers of tears.

"Aggrivane?"

"I never wanted it to be this way, Guinevere." He hiccupped. "I never thought it would come to this. Oh, what have I done?"

My tears answered his in silence. Neither of us spoke until he had regained control over himself.

"When Mordred told me what he suspected, I was irate. More than anything, I wanted to prove him wrong. Then when the signs began to suggest he was right, all I wanted was to get back at you for choosing Lancelot over me. It should have been me. That is all. Not this. Never this."

I took a deep breath, somehow, even after all these years, still finding my center in him. "Even if you had refused to help, told Mordred and Elaine they were mad, they would have found a way. This is not your fault." I wiped my eyes. "Elaine wanted revenge on any other woman Lancelot loved. As for Mordred, when Arthur and I ruled against him on the rape accusation, he promised revenge—and now he's taken it."

Aggrivane kissed the top of my head. "No matter what happens, I will stay with you. I will be with you to the very end."

I snuggled into his chest, finding enough peace there to sleep. I only knew I slept because I dreamed. I was in the Grail castle, but it was as though I could see everywhere at once. Arthur knelt before the Grail, praying so fervently sweat ran down his face. In a nearby room, Bishop Marius blessed the sacramental bread and wine. He added a drop of water from a cruet and a drop of something else from a small vial.

After muttering a few more prayers, Marius interrupted Arthur by placing the host on his tongue with the words, "*Corpus Christi.*" Then he gave him the chalice to drink from with the words, "*Sangue Christi,*" to which Arthur responded, "Amen."

"Go back to the castle and get some sleep, my son. I am sure the Holy Ghost will illumine your dreams with wisdom," Marius urged.

Arthur did as he was bid.

While Marius busied himself cleaning the chalice Arthur had used, a hooded woman approached him from behind.

"Father," her voice was tinged with a familiar lilt, "I trust all went well."

Marius turned, passing something into the woman's waiting hand. He folded his hands before him in an attitude of prayer. "God's will be done." He chuckled darkly.

The woman turned, and I caught a glimpse of her face. It was Morgan.

Before I could see more, the door to my cell squeaked open, and I was jolted awake. I scrambled to my feet.

Mordred stepped in first, trailed by Bishop Marius. Mordred saw Aggrivane and grimaced. "Why am I not surprised to find you here?"

Only then did Marius realize who Mordred was speaking to. "Ah, together again. It ends how it began. Poetic, isn't it?"

"Ends?" I asked, scarcely able to breathe.

Marius looked at me as though it was obvious. "Why yes, our king has made his decision."

Two women entered, carrying one of my gowns and my cloak along with a few pieces of my jewelry. They helped me put on all of it.

When they were done, Marius simply commanded, "Follow me."

I looked at Aggrivane, confused. Did this mean I was free or not?

"But what is my sentence?" I yelled after Marius.

He said nothing, only motioned for me to come along.

I started to follow, but Aggrivane grabbed my arm. "Please. Tell me one last thing. Do you forgive me?"

"Yes. And part of me has never stopped loving you. Whether I meet freedom or death outside these doors, I can be at peace knowing you know."

I thought I heard him whisper his love to me as I stepped into the blinding light of morning, but I couldn't be sure.

⚬⚭ ⚭⚬

Death had come for me.

But she was not an old woman as I had always imagined but a young man, barely more than a boy, sent to accompany me on my final walk.

When my eyes adjusted to the light, he was waiting for me with Bishop Marius. The bishop could hardly contain his glee as he said, "The high king asks me to pass his sentence on to you. On the charge of high treason, you are sentenced to death at the stake. His Majesty asks your forgiveness."

The world tipped, but the boy caught me before I fell. My stomach cramped, and my bowels threatened to empty right there in the street. Terror, more pure than anything I have ever felt, filled me from head to toe. I shook so violently my teeth clicked together.

"I forgive him," I managed to say amid waves of nausea.

They led me to the mouth of the street known as the bloody lane because it was a popular location for duels, revenge killings, and the occasional public execution. My final destination was within sight. Where the road opened to a square, a pyre stacked high with wood was the focal point. Never had a short road seemed so long.

Somehow, word had gotten out already about what was to happen. The street was so packed with spectators that a burly man had to be recruited from the crowd to push the gawkers out of our path. But first, Marius removed my jewelry—save for the sapphire ring Arthur had given me that I managed to hide—and tossed it into the crowd, who fought over it like starving dogs. Punches were thrown and blood spilt, and that was before one of the guards tore my cloak from my shoulders and hurled it at them too. Finally, it came time for my dress, which I opted to remove myself. I would go to my death with no possessions, clad only in a shift for modesty.

As I walked the gauntlet, stumbling and unsteady in my panic, the people shouted all sorts of taunts, curses, and filthy words at me. The same people I had vowed to give my life to protect were now gladly cheering on my death. Garbage and all manner of rotten things were hurled at me. Just when I thought the indignity couldn't get any worse, from somewhere above, someone emptied a bucket of water on me. Well, I'd thought it was water. It turned out to have been a chamber pot.

We finally reached the scaffold. The boy had to help me mount the stairs because I was paralyzed with fear.

"Where is my lord? Where is the king?" I asked as they lashed my wrists to the pole. "Is he not supposed to witness such an act?"

"He was detained. But that is why I am here in his stead, to make sure the job is done." Marius inspected my bindings. "Have you any last words, priestess?"

Priestess. The word was like a trigger in my brain reminding me who I was. I was not some helpless whore but a woman dedicated to the gods. This was not how I would meet my end, not at least without a fight. With that, the panic subsided, and my mind became full of clarity.

"Yes. You can go to hell. And all your kin with you." I spat in his face.

He took the burning torch and touched it to the kindling at my feet. "You first."

The kindling caught in a whoosh of smoke and heat. If I was to have any chance of escape, I had to act fast. Coughing and spluttering, I tried to find a grip for my feet on the uneven, splintery wood. It was not easy, but I soon found a position I could hold for some time.

While the crowd jeered and cried around me, I closed my eyes and concentrated on sending my consciousness down into the earth and forming a shield around me, just as I had done during my priestess trials in Avalon. I imagined the flames staying at least an arm's length away from me, and I pushed back the heat and smoke with every exhalation.

It was not long before the sight took over. I could see through the flames, into Arthur's bedchamber, where he'd woken just moments ago, desperate to get to me and commute my sentence. He tried the doors, but they were locked. Weak, unsteady, and retching, he fell to the floor. Still determined to stop this madness, he crawled to the windowsill, body partially paralyzed by that wicked drop in his communion wine.

He called my name, but over the crowd, no one could hear him. He continued crying, "Stop! Stop! This must stop. I am the king!" until his throat was raw.

When I came back to myself, I was still struggling with my bindings. My strength was beginning to wane. The heat crept closer as my shield slipped. Just as the blackness was about to take over, I heard the familiar clanging of swords and whinnying of horses. I raised my head and forced my eyes open. Riders—Bedivere, Sobian, and Gawain among them—were deep within the crowd, fighting to reach me.

Then the bonds around my hands slackened. I turned to find Mordred hacking away at the ropes. His clothes were drenched to stave off the flames, and he had a cloth over his nose and mouth so he could breathe.

"Promise me you will not seek the throne while I live," he said.

Astounded, I could barely respond. "Yes. I swear."

"Then go. Lancelot waits for you. Go and live."

I looked to where he indicated just in time to see Lancelot ride toward the pyre at full gallop on a massive black horse, trampling people underfoot. Mordred ducked as Lancelot reached through the fire to swing me up onto his horse. My hair and clothing caught as I vaulted through the flames, skin blistering, but I barely felt the pain.

I clung to Lancelot with the last of my remaining strength, coughing out smoke as the horse's hooves beat a steady rhythm on the hard ground. Only once did I chance a glance back over my burned shoulder. We were not being followed. Sobian and our allies were doing their jobs.

We rode until Camelot was a mere speck on the horizon. Smoke from the pyre was still visible, but the dwindling thread at its center indicated the fire had been doused.

Lancelot turned to me and examined my arms, face, and the burned crisp that used to be my hair. "You are injured. We must find you treatment, or you will grow ill. I did not rescue you only to have you die of your wounds."

I nodded, still numb to the pain, but I knew that when it came, it would be excruciating. I needed a safe place to recuperate. "We cannot stay on the open road long. No matter how long Kay and the others hold off the chase, they are sure to send more soldiers after us."

"Where do you wish to go?"

That was a good question. I was free. I could go anywhere. But I was no longer queen, no longer Arthur's wife. What did that mean for me? Where would I be safe? I could not be guaranteed anyone, even my own kin, would not betray me. Avalon was too far away. I knew of only one place where we could be safe, at least for the time it would take me to heal and reevaluate my life without Arthur.

"We ride to Lothian."

Before You Go . . .

Thank you for reading this book. If you enjoyed it, please leave a review on Amazon and/or Goodreads. Word of mouth is crucial for authors to succeed, so even if your review is only a line or two, it would be a huge help.

To be the first to find out about future books in this series, other novels, and insider information, please sign up for my newsletter. You will only be contacted when there is news, and your address will never be shared.

Also by Nicole Evelina:

Daughter of Destiny (Guinevere's Tale Book 1)

Future releases include:

Been Searching for You (a romantic comedy) – May 10, 2016

Madame Presidentess (historical fiction about Victoria Woodhull, the first American woman to run for President) – July 25, 2016

Mistress of Legend (Guinevere's Tale Book 3) – Late 2016/Early 2017

Please visit me at **nicoleevelina.com** to learn more.

*

I love interacting with my readers! Feel free to contact me on Twitter, Facebook, Goodreads, Pinterest, or by email. You can also send snail mail to: PO Box 2021, Maryland Heights, MO 63043.

Author's Notes

Whereas the first book in this series was Guinevere's early life, this story is the one everyone thinks of when they call to mind Arthurian legend. And because of that, it was written with no small amount of trepidation. I knew no matter how I chose to spin the story, I would alienate or offend someone who is a purist of a tradition I didn't follow. That's one of the perils of retelling a legend like that of Guinevere and Arthur; everyone has their own image of what the story should be, of what are the essential truths and elements that cannot change.

Not only that, this story delves into a few controversial and dark issues, including rape, physical and mental abuse, and PTSD. Guinevere's kidnapping and rape by Malegant (or sometimes other characters) is part of the canon of Arthurian legend. Sometimes she goes with her captor willingly, but more often than not, she is the victim of his lust and desire for power. Just how badly she was abused (if at all) varies by the telling, but to leave this event out simply because it is distasteful would be disingenuous to both the tradition and to readers.

I have done my best to treat these issues with respect and not use them simply as plot points but to show how they affected the characters' lives and brought about change, as they do for victims in real life. Therefore, my version of Guinevere suffers both mentally and physically for a lengthy period of time after Malegant's abuse, nearly losing her mind when it is coupled with Arthur's betrayal. It is only after time and Avalon's version of therapy that she can learn to move past her experiences.

Similarly, the Battle of Mount Badon affects all of Arthur's troops as well as the victims and their families, most notably Nimue, for whom loss of her mother was the trigger of a slow descent into madness. While her brother found strength and redemption in his faith, Nimue was unable to cope. I hope that if anyone reading this story has been affected by similar circumstances, you see the care with which I have tried to handle these delicate subjects, and if, God forbid, my writing triggered any negative memories, I am truly sorry.

Celtic Marriage

As the story starts out with Guinevere and Arthur's wedding, my notes begin with the history behind marriage in their time. Celtic marriage was very different from what we think of today. It was rarely done out of love, usually out of political gain for the families/tribes involved. It also was not a religious event but a contractual agreement. The laws governing marriage were set up to ensure children were protected (the stigma of illegitimacy did not exist even if a child was born out of wedlock), make clear the rights of the husband and wife, and protect the property rights of both parties.

Under Brehon Law, there were ten forms of marriage, each diminishing in importance, legal rights, and desirability. Guinevere and Arthur could have had either a first and highest degree of marriage, which takes place between partners of equal rank and property, or a second-degree union in which the woman has less property than the man and is supported by him—it all depends on how you look at it.

When Malegant kidnaps Guinevere, he is attempting to create a sixth-degree union in which a defeated enemy's wife is abducted and the marriage is valid only as long as the man can keep the woman with him. There is also a ninth-degree union which was brought about by rape. This is why, in his mind, Guinevere is his legitimate wife.

The Celts believed in polygamy, so second wives and concubines were not unknown, although how often this was practiced after the Roman withdrawal is unknown. Morgan and Arthur would have had a second-degree union because by the time he married her, she had married into a title and lands with Uriens but was not equal to Arthur. Luckily for Morgan, she was married to Arthur for a while before Guinevere returned because, as we saw in the first book of this series, laws existed that stated a first wife could legally murder the second wife within the first three days of marriage. Still, Guinevere was not only Morgan's competition for Arthur's attention, she was a threat to Morgan's livelihood. In the event of Arthur's death, a chief wife had rights to her husband's estate, while other wives were governed by informal contracts that often didn't require the first wife to provide for them at all or for the husband to leave them anything. So Guinevere would have been within her rights to leave Morgan with nothing after the Battle of Camlann, but that's another story for the notes to the third book in this series.

The transactions around marriage depicted in this book are all based on Brehon Law. Dowries were very important as brides were purchased from their fathers by their husbands for what became known as a bride-price. Some of this was kept in reserve for the woman should her marriage end at the fault of her husband, so she would not be left destitute. There was also a virgin-price that guaranteed the wife's purity, which Guinevere's father falsely arranged with Malegant.

Arthur's Lineage

The family lineage Arthur explains to Guinevere when she first comes to Camelot is one of many used throughout Arthurian legend. The ring he gave her is real. It's called the Escrick Ring. It was found in March 2013 (while I was writing this book) near York and immediately linked to "fifth-century royalty." So naturally, I tied it into my novel with fictitious symbolism relating to Arthur's ancestors.

The Combrogi and Arthur's Military

"Combrogi" is a real term found in Welsh literature that I chose to appropriate in place of the more modern Knights of the Round Table.

Chain mail really was a Celtic invention, but whether or not the Combrogi's saddles would have had stirrups is a matter of controversy. Most historians say they would not have, but at least one Arthurian scholar has put forth a hypothesis that the invention may have been carried to Britain by the Sarmatians, who were sent to Britain by the emperor Marcus Aurelius in 175 AD. As a fiction author, I have chosen to take this unlikely possibility and spin it into a partial explanation for the Combrogi's unprecedented success in battle.

Lancelot's views on training horses may seem very modern,

but they actually have ancient origins. The Greek writer Xenophon (430-354 BC) advocated the kind treatment of horses in his book *On Horsemanship*. "The golden rule in dealing with a horse is never approach him angrily. . .When a horse is shy of some object and refuses to approach it, you must teach him that there is nothing to be alarmed at. . . or, failing that, touch the formidable object to yourself and then gently lead the horse up to it. The opposite plan of forcing the creature by blows only intensifies its fear, the horse mentally associating the pain he suffers at such a moment with the object of suspicion" (28).

Like Lancelot, Xenophon also emphasizes the importance of the relationship between horse and master. "It is best that the stable be placed in a quarter of the establishment where the master will see the horse as often as possible" (20). And again, "If you would have a horse learn to perform his duty, your best plan will be, whenever he does as you wish, to show him some kindness in return, and when he is disobedient, to chastise him" (39). He emphatically states, "Far the best method of instruction is to let the horse feel that whatever he does in obedience to the rider's wishes will be followed by some rest and relaxation" (50).

The Famous Battles of King Arthur

The battles I've chosen to show are only a few attributed to King Arthur by the Welsh historian Nennius, who records twelve great victories during Arthur's reign as Dux Bellorum. There is much debate among scholars over their true dates, locations, and even who fought whom. As a fiction writer, I have picked what best fit my story and will leave it to the historians to hash out the rest.

The name Caw is closely associated with Arthurian legend. There are likely a number of men by this name. A Pictish chief named Caw really did live somewhere near Strathclyde around the years 493-570 and may even have been father of Arthurian "historian" Gildas. I have chosen to make him a rebel and conflate the details with what Nennius tells us of the battles of Arthur, "The seventh battle was in the Caledonian Forest, that is, the Battle of Celidon Coit." I have chosen to interpret that to mean the Caledonian Forest was in modern Scotland. The details of the battle are all from my own imagination, but legend has it that Arthur was victorious.

One of the two battles most people are likely to be familiar with is the Battle of Mount Badon (the other being Camlann, which takes place in next book in this series). Nennius writes, "The twelfth battle was on Badon Hill and in it nine hundred and sixty men fell in one day, from a single charge of Arthur's, and no-one lay them low save he alone." While the name comes from the book *De Excidio Britanniae (The Ruin of Britain)* written by the monk Gildas in the mid-500s, the battle itself is likely to have been real. Someone led a decisive battle against the Saxons sometime between 490 and 530 AD that resulted in a period of peace. That someone has come to be known in myth as Arthur and the battle called Badon. The location is a matter of much speculation, but I've chosen to go with the popular theory of it being at a hill fort near Bath, which the Romans called Aque Sullis.

The use of battering rams by the Saxons is also historical. In his book *Britannia antiquea, Or Ancient Britain brought within the limits of authentic history*, Beale Poste, a nineteenth century historian writes, "We find by the History of Gildas that the Saxons had plenty of battering rams, in the use of which, they were very liberal (234)."

Celtic Views on Death and Burial Practices

The Celts believed in reincarnation. In mythology, the Cauldron of Rebirth was able to revive the dead. Pre-Christian Celts also believed in an after-death Otherworld (Annwn in Welsh mythology), a resting place between incarnations that was a heaven-like paradise.

Graves were oriented west-east. West was the direction of the Otherworld, and Christians believed that this positioning allowed the dead to face Christ when he raised them on Resurrection Day. Single-person burials were the norm, with the dead person's head facing west. Sometimes a mother and child were buried together. Bodies may have been laid in the bare earth, in a stone coffin, or in a hollowed-out log, but coffins as we think of them were rare.

Ogham

Chances are you've heard that the Celts passed all of their knowledge on orally, which is one of the reasons why we know so little for certain about their beliefs. This is true, but the Celts did have a system of written language called Ogham. The earliest inscriptions we have in this language date to somewhere in the fourth century, mostly in Ireland, Wales, and Southern Britain. But some historians and archeologists, such as Lloyd and Jenny Laing, believe it dates back much further than that—even as far back as the Sycthians, who may have been the Gaelic Celts' ancestors dating to about 1300 BC. Ogham is mentioned often in ancient Irish myth, where it is said to have been used for poetry, Druidic spells, and even political challenges. The main source of written knowledge about Ogham is a fourteenth century manuscript called *The Book of Ballymote*, now housed in the Library of the Royal Irish Academy.

When written, Ogham appears to the modern eye like a series of vertical, horizontal, and diagonal lines, the number and shape of which indicate the letters. The alphabet had twenty characters arranged in series of four. Later, five additional characters were added.

The use of Ogham as sign language, which Imogen employs, is very controversial and certainly not accepted by all historians. John Matthews explains in his *Encyclopedia of Celtic Wisdom* that the fingers of the hand and certain locations on the palm represent letters or phrases. A person signing this way would use the placement of fingers across the shinbone, nose, thigh, foot, or on the palm or fingers of the opposite hand to indicate a letter, word, or phrase.

The Grail

No explanation of an Arthurian legend story would be complete without talking about the Holy Grail. So many books have been written about it that I'm not going to go into theories, only explain how I came to the idea you see in this book.

I chose to have a party of knights find the Grail because tradition varies as to which one did the finding. The most popular are Galahad, Perceval (Peredur), and Bors. In my version, Bors is not included because he's not a nice person. Traditionally, though he is involved in the quest, Lancelot doesn't ever see the Grail because he isn't pure. I have chosen to force him to make a choice between Guinevere (as representative of the Goddess) or the Grail. Of course, he chooses Guinevere.

Because there are so many possibilities of what the Grail could be (chalice, cup, cauldron, etc.) and they mean so much to people who believe in them, I didn't want to alienate anyone by picking one over the other. My Grail changes because I really do believe it is whatever you wish it to be. The seals Guinevere sees on the sides were inspired by those on a small chalice I purchased years ago from a New Age store. I'm not even sure what faith it is an implement for. (If you're ever at one of my book signings, I'll have it with me, so maybe you can tell me.)

The Grail Maiden is a title usually given to Elaine of Corbenic because she bore the man who finds the Grail. However, in many of the legends, a woman or angel is guarding it when it is discovered. I have chosen to extend this idea into a kind of special suborder of the Avalonian priestesshood. The stone circle they pass as Guinevere is tracking their progress (called this book the Sanctuary of the Stars) is Avebury.

The Grail Castle can be found in the Vulgate Cycle of Arthurian legend as well as Thomas Malory's *Le Morte d'Arthur*. It is usually associated with Corbenic, Elaine's home, but I have chosen to make it a place that housed the Grail after the knights find it. I placed it on a fictitious island off the coast of Camelot to keep it well within reach of Arthur and Father Marius.

There are many other topics I could cover here, but I think these are the most important, and this is an already-long book.

If you would like to know more about the sources I consulted in writing this book, please visit my website, **nicoleevelina.com**, and click on the "Research" tab under the section for *Camelot's Queen*. You may also which to search my blog, located on the same site, for additional information on many of these topics.

ACKNOWLEDGEMENTS

Thanks to my wonderful editor, Cassie Cox, who challenged me to dig deeper in my reasoning behind the character's actions and helped make this book what it is today, and to Jen K. for her early feedback that took this book from a hulking 160,000 word mess to something streamlined and intelligible. Thanks also to Jenny Q. for the beautiful cover and to The Editorial Department for the elegant layout.

Thanks to my beta readers: my mom, Courtney Marquez, Amy White, Tyler Thomas, and Nancy Corbett. I appreciate your candor more than you could know. You are the eyes that can see what I cannot, and I am blessed to know you. Thanks also to my parents for their unwavering support and love as well as for the home-cooked meals and reminders to sleep.

This was my first National Novel Writing Month (NaNoWriMo) book. The section from when Guinevere is kidnapped through her return to Camelot is what I focused on in November 2012. I would be remiss if I didn't thank the Office of Letters and Light for producing this wonderful event every year and the St. Louis municipal liaisons, Jen Sights and Jennifer Shaw. Thanks to all my fellow STLNaNo writers who supported me in my first year, especially Robert Guthrie, Jen Sights, Jay Noel, and Kim Miner Litton. Your laughter and encouragement (as well as word wars, candy, and pizza) are fond memories always.

As with the first book in the series, I owe thanks to Jamie George and Geoffrey Ashe for kindly and patiently listening to me prattle on in England and for answering my million questions.

I would also like to thank the St. Louis County Library for use of their research facilities, books, and help with interlibrary loan materials.

And last but not least, thank you to everyone who bought, downloaded, or borrowed a copy of this book. I may have been its creator, but you are its caretakers from now on. I hope you will hold this story as close to your heart as I do.

Nicole Evelina is a St. Louis-born historical fiction and romantic comedy writer. A self-professed armchair historian, she spent 15 years researching Arthurian legend, Celtic Britain and the various peoples, cultures and religious practices that shaped the country after the withdrawal of Rome. Nicole has traveled to England twice to research the Guinevere trilogy, where she consulted with internationally acclaimed author and historian Geoffrey Ashe, as well as Arthurian/Glastonbury expert Jaime George, the man who helped Marion Zimmer Bradley research *The Mists of Avalon*.

Her mission as a historical fiction writer is to rescue little-known women from being lost in the pages of history. While other writers may choose to write about the famous, she tells the stories of those who are in danger of being forgotten so that their memories may live on for at least another generation. She also tells the female point of view since the male perspective has historically been given more attention.

Nicole is one of only six authors who completed the first week-long writing intensive taught by #1 New York Times best-selling author Deborah Harkness in 2014. She is a member of and book reviewer for the Historical Novel Society, and Sirens, a group supporting female fantasy authors, as well as a member of the Romance Writers of America, Women Fiction Writers Association, the St. Louis Writer's Guild and Women Writing the West.

When she's not writing, she can be found reading, playing with her spoiled twin Burmese cats, cooking, researching and dreaming of living in Chicago or the English countryside.